BRENT EVANS'

LAND & SEA

RATCHET'S RUN

BLAINE LEE
PARDOE

BOOK
05

"We see our role as essentially defensive in nature. While our armies are advancing so fast and everyone's knocking themselves out to be heroes, we are holding ourselves in reserve in case the Krauts mount a counteroffensive which threatens Paris... or maybe even New York. Then we can move in and stop them. But for 1.6 million dollars, we could become heroes for three days." Oddball from *Kelly's Heroes*

Dedication:

To my son, Alex, who took me on a tour of this future battlefield, little realizing that I was doing research at the time.

Acknowledgements:

I always want to thank the team at Creative Juggernaut—Brent, Eric, and Kevin as well as the crackerjack militia unit (The WarGate Legionnaires) of Walt, Lauren, Jason, and Nick over at WarGate Publishing. Also, thanks to fan Joseph Gudge for his suggestion I incorporated into the story as well. Also, special thanks go out to my grandson Trenton for selecting the right music for this book.

This idea has been brewing for some time. During one of the first design sessions for the LAND&SEA ™ universe, I came up with the idea that morphed into this book. I had seen the movie, *Kelly's Heroes*, for what had to be the fifteenth time and thought that the concept had merit in the events presented in LAND&SEA. Originally, I toyed with doing this as one of our first role-playing game scenario books, but realized that the story really needed a strong fictional treatment. Who knows, though—it might just make it into the game as well.

The inspiration started with *Kelly's Heroes*, but that was just the spark the lit the fuse. The aliens are the enemy…that is for sure. But in many respects, the greatest enemy that mankind faces during such an invasion is not from the invaders, but from his fellow man. This was a story that had to have some great characters and a chance to evolve as the story unfolds.

CYCLE I

Close Captioning Feed— Dale Wharton, Trusted News Network— October 29, 2040

"Good evening. This is Dale Wharton and I'm once more reporting from the front lines in Los Angeles where the war has entered its second year in the City of Angels. Today's stalemate at the front was just another bitter reminder that we are nowhere near the end of this deadly conflict against the alien invaders.

"The Army reports that it has advanced closer towards the City Hall, which has been under alien control for several weeks now. As you can see from this footage, the battle here is intense."

//Footage 71—sounds of explosions and gunfire//

"The Army is still fighting shortages of munitions, along with the Air Force's lack of precision ordnance, despite assurances from the Bobrow Administration that production is increasing. This critical lack of munitions has made progress slow and painfully plodding, fighting for a city block at a time against a ruthless enemy. Those parts of the city that are reclaimed are often left in shambles from the

//Footage 72C—drone view of devastated city blocks//

"While the Army claims today's advances were another step on the long road to victory, it has come at a high cost. Word is that with this victory, the militia unit, Matilda's Maulers, was nearly wiped out. This loss will no doubt feed critics on Capitol Hill to once more question the Army's adoption of the controversial militia program."

//Footage 61B—Senator Ferguson speaking to press: "This militia program has been a debacle since day one. The Army should simply absorb these ill-prepared militia troops, if only to save their lives."//

"The recent setbacks here in Los Angeles have forced the Army to make a number of changes in command. Last week, Lieutenant Colonel Derek Logan, a highly decorated hero from the Russo-Bratva War, replaced Colonel Rand Higgerson here at the front. This move is seen as a positive step by most of the troops on the ground, given the losses attributed to Higgerson's handling of the defensive lines and his inability to mount a meaningful counteroffensive.

"While the debate as to the usefulness of the militia program continues, what can be said here at the front in Los Angeles is that the fighting continues to be bitter and contested. The aliens seem to be adapting rapidly to the Army's style of warfare, making this once thriving city a wasteland of rubble and debris.

"While the world struggles to reclaim its coastal cities, Los Angeles remains mostly under enemy control with no immediate end in sight. This is Dale Wharton for TNN."

Seven months earlier...

Commerce Bank, Beverly Hills, the Western Front, California, the United States of America

Antoine Billings was the manager of the Commerce Bank, tucked away just off of Rodeo Drive, and he was a man wrestling with anxiety. Everyone else in Beverly Hills was panicking; they were frightened by the war. He could not afford that. Moreover, his customers did not want to see him nervous or shaken. *Stability and calm—that was what people wanted to see. It is what they've come to expect.*

The sounds of the war were getting closer; there was no denying that. The reverberations of the aliens' weapons were tightening around him like a noose; he could tell by their intensity and the thin wisps of dust that fell from the ceiling with each new barrage. Several times the lights flickered off for a few seconds, only to come back on. Antoine chose to ignore it. *We've had far worse during some of the earthquakes. This is going to pass...it has to. This is more like when the Russians fired missiles into the city during the war.*

As he sat behind his desk, he tried to contemplate what his next moves should be. When the aliens had first come ashore, he had not panicked. Initially, their dangerous jumping land-piranhas had emerged from large shells that had slithered ashore, killing and injuring thousands. The beachfront communities had suffered the brunt of that onslaught. The images he had seen on the net and television were horrific and terrifying.

After those initial attacks, most sane people stayed away from the coasts. For Antoine, it was of little loss. The only time he went there was on Sundays, in Santa Monica, to sit window-side at Elephante and watch the morning waves rolling in. Those days were long behind him now. The military had showed up, turning communities like Santa Monica into a defensive position.

Now the aliens were back…and this time it was not their ferocious piranhas that came ashore, but the same monstrosities that had attacked Guam and Hawaii. The battle was on, and from the sound of it, it was creeping closer.

The war was going to be terrible for business—it already had been. The Commerce Bank had an exclusive clientele, the richest and most famous of the La social structure. The rich could not tolerate going to a bank where normal citizens would gawk at them. They preferred a discreet establishment, something exclusive. That was what his grandfather had catered to when he had opened the Commerce Bank. "It needs to be the kind of place where the rich and powerful are treated according to their stature," that was what he had told Antoine when he was a boy.

Now the bank was his, and it was about to experience the devastation of war for the first time.

Antoine was keeping the vault open until the last minute, just in case clients showed up. He still had three heavily armed security people on duty, having to quadruple their pay to remain with him. *The poor love to loot when things like this happen, and my bank isn't going to be a victim of their panic.*

Poor was a relative term. The Commerce Bank was in Beverly Hills, as were many of its clients. The poor that he was worried about were those who couldn't afford to live in the Hills or the affluent neighborhoods of Los Angeles or its surroundings. He knew it was a bourgeois view of others, but given his customers, it was appropriate in his mind. *My father always said that if you are going to service the rich, you must think like them.*

Outside he heard new noises, the sounds of explosions—no doubt from the human defenders. Some of the distant blasts were small, some large. A few moments later came the roar of low flying jets over Beverly Hills—a clear violation of the noise abatement laws. *Someone is going to need to tell the military that we don't want them over our skies—it's too disruptive.* No doubt phone calls were being made by the nearby residents.

There had been a rush the day that the invasion had started. The Commerce Bank was small, so more than ten customers showing up constituted a rush. Some of his clients made withdrawals, substantial ones. Others put things into their safe-deposit boxes or took things out. They were afraid; he could see it in their faces. As he had been raised to do, he did not show any concern. He greeted them warmly, with a smile and their favorite drink from the bank's bar. Antoine personally assured them that the Commerce Bank would be there for them, after this entire ugly affair was put to rest. He conveyed to them that their precious assets were safe.

Amid the distant rumbles and booms, he carefully adjusted the small pile of paperwork on his desk, blowing off some of the fallen dust in the process. *This invasion is an inconvenience, hopefully a short one. They will find some flaw with the aliens and crush it.* He had seen enough films about alien invaders to know that mankind always defeated them. *All we need to do is find their mother ship and blow it up, or something like that.* Antoine hoped that they would do it before they did too much damage. *I will need to look at assets on hand when the battle is over. My customers will need to rebuild, and that will cost money.* With his hand, he jotted a note to himself to call the Federal Reserve to make sure that the funds were available for him. *This is what a good banker does, he takes care of his clients.*

Another sound came—this one deep, throbbing, and long. The alien weapon was louder than before, closer. It made his skin prickle with goosebumps, if only for a moment. More dust drifted down, making him brush it off of the shoulders and lapels of his dark gray Brioni suit. *It is likely to be a while before I am able to get a dry cleaner.*

Antoine didn't panic like others, but he was also no fool. He had made arrangements to protect his family heirloom, the bank, beyond security. Provisions had been made to ensure that he could ensure that the Commerce Bank was ready to take care of its clients, even if the war did reach Beverly Hills.

Another explosion went off, this time much closer. The lights fluttered on and off rapidly, almost like a strobe. The crystal chandelier trembled and tinkled, then swayed overhead. The only time he had seen that was during an earthquake.

Have I misjudged the situation? For the first time since the invasion began, he wondered if staying at the bank was a mistake.

CHAPTER 1

Lieutenant Frank "Casper" Ryland looked out into the wastes of Los Angeles at where Bravo platoon's third squad had hunkered down. *That position is about as useful as Anne Frank's drum set.* They had dug into a position that allowed the aliens to easily flank them. They had cover, but it was less than soft—it was fuzzy. Worse yet, from what he saw through his visor's zoomed view, they were holding up their weapons and blind shooting…a complete violation of battlefield doctrine. His eyes saw they were being circled by the enemy—a pair of Foxes and at least one Crab. As they moved, they kicked up dust on the streets. The Fish were effectively using long abandoned cars for some cover.

The obsessive within his personality spoke loudly in his brain. *They have made rookie mistakes and are paying a price for it. There are a dozen things wrong with the position they have chosen.* That was how he kept his people alive—meticulous planning. He wouldn't sleep for a week before a pre-planned mission, thinking over every contingency and any possible reactions. It was what kept

7

the Ghost Legion he commanded alive. It was a compulsive obsession, but where others saw it as a weakness, he recognized it as a strength.

Today's op, code-named Thunderball, was far from planned. This was a rescue mission, plain and simple. That didn't mean Ryland didn't obsess over it—he simply wasn't afforded the time to cope with his manic feelings as much as he wanted.

"You see them yet, sir?" Staff Sergeant Calcutt asked.

"Oh, I see them," he said, zooming back out and stepping down from the fallen mailbox that he had used to get a better view. "They picked the worst possible place to have an engagement." His mind was going over all of the options, the best avenues for reaching them. It wasn't going to be easy. If it was, Colonel Logan wouldn't have sent in him and his Ghost Legion.

"Battlespace Command, this is Casper," he said over the command channel. "I have eyes on target. What is the enemy composition?"

"Stand by," came the all too calm voice of the battlespace commander. The erratic pop-bangs of gunfire from what was left of the trapped squad echoed through the remains of West Los Angeles. Far away, he heard the muffled *whomp* of mortar rounds going off. That was a different battle—his was in front of him. Everything else was a distraction he could ill afford. He took a moment to glance out over what had once been a thriving city. Most of the tall structures showed damage from the fighting. Entire blocks in some areas were laid waste, seas of rubble. A haze of brown dust seemed to hover over the remains, and in some areas, gray and black smoke plumes rose from fires. *The City of Angels looks more like a scene from hell.*

Even with the filters in his visor/faceplate of his Mark III ECH (Enhanced Combat Helmet), there was a stink of the city in the air. A combination of rotting garbage, burning garbage, and stagnant water. Ryland had been to La a few times in his life and remembered the stink of the homeless on the streets, the mix of urine and exhaust. At the time, he hated that aroma. Now, he wished it was back instead of this new fetor that hung constantly in the air. The only consolation was that it was far worse in the Valley.

"Casper, we are currently painting two Crabs, three Foxes around your target. We have partial coverage of the surrounding area but do not show any other enemy activity for a half-mile. Be advised, with our coverage, that is a fifty percent probable reading at this time."

Might as well flip a damn coin. "Copy that," he replied. He turned and faced his squad. "Alright, they are in a shallow position about three blocks up, right in the middle of the street. ACS on. We can assume they have wounded, so we will need the Huskies ready to go."

The ACS, the adaptive camouflage system, was a unit wired into their STG—standard tactical gear. It used nano-image receptors and projectors to effectively hide an infantryman right in plain sight. In theory, it made you almost invisible. The reality was that the more you moved or shot, the more the system degraded. ACSs had a knack for failing at the worst possible moments, overloaded with a blur of buffered image processing. Members of the same unit could see each other; the receptors didn't process images from other cloaked individuals well. Despite the flaws and weaknesses, having some invisibility was always preferable to none.

Calcutt turned to Corporal King who was their joyboy drone operator. "Whisper, that's on you. Keep those hounds of yours close."

King nodded in response.

"I want a fire team on the roof of the BP gas station to the west. The rest of you are with us for the main assault. We are going punch in, get these boys and girls out of the hurt they are in, and get out."

Calcutt gave orders for three of the squad to take the high ground on the gas station. Ryland approved of the choices. One sniper and two of the squad's best shooters would give them good cover. Winston with that hulking sniper rifle might actually hurt the Fish. Small arms fire against the aliens was iffy at best. Sometimes shots got the right angle to penetrate their hides or armored carapace, but it was difficult. If anyone could do it, it was his Ghost Legion. The trio took off, hopping from bits of rubble and debris as if they had been doing it their entire life.

Toggling his comms system, he linked up with the wayward squad. "Slasher Squad, this is Casper of the Ghost Legion. We are here to get you out."

A voice came back, panic oozing between each word he spoke. "This is Corporal Batson. Our LT and both of our sergeants are down. We are surrounded. For God's sake, we need immediate extraction."

"Calm down, Corporal," he advised slowly and calmly. *These recruits they are sending us are easy to scare.* He did have some sympathy for the young man. *He's lost his chain of command and is winging it, ignoring his training.* "The cavalry is here. Do what you are told and you'll be fine. We are setting up to the west of your position for cover fire. We are coming to you from the south, so watch for us there. We will come to you and pull you out. Be ready to move. Understood?"

"Yes sir," he said, already sounding relieved.

Ryland turned to Calcutt. "Shall we?"

The sergeant grinned and gave him a nod. "Alright, Ghost Legion, we are doing this by the numbers. I want Grant and Hollings on point. King and Raffi, you are next. LT is next and I have the back door. You people know the drill—we punch a hole to these wayward children, and we haul their asses out of the AIZ." The members of the squad didn't grumble and assumed their positions like seasoned professionals.

This wasn't their first rodeo in the Alien Incursion Zone. The Ghost Legion had been cobbled together from a number of disbanded units, the ragged survivors. Ryland hand-forged them into a formidable force. They were experts is relief missions and extractions. Oftentimes it was providing security for getting a crippled ASHUR out of the battlespace. Other missions were like this one, saving the collective asses of a trapped unit. The running joke in the unit was that when something was fucked up, the Ghost Legion were the "un-fuckers." The unit had taken that nickname to heart. Their unit patch were ghostly soldiers firing with the flaming letters UF stitched below the ghosts. In a banner over the top was their formal name: Ghost Legion.

The members of the Legion kept low, moving through the rubble of what had been a two story office building. Word came from Winston that they were in position already. Much of Los Angeles, or La, as many people called it, had been turned into a wasteland by the alien incursion. What the Fish didn't destroy, the Army did each time they tried to launch a counteroffensive. There had been five battles for Beverly Hills, seven for West Los Angeles. All resulted in a stalemate. Both sides of the conflict constantly probed at each other, but mounting a large scale counteroffensive had proven difficult. The Fish seemed content to take the city, one ruined block at a time.

As they reached the corner of the building, the point unit stopped, Grant holding up his arm. Ryland opened comms with him. "What do you have, Private?"

"It looks like a straight shot, except for the Crab that is between us and them."

Crabs were nasty warriors for the Fish. They were between ten and twelve feet long and had bodies like up-armored scorpions. Their tails were deadly whip-like weapons, complete with stingers that could punch through blast plate and kill instantly. Their forward torsos rose higher than a human, with a thick exoskeleton making them difficult to take down. Their massive heads and maws were not nearly as terrifying as the two big claws in front of them. Ryland had seen men cut in half by the claws once they clamped on. Often, biologically engineered weapons were fed into the claws, adding to their fright-factor. This one was a washed dull green color on top, and a dull gray to yellow on the bottom. While there had to be some significance to the coloring of the aliens, thus far no one had been able to figure that out.

Despite the intimidation factor of the alien, Ryland was not cringing. He had taken down a countless tally of Crabs since the war started. As ominous as they appeared, they could die like any other living organism. All it took with the proper application of firepower at the right place. "Alright, Sergeant, we need to neutralize that Crab. The last thing we need is to get into Slasher's position and get hemmed in with them."

"Understood," Calcutt said. He rattled out the orders as if they were memorized. Welsh trusted him implicitly. One, the sergeant had a lot of experience—both in Los Angeles and during the last war with the Russians, then the North Koreans. Two, he maintained his calm even in situations when he should be losing it. Such NCOs were what kept their people alive.

They moved out on the count of three—with Winston banging away with the opening shot from his big modified M-24A. The 7.62 round hit the center of the head of the Crab as the rest of the squad moved forward. Welsh didn't see the hit as much as he saw the Crab twist around from the impact, turning to face the new threat.

As it twisted in place, Hollings and Raffi opened up with controlled shots at the head as well. Their ACRs banged away with precise shots—he could see them glancing off of the carapace head. Realizing it had two new threats to deal with, the Crab hesitated.

A moment was all they needed. Private Grant pulled out a double-stacked grenade and thumbed the firing stud. Despite his size, he was more muscular than most of the rest of the squad, no doubt because of his use of Army-authorized muscle building drugs. The grenade tumbled in the air, bounced off the hood of a Prius II, and landed under the rear of the Crab. The explosion was glorious, lifting the Crab upward a few feet and blowing off two of its eight legs, sending them whipping around in the air. Dust and dirt billowed upward from the explosion as the squad moved in closer. Grant dove for cover and his ACS completely failed on impact. *Par for the course.*

As the dust settled, the Crab backed away from them. It lifted a claw and aimed it in their direction. Welsh didn't have to call for them to take cover, everyone dove. High-speed projectile needles sprayed the area around them. A needler, another cursed weapon of the Fish. Much like the Army's rail guns, the needler launched the projectile on some sort of bio-magnetic pulse. Hollings made a moaning sound, which Ryland's earpiece picked up. *He's been hit.*

Winton fired another shot, this one doing some real damage. There was a splatter of gray-green ooze on the side of the Crab's head, spraying out like a garden hose for a few moments. The Crab coiled up, hopefully in agony—then twisted around, firing another spray of deadly needles at the gas station in the distance. Ryland had only seen a Crab retreat once before. They had a nasty tendency to fight to the death. *When they fall back, it's only to recover and bring in reinforcements.* That meant that the clock was running.

Ryland held up his ACR and the targeting reticle in his visor tracked his aim. Once he got the Crab in his sights, he fired—three controlled shots. He doubted any of them punched through the armored body, but he was joined in by Calcutt and the rest of the squad, sans Hollings.

The hulking alien had enough. It whipped around and scurried away as best it could on its remaining legs, moving behind a small strip plaza, breaking line of sight.

"How's Hollings?" Welsh asked.

"I'm fine," he groaned. "Got me in the arm. I've pulled it out already, but my arm is going numb."

"Raffi," Calcutt snapped. "Give him a shot of battery juice. The rest of you, we are going in and getting these greenhorns out of there." Some of the needlers released poison, adding to their charm. Get enough of it in your blood and your organs, including heart and lungs, they would shut down. The medical corps had cooked up battery juice. It helped negate the effects of needler venom, but it left the victim with a two-day headache when it wore off. Taking the shot was still better than death.

They rushed forward to the place where Slasher Squad was huddled. It was an old artillery crater, with the rusted parts of several automobiles lying in the big hole. As soon as they entered, Calcutt had King deploy the GRDs. The two dog-like Huskies bounded in with the troops.

The men and women of Slasher were covered in a thin layer of tan and gray dust. Most lay as flat as they could; the crater was not deep. Sweat mingled with dust to add a crust of filth on them. Some were injured, their wounds dark crimson stains bleeding through their STG (standard tactical gear). Spent brass lay scattered everywhere. The wrappings from bandages mixed in with the debris of the firefight.

"We're here to get you out," Ryland said. "Immobile wounded, go out on the Huskies. The rest we will carry out. Move it, people!"

The Huskies had collapsible carbon rods that held a thin stretcher material you could strap the wounded to. King went to work, furiously working with the survivors to get the wounded slung to the rear of the drone. It was going to be a bumpy ride, but it was better than remaining where they were.

A corporal, no doubt Batson, stooped low and moved up in front of him. "Thank God you came."

"See to your people. Get them ready to move. We hurt that Crab, but he's going to be back with friends." Mentally he marked the time, moving to help support a private with some sort of foot or ankle injury. Glancing around, he saw that everyone was up. "Time to move, people!"

* * *

It took almost an hour to get the remains of Slasher Squad to the safety of the human side of the front lines. One of their most wounded, strapped to a Husky, died during the trip. Ryland wanted to feel bad about the soldier's death, but he couldn't muster it. He had seen too many good men and women die since the start of the war. It hurt when it was people under his command, but for total strangers, it was hard for him to feel sympathetic.

He led the debriefing and BDA session in the company assembly tent and had done what he could to provide guidance to the survivors they had extracted. It was a string of lessons he had shared many times before. In his mind, things needed to be organized—they needed to be structured—including his critique for the survivors.

What Slasher had done was try to improvise, and they'd lacked the skills to do that right. They failed to adhere to their training and they needed someone to explain it to them, in meticulous detail. If he didn't do it, he knew he'd not be able to sleep that night. He had to finish the mission entirely, which meant the debriefing session. Logic said he should have waited until the next day, but he couldn't do that. The mission was not over in his brain until the debriefing and BDA. Sleep was always iffy, but he knew if he didn't explain to them what they had done wrong, he would find no rest. It was the curse of possessing a healthy compulsive disorder.

Every sentence he spoke landed like a mortar barrage on the survivors. They had ignored the orders of the battlespace commander when he had told them to keep moving and instead they had dug in. The position they chose was not good hard cover and left no egress. Instead of fighting their way out of the encirclement, they tried to inflict attrition on the Fish. Their fire discipline was pure shit. Yes, they had lost both sergeants, but rather than fall back on their training, they panicked. As a result, his Ghost Legion had gotten a casualty. He made it sound more serious than it was. The medics had assured him that Hollings was fine, but he used him to make a point. "When you screw up, you endanger not only yourselves, but others."

Ryland saw they were exhausted and dejected by their performance. Most had only a few minutes to clean up before the debrief and still were filthy and naturally defensive. *They always are at first.* Slowly he coached them through their mistakes as if it were a learning opportunity—albeit a deadly one.

Some officers preferred to be supportive, almost to the point of coddling, during such debriefs. Ryland wasn't there to hold hands and sing "Kumbayah." He wanted to save lives, including his own. That meant being blunt and not worrying about their egos or feelings being hurt. *Their first mistake was calling themselves Slasher Squad. I guess Soiled Underwear was taken.* They wore the dejection he generated like cheap Halloween masks, but he didn't waver. *The smart ones will listen to what I say and change what they do next time out. Those that don't will be dead.*

Sadly, this was not new to him. The war was forcing the Army to throw unprepared troops into the fight. The result was a series of minor disasters that left much of the city in the hands of the Fish. The war for him had turned into one rescue mission after another—rather than actually taking the fight to the aliens. Ryland was beginning to feel that even his debriefs followed a fairly similar series of bullet points.

When he had been in college and in the ROTC, his history instructor had told him that a soldier needs to assess their shortcomings, come up with solutions, and apply them. These new recruits didn't seem to have had that lesson. Most had been fired up by the wave of patriotism that had come up at the start of the war. Their training was rushed...it had to be. Losses at the front demanded replacements faster than the Army could make them. Ryland understood the zeal and desire to protect the nation—it was why he had stayed in the Army himself. That didn't change the realities of the conflict. *This is starting to turn into a meat grinder... and we can't afford to do that over the long term.*

There's got to be a way to turn this around, to make this bullshit actually mean something. Saving these snot-nosed college punks who think that Call of Duty 22 *is equal to military training is going to get me killed sooner or later.* Ryland wanted to believe in something else, something after the war. As it was, he only saw himself coming away from the conflict with an endless series of nightmares and far too many scars for a normal man to have.

"Your assessment was pretty harsh, sir," Staff Sergeant Calcutt said as the dejected Slasher Squad survivors left the tent, still stinging from his rebuke.

"I'm trying to save their lives next time they go out. If that hurts some feelings, well, they will need to cope with that, Sergeant."

Calcutt nodded. He was also a seasoned veteran, someone who had been a warrant officer at the end of the Russo-Bratva war but, after an "incident," he'd been busted down to staff sergeant. Ryland trusted the man implicitly and counted on him every time the Ghost Legion went out.

"Casper," he said, leading with his call sign rather than his name or rank…an indication that he was going to offer his own critique. "You are probably right. But these guys lost their NCOs and an officer. They won't ever say it, but they were hurting. You came down on them a little hard, that's all."

Calcutt was right, which made it a tougher pill to swallow. Still, he felt he had no choice but to deliver a critique brutally and bluntly. "I know that. It's not easy for them; it's not easy for the Army to keep losing good people. I'm not here to make them happy, I'm here to make sure they don't turn another op into a QCCF." A Quasi-Controlled Cluster Fuck.

"Understood," the staff sergeant said, taking one step away. "If I may…you might want to watch your bitterness level before you give such a talk, sir. I understand your frustration, all of us do. We serve with you. They are strangers, and all they know is that the guy that saved their asses just told them it was their fault." Before Ryland could respond, Calcutt walked away.

The acrimony was there. There was no sense denying it. Some of it was personal frustration, some was just the war constantly eating away at him. Being obsessive-compulsive, all Ryland had was the next mission. There were no other diversions in his life, nothing that could take his mind off of the conflict. His days and sleepless nights were filled with memories and thoughts about the Fish, flash recollections of battles, and other fuel sources for sleep deprivation. The slow grind of the war was devouring him, turning him into a person that even he did not like.

From his youth, he knew what the solution was. *I need something different, something challenging, something worthwhile. Something that is about me rather than fixing other people's problems.* None of that seemed possible. He had put in for transfer to more traditional combat assignments, but Lieutenant Colonel Logan had shot that down fast. "For the time being, I need my people where they are right now, doing what they do best." He understood Logan's sentiment; he was new in his role and was still getting comfortable with the position. That didn't help Ryland.

I will have to create my own solution. Something is bound to present itself. It has to.

CHAPTER 2

Operation 410C Shake, Rattle, and Roll 1A; West Los Angeles
AIZ, the Western Front, California, the United States

Mark "Punch List" Stevens and his militia unit, Open Hostility, huddled down in an abandoned gym that was part of a small plaza on Exposition Boulevard. Remarkably, the windows were still intact, though they were covered with a dusty film that made them hard to see through, which he was thankful for. His people spread out on the mats and gym equipment for a few minutes' rest. It had been a long morning and they needed a breather. If not for the dust that had infiltrated the interior, there was a weird look of normalcy as he dropped onto a bench and pulled his camelpack's tube for a long drag of water.

They had been sneaking and trudging for three hours to evade the alien patrols. The Fish held most of West Los Angeles in their claws, but that grasp had a lot of gaps and holes that Open Hostility exploited. One of the secrets to staying alive in the AIZ was good use of terrain. His people knew that they were hard to shoot if they couldn't be seen.

Open Hostility was, on paper, a platoon of force. Some were

always left behind at their outpost on the border of the AIZ. Mark liked to go in with the troops when they were given an op in the occupied territory. No matter where his people were, they were his responsibility.

Taking another drag on the water tube, he turned to Kris "the Witch" Vogal, his second-in-command. She was a short African American woman, tough as nails, with a highly limited sense of humor that leaned strongly towards sarcasm. While she had no known ability to take a joke, her skills and experience made her damned effective. Vogal had failed out of her Ranger training when she had been in the Army and failed out of ASHUR qualifications. That didn't matter to Stevens. The fact that she had made the cut in the first place was enough for him. She had come to his construction company after mustering out of the Army, and he found her to have a lot of talent, especially in working with metal. "Hey, Witch, how much farther do we have to go?"

"Another block," she said firmly.

"Why are we doing this again?" asked Chad Corvin from the triceps press machine that he was using as a chair.

"It's simple," Stevens said. "One of the Army's precious ASHUR rigs has been crippled and we have to go in and help them recover their hardware."

"Yeah, but why are *we* doing this?" Jon "Wrench" Offerman asked.

Stevens knew whining when he heard it. "We are doing it because the Army has other missions that are of higher priority."

"And we're expendable," Roth said from his position on the

floor near a weight rack.

"That's not true," their Army liaison, Warrant Officer Shelly Reese, snapped. Most warrant officers were best described as grizzled. Trapped between being an officer and enlisted, they were rough and pragmatic. Warrants focused on results. Reese didn't fit in that mold. She held the Army up on a pedestal, even when the evidence pointed the other way. Offerman was her closest friend; the rest of the unit gave her some distance because they saw her as a true believer in the military. Stevens appreciated her naiveté at times… other times, far less so.

"Oh, it's true," Corvin said. "If this was so damned important, they would just chopper in and extract the rig."

"Can the chatter," Vogal said firmly. "They aren't going to chopper in because the Fish like shooting down choppers. We are going in because we drew the duty. They don't hate us and they don't want us dead; they just want us to do the job because they know we can do it and do it right." There was a lot of truth in the Witch's comments. Open Hostility tended to get the tough assignments because they could pull them off. Everything from diversionary attacks to "aggressive probes" put them on par or above most regular Army units.

"Why do we get the tough ops?" Offerman pressed.

Bigalow jumped in. "I spoke with some chick in the Condor Company. You know what kinds of duty they get? Garrison. They protect convoys. They hold the line. On the other hand, we get to sneak around like a bunch of rats behind the lines recovering some scrap metal."

Bitching was part of military life, even in something as informal as militia units. That was a fact of life that Stevens understood. He cut off Bigalow quickly. "We get these assignments because we are good at them. Condor Company? Seriously, Bigalow? Have you seen them? Most of their gear is Amazon.com cheap Chinese knockoffs. I know their CO. They're more a social club with weapons than a militia unit. They don't get these jobs because if they did, they'd be dead."

His words sucked the life out of the complaining.

Reese shattered the quiet. "He's right, you know."

"You have to say that," Jennings said from her spot in the corner of the gym. "You're our liaison." Her words were as effective as a well-aimed shot. Reese's face went red. She was good, if not overly enthusiastic and idealistic. She saw her role as a patriotic one, as if she were working with minutemen during the Revolutionary War. They labeled her a "true believer" and it stuck. Stevens liked her, but at times her zeal and adherence to the rules was as irritating as sand under his STG armor, grinding and grating at his skin.

"Can it," Stevens said. "Rest time is almost over anyways. We have a job to do and it's important. ASHURs are too valuable for the Army to leave them behind, even if they've been trashed." His words were from the heart. Mark had seen them in action during the Russo-Bratva War. He had helped take down a Cossack-class Russian rig in one firefight. In the ongoing war against the Fish, they had been the best edge that mankind had. Tanks in urban environments were cumbersome and vulnerable. ASHURs could move fast, had a lot of firepower, and could get into places traditional armor could not reach—like rooftops and narrow alleys. Their speed and size made them difficult to hit, and they could dodge and duck and move in ways that made them hard to target.

The combat rigs had dramatically altered military tactics and doctrine. There were a handful of elite units that were all ASHURs, but for the most part, there was just one per platoon. ASHURs operated hand in hand with a unit, but their pilots were trained to be solo operators as well. Where normal military doctrine called for engaging the enemy at a distance, ASHURs had a tendency to operate up-close and personal with the enemy—their armor allowed for that kind of engagement. They often could shatter a well-disciplined human unit and were not afraid of entering a kill box unless the troops were armed with anti-tank weapons. Even in those instances, their speed and proximity often made the use of such weapons as much as a danger to the ASHUR as the personnel it was attacking.

Every government on the planet wanted ASHURs and used them in different capacities. They were highly prized, even battle weary ones. More importantly, recovered ASHURs could be rebuilt—which was easier and cheaper than replacing them.

Recovery meant that the technology wouldn't end up in the alien's claws. No one knew for sure how the Fishtech worked or if they could use human military gear, but no one wanted to take that risk. The aliens used biological engineering on a scale that was beyond comprehension. Their weapons and ammunition were organic in nature. They incorporated metal into their bodies and organs as well. Some could heal their wounds and injuries in a matter of minutes. Even their communications were a mystery. How they functioned and worked was species still a vast unknown for mankind. It was that deep enigma that added to the fright that they generated.

Stevens rose to his feet and the rest of Open Hostility followed suit, without a word needing to be spoken. The people in his militia unit all had some combat experience before the alien invasion. Even Sprang, who had served in the Coast Guard, had seen action against the Mexican cartels. Mark knew a few of them from the construction company he had owned, the rest had come through referrals. The company was gone—he had lost everything when the Fish had waded ashore. The way Mark saw it, he could reenlist or pull together a militia unit. Rather than tell his people to hit the unemployment line, he gave them hope in the unit he founded. In his mind, he was still putting food on their families' plates.

His people knew the drill. When Stevens stood, the time for griping was over. It was time to do militia shit. They made their way to the rear of the gym and emptied into the street behind the plaza, crouching low. Moving single file with the Witch in the lead, they crept past a series of dumpsters that were now blocking the access to the parking lot.

The apartment building behind the plaza was a three-story affair with a semi-underground parking garage. Rather than move around it, Vogal opted to go through the garage. It took a moment for them to pry open the security door to get in. Mark approved of the path. Moving outside made them exposed. At least the parking structure would give them a good defensive position if the Fish came at them.

It was dimly lit, the days of the electric lights having evaporated along with much of the city's electrical infrastructure. The floor had an inch of stagnant water, no doubt from a shattered water main somewhere. Open Hostility sloshed through it, moving around abandoned cars, coming up on the ramp at the far side of the structure. The Witch paused and Stevens came up alongside her. "I make our target on the other side of that row of houses," he whispered, looking at the street in front of them. One of the houses was a gutted shell, burned to the ground. The two next to it showed damage from the fire, looked merely vacant.

"You want the left or right?" Vogal asked.

"Left," he said. It was a random choice. Neither passageway looked more promising than the other. While the street looked empty, there was no way to know if the enemy had eyes on it.

Using hand signals, he gestured for his alpha fire team to break to the left and straight; Vogal did the same with bravo fire team to the right. When she finished, she gave him a nod and lowered the visor on her helmet.

They scurried across quickly, silently, moving on both flanks of the burned out building. It was a narrow passage that reeked of charred vinyl siding. Moving past the tiny fenced-in yard, he saw the street beyond. Looming in the middle of it was what looked like a statue. It was a Komodo-class ASHUR, standing erect around the glitter of spent brass in the street. It was one of the Gen Three rigs, sleeker, deadlier. This one had been through hell, that was obvious. Its right arm was missing, nowhere to be seen. Its legs had lost most of their armor, and hydraulic fluid dribbled out on what was left, puddling at the feet of the beast. The cockpit canopy was open, but it had been breached in several places—melted through by a Fish acid squirter. There had been a firefight all around the Komodo. The signs of battle were everywhere...a crunched Carl Gustaf tube, magazines tossed about, even bits of STG armor and parts of the ASHUR rig. A helmet rested against one of the metallic feet of the rig. *There is a story here; there was a great fight. Now all that remains is the debris and tech.*

He held up his fist to signal to Vogal to hold their position, then activated his communications system. "Battlespace Commander, this is Open Hostility Actual, Op four, one, zero, Charlie, Shake, Rattle and Roll, one alpha. We are in position."

"Roger that, Open Hostility Actual," came the disembodied voice. "The recovery team is closing on your position now. ETA looks to be about ten minutes."

"Confirmed."

He used hand signals to Vogal to cross the street. *She's smart. There's a house there with a low stone wall. It will provide them good cover.* While she deployed, he ordered his unit to spread out along the street opposite of them. His two best shooters, Jennings and Nardo, used the downspouts of the buildings adjacent to the burned out structure to climb up and take the high ground. Likewise Corvin from bravo fire team climbed up a tree that was growing next to the sidewalk across the street and assumed a position there. Stevens pulled Grant over and assigned him to watching their rear, covering their exit if things went south.

The waiting was the hard part. ASHUR recovery could come in a lot of different forms. This was a truck, a lumbering out-of-date diesel from the sound of it. Even three blocks away, over the distant firing and occasional booming of the AIZ, Mark could hear it coming, right down to where the driver was grinding gears. It finally came into view and he was surprised by the sight. It had been a tow truck in its previous life. Clearly the Army had commandeered it, painting it with dull flat green and gray paint. It was so badly dinged, that even from the distance, he could see streaks of the original bright red paint showing through.

He hated the sound it made as it got closer. It turned around when it came up on the rig and two techs bounded out and began winching out the cable and lowering the bed to drag the ASHUR up. As they did, he moved out to join them, his ACR at the ready.

"Thanks for the support," one of the E4s said, hooking on to one of the ASHUR's numerous handholds. The bed came down on the street hard, with a boom that made Stevens wince. *That had to have been heard for blocks.* His eyes darted both ways down the street.

"You guys have to move and move fast," he said. The winch whined loudly as it dragged the ASHUR to the edge of the bed. It stopped for a moment, then fell over on the bed of the tow vehicle. The booming thud reverberated everywhere, shaking dust off the leaves of the tree where Corvin was still holding position. *These guys are practically broadcasting our presence here.* Then came the metal scraping of the rig being dragged farther on the bed.

"We have incoming," called down Jennings from his position on to the tactical channel in their helmet comm systems. "Due west, four blocks."

The voice of the battlespace commander came on next. "Open Hostility Actual, we show two Crabs and supporting forces moving on your position quickly. Advise you get out of there now."

Thanks, Captain Obvious! Stevens looked over at the E4 watching the ASHUR being loaded. "Raise your bed and get moving."

"I still have to strap it down," he said.

"Raise the fucking bed and get moving or we are going to be overrun," he clarified.

The E4, a young kid, lost all color in his face in that instant. He turned to the driver. "Raise the bed now!"

Battles were a form of math, a silent series of rapid-fire calculations that led to decisions and actions. It was something that Stevens had learned when he had served in the last war. The size of the coming force meant that his people were not going to be able to simply sneak their way back to the front lines. The Fish would either go for the recovery vehicle, his people, or both. If he made the wrong choice in that instant, it could cost people their lives, something he was opposed to doing.

He tapped his wristcomp to broadcast to the entire unit. "This is Casper," he said using his call sign. "We have baddies closing on us. Everyone, on the truck. We will fight from there."

Open Hostility didn't need to be told twice. They scurried aboard the vehicle, moving to use the ASHUR as partial cover. Corvin came last, stopping long enough at the former battle site to grab the helmet and a few magazines that were on the ground. Stevens understood. Battlefield salvage was a big part of being in the militia. *We can always use the ammo, and who knows, maybe the Coyote will want the helmet.*

Vogal barked out orders to Roth who wedged a claymore mine on the back of the truck, up against the footpad of the ASHUR. "Let's roll!" Stevens called, banging on the cab as the pair of E4s scampered in. In the distance, the dust cloud from the approaching enemy was visible, closing fast.

The truck lurched and started off at what seemed like a leisurely pace. Stevens zoomed in his helmet's visor and saw the Crabs and what looked like eight to ten Frogs moving towards them. "Weapons free," he signaled. Turning to the cab, he banged again and called out, "Punch it, God damn it!"

"It isn't exactly built for speed," the driver said as the vehicle lurched a few miles per hour faster. Weapons fire began from his team. Nardo, Jennings, and Corvin led with their sniper rifles. "Not exactly the most stable firing platform, boss," Corvin grumbled as the vehicle bounded around with the suspension of an old dump truck.

As the Fish closed the distance, Stevens turned and tried to steady his aim as best as possible, lining up one Crab and firing controlled single shots, one after another. It was doubtful that they were doing much damage, but he hoped that one of them might hit a gap in their armored hide. He saw the lead alien twitch slightly under impacts from the sniper shots, but otherwise was undeterred as it closed in on the back of the tow truck.

"Be advised," the voice of the battlespace commander said in his ears. "The enemy is almost on top of you."

"You think?" he said, only half regretting it.

Suddenly there was a rolling deep booming noise that raced out in ripple-like waves through the streets between the two forces, concussing up toward the truck. Stevens's vision tunneled and his ears and brain ached worse than any ice cream–induced brain freeze he had ever endured.

It was a sonic blaster—one of the wonderful weapons the aliens brought to the party. Glancing at his people he saw that many were like him, doubled over in pain. Even with their visors down, he could make out the agony the weapon inflicted.

Stevens rallied himself; there was little choice. His eyes watered as he moved, his brain felt like it was sloshing from one side of his head to another. Rising as the truck hit a pothole, he almost lost his balance, steadying himself on the Komodo. He aimed with icy precision, his targeting reticle inside of his visor showed he had the Crab in his sights. Squeezing the trigger, he couldn't even hear his gun fire, his ears were so badly popped. Only the slam of the weapon into his shoulder assured him that it had fired.

His shots slapped into the carapace-hide of the creature's midsection, not even slowing it. The forward Crab was followed by its comrades and was almost on top of them. Stacked grenades flew from his side, landing in front of the creature and going off as it passed. One of the Frogmen was cut in half by the explosion—which un-popped his right ear painfully. The lead Crab slowed, just long enough for the other one to pass it. *Good, that means it's hurt!*

A spray of needler projectiles tore into the rear of the truck, causing everyone to fall flat or dive behind the Komodo. More grenades flew at the new Crab, more blasts went off. Rising once again, Stevens saw the creature a mere ten feet behind the vehicle, its claws jutting in front of it as if he were trying to grab the end of the bed of the tow truck.

To hell with fire discipline...he switched to full automatic and aimed for the large flattened head of the creature, emptying his magazine in a stream of hot jacketed metal. He saw the flicks of the deflected rounds but at that range, some had to have gotten through. His shots were not the only ones, the rest of Open Hostility poured fired into the alien.

It hopped, lunging for the bed of the truck. Mark had seen many Crabs in the battles for La, but never this close. The Crab landed hard, making the entire vehicle lurch, and he grabbed the ASHUR to avoid falling. A flash of panic hit him as he saw the creature rise from behind the fallen Komodo. Its massive claws were open extended, swinging out, preparing to sweep his unit like giant scythes. Its deadly tail stabbed down towards Bigalow, missing and hitting the bed of the truck, punching through the steel plate, then whipping sideways in recoil, cutting Bigalow's shoulder in the process and almost throwing him off the truck. Stevens's reloading felt like it was in slow motion. Vogal moved beside them, her ACR unleashing everything she had in her magazine.

There was a *whomp* from the rear of the truck, different from the sound of grenades going off. It was Corvin's claymore. Hot shrapnel tore into the underbelly of the Crab where it was weakest, ripping the alien's midsection and blasting it in half. The tail and rear portion of the creature hissed for a moment and sprayed a grayish black ooze skyward, then flopped off into the path of the pursuing aliens.

The front part of the Crab collapsed forward onto the Komodo, falling limp. The creature's huge head came to rest right in front of Stevens, only two feet away. It made a groaning noise, something deep and muffled. He hoped it was a dying gasp, but with the aliens, you never could tell. He moved back a bit, then stuck the barrel of his ACR right between the eyes and fired a round—simply to be sure that it was dead. Even though half of it was gone, you couldn't trust a Fish.

* * *

It took an hour for the truck to reach the edge of the AIZ and the safety of being out of enemy controlled territory. Their egress point was an Army controlled outpost, a barricade that blocked off six city blocks from potential enemy intrusion. It looked formidable, with all of its razor wire and carefully crafted obstructions, but Stevens had been around long enough to know that such defenses were child's play against an all-out alien assault. *We do the same thing at our outpost. It's more to make us feel safer than provide true safety.*

His people had suffered minor wounds. Bigalow had a sprained shoulder; Clarkston, Roth, and Nardo had been hit by needler spikes. None of the projectiles had gotten through their blast plates. Even with the STF, the sheer thickening fluid of their armor, they were all badly bruised from the kinetic force of the impacts.

They drove to the repair depot before the truck finally stopped. One of the E4s in the cab nearly passed out when he saw half of the

Crab on top of the Komodo they had recovered. In the flurry of their flight, no one had told the techs that they had picked up part of a hitchhiker in the process. The sight of the Crab carcass attracted a crowd. Most of the techs didn't get a chance to see the enemy up close. They eyed it with fear and awe. One took a metal rod and poked at it. Stevens understood their marveling at the creature. No doubt they had been told all sorts of stories and propaganda about the Fish. Seeing one at personal range was bound to shake some of their resolve, or worse, confirm their darkest nightmares.

A young lieutenant, probably fresh out of OCS, stormed over and began a lecture about the rules regarding bringing aliens into the base. "You are breaking protocol! You are putting us all at risk!" he barked up at Stevens. The commander of the militia looked down at the lieutenant as if he were mentally disabled. *The damn thing nearly killed us, and now this kid is telling me we are introducing some sort of threat.* The rules that the Army had were quaint...in some cases downright entertaining in their levels of stupidity. That was the advantage of being militia—the rules were seen more as rough guidelines. "Lieutenant," he said slowly. "Our mission was to recover this rig. We did that. I can't be responsible for the fact that we picked up a hitchhiker along the way." It was the most polite way of telling the officer to fuck off that Mark could come up with.

Open Hostility went to a set of tents used for teams to rest up before returning to their posts. Everyone got mostly hot showers, a chance to wash off the dust of La from their skin. They also got a chance to get reloads and replace any damaged gear. Corvin proudly told him that the helmet he had salvaged was in good working order.

They got some grief about replacing their stackable grenades. The staff sergeant in charge of resupply gave a long story about them being in short supply. It was as if the irony was completely lost on him. The debate ended when Stevens suggested that he would love to talk to the sergeant's CO about him getting some first-hand experience and going out on a mission or two with Open Hostility. Replacements were miraculously found with the suggestion and provided.

They got a fresh meal before heading back to their own base. It wasn't half bad, even by Army mess standards. At least it was a meal that they didn't have to prepare. He was even able to convince one of the supply trucks to drive them back to their tiny base.

Reese prepared the combat action report and BDA for the unit, submitting it to him for approval. He signed off on it without even looking at it, using his finger on her digipad in a sweep that looked nothing like his signature. "Aren't you even going to read it?" she asked.

"Why, did you lie in it?"

That question flustered her for a moment. "Of course not. It's just that it is an official report."

"I know," Mark said. "But does it *really* matter?"

"They go up through the chain of command."

"Reese, you're a good liaison. You need to learn one thing, though. Paperwork and administrative bullshit won't end this war. It doesn't get us any new equipment, it doesn't give us a single round of ammo more. You write a damn fine battle assessment, but in the end, it is just a waste of time."

"It's part of my job."

"It is. It's just not necessary. It doesn't help anyone. All it does is make sure that your Army CO can check a box on your evaluation that says you turned it in. Nothing more, nothing less."

She looked dejected, and he felt bad about it, but by the same token, it had to be said. *Reese likes doing things by the numbers, by the book. Out here, the book doesn't mean shit. She still hasn't wrapped her mind around that yet.*

"Don't take it personally, Shelly," he said, attempting to ease her angst. "You have to do what you have to do in order to get through this clusterfuck of a war. If that means writing reports on what we do, then do it. I'll sign them. Just don't expect me to be joyous about it. My job is to keep these people alive and combat effective. I have to lead them on ops that most people would run from. That's my job. Yours is to make sure we are coordinated with the Army."

He paused, letting his words sink in. "Now that you've submitted your report, let's go check on the others. Something tells me that we aren't going to have much downtime."

"Have you heard something?"

"No," Stevens said. "Not yet. It's just a nagging hunch. With this sector getting a new CO with Colonel Logan, he's going to want to make a mark for himself so he doesn't end up like the last man in command here. People in those positions have a tendency to put us into action just to show they are the biggest swinging dick at HQ."

A part of him regretted the "dick" comment—but Mark did nothing to take it back.

CHAPTER 3

Headquarters, Foxtrot Sector, the Western Front, West Los Angeles AIZ, California, the United States

Lieutenant Ryland entered the principal's office of the commandeered Catholic school that served as the sector headquarters. The furniture had been kept but most of the other trappings of the office's prior user had been removed, except for the crucifix hanging on the wall behind Lieutenant Colonel Logan. Standing before the new commanding officer for the sector, Ryland couldn't take his eyes off the lurking crucifix. It was hard not to feel as though he was being brought before the principal for some sort of discipline, even though he had committed no transgression.

Logan was an older officer, which was something that Frank appreciated. He commanded the 7th Infantry Division's 1st Striker BCT—and with that, all of Foxtrot Sector. Logan was in the National Guard when the war started, called up to active duty. Other than that, Ryland didn't have much of the older man's background. There were rumors that had been circulating since his arrival, but he had disregarded those. *With so many unknowns in this war, there are more rumors than bullets in the air.*

With a hand gesture, Logan motioned for Ryland to take a seat. "I saw your after-action report from yesterday," the lieutenant colonel said. "Damn fine piece of work, saving those trapped troops."

"To be blunt, sir, we shouldn't have had to go in in the first place. They screwed up. If they had followed orders, I wouldn't have had to risk my personnel to try to get their collective butts out of there. They weren't ready, not for the kind of fighting that the Fish are throwing at us."

Logan winced at the biting assessment. "True. We are throwing in green troops into situations that they aren't prepared for. We'd spend years preparing them to fight a war against an enemy like the Russians or the Chinese, and now they are facing aliens with weapons and troops right out of a science fiction film."

His words were refreshing to Ryland. *At least he's a realist.* "Putting them out there on these patrols, even the ones that seem safe, gets people killed and wounded."

The lieutenant colonel sighed and seemed to relax in the wooden chair. "That's true. By the same token, we can't coddle them until they are ready. I don't have the luxury of time on my hands. The Fish are not letting up pressure on us. That means that some raw troops are going to have to earn their stripes out there." He gestured to the window which did not offer a good view of West Los Angeles —but it was enough for Ryland to get the point.

"Sir, it is better to use these new troops as replacements than have them serve together."

"I know that, Lieutenant. We are both burdened by the orders from headquarters. I proposed that very change two days after getting stuck with this job. The commanding general said no. He believes that breaking up these units would be a blow to morale."

"Morale is important, but it's a nicety. Death ranks higher in my book."

"Mine as well. My Boss doesn't seem like he's interested in my opinion."

"Yes, sir." There wasn't much else for Ryland to say. He was just starting to build a relationship with the lieutenant colonel. While Derek Logan seemed like a reasonable man, it would take some time to validate that and earn his complete trust.

"Do you know how I got this job?" Logan said after a long moment of silence.

"No, sir. How?"

"I got this position because the man ahead of me did everything by the book. He followed every Pentagon directive. He adhered to the rules from his commanding general. In doing so, he got a lot of people killed and lost a lot of ground to the enemy."

It was a candid and icy assessment, one that Ryland thought remarkably accurate. "I tend to agree, sir. Colonel Higgerson was a good man, but he was a byproduct of the last war. Even the way he allocated ASHURs showed a counter-Russian way of thinking."

Logan pulled up his digipad and stabbed at it quickly. "He said you were a reckless element," Logan read, squinting at the pad. "He felt you were unorthodox. That you 'chaffed at following proper military doctrine.'"

These words were a surprise. Apparently Colonel Higgerson had been keeping notes about him. While they all were true, the practice of keeping such notes was often a ploy to ruin a man's military career. *That rat-bastard! He was sabotaging me all along. All I was doing was telling him the truth. The other officers were more interested in kissing his ass and telling him what he wanted to hear.* "Sir, if I may—"

"No, you may not. Let me tell you what I think. I've perused your reports and BDAs. I've seen the emails you sent Higgerson. You told him the cold hard truth. The problem was he didn't want to hear that. What he wanted was some mindless human GRD rather than a good officer who could think and act on his own. So he left me this little log file on you and a few others that he felt responsible for him losing his command. A nasty little parting shot."

Ryland felt his jaw lock forward, despite the honesty. He was still pissed about Higgerson's sabotage. *I wonder how many people were privy to those comments? How much damage did that bald-headed bastard do?* "I was unaware that the colonel harbored such resentment towards me," was the best that he could muster.

"Lieutenant," Logan began in an almost fatherly tone. "Understand this. I don't care what Higgerson thought about you. You can't polish shit, and he was piled high and deep. You get a clean slate with me. I am all in favor of following fancy rules of engagement or directives from on high, but I'm more interested in taking back the city. Victories have a great way of redeeming any snide remarks by a washed-up officer."

That's a relief. "Thank you, sir."

"The problem I'm facing right now is that the number of

missions that command has piled up for me overpowers my ability to mount the kind of counteroffensive I need. That means I have to take advantage of the resources at my disposal. Your Ghost Legion has a damned good reputation for brutal efficiency. That means you and your people are going to be rotated out into the AIZ quite a bit in the coming weeks."

That was not good news. His people were exhausted already. The Ghost Legion was good, but they were tired. What the lieutenant colonel was telling him was that they were going to be pushed even harder. "Sir, there has to be another way. My people are pretty strung out as it is."

"I understand," Logan replied. "I also don't have much of a choice."

"You could offload some of our ops to the militia."

That comment brought about wrinkles on Logan's face and a tinge of crimson rose to his face. "Between you and me, some of these militia units are about as useful as a box of hair."

Ryland understood what he meant. Militia units came in all different flavors. Some were former street gangs, some were biker clubs, others were just some good-old-boys looking to perform some legalized alien killing. Word was that the California governor was even forming penal units, taking murderers out of prison and having them fight with a pardon dangled in front of them as an incentive.

Not all militia units sucked. The Wranglers, Open Hostility, Angel Flight, the Crimson A's…they were all good, almost as good as his own Ghost Legion. The rest spread out on a spectrum between fair and a walking bag of dicks. While some lacked the skills, the

Army had embraced the militias despite knowing little about how to utilize them. The lack of control over such forces made a lot of commanders use them for light or rear area duties. Higgerson preferred to use them as "Ukrainian Mine Detectors," likening them to blindfolded chumps randomly stomping the ground before them to find landmines. It was an ugly comparison implying stupidity that Ryland didn't find entirely accurate.

But that wasn't all. Regular Army officers and staff tended to view militia as second-class soldiers. There wasn't the kind of trust with militia that reg-Army officers had with trained personnel. A militia unit had to prove itself in order to earn respect with many officers. Even with victories and successes, there were a handful of officers that would never come around to respecting them.

"Sir, not all of the militia units are messed up. Some are a hell of a lot better than the replacements and new units we are getting. The ones with personnel that are staffed with veterans, for example, are almost as good as our best forces in this sector."

"That may be, but they don't follow orders well. Some disengage from the enemy at first sight. I can't prove it, but some seem to be into this for the looting and salvage more than the fighting."

That was true. One militia team had "liberated" a group of G-Wagons from a Mercedes-Benz dealership in the AIZ and had turned them into their own high-end Technicals. There were a lot of stories of militia units selling arms and ammo they had recovered on the black market.

"I think this is a case of a few bad units giving the rest a bad name," Ryland offered. "A handful of these troops would be helpful in offloading some of the missions you might be looking to shift to us."

Logan said nothing for a long minute. He rested his elbows on the principal's desk, templing his fingers in front of his face. The gaze from his hazel eyes was as penetrating as an anti-tank rocket. The silence was enough to make Ryland want to speak, but he held back that urge. Finally, Logan lowered his hands to the desktop. "I'll take that under advisement, Lieutenant. Prep me a list of units you'd recommend. I won't promise you anything at this point, but I will look it over and do some digging. Command is expecting me to mount a counteroffensive and I'd appreciate your input as to the quality of such units. Ultimately, it doesn't matter to me who goes out and fulfills a mission, as long as it gets done and done right."

Ryland nodded. He was about to ask if there was anything else that Logan wanted, when a knock on the door interceded. His clerk, a young corporal, leaned in. "Sir, Ratchet is here with her entourage."

"Ratchet—the singer?" Logan asked. Ryland simply shrugged.

"Yes, sir," the corporal said.

"What does she want?"

"Sir, she wants to talk to someone about going into the AIZ to recover something for her."

Well, there's a first. A lot of people fled La when the Fish had invaded. *You have to wonder what Ratchet thinks we are going to do about it.*

Logan rolled his eyes and sighed. "Lieutenant, can you sit down with her and inform her that the US Army is not an asset recovery team at her disposal?"

"Yes, sir," Ryland said, rising to his feet.

"Tell her to fuck off, but don't use those words," the lieutenant colonel said, allowing his wrinkled face to crack a thin smile. "These damned celebrities will talk to the media about their little problems and the last thing I need right now is a public relations problem."

With a nod, Frank Ryland stepped out into the adjoining office.

* * *

Ratchet looked entirely out of place in the teachers' lounge that had been converted into a makeshift conference room. She—he assumed she identified as she—wore a cut-off T-shirt that barely covered her breasts. He was fairly sure they were controllable implants. As she walked with a wiggle, he saw her rear end and assumed that it too had a bio-pump system to improve the looks of her booty.

Her mocha skin was perfect in almost every way. Her hair extensions were high-end, with UV color tinting that could be changed with a special light brush. It was the kind of add-ons that only the super-rich could afford. She wore makeup, something that Ryland hadn't seen in a long time on another human. He caught a whiff of her perfume and felt his face go red. *No doubt she's using some pheromone enhancers in it...all part of maintain her sex-appeal image.* Flanking her were two hulking bodyguards, but Ratchet looked more like she was on her way to a movie set than visiting a combat zone.

He offered her a water, but her bodyguard gave her a bottle—

obviously something imported by the label he couldn't read. Oddly it made sense. *The rich will always get their perks, while we struggle to get deodorant and toothpaste.* He settled down in a seat across from her and she eyed him with an arrogant disdain.

"Why couldn't the colonel meet with me?" she demanded, taking a sip from her bottle.

"He's a very busy man."

"*I'm* very busy too."

There's a war on, in case you haven't noticed. Frank had to temper his inner voice. "What can we do for you?"

"I need the Army to recover some personal goods for me."

"I see…" was all he could muster without yelling at her for her haughtiness or busting out laughing.

"There's a little bank in Beverly Hills," Ratchet continued. "The bank is called Commerce, and it is just off of Rodeo Drive at Wilshire. I have a safe-deposit box with them, and I would like the contents of that box."

Ryland cocked his head. "I've been up there a few times and I don't remember any bank there."

"No doubt. It is there for exclusive clientele. It's what I would call *discreet*. Just a simple door and a tiny sign. Those that need to know about it, know about it." She had a way of talking down to him that he found amusing as much as insulting.

She's talking down to me without even realizing it. "You *do* realize that Beverly Hills is in the AIZ. It's occupied territory."

"Of course," she said, taking another fast sip of her water. "That's why I'm here. You are in the Army. I pay taxes, which means

I help fund the Army. I probably pay your salary. All I need you to do is to go in there and get me my possessions."

It was hard to not laugh at her, but somehow Ryland managed. "I'm sure it looks that way, from your perspective, but what you are asking for is dangerous and a bit unreasonable."

"Send in some of your Ashcans or whatever they're called, or a tank, I don't care. I'm not asking you to do anything but get into that vault and get out my belongings."

She's used to everyone in the world jumping when she makes demands. The problem is that the Fish are not from this world. "Miss Ratchet—"

"Just Ratchet."

"Like Madonna?"

"Who?"

"Sorry, I like the oldies."

"No one listens to that old crap. My stuff is fresh, crisp and spicy," she proclaimed proudly. She winked at him, as if that might sway Ryland.

He remembered that Lieutenant Colonel Logan didn't want a public relations incident, so he held his tongue even more than before. "Ratchet—you see, for us to go in there, people are likely to be killed. The Army doesn't run asset recovery missions. We are fighting a war just to hold on to what we have. We don't have enough personnel to engage in these kinds of missions."

"What about my possessions? I didn't have time to get them out when the Fish came—I was in a photo shoot in New York. Are you telling me that my stuff just has to sit there until you win this little war of yours?"

"It's not a little war," he corrected her in a controlled tone of voice. "These aliens have hit every coastal city. No doubt you've seen the news. We are fighting just to contain them at this point."

"I don't care about that. The war is your problem. The things I have in that vault are important to me and I want them."

She doesn't understand the concept of "no." "We just don't do those kinds of operations. Sending a team in that deep behind enemy lines means they would run the risk of being overrun, captured, or slaughtered. It would be suicide."

"Well, can't you just send your army-people in there and secure Beverly Hills? You don't have to hold it long, just long enough to get my things out."

"The Army doesn't work that way."

"Shouldn't it?" she demanded.

"No. If we were to do this for you, then everyone in Hollywood would have us attempting to get to their mansions or into movie studios. Surely you understand that you can't run a military based on special requests like this."

Ratchet crossed her arms, almost like she was pouting. For a few moments, she said nothing—but glared at him with her dark brown eyes. "This is about money, isn't it?"

"I'm sorry...what?"

"Money. Fine, I get it. I will pay you a half mil to go and recover the things that belong to me. I don't care about anything else in that vault. You can take whatever else is there, but I will pay you to go in and get what is mine."

Ryland understood that she was used to using her wealth as lever. A half a million dollars was a lot of money; it was hard to ignore it. *What good is that kind of cash if you are dead?* Ratchet did offer something else, the rest of what was in the vault. *If that is the kind of place that the rich and famous store their stuff, I can only imagine the kinds of things that are in there.* Suddenly the bank and its contents came into a new focus with Frank. *What's in there could be worth tens of millions of dollars.* Yes, it was far behind the lines—but it was just sitting there.

For the moment, he suppressed the greed that tugged at the back of his mind, and instead focused on her request. "What kind of security does this mystery bank have?"

One of her big bodyguards spoke up. "Most of the usual stuff. Laser grid with alarms and lockdown. The vault door can't be reached except through steel bars. Word we have is that the vault has a gas system in it, should anyone try to enter without the right combination." The way he spoke, he was experienced in such matters.

It sounded formidable—but by the same token, it was not impervious. Explosives and a lack of electricity would negate some of the defenses. Frank caught himself contemplating the risks versus the rewards for a moment, then reeled himself back into reality. *There's no way we could do it—Beverly Hills is too far behind the lines.*

"I am deeply sorry, but there's just not a lot the Army can do for you on this matter."

"You're just not man enough to do it," she verbally prodded.

He smiled a little at the attempt to insult his manhood. *I have been through hell and back, you spoiled little bitch. I have been fighting and bleeding out there so that you have the right to flaunt your wealth and fame. If you think you can goad me into action with mere words, it's time for you to graduate high school and get into the real world.* "Have you ever been out there? Have you ever seen the enemy?"

"I've seen the vids on the net," she snapped back.

Frank chuckled. "Don't play little games with me about my masculinity or willingness to fight. I've been out there, putting my life on the line so that people like you are safe and sound at night. I've seen the aliens face-to-face. I've been wounded more times than I can remember. You talk like going out there is some stroll in the park. It's not. Death is waiting behind every corner, behind every mound of rubble or abandoned car. Almost every form of death comes slowly, with pain and agony. That is why I won't risk the lives of good men and woman so that you can have your things back."

"Fine," she spat angrily. "Who *can* do something about it?"

He drew a long breath in through his nose before responding. "The militia units wouldn't undertake it. I suppose you could go and talk to some PMCs. They have the kind of resources to pull something off like that, though I doubt any of them would be interested, given the risks involved." That wasn't quite true. PMCs—Private Military Contractors—might actually take a look at what she offered. Frank was hopeful that his words would dissuade her from pursuing that option.

"Well, how do I get in contact with one of these PMCs?"

"Most are under contract right now. You can Boink them, I guess," he said, referring to the search engine.

"Who would you recommend?"

She's persistent, I'll give her that. Whatever is in that vault must be worth a great deal. He took a moment to consider. Each PMC had their own strengths and weaknesses. He wanted to choose someone that would have the brains and balls to turn the mission down. After all, mounting such a push into the AIZ was going to result in carnage and death. "One of the more legitimate ones is Spartan Associates. You can try asking them, but chances are they will tell you the same thing I did."

"We're done here," Ratchet said, rising and leaving with her bodyguards opening the door for her.

Good luck with that. They are not the kinds of people that maintain web pages…not the good ones, anyway.

CHAPTER 4

Outpost 46— Op Red Rover 2, the Western Front, West Los Angeles AIZ, California, the United States

Open Hostility didn't have a formal operation looming for the time being. As a result, they received two days' rest and refit, then rotated to a defensive position on the border of the AIZ. Mark Stevens hated the assignment. *You can't win a war by playing defense.* At the same time, he didn't complain because he knew the Army would be more than happy to throw his militia force out against the Fish as a response. As a former vet, he understood that complaining about your assignment, good or bad, was integral to the military mindset.

Their position, Outpost 46, was a road intersection. Hesco barriers had been piled two high and four deep as a berm to block off the street, except for a narrow passage large enough for a vehicle. That gap had temporary barricades and steel caltrops there as a deterrent for any aliens that might chose to try to rush it. A tower had been erected with an old, beat-up M2 poised in it. Five big weathered and damaged yellow metal cargo containers had been dropped off by the Army Corps of Engineers and outfitted as quarters and storage. They had piled sandbags around them, though no one really felt that they would be much of a defense if the Fish came in force. Two of the container units were used for bunk beds, the third was a common area—which had a television that could only get two channels, a table, a sofa that had been scavenged from an abandoned house, and some chairs. The lighting was bright LEDs, too bright for his tastes. Still, Outpost 46 was home, and it had the illusion of being quasi-safe.

They had originally set up in an abandoned apartment building, but the Army had deemed it too far from the outpost, so they got the storage containers as shelters instead. It was a bit frustrating to Stevens; most of the apartments were empty. A few locals had opted to stay behind, despite urgings to leave. It had been like that in Alaska too. *Some people just can't bear to leave, so they stay behind.* It had been that way since the beginning of warfare, he reckoned. *You have to wonder how many civilians remained behind during the battle of Stalingrad. How many ended up dead because they refused to move on?*

He checked the troops at the outpost, making sure that the first watch was in their designated positions. On either side of the street were office buildings that had been abandoned since the start of the fighting. He had two of his people up there, observing from a better vantage point.

There was always a chance that the Fish would attack. It was an ominous threat that never seemed to materialize at his outpost. Others got hit, some were overrun—forcing the Army to try to take them back. Occasionally his people would get a sighting of a Fox or some other alien a few blocks up from their position, but so far it had not resulted in a general offensive operation.

As Stevens stood surveying the tower, Barry Roth walked over to him, his greasy short black hair spiked with sweat and held in place by the ever-present dust. "Sir, the Coyote is here."

Stevens cracked a smile. Don "Coyote" Sims was a freelancer among all the militia units. The man was a scavenger of the highest caliber. There were two stories about him and his relationship with the black market. One was that he was one of their best field contacts. The second was that he *was* the black market in greater La. As Roth finished, Mark could hear the rumble of that truck getting closer. When the Coyote showed up in his old surplus Army truck, it was time to barter or buy just about anything.

No one knew much about Sims before the war, but the rumors were entertaining. Some said he was a loan shark, a hustler, an ex-con—hell, one rumor even said that he had been a commodities broker that had been forced into his new line of business. Stevens didn't care where he came from and never bothered to ask. There were rumors that he stole many of his weapons from the Army, but that didn't seem likely. After all, if he had, the Army would have tracked him down long ago. What mattered, as far as the commander of Open Hostility was concerned, was that the Coyote could provide things that were needed.

"Alright, break out the stuff," he said as he saw the olive green truck lumber around the corner and pull up next to their storage container homes. It coughed up a black billow of diesel smoke until it finally shut off. The Army's newer trucks were hybrids; this one was an antique in every aspect.

Sims bounded out of the passenger seat, wearing a fresh jumpsuit —obtained from who knows where—with a big smile on his face. "Ah, Lieutenant Stevens—good to see you again!" He beamed, walking over and giving Mark a firm handshake. Coyote was one of the few people that referred to him as a lieutenant, the designation that the Army gave him for commanding a platoon's worth of militia.

"Coyote," Mark acknowledged back. "I hadn't expected to see you for a few days."

"I was in the neighborhood. The Westside Irregulars were in need of resupply after their op three days ago, and after I helped them out, I thought I would stop by my favorite unit and see if you needed anything." There was almost a singing tone to his voice that sounded more like a used car salesman than a reputable purveyor of military hardware. "Besides, word was your folks did a hell of a job not too long ago, rescuing an abandoned ASHUR."

Where the hell does he get his information? The Army's G2 should hire this guy. Then again, I doubt they could afford him. "We did alright," Mark conceded.

"You brought back half a Crab," he said. "Do you know what that could have gone for to the right buyer?"

"You know it's illegal to traffic in alien flesh," Mark said with a grin. There were a lot of companies out there that wanted any bit of Fish tissue or organs or whatever they could get their hands on. There were also laws against anyone selling or buying alien parts.

"Oh, I would never be involved in something so unsavory," Coyote assured him with false honesty. "I was just making a point."

"Right…" Mark said. "We did get a few things on the last two ops." Turning, he gestured to Roth and Nardo who carried out a footlocker and put it at the feet of the Coyote.

Opening it up, he immediately pulled out the ECH helmet they had recovered on the last op. "You know, it's hard to get these things. A lot of civilians want them now. This one is a little banged up, but I'd be happy to front you one hundred for it in credit."

Kris Vogal walked over. "You can do better than that, Coyote, and you know it."

He turned to see her and grinned. "Aw, come on, Witch, you know that guys are dropping these all over the place."

"Not one that works. We checked this one, it's good," she pressed, standing next to Mark.

"Alright, one twenty-five."

"One fifty," Mark said. "Anything less than that and we'll keep it."

"Fine," scoffed Coyote. "You know you're robbing me."

"Sure we are," Vogal said. "You would know all about that."

"You know, I get the feeling sometimes you don't trust me."

"We don't," Mark said flatly. "You're just about the only store in town."

"Let's see what else you have here," Coyote said, dipping into the footlocker. "Ammo belts—those are hardly worth my time. Oh, an ACR cleaning kit—those are nice…" He rummaged through the footlocker for several minutes. "Look, the rest of this stuff is pretty run-of-the-mill. I will give you two hundred to take it off your hands."

The back and forth continued, with Vogal taking the point on it.

Eventually they settled on two thirty in credit.

With that part of the exchange finished, Coyote turned to Stevens. "Now that we've done the hard stuff, what can I interest you in?" He started walking back to the truck where his driver had already pulled back the rear canvas flap.

The inside of the truck was filled with hardware, boxes of all sorts of equipment and sundries. It was a mobile Walmart of death, carnage, and rare pleasures at the front. Where the outpost almost always had a stink in the air from garbage, burned or rotting, there was almost a sweet smell coming from the rear of the truck. *That's deliberate; this guy knows how to sell stuff.* Coyote stood before it and gestured proudly at the contents of the vehicle. "Whatever you need, I either have it or can get it."

Stevens looked over at Vogal and gave her a nod. "Three things, Coyote. Toilet paper, toothpaste, and a grenade launcher," she said.

He chuckled. "That's a pretty big spread. Toilet paper is a rarity, you know that. Most of the good stuff came from China and the cargo ships are not running. Same with toothpaste."

Vogal waited a heartbeat, then flatly stated her request again. "Toilet paper, toothpaste, and a grenade launcher."

"That's going to exceed what you have traded today," Coyote warned.

"We have open credit with you to the tune of five hundred," Vogal said.

"Four eighty-eight, actually," he corrected.

"Whatever."

Coyote frowned at her request. "Look, I wouldn't do this for just any unit…"

Mark smiled at the sales tactic as it unfolded.

"…I do have two packages of prize Charmin—I'm talking double ply. It's pricy—"

"We'll take that."

"Now, toothpaste I don't have much of, other than some stuff someone liberated from a destroyed Dollar General. It's past its date, but at least it's mint flavored. I've got three tubes."

"Fine," Vogal said, clearly more happy about the toilet paper. "Now about the grenade launcher…"

Coyote climbed into the truck and rummaged around, finally emerging with an old grenade launcher. "It's not much, but it works."

"It looks like it last worked during the Vietnam War," Vogal quipped as he handed it to her.

"What can I say? They're emptying the arsenals and using whatever they can get their hands on. I can throw in ten grenades with it."

"Don't you have anything built in this century?" Mark asked, eyeing the old weapon with a bit of contempt.

"Not this week. Supply and demand. Everyone wants the newer stuff."

They haggled for some time over the costs, eventually leaving with one ten in credit with the Coyote. As he and his driver secured the back of the truck, Mark was suddenly distracted by a call from Clarkston.

"Punch List! We've got company." He pointed off down the

street.

There were ten of them, all wearing long white robes tinged with light brown and gray dust. They wore flip-flops. One held a large triangle with little crossbars of small metal bells and was ringing them as they walked. Each had a hood that covered most of their heads. The newcomers trudged on in unison, heads held high. Even Coyote paused as the sight of them approaching. "Well, there's something you don't see every day."

What the hell is this shitshow? Stevens walked over to the tall leader, an older man with salt-and-pepper hair poking out around the edges of his hood. "Excuse me, this is an active military area," he said, holding his hand up to stop them. Vogal moved in alongside him and so did Coyote, though why the scrounger was there was lost on him.

"Let us pass, my son," the man said in a low tone.

My son? Oh geez, today must be my lucky day! I've got the religious nuts showing up at my gate. "I'm afraid I can't let you do that," Stevens said. "Past that line is the AIZ."

"We know where the so-called aliens are," the man said. "It is our intent to open a dialogue with them." As if to make his point, the girl with the triangle with bells gave it a shake to make all the little bells tinkle.

"Oh, this is going to be good," muttered Coyote. Mark cast him an angry sideways glance that shut him up.

"I don't think you understand," Vogal weighed in. "You try to cross through our little outpost, and you people are going to be killed."

"We will not," the man assured her. "That's the problem with humankind. So far, we have only tried to deal with these divine visitors with brutality and force. I have been channeling with these creatures. You don't understand them the way that we do. We are going to open a dialogue with them." There was a creepy cult-like way he spoke that convinced Mark fairly quickly that they were crazy rather than enlightened.

Organized religion had been caught in a quandary with the arrival of the Fish. There was a fundamental question that had to be dealt with—if God made man in His own image, where did the Fish fit into the equation? Clearly they were more technologically advanced than mankind; they traveled from another world. The pope had been trying to assure the world's Catholics that nothing in their doctrine had changed. He had even called for a "crusade" against the alien invaders. Rumors persisted that the Vatican was assembling some sort of Special Forces to take the war to the new threat. Other religions tried to twist the words of the Bible, Torah, or Quran to explain the arrival of the Fish. All of their hand-wringing and vacillation was enough to make Stevens thankful that he didn't attend church.

"Look," he firmly said. "I don't know if you have some sort of connection with the aliens or not. I don't care. I do know this: I have orders to not let anyone go into the AIZ without authorization. I recommend you go to HQ and plead your case there. If we get orders to let you in, we will."

One of the women, a tall redhead, spoke up as more of Open Hostility walked over to see what the commotion was. "Your military has no sway with us. We all know that your kind have caused these problems. They are not alien invaders…they are creatures of the sea. They have come from Mother Earth as a warning and punishment for what we have done to the oceans of the world. It is divine retribution for humanity's pollution of the world."

"No," Vogal said. "They came from space."

The redhead frowned. "Your disbelief and fear are what has started this war. Let us pass, and we will end it."

"It might be entertaining to let them on through," muttered Coyote from Mark's side.

"You're not helping," he growled back, then turned to the man that first spoke. "Look, it doesn't matter where you think these things came from, I want to assure you, they came with the intent of waging war. We didn't start this, they did."

The man smiled. "You know so little of how things work in this world—being a man who kills for a living."

"Hey," he snapped. "I owned a construction company before all of this shit went down. We aren't the Army, we are militia. The only reason we are here because they chose to bring war to us."

"We will sit with them, we will connect to them. We will end this senseless war."

Vogal leaned in so her voice wouldn't carry as she cupped her hand to Mark's ear. "These folks are not the sharpest knives in the drawer," she whispered. He wanted to grin at the Witch's comment, but let it pass. "I'm going to grant you, this war is senseless. You need to understand that these creatures have never shown any inkling of trying to communicate with us. Remember when they sent those

Goblins ashore in the big shells? They don't want to commune or connect, they wanted to kill."

The redhead spoke up again. "You are ignorant to what Mother Earth is telling us." The girl with the triangle rang the bells again, this time with an aggressive shake.

A breeze blew through the street, swirling dust in the air around them enough to make Mike squint to avoid any getting in his eyes. "I don't know Mother Earth. She's never paid us a visit up here. I do know Death though, and he rides on through every day. Part of my charge is making sure people like you don't show up here and do something stupid that gets yourselves killed." He paused and his Army liaison, Shelly Reese, gave him an assuring nod of support— not that he needed it.

"So, here's what's going to happen. You are going to turn around and leave. I don't care where you go, but you are not coming through the grid coordinates that I have assigned to me and my people."

"You can't stop us. We will find a way through. We are humanity's hope," the man spoke as if he truly believed what he said.

"I assure you," he said, patting his M18 sidearm in its holster, "I *can* stop you. More importantly, I *will* stop you."

"We have rights!" the redhead barked back.

"This is war," Vogal said with a smirk. "It trumps your rights."

The man surveyed them all, one by one. Stevens could feel his disdain as he did so. "You are all guilty in the eyes of Mother Earth. You have attacked these creatures, her messengers. You are being misled into fighting a war that is unnecessary and unjust."

"You may be right," Stevens said. "But you need to be right somewhere else. All of these folks have faced the enemy. Almost all of us have been wounded. We've lost friends and comrades. This fairytale that you are embracing about the Fish being a harbinger from Mother Earth, well, it's wishful and horribly misplaced thinking. This bullshit you are peddling, no one here is buying it."

The man scowled but turned away. The last to make the turn from the robed group was the woman with the bells, who shook them again aggressively at him. *Only in fucking California!*

"Well," Vogal said as they departed. "You have to admit, you don't see that every day."

"Yeah," Mark said wearily. "It just serves as a reminder."

"Of what?" she asked.

"A reminder that we don't get paid enough for this level of bullshit."

He embraced the truth in his words. Sanctioned militia were compensated, but it was a pittance of what he had made when he owned his own business BI—Before Invasion. There were other "perks" too, like free Army medical care, which had only scant resemblance to actual medical attention. While it was a living, no one got rich out of being at war, other than the companies that made arms and munitions.

With that stark comment, Mark Stevens walked away to go check the perimeter defenses once more.

CHAPTER 5

Firebase Dragon, the Western Front, West Los Angeles AIZ, California, the United States

Lieutenant Sutherland MacLeod stood at attention in the apartment room that his unit had commandeered as their HQ. As MacLeod stood before the coffee table desk that his CO was using, he glanced outside toward the distant rumble of an explosion that bounced through the buildings of La. Their firebase was a series of reinforced buildings, stacked Hesco barriers, walls of rubble, all ringed with razor wire. The apartments were generally considered safe, though the Fish had lobbed shell-like cocoons filled with ravenous Goblins over a few days ago, shattering the illusion of safety in the base. It had taken some time to kill them all, and a lot of people bore scars from the attack. It was just one more of the war crimes that he held the Fish accountable for.

Captain Bechdoldt crossed his arms and glared at MacLeod as he asked him to take a seat. Sutherland knew why he was pissed and it oddly didn't bother him. "I suppose you know why you're here," Bechdoldt said as his jaw set in anger.

MacLeod wanted to grin, but knew that would be a horrible

mistake. Denying his actions was also something that he wasn't prepared to do. *I'm better off simply admitting what I did and getting this conversation over as quickly as possible.* "Yes, sir," he replied. "I went out into the AIZ yesterday on an unauthorized mission."

"Do you have any idea what a pain in the ass you are at times, MacLeod?" Bechdoldt snapped as a red tint washed over his face.

"More or less, sir." That was the truth, and MacLeod was more or less proud of it.

"That ASHUR is not your personal plaything. It's not yours; it's the Army's. You can't just pop into a combat zone and fight your own personal war."

"Sir, Army doctrine gives ASHUR pilots a fairly wide discretion as to how they are deployed in battle." That was one of the things that made ASHURs effective, apart from their speed and firepower. ASHUR pilots had discretionary authority to deploy as they saw fit. They weren't locked into military doctrine. That unpredictability and rapid deployment had been instrumental in winning the last war.

"You have discretion on authorized missions. That doesn't mean you get to pop out across the front without authorization. You are more than aware of that, Lieutenant. This isn't the first time we've had this talk."

"Sir, I saw an opportunity to inflict damage to the enemy, and I took the chance to do so. I might add, I killed a Crab and more than a dozen Frogs."

"The body count doesn't mean shit if you go off and get killed. What if you had run out of ammo? What if you had gotten stranded out there, alone? That ASHUR rig cost a pretty penny to the government, not to mention what was spent to train you as a pilot. Being out there without infantry support, you could have gotten killed."

"Not likely, sir."

"Don't backtalk me while I'm chewing your ass, Lieutenant."

"Sir," MacLeod pressed ahead, despite the warning. "I had a GRD with extra ammo with me. Battlespace command knew where I was, and I wasn't so far out that I couldn't signal for help if I needed it." *Which I didn't.*

"Because of your little stunt, I had to fill out paperwork for an hour explaining your actions, justifying them. I had to listen to the snot-nosed battlespace commander bitch about how you are a 'disruptive element' in his command. And now I have to document why your ASHUR isn't combat ready. Frankly, you're more of a pain than it's worth."

"That wasn't my intention, sir. I just want to win the war."

Bechdoldt was attempting to smother the flames of anger that were burning in his mind. He drew a deep breath and ran one hand over the salt-and-pepper stubble of hair that he wore, using the moment to gather the right words. "I would love to bust your ass down in rank, but you've had that done twice before to little effect."

By better officers than you... "It isn't about my rank, sir." *It's much bigger than that.*

"I have read your service record. Revenge is a bad motivation. I know you've lost good people out there, but going out on some hunt for vengeance won't bring your comrades back."

"Yes, sir," he managed. Bechdoldt was right, he was out looking for revenge. His first CO in the war, Captain Byrne, had lost his life to one of the enemy Bosses. MacLeod had injured the bastard, leaving him a scar, but the enemy had managed to get away. Since then, MacLeod did everything he could to get out and hopefully lure that Boss into the open. *Byrne was a hell of a soldier...he didn't deserve to go out with his spine snapped like that. That big shiny bastard is going to pay for his death.*

"Do I have your word that you won't do this kind of stunt again?" Bechdoldt asked.

"If that will help, then yes sir, I will not undertake unauthorized mission beyond current op parameters." He said the words but there was nothing behind them.

"You know, I don't believe you."

"I wouldn't either, sir."

"I would reprimand you, have you get transferred to another sector—but our new CO, Lieutenant Colonel Logan, is encouraging aggressive action. I go and bust you and he's likely to be chewing my ass in response. So you see, you've put me in a nasty situation."

"I'd offer my apologies if that would help, sir." Secretly, he liked the sound of the new CO. *We aren't going to win this war fighting defense.*

"I have to demonstrate that there are repercussions for insolence. As such, you are restricted to quarters for seventy-two hours," Bechdoldt said firmly. "I don't want to see you anywhere on the base, especially at the repair bays. Stay in your quarters—understood?"

"Yes, sir."

The captain dismissed him and Sutherland walked outside. He took the stairway down where he met Corporal Rachel Swift, his rig's tech, at the bottom of the stairs. "How'd it go with the captain?"

Narrowing his glare at her, MacLeod tipped his head. "I'm restricted."

"Well, if it'll make you feel any better, it's going to take me two days to get the Steel Hyena repaired," she offered.

"Get on it and text me updates. I can't leave my room, but I'm not cut off entirely. I want the Hyena ready as soon as possible."

"You're not talking like someone that has been ordered to sit in their quarters and be pensive."

MacLeod cracked a grin. "Just get to work on it, Swift. There's a war on and I have no intention of sitting it out."

CHAPTER 6

Starlight Inn, the Western Front, Le Brea, California, the United States

Albert "Shredder" Dawes and his second-in-command, Ted "Reaper" Wallace, sat across the table from Ratchet and maintained a smile, despite what she was proposing. His company, Spartan Associates, had rented the first floor of the Starlight Inn shortly after the invasion and been using the hotel as their base of operations. Thanks to their defense, Le Brea hadn't completely fallen to the Fish yet. It was a pocket that was flanked by the AIZ, but was friendly territory.

They had rented out two floors of the Starlight Inn once action had commenced in the city. The tourist trade was gone, and the owners were happy to have a heavily armed security company in residence, especially when the other option was the Fish. The Army and militias lived a far rougher life than the personnel of Spartan Associates, but from where Dawes sat—that was their choice. *In this kind of war, there's no excuse for not using what people left behind.* The Army and the militias were "encouraged" to not occupy the homes of those that fled. Dawes's people didn't suffer under that kind of restriction.

Spartan Associates had been his pride and joy from day one. He had convinced several of his veteran buddies to come work for him, providing protective services to celebrities in Los Angeles. As time passed, they had branched out, undertaking several quasi-legal operations for clients. Spartan always was discreet and professional. When the war broke out, he was taking short-term assignments both from the Army and interested private parties. The private sector paid a lot to recover things like data backups or precious goods, whereas the Army simply used his team for combat ops at minimum wages.

Dawes listened to Ratchet's story with keen interest. He had never heard of a secret bank in Beverly Hills, but it made complete sense. Spartan Associates had done enough private security for celebrities before the war to know there were hidden hotels and restaurants scattered throughout the city that were not for the general public. *Of course they have a covert bank...because that is what rich people do. They're too good to bank like the rest of us.*

"So you are asking us to punch through enemy-held territory to recover what you have in your safe-deposit box?"

"That's right. All I want is box 435."

He chuckled, not just because it was a ridiculous request, but as a negotiation ploy. "Ma'am, I would be sending my people into harm's way. A half-million dollars may sound like a lot of money, but we run the risk of losing men and women along the way."

"Alright," she said, shifting in her seat and leaning forward across the table. "Then how about 750?"

This time Dawes shook his head. *She buckled pretty quick, which means I can press more.* "We are talking 1.5 million or it's not even worth considering." *Let her chew on that. She'll come back at a million and I'll take it.*

"Agreed," she said, surprising him slightly, though he didn't show it.

"Okay, we will need 250k up front for the gear."

"No problem."

"And I want you to know, there are no guarantees. We will do everything in our power to recover what you have there, but there's a chance we won't."

"Fine, but if you fail, it's only 750k, sans your up-front payment," she replied. *Apparently she's shrewder than I thought.*

"Look," he said firmly. "Realistically, you aren't going to get anyone to even consider taking this mission. Most people that do what we do are fully committed to their contracts. Spartan Associates builds in some slack for these kinds of runs—but most of our stuff is not as risky as what you are proposing. We have to not only get there, but haul in enough explosives to get into the vault, then find your box...all of that takes time and will attract the attention of the aliens. For all we know, this bank of yours is already a mound of rubble. We are going to need more than that to make it worthwhile."

"What are you thinking?"

"A million—win, lose, or draw."

Ratchet went quiet for a moment. One of her heavy associates leaned in and whispered something in her ear. *He's probably warning that we might fail—that she might lose a million dollars.*

"I know you are probably hesitant. You need to understand, this is a seller's market and I'm the seller. My competitors are likely to send you off without even talking to you. But hey, you are welcome to shop around." Dawes knew that the best way to accelerate a decision was to pretend you weren't interested.

"Alright, Mr. Dawes," she said. "You have a deal." She slid the safe-deposit box key across the table.

"Great. And just so we are clear, this is a cash deal."

"Again, no problem. I will get it to you in the next two days or so, if that's agreeable."

Dawes glanced over at Ted sitting next to him and got a light nod. "Well then, Ms. Ratchet, we have a deal." Albert rose and extended his hand.

She held out her fist, and he balled his and gave her a bump. Since the pandemic, an entire generation of people shunned old-fashioned handshakes still. It didn't matter to Dawes. All that he cared about was that her money was green. She and her two bodyguards left the room and he waited, making sure they were out of earshot.

Dropping back into the chair, he turned to Wallace. "Well, that was interesting."

"What do you make of her?" Dawes asked, taking the key and fondling it as he spoke.

"She's all fired up about getting the contents of that box," Wallace drawled in his south-Texas accent.

"It's interesting that she didn't use a middleman. Most people of her caliber don't like getting into the nuts and bolts of this. I wonder why she didn't send a lawyer or her manager."

"Maybe she reckons that the fewer people that know about this, the better."

Dawes's eyes narrowed in thought. *It is possible. Maybe whatever is in that box is embarrassing to her, or something she doesn't want in the wrong hands.* What could be in that deposit box that was worth her undertaking the negotiating herself? "She was a little heavy with the pheromone-laced perfume."

Wallace chuckled. "Boss, I've been sporting wood since she walked in. Yeah, she was trying to manipulate us a little bit with some chemical sex appeal."

"I get the feeling there is more in play with her than what we saw. I can't say she's hiding something. I feel pretty sure she didn't show us all of the cards in her hand, though."

"I don't know much about her. I mean, she's a hip-hop singer— won some Grammys and all. I don't listen to that crap. She was in two movies, neither of which were big blockbusters. She's not a typical Hollywood partier. TMZ-2 doesn't even cover her unless she's on a red carpet somewhere. She's got Grammy Awards, but those are a dime a dozen. From what I was able to learn, she's almost squeaky clean."

"In this town, that alone is suspicious."

"Agreed. And interesting, especially given what she wants us to do."

"I don't trust her. She was too quick to close the deal with us. When I said we needed this to be a cash transaction, she didn't flinch."

"That there was my favorite part of the whole conversation. With the inflation hitting us since the war started, we might be able to buy a loaf of bread by the time we get her precious box," his second-in-command said.

"My thinking is simple—I wanted to see how she would react… that and there's no point in giving money to the FedGov," Dawes replied.

"What the hell is so important for her to drop that kind of cash?"

Indeed…whatever is in box 435 must be pretty important or valuable. "It doesn't matter. Whatever it is, it is worth more than what she's paying us."

"So, we're actually going to do this?"

It was an interesting question. They stood to make a million dollars by doing nothing and telling Ratchet that they tried to get to the vault and failed. It was tempting, and he certainly was giving it some consideration. *After all, why risk our lives on a bank heist?*

In that moment, Dawes considered the mission in a different light. *What Ratchet has provided us is information that is worth a great deal more.* "Let's mull this over. So, there's a bank hidden in Beverly Hills, that is filled with celebrities' money and goodies."

"That's what she said."

Albert grinned. "There is potential there, a lot of potential. Think about what kind of cash we might be looking at. I mean, if we were to do it, why wouldn't we simply take it all?"

"The Army is likely to have a say in matters," Wallace countered as the voice of logic and reason. "You know the rules. Picking up military hardware is okay. Looting and robbing is punishable by death or imprisonment."

It was a sobering fact. There had been several publicized instances of individuals, militia, and PMCs that had been caught looting. The perpetrators had been tried and sentenced to death or a lifetime in Leavenworth. The Army had made examples out of them with a clear warning to anyone that was contemplating exactly what Dawes was considering. "Well, that assumes we are going to be caught."

"How can we not be? I mean they are going to see us go into the AIZ and come out with what, a few vehicles filled with stuff? We have to pass their checkpoints. Questions will be asked and frankly, with us hauling that much stuff, we could be facing a firing squad."

Dawes made a wince. *It probably wouldn't be that bad. I could probably talk our way out of getting a blindfold ad cigarette. Wallace is raising hurdles that we need to overcome.* "That all presumes we are caught. I would think we have enough brainpower to figure a way to avoid that. We can circumvent the Army. If anything, that's going to be the easy part of this."

"There *is* no easy part to this."

"Come on, Ted, you are always doom and gloom. I think this is more of a matter of logistics than anything else. It's a matter of securing the bank, getting into it, and transporting what is in there out."

"Transportation is problematic. There have been, what—five battles for Beverly Hills so far? Many of the streets are more craters than concrete. We were up that direction a month ago on the Rodriguez job. You remember how bad the ground is up there. Add in that there were several attempts by less reputable folks to loot the stores up on Rodeo Drive. Just walking up there is a problem, let alone having transportation in and out."

Albert Dawes didn't have an answer to that, but was confident that he could produce one. "Yes, the ground up there sucks ass, but we will have a lot of money up front to get us the right equipment to overcome those obstacles."

"Assuming you are right, we have to do this under communications blackout conditions. If the battlespace commander for that sector picks up on us, it will draw a lot of unwanted attention."

"Any attention in the AIZ is unwanted," Dawes said. "But yeah, you are right. This is a stealth run."

"And then there's the obvious. The Fish are not going to like us poking around in their backyard."

Dawes leaned back in his chair in thought. The aliens were the random factor in all of this. He could game against human beings. He understood how people reacted. The Fish were an entirely different matter. They had their own logic, their own tactics and responses. There was a level of unpredictability about how they acted at any point in time. *If we stir things up too much, they are likely to respond with brute force.* With the aliens, that was always bad news. "We might need some sort of diversion, something to keep the aliens occupied while we do this."

"You are talking one hell of a diversion."

"We will come up with something. If we do this right, we might be able to get the Army to do the heavy lifting on that part of the plan."

Wallace studied Dawes's face. "So, you are really thinking about doing this?"

Grinning back was something he didn't even try to control. "Let me put it this way, I can't envision us going all of the way in to just bring back the contents of one safe-deposit box."

"We could just lie and tell her we tried and failed. We make a cool million."

Wallace was right. The smart and safe play was to not undertake the mission. Scamming the client would be easy. Lesser PMCs would do that to Ratchet without any hesitation. Spartan Associates was his company, though; he had built it up from scratch. He had done so through doing professional work and leveraging referrals from satisfied clients. "Imagine the hit to our reputation if we fake this."

"I'm not sure reputations are worth the pain in the ass associated with a run like this," Wallace cautioned.

"Think about it. If we do this and give Ratchet whatever she has in her safe deposit box, she is going to tell her friends about us. She will have no idea that we plundered the rest of that bank. Her friends all have houses that are behind enemy lines. The celebrities all have safes or hiding holes in their mansions. Ratchet will talk, and it will bring us a line of celebrities who all want their shit back."

He could read Wallace's face to see that he understood the implications. Ted's eyes went wide and he made a faint O with his lips. "Okay, I see where you are going with this."

"Good. We need to start planning this out. But first, we are going to need to convince the Army to let us get an op near the La City Hall."

The mention of the Los Angeles City Hall made Wallace cock his head. "What do we need at City Hall? I mean that place has been behind the lines for weeks."

Frank Dawes smiled. "If I'm going to rob a bank, I'm not going in blind. They will have the plans on file at City Hall, even if it is behind the lines. We need to get the full layout of that building before we go rushing in. If I'm going to rob an exclusive bank, I'm going to do it right."

Chapter 7

Headquarters, Foxtrot Sector, the Western Front, West Los Angeles AIZ, California, the United States

Lieutenant Ryland woke up again and checked his watch, wincing at what he saw. 0230 hours...*again!* He rolled over on his cot and fidgeted, trying to fall back asleep, though he knew it was a wasted effort. This happened a lot in recent days. There were meds for it, pre-PTSD drugs, but he scorned them. The Army had embraced a whole series of drugs and despite their reassurances, he was unsure what the long-term effects were. Some troops were pumpers, using crafted steroids to bulk up—others used the drugs the Army provided to deal with a myriad of mental problems. For Ryland, it was better to go without sleep than risk being hooked on some pharmaceutical.

Sitting up, his mind was racing as if he had slammed several cups of coffee. It had been the same ever since he had met with Ratchet several days before. His mind kept focusing on what she had told him. A bank that rich people used, exclusive, sitting out there, waiting to be liberated. His brain could not shake the thought of the bank. It was tantalizing to consider, but not nearly as engaging as

79

trying to figure out how to actually rob it. Ryland couldn't imagine what might be in the vault, but whatever it was, it was worth a lot of money.

Everything about him had been to conform to the mold of a good soldier. In college he had joined the ROTC. His father had referred to his service there as being, "The equivalent of the flag squad for the real Army," but Frank took pride in it. In his mind, the military was a career path. At the time, he thought he would serve for a few years, take what benefits he could, and then move on to some other career…perhaps go on and get an advanced degree.

Of course the Russians had fucked that up. *Or we fucked it up… it was hard to tell the difference.* While the whole world had suffered from the cyberattack, many people felt that the US actions against Russia had gone too far. The Europeans turned against America, cracking the proverbial spine of NATO. When the inevitable showdown between the superpowers came, it was not a nuclear exchange, but a brutal naval and land war. The North Koreans used the chaos to surge across the DMZ. In Korea, the enemy bodies got stacked, but at a vicious cost. America drove the Russians out of Alaska, but it had come at a high price in terms of national prestige and honorable dead.

Frank had endured a lot of sleepless nights during that war but that was hardly new to him. He'd had the same issues throughout his life. Even as a child, he was an obsessive compulsive. He would fixate on a something and it would intrude on his sleep, gnawing on his thought processes. It created anxiety that could not be shaken. Sometimes it was songs, sometimes something he read, other times it was simply interesting topics. When he became obsessed with building his physique, he worked out for hours at a time, studied how to improve certain muscle groups, buried himself in that effort. He became an expert in the subject…not out of desire, but as a coping mechanism. When he latched on to something, it could consume his thinking, slithering into his sleep patterns. His parents had tried to get him help and the family doctor had suggested medication, but his mother was against drugging him. "You are going to have to learn to cope with these feelings. Drugs are a crutch."

Ryland knew his people sometimes struggled with his need to have order and his focus on details. They called him "overly meticulous," at least that was what they said in front of him. As much as they griped about it, there were times it saved lives. As much as they moaned and groaned, most understood that his focus was on them doing their jobs right which would, hopefully, keep them alive.

What Ratchet had presented him was something his mind had grappled with and he couldn't shake it. Robbing that bank became his new fixation. It was a problem that demanded solving, even though he had turned down her demand. It was a puzzle, and he loved the joy he felt when he beat a mental puzzle. Finding some way to get to the riches from the vault and get them out was a challenge that was worthy of his intellect. Thoughts of ways to beat the enigma kept him up at night.

What intrigued him was the concept of treasure being the goal. As a kid, his favorite movie had been the classic film, *The Goonies*.

His love of that film was fuel for the mental fire he was trying to cope with. The search for a pirate's treasure was a fascinating concept to him. Having boundless wealth solved problems; the movie had ended on that note. The same applied with Ratchet's mysterious bank vault. It was the prospect of riches that fed his desire to solve the problem.

Frank rose from his cot and stretched. Every muscle ached. Some of that was the stress of combat, some was the lack of sleep. Sitting down on the small folding camp chair, he stared out into the pre-dawn darkness outside of the tent. There was a rumble in the distance, not thunder, but an echo from an explosion. Even in the blackness of night, it was a reminder that the war was not far away.

Stretching his legs out, he couldn't shake the memory of the conversation with Ratchet. *There's a bank out there filled with all sorts of wealth.* It was the kind of money that might let him leave the Army once and for all and actually enjoy life. For him, everything was tied to his military service. What was in that vault could alter that equation. *If I stay fighting this war, I will eventually get killed— or worse. If I had the means, the money, I could walk away from this hell.*

It was idealistic thinking. Chances were the Army wouldn't let him retire with an invasion underway; they at least would put up some sort of fight. It was possible, though. There were ways to manipulate the system, and he was an insider. He understood the rules of the game he was playing. *If I left now, I would just end up working in some tank or ASHUR factory. But with the contents of that vault, I could find a place somewhere quiet, far from the coasts, and live some sort of life.*

It wasn't all about self-indulgence. He couldn't possibly pull off such an operation without help. While he had no idea how much was in the vault, given the dollars that Ratchet was throwing around for just her safe-deposit box, there was an implication that there was a tremendous amount stored there. *It would be enough for everyone to get a fair share.* He would be able to take care of his entire team.

The night before, he had arrived at some thoughts around the vehicles. Trucks would be slow and cumbersome on the blasted roads. ATVs, however, would be perfect. Small, fast, and quieter than a truck, a few of them could be used for transport without the risks that larger vehicles presented. The biggest vehicle they could take would be a Jolt recon vehicle, but he discarded that thought— Jolts weren't as maneuverable for what he felt they needed. Speed was important on a mission like this, as was good intel. Given his position, he would be able to assess the best routes to get to Beverly Hills, hopefully evading enemy patrols or positions.

Some logistics were still too over-the-top for him to process. Reaching over to the small cooler he kept in his tent, Frank pulled out a bottle of water, wet from the melting ice he kept there. Cracking it open, he took a large gulp and closed his eyes in thought.

In the dark of his tent, his mind shifted to the problem of how to put together a team. His people were loyal, of that there was no doubt. But taking an entire platoon in was something that might attract a lot of attention with the command staff. *I need a platoon, but taking all Army personnel is a risky proposition.* Some of his people, while loyal to him, held the Army in high esteem. Their sense of honor and loyalty to the nation would work against him. They might feel compelled to inform his superiors what he was doing. *That would be a short trip to military prison.*

Of his platoon, there were some he could count on that wouldn't talk. Staff Sergeant Calcutt—a man near retirement age…he was a man that might be looking to augment the benefits the Army offered when mustering out. Winston and King had gotten in trouble before running some sort of betting pool on professional pickle ball. Their greed got them in trouble and a good slap on the wrist by the provost marshal, but it also showed Ryland that they wanted to make some money while in the Army. *I am willing to bet that I can channel that greed to my advantage.*

Private Raphael "Raffi" Wix had only a few months of nursing school left when the Army had called her up to active duty. With her training, she had hoped to be assigned to a hospital where she might be able to complete some of her learning. Instead, the Army, in its infinite wisdom, had made her a rifleman. Despite her official designation, she had served as the Ghost Legion medic, something that Ryland had pushed for. Raffi carried a lot of resentment for what the Army had done.

Private Bishop Grant was in the war because it gave him a chance to blow things up. He was a farm boy from Iowa. His parents had lost their family farm in the last economic recession after the Russo-Bratva war. A chance to make some money to help his parents get back on their feet would be a big incentive for the hulking Grant.

Avery Slocum was his next mental choice. From Ryland's talks with the kid, he knew he had big dreams in life. He wanted to own his own body shop, like his brother did. He was banking his pay for that dream, but on an Army private's pay, even with the combat bonus, he was years away from making his hopes a reality. *If presented with the chance to earn enough money to get his business started, he will likely leap at it.*

In his mind, this was a good team—balanced, trustworthy, and skilled. Still, it lacked the kind of firepower needed. *If I can't trust other Army personnel, who can I bring in?* Leaning back in the chair, he stretched his legs out in front of him and drew another long sip from the water bottle.

It hit him...*the militia.* Most regular Army personnel viewed the militia members with a great deal of mistrust. It was understandable. They were irregulars, volunteers who, in many cases, didn't measure up to military standards physically, psychologically, or ethically. Matters weren't helped by their reputations. Some units fled after firing just a few shots at the enemy. Others didn't follow orders well at all. Even when they did follow orders, they tended to do it their way—not the Army way. It frustrated officers who tried to shuffle off most militia to mundane duties and details.

That wasn't the case of all of them. Frank's compulsion for lists made him mentally prepare a list of possible militia allies. Colton's Cutthroats were widely heralded as an elite unit. So was Andrew's Panzer Company—APC. The Malibu Mafia were known for being incredibly ruthless both on and off the battlefield. Ryland had worked with the Westside Irregulars and had found them almost to be zealots about taking the fight to the Fish. Once a street gang, they channeled their xenophobia of other races into a hatred for the aliens.

Then he mentally hit on Open Hostility. His brain focused on that one for a long moment. Mark Stevens was a vet, a man who had lost everything with the invasion. Many of his people worked with him in the private sector before the invasion, which spoke to their mutual loyalty with their commander. In some respects, they had been forced into the militia life when Stevens's business had been lost. Frank had worked with him on two ops before and had found Hostility to be a solid group of people—all steadfastly loyal to their commander.

What made them more appealing was that they also didn't strictly follow the rules. They often bent the parameters of missions to be successful. Stevens did what was right, rather than check boxes off some Army checklist. Such a level of moral ambiguity might make him willing to entertain a proposal from Frank about making a run on the bank.

It would be tricky to approach him. He had been in the Army before, meaning that some of that Army sense of loyalty was probably still there, if not buried deep in his soul. *Still, this kind of money we could score at the bank might be enough for his unit to walk away from the war and return to some sense of normalcy.* In Frank's hypothetical mental list of units to consider, Open Hostility moved to the top slot.

Our goal isn't to fight the Fish, but to avoid them. The aliens were the biggest risk to such an operation, far more than the Army. Evading the Fish was something he desired, but he knew that it wouldn't be entirely possible. They were difficult to predict, erratic. The odds were that his people were going to have to engage the enemy. *We will need some firepower…something that can tip the scales more to our side.* A tank—or better yet, an ASHUR—would be a great addition to any force going that deep into the AIZ.

The problem was finding an ASHUR pilot who would be willing to take part in such a mission. Talk to the wrong person and they'd spill the beans to Lt. Col. Logan. ASHUR pilots were the best that the Army had to offer, and as such, the majority were career Army personnel—right down the olive drab underwear. *I need someone whose values are a bit flexible. Someone who has the skill to undertake this mission and is willing to do so.*

A few names came to his mind as he took another sip of the water. Setting it down on the plastic folding table, he rubbed his wet hands through his sandy hair, brushing it back. The cold water from the cooler felt soothing as he thought through the options. *Darrel Tapper is a good pilot, but he's a talker…a braggart. I can't risk him letting the cat out of the bag.* Maria Snell was his next choice. *She'd probably be willing to do it, but would want to be in charge of the op. No, if we do this, I need to maintain control.*

Then his mind summoned up another candidate, Staff Sergeant Sutherland MacLeod. His call sign was the Steel Hyena, even though that wasn't the class of ASHUR rig he was qualified to pilot. Word was he had earned it by being a little crazy, which might just be useful on a mission like this. Ryland was tempted to skip over MacLeod. Because ASHUR pilots were so elite, it often went to their heads. Some were egomaniacs, others were aloof. They tended to congregate with each other over other officers, no doubt sharing some special bond with fellows who had excelled to win the honor of piloting a rig.

MacLeod was different. He had no problem calling his fellow pilots egotistical asshats, and did so often. As a result, they often didn't invite him to take part in their reindeer games. If they thought that bothered MacLeod, he didn't seem to show it. He acted more like a rebellious warrant officer than a front-line staff sergeant piloting a sophisticated war machine. From what Ryland had heard, MacLeod often disregarded orders, doing what he thought was best. It frustrated his superiors, but many saw him as a genuine hero of the common soldier. Before arriving in Foxtrot Sector, MacLeod had been bounced by two other commanders who had gotten fed up with his unique brand of insolence and disregard for combat doctrine.

MacLeod might just be the right person. He has no love of the Army and is an independent operator. Frank mulled over the pros and cons of involving him, and to his surprise the mental tally favored the wayward ASHUR pilot. *I will have to overcome his idiosyncrasies but that is on me, not him. Besides, he is a solo operator, which means he would be less likely to talk to anyone else about what I might be planning.* MacLeod would be the best possible person, if he chose to undertake such a mission.

Frank finished the cool water and sat in the folding chair with his eyes closed. His mental list of what he needed for such an operation was shaping up. *It might just be possible.* Of course, it was just a mental exercise—one of his many little obsessions that tormented his sleep. There was a big difference between actually executing such a plan and mentally planning for it. He tried to tell himself that it was just a hypothetical exercise at this point, but there was a nagging voice in his head that kept treating the entire affair as if it were real.

I'm not there yet. For now, this is just a thing to think over, to contemplate. Such thoughts did not help him return to his cot and sleep, though. All he could do was sit and think about the vault and how to get its contents into his hands and to safety off the front lines. For now, it was an obsessive brainteaser, something besides the war, that kept him up at night.

CHAPTER 8

Outpost 46— Operation 888 Meatloaf 14F, the Western Front, West LosAngeles AIZ, California, the United States

When Open Hostility got the orders for Op 888 Meatloaf, Mark Stevens's eyes rolled. They were to make an incursion into the AIZ and act as a diversion for a regular Army unit that was attacking down the line. He hated diversions. They were intentionally loud and disruptive and done in a place where being loud and disruptive brought death. In his mind, this was the new sector commander, Lieutenant Colonel Logan, attempting to show that he was more aggressive than his predecessor. He was willing to demonstrate that by putting Mark's people in harm's way.

The only good news was that Hostility had been given some explosives to get the Fish's attention. Usually Stevens skimmed off several of the blocks of demolition material for future missions, pretty much standard procedure for a militia unit if you wanted to keep them operational. There were times he felt that he was fighting the Army's logistics as much as the aliens. Today, however, he didn't do that. *We are going to need all of the boom we can get.*

The easiest way to execute such a mission was to sneak in, plant the charges, set them off over a period of time—then bug out before the Fish showed up in force. That would meet the mission parameters and no doubt that was what the Army expected him to do. Easy wasn't always the right way. *This war isn't going to be won by making noise. It is going to be won by killing the enemy. That's how we did it up in Alaska with the Russies. If I'm going to set off explosions, I'm going to do it to kill the enemy.*

He had picked his target carefully. While it was a good two-mile hike, the Westside Pavilion offered a great deal of opportunity. Two miles was considered deep in the AIZ, but the site he had chosen for the diversion was too good in his mind. The shopping mall had been abandoned for some time, and it was big, which offered a lot of potential fields of fire. Westwood Boulevard offered a good exit path to the I-10 and back to an Army outpost. More importantly, most of the pavilion was still intact. Also important was the fact that their diversion was not near their own outpost. The Fish didn't seem to demonstrate a tendency for vengeance, but it was a concept that few people wanted to test.

The mall was also close enough to where the Army was going to run its operation that his diversion would do some good. He and his liaison Reese had spent hours going over the plan with the Army to make sure that it was going to meet his needs and those of the other assault team. Being a diversion was almost as bad as leading a raid. It was like throwing a rock at a wasp's nest and not running until the last minute. Miss your timing and you got stung. With the aliens, it was much worse than a wasp sting.

The pavilion had, in its heyday, been the hottest shopping venue in West Los Angeles, the grand dame of shopping. The cities constantly evolving demographics, and the damaged neighborhoods from the Russian missile strikes during the last war, had left much of the mall almost empty when the Fish had come ashore. He had visited it in his youth and didn't savor that it was going to be a battlefield now. Like most people, he longed for the days of normalcy, when life's biggest complication was where to go for dinner or if you could find a parking spot. *The old girl is going to serve one more purpose, deceiving the enemy.*

Mark had spent some time with his people, going over what he had in mind. He had Wrench go and contact Coyote for some of the unique supplies he intended on using. It had eaten up much of their remaining credit, mostly because Ratchet wasn't a great negotiator— but they got what they needed.

Suiting up for the run, he checked his own battered STG. The Kevlar III weave showed fraying in some spots from previous hits by needlers and enemy claws, but for him, it didn't warrant replacement. His thin layer of sheer thickening fluid was nearly at the end of its useful life, but still hardened when hit—so he didn't see the need to change it out. Two of his blast plates had been damaged. If this had been the Army, he would have swapped them out. As it was, getting replacements was an ordeal for Reese to secure the paperwork and approvals.

Putting on his enhanced combat helmet (ECH), he tuned out a number of the pop-up screens that loaded by default on the inside of his visor. The ECHs were great; they integrated weapon aiming with a reticle synced to his ACR, and they could provide a full feed from the battlespace. The visor was also good for night vision, a vast improvement over the light-enhancing imaging systems of the last war. The problem he had was that they gave him a headache. It was common with soldiers; all of that data meant you got massive eye strain. On top of that, normal eye movement could activate certain features. Yes, the Army had pills for that, but he was not a fan of taking things that affected his brain—so he simply disabled the features he felt he could live without.

Mark assembled his squad near the gate leading from their outpost into the AIZ. Twilight was coming, and soon it would be dark, and darkness brought dangers, so planning was important. Going over the details of the op took a valid investment in time. No one ever complained about being overinformed in a combat zone, especially when their lives were on the line. The afternoon sun was reddish-orange in color, mostly from the smoke that rose in thin streaks from the city. The lack of breeze was appreciated. At this time of year, West Los Angeles was in the 60s during the day and 50s or less at night. With their gear on, the militia members would have parts of their bodies drenched in sweat, while the exposed parts of their skin were cold.

For the most part, they were enthusiastic about the mission. They had hours, time that was going to be needed for the op to go off without a hitch. Reese handled the communications, coordinating with the Army unit that was going to lead the attack that Open Hostility was diverting attention from. She had the only critique to the mission. "I'm fairly sure that this wasn't what the explosives were issued for."

Stevens's response was blunt. "The Army wants explosions; I'm going to deliver that." She gave him a sneer in response, but ended her protest.

They set off in a long single file, quietly navigating the debris and rubble. A few times Hollings, taking point, signaled for a stop as he and Winston checked a street crossing or the end of the alley to make sure that it was clear. The caution was welcome. The Fish didn't use drones to map the battlespace, but they did seem to have an uncanny picture of many of the battlefields and skirmish sites. No one had figured out how they knew the ground so well, but they did. *It's just one of a thousand questions we have about them.* He had to trust that someone out there was attempting to get those answers.

It was a slow go, as planned. By the time they reached the Westside Pavilion, the sun was already setting and darkness was descending. The mall had been redone about ten years earlier, though you would never know it from what he saw. Many of the windows on the lower floors were broken. The stores had been looted, there were a few stray pieces of clothing lying about, covered in a film of dust. It was a human reaction to fear—to smash and steal. During the invasion months earlier, Mark had seen the footage of people running out of a Target with a television. Why they stole something as worthless as a TV was a mystery that he never could figure out.

Looking at the mall, he noted a few of the big topside curved atrium windows had been broken as well. The mall was dark inside, seemingly devoid of life. The building was now just a shell, abandoned and of little value. Abandoned cars, some of which were burned and now nothing more than rusting shells, littered the drive in front of the structure. "Alright, I am going to take Bravo topside and get set up. Alpha, you're with Vogal. Take the explosives and rig them per the plan."

Vogal and her people set out, while he led Bravo around the building. It took several minutes to find what he was looking for, a roof access ladder. They had to cut a padlock to open the gate to it, but Corvin had a cable saw and made short work of it. They went up the ladder to the roof, coming down on the gravel roofing material that crunched loudly under their feet.

From the roof, the view of the city in evening twilight was spectacular. From where they were poised, you couldn't see the rubble of the streets. Collapsed buildings were out of their line of sight. In many respects, it was a reminder of what the city had been before the invasion. While it felt somewhat nostalgic, he also experienced something else—a moment of dread. Urban combat in La was usually at deadly close ranges. Here, on the massive mall roof, he felt strangely exposed and vulnerable.

"Alright, fan out, find us another exterior ladder down—just in case we can't get to this one. Check all of the sides and make sure we don't have any aliens on the ground. Deploy your P-Drones so that we can map out any incoming threats," he ordered. His people fanned out as quietly as possible. Within fifteen minutes he had a good idea of all the rooftop access points and was sure that the enemy wasn't waiting too close. The rooftop was tricky ground to be on. If the enemy surrounded them, they would have to punch their way out—so multiple accesses was necessary.

That was where the P-Drones came in. Small, the size of a human hand, they could run for two hours on a charge, transmitting images and sensor data to the battlespace commander. Moreover, the small semi-autonomous drones could get into places where humans couldn't. They buzzed along the rooftop, then dropped down, mapping the area around the mall as well.

Turning to Reese, he spoke one word, "Time?"

"Forty-eight minutes," she replied. "I'm tied in with the battlespace commander and the main assault force is still on schedule. They will move after we give them the diversion."

Wonders will never cease. "Good," he replied. Using his own wristcomp, he connected on a command channel with Vogal. "Witch —what's the word?"

"This place is a mess. Some busted pipes down here have flooded some areas. We are still setting charges. There's a lot of supports down here we have to rig."

"Make it snappy," he said, checking his wristcomp. "The clock is running."

He killed some of the time while Vogal did her work by walking the roof, peering down the skylights into the darkened mall. *Just ten months ago, this place would have been lit up. The city would have its traffic jams. There would be noises and smells that are long gone.* He hated the fact that things were different. *Even if the Fish leave, how long will it take to rebuild this? Will they even try?* A mix of depression and anger swirled as he waited.

Finally, Vogal's voice came in his helmet's earbuds. "Punch List, we are good down here. We are pulling back to the entrance."

"Alright, people," he said to his roof fire team. "It's show time. Corvin, break out the lighter. Aim them for the north end of the roof.

If we are lucky, that's where they'll come first."

Corvin grinned and knelt down. Out of his ruck he pulled a handful of long cardboard tubes. It took a few attempts to get the disposable lighter to ignite, then he touched the fuses on two of the Roman candles that they had purchased from Coyote.

The dull *thunk* of the Roman candles sent balls of bright light streaking into the Los Angeles night. The fireworks burst in the air over the Westside Pavilion with brilliant eruptions of crimson, green, and yellow light. After the first Roman candles finished, he used a commercial fireworks mortar and launched an even larger display of fireworks. As Mark and the rest of the team on the roof looked up, it was hard not to think back to the Fourth of Julys of their childhood. He only had three of the big mortar bursts, then Corvin switched back to Roman candles again.

A crackle came in Mark's earpiece. "Punch List, this is Battlespace Command. Is that you with the fireworks?"

"Roger that."

"We gave you explosives to use for the diversion."

"Understood. We will be using them. We first wanted to make sure we drew the baddies in," he replied as the last of the Roman candle tubes fired its balls of sparks and color off to the north end of the pavilion roof.

"Your mission is to get the attention of the enemy," came back a scolding retort.

"If our little fireworks display didn't work, trust me, you'll see the boom." He was confident that it would work, based on his experiences in fighting the Fish. They had seen the aliens react to bright lights before, especially during night ops. *The Army thinks they know the Fish better than those of us with boots on the ground who are facing them.*

Shifting in place, he boosted his external audio to see if he could hear any activity as a result of their demonstration. His night vision on the inside of his visor showed nothing thus far. For a long few minutes, there was nothing. Being wrong didn't bother him nearly as much as having to explain it to the Army. He didn't want to have to fight the Fish, but that was their job. It struck him then that his life was caught in that dichotomy…between having to fight and dreading it. *I'm shocked they haven't shown up. Maybe their forces are elsewhere. Come on, you bastards—we baked a fucking cake for you!*

Then he saw it, a rising cloud of dust to the north of the mall. It was something on the ground, something large, and it looked as if it was getting closer. Hollings called it out before he could. "Motion to the north," he said on the tactical channel as Stevens used a flick of his eyes to dial down his external comms. Things were about to get loud.

"Alright, people, look sharp," he said, then danced over to the battlespace channel. "Battlespace command, this is Punch List. We have enemy motion north of our position and closing. Can you confirm?"

"Stand by," came the call voice with a long pause.

"Punch List, be advised, we are showing a large body of Class Fives heading your way. Drone shots and target counts show the numbers to be over fifty—moving fast."

Class Fives—Frogs. That wasn't entirely bad news—there were worst things that the Fish could send at them. Frogs, or Frogmen, were giant genetically engineered bipedal Frogs. They were the nastiest of biological weapons. They were mindless, insensitive to pain—hell, you could blow an arm and leg off one and it would continue to try to crawl to kill you. They could spit a blob of some sort of goo that if you inhaled it or it stuck to your skin, it could send you into toxic shock and could kill. Their claws and bites were nasty as well. The only good news about most Frogs was that they were not bulletproof. They relied on mass attacks to overwhelm their targets.

Well, at least our diversion is working. Switching back to the tactical channel, he spoke to all of Open Hostility. "We have incoming Frogs, numbering around fifty. Keep them distant and watch your fire. Remember, these things keep coming after you hit them, so triple-tap these bastards. Don't let them get close enough to squirt you."

His people on the north end of the mall fell back as the dust cloud got nearer. "They are close," Corvin said nervously.

"We are outside and clear of the structure," Vogal said from below. "At least some of them are going to come in at our level."

"Stay outside and get good fire zones established if they do," Stevens replied. "Roth, set our repel lines on the south side so we can join the Witch and the rest." His heart was pounding in his ears as he saw the dust reach the far end of the mall. They all drifted back a few steps, with the exception of Clarkston, who knelt down and braced for battle.

For a moment, the cloud dissipated, and he wondered if they were all entering the mall under his people on the roof. *If that's the case, we need to get down off of here and fast.* Then he saw a number of clawed hands grapple with the edge of the roof, pulling their owners up and over. "Fire at will," Mark ordered as he brought his own ACR into play. The red targeting reticle in his visor aligned with the weapon and he squeezed off a pair of rounds at one of the first Frogs to make a visible target. Someone else hit it too, sending it toppling backwards. Suddenly there were a dozen targets—then even more as they scaled the exterior walls of the mall.

The Frogs rushed forward grunting, first individually, then slowly syncing their guttural roar in unison. It was a deep roll, a throbbing sound. Stevens did what he could to mentally tune it out, focusing on his firing. The rooftop was alive with gunfire from Open Hostility at the charging enemies.

The oncoming mass of alien flesh surged toward them in savage jagged hops. One Frog was blown apart with a half dozen shots. Another lost its arm-limb at the elbow joint, but rushed on as if it meant nothing. Three were dropped almost simultaneously, one got back up rushing forward as if it wasn't already dying. Mark gritted his teeth as he carefully aimed and fired at the rushing surge of aliens heading for him.

Small groups of the aliens, forming up like skirmishers, lunged forward faster, far ahead of their comrades, moving in quick small groups, racing in rapid large hops at erratic angles, making it hard to target them. Behind them the rest of the Frogs seemed to organize and lunge forward as one, a dark wall of grunting flesh. In his night vision, it was a wall of angry grunting flesh that barely showed up in the darkness.

The advance Frogs were on top of his people in a matter of seconds. Two more of the charging Frogs were dropped as they leapt for his people. One sprang between them as they fell, bounding high and fast in the air. For a moment, it drew all of their fire, but nothing seemed to take it down. In another large spring, it landed on Clarkston, ripping away at him with his claws. The big poison sacs behind its head swelled then deflated as it spat down at Clarkston's head. The glob of toxic goo covered Clarkston's visor and his screams filled the tactical channel.

Eight shots tore into the attacking Frog's head, obliterating its head in a spray of gray goo. The body went limp and flopped down on Clarkston who was frantically grasping at his ECH. The roar of gunfire intensified and in that moment, Stevens knew it was time to get down. "Offerman, grab Clarkston and hit the ladder. The rest of you, time to go!" Stevens reloaded quickly, firing two rounds at a time, giving Offerman the cover he needed to grab Clarkston's shoulder straps and pull him clear of the dead Frog on top of him.

"Witch, we are coming down," he said as he drifted back to the far wall, making sure his people were starting their descents on the line. For a moment, he switched to full auto, and sprayed the bulk of the Frogs that were starting to reach the middle of the mall roof. He hit at least a half dozen of them, some multiple times. A few dropped, but not nearly enough.

Swinging his legs over the ledge and hooked on to the rappelling rope, he signaled Vogal. "Blow it, Witch—blow it all!"

There was no verbal response as he kicked off, only a rolling series of explosions from inside of the abandoned mall. Windows blew out everywhere, showering shards of glass on the road and sidewalks. As he reached terra firma, he looked into the structure through one of the window openings as the roof, three stories up, came down with a thunderous roar. The exterior walls and some of the roof remained intact, but the bulk of the roof came down thanks to the Witch's explosives. Concrete instantly ground into powder billowed out on Open Hostility as Vogal and her team moved over to join them. If it had been daylight, it would have been spectacular to watch. In the dark, with the night vision straining to get enough ambient light to amplify, it was simply loud, and the dust slid around his helmet filters and made his throat raw.

He had to assume that at least a few of the Frogs on the roof survived. There was no time to validate that or deliver the killing blows. No doubt the collapse took out the majority of them. "Alright, people, time to move."

"Problem here, boss," Offerman said. His gloved hands tore at the now hardened goo that the Frogs had blasted into Clarkston's face. Frog goo was like that, it solidified to a brittle but still toxic substance. He got it off and pried open Clarkston's visor. Even with the night vision and the rolling dust everywhere, Stevens could see that he was pale and nonresponsive.

Shit...he's already in shock! "Someone, stab him with an EpiPen," he ordered. "We will have to treat him when we get clear from here."

* * *

Four hours later...

Stevens sat next to the gurney with the remains of John Clarkston. A sheet covered the dead man's body and face. Mark stared at his former employee and militia member and wept alone, in the quiet of the room. Sniffling, he smelled the disinfectants that the nurses had used to remove the last bits of the Frog's spray. The sterile aroma was in contrast with the sweat and filth that covered his duty fatigues.

The battlespace commander had chewed his ass for "wanton destruction of a civilian structure." Stevens had almost punched him. If not for the intervention of his liaison, Reese, he probably would have knocked the lieutenant out.

Mark remembered the first day that John had showed up at his construction company and had asked for work. John was a punk kid with the right attitude. *He didn't know shit about carpentry but was willing to learn—which set him apart from a lot of kids his age.* Stevens thought back to the life he used to have, to happier times. It felt as if it was a different life, not even his.

Now I need to find his family and tell them what happened. I will tell them he died a hero. That won't ease their pain any more than mine, but will at least give them a drop of pride in their grief. He found himself momentarily angry at Clarkston for not falling back farther when he had the chance. *He knew how fast the Frogs could move. If he had drifted back just a couple of feet, he might still be alive.* Then he suppressed that anger. Clarkston was dead and there was no point in blaming him for it—the responsibility resided with Stevens. That was a specter that he could not shake.

Clarkston wore a simple braided bracelet of paracord on his right wrist. Mark pulled the sheet back and saw that it was still there. His first inclination was to remove it to send back to his family. He pulled it off and felt it between his fingers, rubbing it. In that moment, Stevens decided to keep it for himself. He put it on his own right wrist—a reminder of Clarkston and the fragility of life. *I need to carry this with me…*

Mark wiped the tears from his cheeks. Looking down, he saw the moisture mixed with the dust that still clung to his fingers. Clarkston was the first member of his team that had died in battle. Everyone had scars from the fighting, but this was the first death. It tore at his soul.

He heard footsteps beside him and turned to face Kris Vogal. She put her hand on his shoulder.

"You okay?" she asked in a soft voice that he didn't know she even possessed.

"Not really. I'm not sure I'll ever be okay."

"It's not your fault, boss," she said. "John should not have stayed that far forward. I thought he knew better."

"It is my fault. I formed this unit. He was my responsibility," he replied, looking up at her.

"That thinking will eat you up. This is war. We all knew what we were signing up for, including Clarkston."

Maybe this was all a mistake. I took a construction crew and turned them into a militia unit—now people are dying. "What are we fighting for? All we were doing was diverting attention from the real attack. Was it worth it?"

"That's for the brass to judge," she assured him. "We have been lucky up until now…fortunate that none of us bought the farm before now. Sooner or later someone was bound to die."

"You're right," he muttered. "That doesn't make this easier."

"We're militia," she said with a hint of pride. "If we wanted easy, we would have joined the Army."

Her words made him smile, if only for a second. "You know what, Kris, there's got to be something redeeming from all this shit…something to make the war worthwhile."

"Boss, if you find it, sign me up," she replied. Slowly she turned and walked away.

As he sat there alone with his dead friend, he wondered if there was a hope for a future at the end of the war…or if the war even had an end.

CHAPTER 9

Los Angeles City Hall, Golf Sector, the Western Front, West Los Angeles AIZ, California, the United States

As Albert "Shredder" Dawes led his people through the maze of abandoned vehicles that littered the streets, he looked up and saw the looming tower of the Los Angeles City Hall. The structure was massive, with thirty-two floors—stark white in the night. With a blink pattern, he zoomed out his helmet's view of the structure and took it in. Despite all of the war and carnage at the street level, the old building looked remarkably intact. For that, he was thankful.

His Siemens C15 helmet optics were better than the ECHs the US military used, as was his body armor. Spartan Associates was not burdened with the Pentagon's purchasing system and the need to buy things from the lowest bidder. That was one of the reasons his people were so loyal to Dawes—he spent copious amounts of money to make sure they would survive any alien encounters.

Entering the AIZ always came with risk. You had to play by some basic rules, the first of which was informing the Army that you were going into their battlespace. Inevitably, that was declined. Dawes had done what he had done before; simply telling them he was going in regardless of their decision. That brought about the inevitable disclaimer discussion. "We cannot and will not be held accountable for any injuries or loss of life from you entering a combat zone…Military resources will not be utilized in an attempt to extract you or your people." There were forms too—where he signed away his rights to sue, as if the pieces of paper meant anything. It was a routine that he knew all too well.

As they approached the building, there were signs of battle damage on the lower three floors. Black scorches showed on the stark white concrete. Most of the windows were either blown out or jagged shards clinging to the openings. There were four cars, including one police cruiser, that were burned, rusted hulks—no doubt from artillery or mortar fire. The pavement near them was stained, not from the fire, but from the leaking battery acid. Spent brass was everywhere on the ground, to the point where he watched where he put his foot down so he didn't slip. Even with his night vision gear, he could make out the bullet pit marks on the outside of the structure. Yeah, there was a fight here—maybe more than one. He wasn't surprised at the sight. The military fought hard for every block of the city. Structures like city hall were symbolic; so the fighting was bound to be more for that particular block.

The darkened building was bound to be a maze of cubicles, all of which had to be navigated. There would be no power to the structure either, not that he would have dared turn on a light and alert any aliens nearby. There was also the risk of getting in the structure, and the Fish showing up and making exiting impossible. "Alright. Agis team, you follow Reaper and are responsible for keeping the door open. I'll take Leonidas team in and secure the plans."

"Don't worry, Chief," Wallace replied. "We have your backs."

"You'd better. Otherwise payday comes late this month," he quipped, making his way to the twisted metal framed glass door for the building. It took a few jerks to pry it open, but it squeaked and moaned, finally opening enough for Leonidas team to enter.

The hallway was dark and abandoned. The disturbed film of dust on the floor indicated that someone or something had been in there recently. His night vision visor picked up a spray-painted spot on the wall, a crude Fish with a circle around it and a slash diagonally across it. Dawes shook his head at the sight. *Even in the middle of a war zone, kids take the time to spray their art and tags on shit.* Part of him admired the guts of someone doing it. After city hall fell, they were here and left a mark to prove it. It was either bravery or raging stupidity.

They had done their research before their penetration. The city planning commission had the original blueprints for the Commerce Bank, which had been built in 1968. While the city maintained all of its records digitally since 2024, the older hard copies of blueprints were kept in storage on the tenth floor. Finding it was going to require some digging, but Dawes had planned for that as well. It was going to take time, though, and being behind enemy lines made that a tense and possibly deadly proposition.

The owner of Spartan Associates signaled for his people to sweep the hallway. They crouched low, moving briskly, checking doors and halls as they went. He got a gesture from Diamond Jones that the path was clear.

Moving in on the stairs, they began the climb. Two stories up, there was more graffiti; at the third story, there were signs that someone had used the landing as some sort of bathroom. Feces and the reek of urine were strong. *This building has to have a hundred toilets, but someone thought this was a good place to take a shit.* Dawes doubted he would ever fully understand human behavior.

His knees didn't protest until he got to the eighth floor, and then it wasn't bad. When they reached the tenth floor, he could feel the moisture of his body sweat starting to soak his undershirt. *It's the little things you miss—like elevators. I swear I will never take them for granted ever again.*

The Leonidas team fanned out when they arrived at the tenth floor. There were no signs of human or alien occupation this high up. The layer of dust on everything was undisturbed. The air had a dank, slightly musty odor. Without power, the stale air had simply not been recirculated since the block had fallen to the aliens. *I hate to think of what kind of mold is growing in the ventilation system after all this time.*

The door to the planning office was locked, which team member Roberta Fisher circumvented by breaking the glass door, reaching inside, and unlocking what remained of the door. The shatter of the frosted glass seemed much louder than it was because of how silently they had been moving. "Makes you wonder why they even bothered to lock it in the first place," she muttered as the door opened.

The office had a counter that was backed up with cubicles. Behind the counter was a computer. "Treacher—this has your name written all over it," Dawes said.

The youngest member of their team, Danny Treacher, moved behind the counter and set down his ruck. He pulled out a battery pack and a number of flash drives, plugging them into the computer. *If there is any system here that has their filing system, it will be this one...for citizens coming in and asking for blueprints.*

The monitor's glow lit up Treacher's face as he settled into the chair and took off his helmet. His fingers danced across the keyboard and he swapped out several of the flash drives. "Their server is down, obviously," he said as he worked. "They likely had a copy locally. I just need to break the ID and password." The apps he had installed on his flash drives were running while Treacher opened the desk drawers.

"Ah, of course," he said, pulling out a sticky note with an ID and password written on it. Grinning, he entered them and the display changed colors and more text flickered across it. "The weakness of every bureaucracy...people."

He worked the mouse and keyboard with fury. "Geez, what is this stuff programmed in—dbase?"

"Less chatter," Dawes said.

"Got it," he said a few minutes later. "Commerce Bank Plans— one set of plans with a revision in 2017. The location is given as C-17-3J. With the server down, I can't get the digitized revisions, but the plans are in that location."

"Excellent. Alright, people, let's find the storage."

It took less than three minutes to locate the massive library. The roller-racks were cumbersome to work since they had to move three of them with the hand cranks to reach row C. They then found the rack and drawer number. He switched off his night vision and turned on his Maglite so that he could validate the prize. Flipping through the big folder, he found the blueprints marked for the Commerce Bank.

There would be plenty of time to read it elsewhere, but he wanted to make sure that they had the right set of prints. "Good work, Treacher," he said, pulling out a collapsible plastic document tube from his ruck. Uncapping the end, he rolled up the curling prints and slid them in. "It's time for us to go." Activating his night vision visor, his eyes strained for a second to adjust to the greenish-gray blur. Some colors were visible but distorted, and it took a moment for his brain to adjust to the change.

The Leonidas team made their way to the stairs with crisp military efficiency. They didn't rush as they started down; rushing generated noise and noise could be dangerous. At the fifth floor landing, Dawes stopped. "Shredder to Reaper—we are on our way. How's the path home looking?"

"Stand by," Wallace's voice said in a low whisper. The fact that he was whispering was enough for Dawes to hand-signal his team to halt on the stairs.

A full two minutes ticked by. While impatient by nature, Dawes knew better than to distract his second-in-command…especially if he was in a tense situation. Finally came a *crack-hiss* in his earbud as Wallace spoke. "We just had a Fox pass us, sniffing around. He's left our LOS. He was moving a little quick for a leisurely stroll, if you catch my drift."

"Roger that." Dawes turned to his people in the stairwell. "Let's hoof it." Their normally quiet stride had become a fast gait down the stairs, kicking up dust as they went.

They reached the ground floor and assumed flanking positions along the walls on the way to door out. "We are on the ground, Reaper."

"You are clear. We are across the street from you, in the café."

Switching to his team's comms channel, he spoke in a low whisper. "We are going to the café across the street. We move as one, in pairs. Watch the street as you move." As he moved to the door, he forced it open again with a heavy shove. *Here we go…*

The somewhat fresher air was cooler and rose through his faceplate filters, making his sweaty face feel cold. Dawes crouched low, moving fast, careful where he put his feet and navigating around the burned-out cars. The café's front windows were shattered and the glass crunched under his feet as he went in through the huge windowsill. Once inside, he reeled around with his AAC Wolverine assault rifle to provide cover. His team came across as he had ordered. The last two, Treacher and Jacobs, started across when a loud noise erupted down the street. Leaning out a little, he saw a Crab looming in the distance, moving rapidly down the street right at his exposed people. His mind went over the position, the roads, and surrounding buildings. Running and evading was not practical.

"Cover fire," Dawes ordered over the unit's command channel. Shots peppered out into the darkness at the approaching alien. The creature grabbed a scooter that was in its path with one claw and tossed it into the exterior of city hall, the metal crunching loudly. In Dawes's night vision, it looked to be an almost pinkish color, yet despite that gaiety, it was a vicious and deadly foe. Treacher reached the café as the Crab raised one big claw and pointed it at their position. A blue vein that wrapped around the arm and claw pulsated, like a snake digesting a large rat, moved forward to the end.

There was a hissing sound, loud and sinister—like a leaking tire about to lose all of its air. From the end of the claw, a cone of white emitted, slamming out some fifty feet, washing over Jacobs just before he reached the window. Jacobs let out a horrific scream as he collapsed.

Dawes recoiled and the air around him went crisp with a stinging cold. Jacobs uttered a whelp, collapsing just before he reached cover. *Shit—a freeze sprayer!* The liquid that the Fish fired was a biological mystery in terms of its composition. It was a super-freezing fluid, almost like liquid nitrogen, but weaponized.

He and four of his people wheeled back to the window and fired away with their Wolverines at the Crab. The majority of the shots landed on target, sinking into the Crab's thick hide. There was no illusion that they were deadly—the carapace of the aliens had demonstrated that they could absorb the bullets without serious penetration. Jacobs, moaning, writhed, but Dawes and the others could not focus on him—not with the enemy still closing.

The sustained fire seemed to make the creature's charge down the street grind to a slow halt. Someone grabbed Jacobs and hauled him into the café as the rest of Spartan Associates blazed away at the

Crab. It raised its claw again to fire. "Aim for that vein!" Reaper called out. The streams of full-metal jacketed death stabbed at the extended claw, knocking it about under the kinetic force of the impacts as the mercenaries aimed at the vein and the bulge that was forming for another freezer blast.

Three bullets slammed into the bulge almost at the same time. One managed to penetrate the sac, and a spray of bluish-white mist and water splattered the side of the Crab. The air swirled around the creature with snow-like crispness as the moisture in the air seemed to crystallize instantly.

The alien loosed a wail, not entirely animal, not any noise of any creature that Dawes had ever heard. It whipped around in place, hitting a streetlight pole with its massive scorpion-like tail, sending it flying back at the café, forcing them to fall back inside for a moment.

That moment bought Dawes time to reload, returning to the window to fire again. The Crab had started to retreat, but that did not deter them from adding persuasion in the form of firepower to its decision. Its damaged claw seemed to shimmer blue from the ruptured vein. As shots hit the narrow joints of the limb, it shattered. The hulking claw fell on an abandoned Fiat, crushing it inward and exploding the glass as it crumpled. The Crab continued to scurry away, seemingly oblivious to having lost such a large appendage.

Looking down at Jacobs, Dawes saw the young man sprawled on the floor. A frost still clung to his body armor. His hand, still gripping his Wolverine AR, looked locked as if trapped in some sort of spasm. He was not shivering…no, it was far more…quaking.

Kneeling, Dawes could feel the cold emitting from him, frigid, penetrating.

"Is…it…bad?" Jacobs managed between quakes.

It was a question that Dawes didn't want to answer. The freeze sprayers were rare with the Fish, but were devastating. Whatever it was they sprayed did massive tissue damage and was stabbing deep into his body. Those that survived bore ugly scars and took a long time to recover. "Don't touch the affected areas," he cautioned, "that stuff will seep right through your gloves." In the back of his mind, he didn't assume the Crab defeated. *It will be back, probably with friends.*

The recommended way for dealing with freezer spray was to remove and discard the gear that had been touched with the mist. The problem was that took time, and while they had some cover, it was far from a great position. If they took the time to get Jacobs clear, they might find themselves facing a counterattack. *I hate doing this, but it is him or all of us.* "Get a tarp or blanket under him —we will carry him out."

"Sir?" Fisher asked, knowing they weren't doing what was recommended. Dawes could feel the eyes of the others bore in on him.

"You heard me," he said in a low tone. "That Crab could be on its way back any time with friends. We will get him out of the AIZ and the medics can treat him then."

Someone broke out a plastic tarp and they carefully lifted Jacobs up and put him on it. Fisher tried to pull the Wolverine AR from his grip, but his blue-white fingers refused to release it. Her last little tug was successful, but with it came the tip of his trigger finger. Jacobs didn't seem to notice that it had broken off. None of them said anything to him about it; there was no point. She broke the fingertip off the trigger and tucked it in one of her belt pouches—embracing the thought that it might be reattached. Jacobs's shivers were almost violent as they picked him up.

They made their way through the occupied city at a faster pace than when they had entered. He never had to give an order to do so; his people knew that Jacobs was more badly injured than even Jacobs did. They came within sight of Outpost 44, their designated exit point, when Dawes started to have violent convulsions. They stopped, gently setting him down on the sidewalk.

Jacobs's eyes were open wide, staring into the sky in panic. His lips were blue, almost purple in color. His skin was pale as his body seemed to struggle with the damage it had endured. Half of his face sagged, as if he'd had a stroke. "Hurts...deep...down..." he managed to say with a weak voice. His body was so cold that when he spoke, his comrades could see the wisps of frozen air as he exhaled.

"We're almost to the medics," Dawes said. "Hang tight." He started to rise, to give the order to move out. Without warning, Jacobs's body jumped, he drew in a huge breath of air—then collapsed limp, unmoving.

"Fuck," Reaper said.

"Give him CPR," Treacher suggested.

"No," Dawes said. "You saw his finger. You start pounding on his chest, you'll break his body apart." There was a grim resolve in his voice. *There's nothing we can do for him at this point—he got a full dose of whatever that Crab was firing.* He wanted to curse, then scream, but he knew now wasn't the time. *We need to get out of the AIZ. There will be time for screaming later.*

"Pick him up," he commanded. "Let's get him out of here."

* * *

The next morning...

Starlight Inn, the Western Front, Le Brea, California, the United States

The hotel room that Spartan Associates and Shredder Dawes used for his office felt strangely small to him. They had gotten an ambulance for Jacobs, but he was so far gone that the defibrillator the EMTs used didn't even make his body twitch. They had wrapped him in blankets, more to protect themselves from any residue from the Crab's weapon than to try to warm Jacobs.

Reaper knocked and cracked open the door. Dawes waved him in. "Were you able to get ahold of Jacob's family?"

Dawes shook his head. "He was from Jacksonville, Florida. His family relocated when the invasion came. I've got feelers out to find them, but a lot of people have packed up and moved from the coasts. They could be anywhere."

Wallace nodded. "I think you should say something to the team. He's the first member we've lost. This is a real hit on morale."

"You do it," Dawes said. "I suck at those things."

"They probably want to hear from you, Chief," he replied.

Dawes sighed. "You're probably right."

"What are you going to say?"

He paused, leaning back in the expensive black mesh Herman Miller office chair that they had appropriated for his makeshift workspace. "All the usual stuff. I'll tell them the truth. This is a dangerous business that we are in. The Fish are dangerous, regardless of the precautions we take." He hesitated. "I'll tell them that when this next job is over, they are all going to get some damn huge bonuses—and that they will have a chance for a few months of R&R, if they want it."

Wallace nodded, but the wrinkles on his brow said he wasn't entirely comfortable with the news. "Sometimes bonuses aren't enough."

"Well, you're wrong. I recruited these folks. None of them wanted to sign up for the militia program because it didn't pay enough, nor did going back into the service. They didn't want to throw their lives away under military leadership. Trust me, they will respond well to big bonuses. Money soothes a lot of hurt feelings."

"If you say so."

"I know so. This Commerce Bank has a big vault and services some of the richest and most elite clients in La. I don't know what they have there, but it has to be worth a lot. And when we take it, we are all going to be stinking rich."

Wallace cracked a smile. "From your lips to God's ears."

"I don't need God. I just need a good plan to get in and out of there."

CHAPTER 10

Kickass Bar and Lounge, Foxtrot Sector, the Western Front, West Los Angeles AIZ, California, the United States

Ryland wearily made his way into Kickass. During its heyday, the bar had been a strip club. With the arrival of the Fish, the strippers had left for more fertile ground. The owner would have closed if it hadn't been for the military presence. Ryland looked at the brass poles, now long abandoned, and wondered for a moment if it would ever return to its past. *Doubtful...too much has changed. Even if the Fish left today, things would take years to come back.*

The impetus for his visit was Sergeant Calcutt's birthday. In recent years, the Army had fewer regulations about fraternizing with the enlisted troops—a byproduct of the 2020s. There were guidelines, but for the most part everyone looked the other way. He had used a few favors to get a night pass for his entire platoon to celebrate. Ryland had waited for a few hours to let the troops celebrate without the presence of an officer. There was a value in unwinding, or so he had been told. The reason he had come was because Calcutt was a damn fine NCO—that and he knew he couldn't sleep.

The other reason for coming was that, if the chance presented itself, he could talk to his people about the bank opportunity that Ratchet had presented to him.

Nightly his mind was filled with thoughts of robbing the Commerce Bank. Scenario after scenario played out in his mind, ensuring he could not rest. His obsession with it had become consuming. Ryland had taken to scribbling notes about his ideas in a small journal. He had pulled maps up to determine the best approach. Planning the heist was the only thing that gave him any sort of release and sense of accomplishment. A part of him hoped that going out to the Kickass might just take his mind off of it, give him something else to think about. Deep down, though, he wanted to talk about it—to get it off of his chest. *I need to tell others about it—that's the only way I will get peace.* He knew from experience that talking about something he obsessed about was a release; it bled the pressure off his troubled mind.

The bar wasn't as full as he had expected. It hit him slowly—*we're a few days out from payday. This place is probably packed once they get the money dumped into their accounts.* No matter how many centuries passed, soldiers behaved like soldiers. When they had money, they found ways to spend it, be it in bars or on members of the opposite sex.

Walking to the back, he found a private room with the members of his platoon. No doubt that room had been used for private dances back in the day. When they saw him, smiles broke out, drinks were lifted. He ordered a black Russian from the serving person, who gave him a look of scorn. The drink had been renamed a Crazy Putin after the Russo-Bratva War, but he stuck with the old name.

He raised his glass to Calcutt and offered a toast. "To one of the best damned sergeants in the Army—Walter Calcutt." Drinks were hoisted and even the usually rigid Calcutt seemed to lower his guard and smile.

It wasn't until the second round of drinks before he asked Hollings how he was doing. He had been hit two weeks earlier rescuing Slasher Squad. Despite treatments, his wound got infected and he had spent a few days at the hospital. Hollings proudly showed him and everyone else his healed scar, rather than simply state that he felt better. "This is a strip club, but no one is going to shove dollars in your pants. Put your shirt back on," Calcutt said, his voice slurring from the celebration.

"Lieutenant," Raffi asked. "Any word on our next op?"

Ryland shook his head and finished off his drink. "None yet. Our new CO has been aggressive as of late, but not enough to put us in." It was the best summary as he could offer. It was never good to complain about commanding officers down into the ranks. Lieutenant Colonel Logan was a good man, but was more worried about not making the mistakes of his predecessor than waging a true plan to take back Los Angeles. A few blocks had been reclaimed, though all that the Army had gotten was rubble and ruin for their efforts. He was more aggressive than Colonel Higgerson, demanding well planned and thought out offensive operations. He was also an opportunist, wanting to exploit any mission that was successful beyond what was anticipated. For that, he was both thankful and nervous. *Aggression without a plan is recklessness.*

"I heard that there's a new kind of Fish, some sort of super-Frog that they're fielding," Avery said. "Any truth to that?"

Ryland lifted his empty glass and managed to make eye contact with the waitress, then turned back to Avery. *Most of the time, rumors are pure bullshit, but this one has some basis in reality.* "I got a briefing on that. Down in Texas, they claim there are Frogs that are bulletproof, that can use weapons. So far, we haven't seen any here, but that doesn't mean we won't."

"Smart Frogs," King said, shaking his head. "They are bad enough without making them tougher and better armed."

"You have to wonder, what do they want…you know, the Fish?" Finn asked. "Why come all this way, land in the oceans, and then come at us?" It was a default question, one that came up often with almost everyone. No one understood the enemy, at least not very well.

"It doesn't matter why," Grant said, his Iowa twang loosened and amplified by his drinks. "All that matters is that they are here."

"I just wish they'd leave," Winston grumbled. "We keep going after them—they keep coming after us. I get tired of this back-and-forth shit. Just once I'd like to get a mission that meant something, either personally or militarily." His comment brought the bulk of the platoon to raise their glasses in a toast. As they did, he noticed a little twitch under Winston's left eye. Stress—a telltale sign. *He has a little nervous flutter with his left hand fingers too. This damn war is starting to get to him. I need to make sure he gets some time with one of the shrinks before it manifests itself in other ways.*

I feel the same way they do…I want to do something that

matters. Maybe that was why his obsession with the bank robbery had such appeal. It was something tangible, something that had purpose. "We do what we have to in order to get by," he said. "Sometimes that means following orders. Sometimes that means taking things into our own hands."

The waitress came with several drinks, including his. Ryland embraced it, savoring for a few minutes the warmth that it gave him. In the back of his mind was that niggling thought of talking about Ratchet and what she had said. He held back, though. Yes, the people he had mentally chosen for such a mission would know enough to keep it quiet, but there were others in the platoon who would spread the word. If everyone in the Army knew about it, everyone would plan the same thing he had been.

The party continued for another two hours. Slowly, in ones and twos, the members of the Ghost Legion retired. Sergeant Calcutt's eyes were half-shut from the toasts made to him. Ryland remained, nursing his fourth drink to avoid letting himself get drunk. As time passed, soon it was a small gathering. Calcutt, Hollings, Raffi, and Winston. Grant was there, but was so intoxicated that he would likely have little to contribute, nor would he remember much.

"Lieutenant," Calcutt said. "I appreciate you arranging a pass for this."

"You should know by now I try to take care of my people."

"You aren't the problem," Winston said. "The people over your heads don't seem to know how to wage this war."

"They never had to fight a war like this. All of our coasts invaded —the enemy using technology that is so damned strange that we don't have good defenses for some of it. For all their training and doctrine, they didn't have anything in their war plans for something this bizarre." Even as he said it, it felt as if he were defending the Army's senior command, and he hated doing that.

"I just wish we had something worth fighting for," Raffi said, slumping back in the seat. Glancing at her face, Ryland saw the wrinkles and a hint of gray in her short hair. *She's aged a good ten years in just a few months at the front.*

The door was open with her statement, and Ryland stepped in. "Funny you should say that. A strange thing happened a couple of weeks ago. You know that singer, Ratchet? She showed up, asking the Army to go to some secret bank in Beverly Hills and retrieve some stuff from it that she had there."

Grant, who he had assumed was out, leaned forward. "Let me get this straight, you met Ratchet?"

"Yeah," he replied with a hint of pride. "I did."

Calcutt leaned in over the round table. "Forget that," the grizzled sergeant said. "Tell us about this bank."

* * *

It had been an intense discussion for over two hours as Ryland poured out his thoughts about the bank job he'd been planning. With it came a wave of emotional relief. It was as if a dam of thought that had been building pressure in him was finally broken, and the torrent of what had been tormenting him flowed out. Relief washed over him as he finished answering their questions…relief and immense satisfaction.

No one had voiced dissent to the idea of robbing the bank. In fact, there was an excitement that seemed to purge the alcohol from their systems. Even Grant, who had been on the verge of passing out, asked good questions about how they could mount such an operation without raising attention. The answers flowed from his mouth. They were lucid—well thought out. Long sleepless nights of planning and thinking through the operation had paid off.

Ryland's people agreed with much of what he had planned. Their questions helped him voice refinements to the plan. Raffi and Hollings gave him some new thinking as to how to mislead the battlespace commander. Winton suggested using light ammo trailers with the ATVs to help them transport more. All agreed that additional firepower from a militia unit, preferably one like Open Hostility, was a necessity. By the time they had gotten to that point of the discussion, the waitress had simply stopped visiting their room.

"You have to wonder what the rich folk keep in a bank like that," Calcutt posed.

"Probably things they wouldn't store in a normal bank," Winston said. "I mean, look at Ratchet. She's won Grammys, has platinum records. I'll bet that's the kind of shit she keeps in a box in a bank like that."

"What about money?" Raffi asked. "These rich celebrities have boatloads of it. I bet there's a fortune stored there."

"Gold," Hollings said. "I would bet my next payday deposit that they have gold and silver bars stuffed in those boxes. Not to mention jewelry. You've seen them at those red carpet events, wearing all of that expensive stuff. There's no way they would keep that kind of bling in their houses."

"We don't know what is there," Ryland said. "We only know one thing—there is a bank there, a private little bank for the rich and powerful. The only way to know what is in there is to go and see for ourselves." *There, I said it. Now to see if they are really interested or if this is just drunken speculation.*

It was a good twenty seconds before anyone responded. It was Raffi that broke the silence. "We have to find out."

"I agree," Hollings said. "This is the first op we've ever heard about that I am excited to go on."

"We could probably afford to retire on what we find there," Calcutt said. "If it offers me a chance to enjoy a little life away from the war, I'm all in favor of it."

"To hell with retiring," Winston spoke up. "I just want to be able to make sure my family is taken care of."

King hesitated. "To be clear, we do this—we are risking our lives, and a court-martial for looting, if we are caught."

Grant cut him off, his words slurring. "Then we have to make sure we don't get caught."

The eyes around the table turned on Ryland. "This would be breaking a half-dozen regulations. King's right. If we get caught, the Army will want to make examples of us just to make sure no one else tries this kind of stunt. We will be lucky to end up in Leavenworth. If we botch this, our military careers are over."

"I never wanted a military career," Raffi said. "I joined this to get my college paid for."

Across from Ryland, Calcutt stirred. "Sir, I have been an Army man my entire life. I joined up at eighteen and nearly died at the Battle of Nome fighting the Russies," he said, slurring the last word heavily. "The Army is my life, my home. Even with the draw-down after the last war, I chose to stay.

"When the Fish came, I felt like I was fighting to save my country—hell, save mankind. To be honest, it has been a meat grinder. We have been slogging it out to take back every mound of rubble. These fucking aliens—" he paused, searching for words. "They are demons right out of the gates of hell. They use biological warfare on us. Their monsters are a match for our ASHURs in the field. The Army seems content sending us out to fight and die without any real strategy other than us shedding blood. Every person at this table has been wounded at one point or another out there. We've lost good people along the way too.

"I had hoped to muster out at some point, retire. I've earned it— we all have. With the aliens coming ashore, none of us know how much time we have left. I would like even a few months away from all of this, just so I can remind myself what it is like to be man. But I know if I stay here, it's only a matter of time before one of those Fish gets lucky and kills me." Tears sprang in the corners of Calcutt's eyes.

"So what are you saying, Sergeant?" Ryland asked.

"I'm saying we do it! We take a stroll into Beverly Hills and take whatever is in that bank. If nothing else, it gives us something to fight for that is worth it. It's an op with a meaningful outcome…

beyond just fighting this war."

Nods around the table, accompanied with smiles, gave Ryland the answer he had hoped for.

Winston spoke up, "Sir, they aren't going to let us pack up and leave once we pull this off. I mean, we are in the Army. What good is the money if we are stuck in the Army and can't enjoy it?"

"Good point," Ryland replied. "For this to work, the Army is going to have to think we are dead. Yeah, it means going AWOL, but it is going AWOL with style. We will need a good plan for that."

That comment brought out a number of grins around the table. "Alright," Ryland said in a lower tone. "Assuming we undertake this, I can't stress enough the need for secrecy. My grandmother used to say, 'Loose lips sink ships,' and she was right. No one can know about this, including other members of the platoon. I will recruit any additional help that we need. If anyone violates this, they are putting us all behind bars."

"Let's give this thing a code name, something that we can refer to that won't attract a lot of attention," Raffi said.

"Good call," Ryland replied. "Let's go with Sundance."

"Like the festival?" King said.

"Yes and no. I was thinking more along the lines of the Sundance Kid—a famous bank robber."

King cocked his head slightly. "Never heard of him."

Raffi turned to him. "You never watched that movie—*Butch Cassidy and the Sundance Kid*?"

"No. When was it made?"

"The 1960s," Calcutt said.

"Wow, that's ancient. Is it in color?"

Most of them rolled their eyes at King's comment. None of them had been alive in the '60s but they didn't consider it ancient. "For a guy who's a genius with GRDs and computers, there are times you are stupider than a Blackhawk ejection seat," Raffi sniped, making King lean back in his seat, his face beet-red. The comment brought a low mumble of chuckles from the table.

"Lieutenant," Hollings asked, changing the topic. "Is there anyone else that Ratchet may have told about this?"

That was a poignant question. "I was the only one she talked to in the Army that I know of. I sent her to talk to one of the PMCs—Spartan Associates."

"Do you think she went?" Raffi asked.

He had to concede that, giving a nod in response. "Probably."

"Do you think they might take the bait?" Calcutt asked.

"I don't know." In all of his night-long musings about robbing the bank, it never dawned on him that there might be competition. Worse yet, he might have been the person that set that in motion. "It's possible. SA is run by a pretty smart cookie—Shredder Dawes. I'm sure they'll be tempted, but they know the risks as much as we do. Where we will need to work with a militia and can use some Army assets to assist us, they would be going in cold turkey. Dawes isn't the kind of person to risk his people's lives.

"On the flip side, they are a for-profit company. They might just feel that the potential profit would make it worthwhile." *What if I've read Shredder wrong? Would he be willing to take the risk, despite the odds? I hope I'm right. Even if he does decide to try it, we are more than a match for this kind of mission. They are just mercenaries—well funded, but generally not willing to take a risk on the unknown.*

"Sir, we need eyes on Spartan Associates," Calcutt said. "We need to monitor what they are doing."

"Good call. Put one of our people on it, but don't tell them why we need them tracked. I will run some checks from battlespace command to see if they made any recent forays into the AIZ." His words seemed to ratchet-down some of the concerns. Now he had something new to consider, though—that Spartan Associates might just make a play for the same target, for the same reasons.

"There are a few more members of our unit I want to bring in on this. In the meantime, we need to prepare. I need to bring in the other assets to the mix."

"Is it wise going to a militia unit?" Calcutt asked.

"It's got to be better than involving another Army unit," Ryland countered. "Besides, we need a little moral flexibility with an op like this. The Army sometimes acts as if it has a corncob shoved up its ass. Logan is pushing for new offensive missions so he doesn't get shipped off to someplace worse. Everyone is on pins and needles with the new man on the scene; they are all looking to impress him. The last thing I need is someone who getting all patriotic about things and ratting us out. Agreed?" He got a set of head nods all around.

Now all I have to do is convince Open Hostility and the Steel Hyena to join us…

CHAPTER 11

Outpost 46, the Western Front, West Los Angeles AIZ, California, the United States

Mark Stevens and his people crossed out of the AIZ at their outpost, moving slow and wearily. They had just returned from Op 3317B—Thunderbuns. There had been a lot of jokes when the code name for the mission came out. The general consensus was that the Army was running out of good code names.

Thunderbuns has been a reconnaissance in force, poking and probing into what remained of West Los Angeles. It had been mostly uneventful. An enemy Fox was spotted and they huddled in an abandoned duplex for two hours, watching and observing the creature. The Foxes had long arms, almost gorilla-like. Their skin was an alligator-like hide. Their massive snapping jaw jutted out far in front of the rest of their reptilian face, with a pair of upward jutting fangs. They could move fast, making them hard to hit, and with their thick hide, harder to injure or kill. The Fish used them for recon. While they served the same function that his militia was doing, it was impossible to see the Fox as a kindred spirit.

Once they were sure the enemy had not detected them, they began to make their way back. It was a long slow trudge, but otherwise uneventful. They had fed battlespace command the data on the Fox and the ground they had covered and had even gotten a "Job well done," from the battlespace commander. Corvin had been quick to quip, "Getting a compliment from the Army makes me nervous. If we do a good job, they're bound to give us a shittier assignment next time." Stevens wanted to rebut the sentiment, but he couldn't.

There had been a sense of relief when they had seen the tower of the outpost. They didn't feel truly safe until they crossed the barricade—and even then, there was always the threat of the Fish showing up and wreaking havoc. Stevens made sure his people got to cover, half heading for the showers, the rest heading for a quasi-hot meal. There wasn't enough hot water for everyone to clean up and wash the dust off, so they went in shifts.

He went to his quarters, a lonely tent, and pulled off his STG and helmet. His hair was wet with sweat, and when he rubbed his face, he could feel the grime that had stuck to it. Taking off his fatigue shirt, he noticed the paracord bracelet that he wore…Clarkston's. *Well, buddy, we all made it back from this op.* Wearing the bracelet made him feel that Clarkston was somehow still with the unit, still fighting the good fight.

Vogal came in behind him; he could hear her footsteps before she arrived. Her stride was always fast, always the same pace. "Boss, someone is here to see you."

"Who is it?"

"Army—some lieutenant."

He suppressed a sigh. "What have we done now?" Visits by the Army were rare. Usually they communicated through Reese, their liaison. When they showed up, it was usually to complain on a grander scale.

"I don't know. He isn't carrying a pad or a clipboard, so it can't be too bad."

"It's always bad when the Army shows up."

He grabbed a fresher dull green fatigue shirt and pulled it on, not bothering to button it, then followed Vogal to where he saw the visitor. The lieutenant was of medium build, clearly muscular, more than most lieutenants he had met. His hair was a dull brown, cut short, with just a hint of gray along the front. His fatigues were not freshly pressed but were worn, not as bad as Stevens's, but worn all the same. *This is a fighting lieutenant, not some desk jockey.*

Mark stood in front of him and planted his fists on his narrow hips. "I'm Mark Stevens, CO of Open Hostility."

"I'm Frank Ryland," he said, extending his hand. Mark gave it a firm shake. "I was wondering if we might be able to sit down and talk in private."

He had heard of Ryland—call sign Casper. His reputation was that of an up-front leader. *He goes out with his people on ops and bring them back alive—what was their names? Ah, the Ghost Legion…that's them.* "Privacy is a rare commodity up here. We can go to my tent," he said, gesturing towards the tent. He led with Ryland and Vogal in tow. Behind him, he heard Ryland introduce himself to the Witch. When they got there, he held open the tent flap and both the lieutenant and Vogal entered.

Seating was a pair of empty ammunition crates, turned on their end. Stevens sat down on his cot, his long legs angled awkwardly spread. "I should probably send for Warrant Officer Reese; she's our liaison."

Ryland shook his head once. "We don't need her here at this time."

That struck Stevens as strange. Reese was always at the table when the Army was involved. *Maybe this is all about a problem with her?* He couldn't imagine why she wouldn't be sitting in on the conversation, but gave a nod of agreement rather than question it further. "So, to what do we owe the honor, Lieutenant?"

Ryland's eyes darted to Vogal. "I was hoping to speak with you privately, Mr. Stevens." Ryland turned to the Witch. "No offense."

"None taken," she said, looking over at Stevens for a cue.

"Vogal is my second-in-command," he said firmly. "Anything you want to share with me, you can share with her." Most people wouldn't spot the thin smile of approval she allowed to creep onto her usually stern face. "And you can call me Mark."

His response seemed to make Ryland a little uncomfortable; he shifted on his ammo crate seat slightly. "I understand your unit was formed from former employees of yours," Ryland said.

"That's right. The war put me out of business. I felt that the militia program was the best way to take care of my people and make sure they got paid."

"So, how's that working out for you?"

It was a strange question, but Mark took the bait. "We're

surviving. We get some pretty difficult assignments; I assume that is because we are good enough to pull them off."

"That's the truth," Ryland confirmed. "You aren't on the same tier as Colton's Cutthroats, but Open Hostility is on the same path. I sit in on the mission assignment meetings, and so far no one has anything bad to say about your performance. For militia units, that's saying something. If anything, everything I've heard is quite complimentary…that your people are top notch."

That news made pride swell in him, if only slightly. *This is the first time anyone in the Army has ever said that to my face.* "That's good to hear," he replied, casting a nod at Vogal whose smile actually grew. "I'm sure the rest of my people will be glad to hear that."

"It's the truth. Let me ask you, Mark, what are you looking to get out of the war."

"What do you mean?"

"Well, you said that you started this unit so that your people wouldn't be unemployed…so they could get paid. Is that why you are fighting?"

It was another bizarre question and wasn't easy to answer. "I'm not sure how to respond to that." Glancing at Vogal, all she had to offer was a slight shrug. "We are not mercenaries, not like the PMCs out there. They get to pick and choose their missions, and money drives everything they do. We aren't like that. We are loyal to the United States. We are fighting for our country. If we don't stop the Fish now, who knows when they'll be stopped? Yes, the money is damned important, but it's not the motive. My people all have families somewhere. Most of them don't spend what they make, they send it to their loved ones. This is their living now. It doesn't pay great, but it's better than being unemployed and wandering the country looking for a job." Stevens paused, then offered a question of his own. "Why are you asking?"

The lieutenant took a moment to gather his thoughts. Mark could almost hear the gears turning in his head as he searched for the right words. "To be blunt, what I'm going to tell you could end my military career. I'm trusting you to not say anything to anyone. It's a big ask, I know, but it is necessary."

Intrigue grabbed on to Stevens, and he found himself nodding in response. "Sure—why not?"

"Have you heard of Ratchet?"

"The singer?"

"That's her."

"I'm not into that neo-rap, hippity-hoppity, boom-bang stuff she sings."

"Me either. You see, she paid me a visit not too long ago. She wanted the Army to go to some super-secret bank in Beverly Hills. It turns out that the rich and powerful have a little hiding hole for their most precious stuff." Ryland paused, quite deliberately, from the look on his face.

"Go on."

"Well, this bank of theirs is behind enemy lines. The Fish aren't likely to have an interest in a bank vault. That means that all of the contents of that bank are sitting out there, waiting for someone to retake Beverly Hills, or…"

"…or…"

"…go in and take it." The lieutenant stopped and cracked his own grin.

Stevens was caught off guard. *Is this guy suggesting that we rob a bank behind enemy lines?* He had to admit, what he was suggesting was incredible. *This isn't any surprise.* It would be hard to picture someone like Ratchet just walking into the local Bank of America branch like a normal person. *Of course they have their own special bank—a special bank for special people.*

A part of his mind hesitated. *Maybe this is some sort of loyalty test.* His distrust of the Army ran long and deep. "Robbing a bank would be a violation of military law," he responded slowly. "Anyone doing that would find themselves facing jail time, or worse."

"Assuming they got caught."

"Look, Lieutenant, the battlespace commanders have every bit of the AIZ they can monitored. Beverly Hills isn't far as the crow flies, but you would have to take more than people that far in. It's farther than most ops ever even consider. You'll need vehicles to transport whatever you find there, and the only way out is through the Army's lines. Someone is going to see all of this activity and know something is wonky."

"On the surface, it might look that way," Ryland countered. "A regular Army unit going rogue would be probably caught. A militia unit, one with their own egress point in and out of the AIZ, would stand a better chance. What you would need is someone on the inside, who could make sure that the battlespace commanders were blind to the operation. It can be done, but it requires cooperation—

militia and military."

It was in that moment that Stevens realized this wasn't a test. What Lieutenant Ryland was proposing was something he had given serious thought to. His own brain started coming up with a lot of reasons why this was a bad idea, but the excitement overrode those thoughts. *Rich people have a lot of rich stuff. Damn! I bet that vault is full of all sorts of great shit.* His imagination was beating down the logical parts of his brain like a pro boxer on speed. "Are you proposing what I think you are proposing?" he finally asked.

"I am."

Stevens looked over at Vogal who had nothing to offer other than her wide eyes looking at him in stunned disbelief. Turning back to Ryland. "Why me? Why us?"

"Because you're not die hard fanatics. You are fighting to keep your people fed. And you're good. I've looked at your records. For all of the ops you've been on, you've only lost one of your people. Open Hostility is all about you taking care of your people. Well, if they and you undertake this mission, they may be set for life. You can walk away from this war and no one will say a thing."

"But you can't," Vogal said. "You're Army-green, I can practically smell it on you."

"For my team to do this, they will have to disappear. I'm cherry-picking the people I take in. A lot of shit can happen out there, you know that. Don't worry about my team, we will be a fading memory."

"Why you? Well, we can't do this on our own. A missing squad is a sad thing. A missing platoon, well, that's a disaster, albeit a small one. Beverly Hills is a ways from here, and getting there with the gear and transport, and keeping the Fish at bay, that takes more than what I can bring to the table. I need you and your people, Mark—people I can trust—plain and simple."

"This is wild," Vogal said.

It was hard to argue with that. Yet it was also enticing. "This is incredibly risky," Mark said.

"Every op is. This one has big risks, but for the first time in a long time, it has a big reward attached to it."

"If we were to do this," Vogal weighed in, "security would be critical. If word gets out about this, everyone will be trying to get to Beverly Hills and hit this place."

"Agreed. My team, the Ghost Legion, is small and tight. I assume you are able to keep your people from talking."

Mark's mind was thinking about the distances and the alien threats. "We are going to need more than just our unit and your squad. There's a good chance of the Fish finding us. They will move to cut us off and wipe us out."

"I'm going to line up some ASHUR support," Ryland said. "One rig should be enough."

"Transportation is going to be challenging. A lot of the roads are clogged with abandoned cars and debris up that way. The Army's tried to retake the Hills several times already," Stevens said.

"We are arranging four-wheelers, ATVs with ammo trailers. Small, easy to navigate…they should suffice."

"How are you going to keep the battlespace command from seeing us?"

"We will pull our ID chips before the run and shield them from tracking," he said. "Also, I have some pull at headquarters. I can give them something else to focus their attention on. We will make our penetration using the ruse of an actual op. The new lieutenant colonel wants aggressive action, so that's what this will look like from their perspective."

He's thought this through. Ryland's response only made it seem more possible. "I'm not committing just yet. Let me hear what you have in mind for this."

Ryland began to unload his thinking. It was remarkably well organized. The lieutenant rattled off the team assignments, the approaches that he was exploring, how they could breech the vault— even his calculations as to what they might need in the way of transportation. The level of detail was staggering and suggested that he had been planning this for some time. Ryland spoke quickly, his words a blur as he laid out the plan he was considering and what role Open Hostility could play in it. He went on for nearly forty-five minutes, seeming to not take a breath the entire time, he spoke so fast. There was no gap in his torrent of words to even ask questions. When finished, he sighed and tilted back on the ammo crate seat. "Well, what do you think?"

"It's—impressive," Stevens managed to say, still somewhat staggered by the amount of information that had been dumped on them.

Vogal jumped in. "You've clearly put a lot of work into this."

"It literally keeps me up at night," Ryland admitted.

She dipped her head. "What if we get there and there's nothing? What if someone gets there before we do or already has looted it and it simply hasn't been discovered?"

"Then we fall back, return to our posts, and pretend none of this happened," the lieutenant replied. "The Army will be none the wiser and as long as we don't say anything, no one will know what we tried. They can't put us on trial for *failing* to loot a bank."

Stevens leaned in. "I feel like saying, 'This is just crazy enough to work.'"

"It's dangerous, I admit it. But for the first time in this conflict, we have a chance to do something for ourselves. I can take care of my people—you can take care of yours. In the end it's your call."

Stevens shook his head. "Wrong—it's not my call alone to make. We're militia. We are more like family. Oh, I know the whole Army line about people being part of a brother and sisterhood thing. We aren't the same. I can order my people to do this, but in reality, they need to want to do it if we are going to be successful."

"Far be it for me to throw a wrench in this, but not everyone is likely to want to undertake this," Vogal said.

Stevens quickly went through the roster of the forces, and then knew the stumbling block. "Reese."

"Reese," she confirmed.

"Your liaison?" Ryland asked.

Stevens nodded. "She's the only person in Hostility that is likely to oppose this. Reese is the strangest damned warrant officer I've ever encountered. Most of them are realists. They exist between officers and enlisted personnel and relish that role. She's a real true believer in the cause. Reese plays by the book. If she gets wind of this, she will go over my head, your head, and your lieutenant colonel's head to get her point across."

Ryland paused for a moment. "I could arrange for her transfer."

"No good," Stevens replied. "We might get someone just as bad. Besides, she's the kind of person to question a transfer without some sort of reason. It's probably better to keep her around, but work around her."

"The devil you know versus the devil you don't."

"Right. We just need to put this in front of my people without Reese there. I can have her go to HQ to get supplies, or something like that. Once she's out of the picture, I'd like you to go over this with my people. If they buy into it—then we go."

"And if they don't?"

"My people aren't snitches or bitches. Your secret will be safe with us."

"Alright then, Mark, when do we do it?"

"Give me an hour to get Reese out of camp. In the meantime, the Witch can show you around, make it look like an inspection."

Vogal nodded. "Be prepared to be unimpressed."

* * *

They were packed inside the shipping container they used for common space. Reese was gone with a hastily prepared list of material and supplies, though she did question why Lieutenant Ryland was there in camp before she departed. Stevens had said that they were old friends, and he was just stopping by to say hello— which seemed to be enough for his liaison.

The summary of the operation code-named Sundance was shorter than the one Ryland had given Stevens and Vogal. It was concise and to the point—right down to the part where he said they were going to be violating regulations and facing prosecution if they were caught. Open Hostility didn't say much. They sat, absorbing the words. Mark knew that his people were still tired from their last run in the AIZ, and that getting them fired up was going to be a challenge.

When Ryland finished, he asked for questions. Nardo raised her hand. "Boss-man, where do you stand on this?"

All eyes locked onto Stevens. *They aren't going to commit to a stranger. They want my buy in.* "I formed this unit to put food in your guts and get you paid. Me? I'm all-in. I lost everything to the Fish. You all know that. I've killed enough of them to suppress my urge for revenge. This is a chance for me to walk away from this war and maybe enjoy life just a little. If we do this, it means that everyone walks away with enough to buy themselves some much deserved peace and quiet. So, I'm in. But all of you have to make that call for yourselves."

"Robbing a bank in the middle of a war…" Sprang said with a wicked grin. "Count me in!"

"Why the-fuck-not?" Bigalow asked.

"If we don't do it, someone else is bound to," the hulking Guideon said.

"What about you, Witch?" Nardo asked, looking over at Vogal.

"I can die rich or I can die poor. Why in the hell would I want to die poor?" she replied. The entire tiny room erupted with laughter.

There were no dissenting votes when Stevens asked for a show of hands in favor. If anything, his weary people were energized by the shot at, what Ryland called, "Hidden treasure." He could see it in their eyes, that look that was a mix of greed and excitement. Strangely, the biggest boost to their morale was the very thing that would end their military careers as militiamen.

When they were finished and sworn to secrecy, Ryland made his way over to Mark. "You know, some of the supplies we need, like the ATVs, those are going to be difficult to obtain. I might be able to get one or two, any more than that and it'll start to raise some red flags on my side of the fence. By any chance do you have a source?"

Stevens did—the Coyote. "I do. At best, he's an untrustworthy conniver. His only real talent is being able to get things that no one else can, almost always at a price."

"You think he'll be suspicious with a request like we have to make?"

"Yes. He'll want a cut. He's also the kind of person that if we don't give him a cut, he'll rat us out for whatever reward he can get. His lack of scruples is one of his few trustworthy characteristics."

"Good to know. I'll get you a list and we can work from there."

The Coyote, the Witch, and a ghost named Casper—who would have thought of assembling this group to rob a bank!

Chapter 12

Staff Sergeant Sutherland MacLeod walked around his Rattlesnake ASHUR rig, eyeing it the way he would a steak that was overcooked. His technician, Corporal Rachel Swift, stood in her filthy, lubricant-stained jumpsuit, watching his every move. Tugging at the replacement armor plates she had recently attached, they seemed to be holding fast. He gave the armored elbow hydraulic line on the right arm a firm tug. It was the one that had been damaged by the Crab that he had killed. The line was tight, but there was no way he was going to let her see any hint of satisfaction. For him, it was enough that he was putting her through the drill of double-checking her repairs.

He'd spent more time in the repair bay of Firebase Dragon than in the field. He hated the stink of hydraulic fluid and lubricants, mixed with the body odors from the technicians. As much as he detested it, it was a part of his life—a cologne that great ASHUR pilots wore with distinction.

MacLeod had a love-hate relationship with his senior tech,

Swift. She was good—her only problem was that she knew it. He felt that it was one of his primary duties to keep her ego in check by criticizing her work. She put up with him, mostly due to rank, though he suspected that she actually admired his skills.

ASHURs were the best line of defense against the aliens. He had been on so many operations that he had lost count. That also meant his rig spent a lot more time in the tech bay. The average civilian didn't understand that for every two hours in the field, the rigs had to spend an hour in the bay being worked on. It was the math of combat effectiveness, so it was part of his life, one that he loathed.

Nor was Rachel looking for his validation. "It's all tight; you know that. I don't see why we have to go through this ritual every time I make repairs to this rig."

"All I know is that I nearly got killed last time I was out. Since I'm one of the best pilots in the west, I can only presume it's some failure on your part."

Her eyes narrowed on her grime-smeared face. He knew his last salvo of words had hit. A part of him was looking forward to Swift's rebuttal. *She's going to question my piloting—I know it.* Her mouth opened, but her eyes shifted off to someone moving in behind him.

Turning slowly, he saw the lieutenant. His cloth name tag read Ryland, a name that meant nothing to him. "May I help you, Lieutenant?"

The officer seemed to eye him cautiously. "Sergeant MacLeod, I presume."

"Yes, sir," he said, crossing his big arms on his larger chest.

"I'm Lieutenant Ryland of the Ghost Legion."

"Alright," was all MacLeod said. He had heard of the Ghost Legion. Supposedly they were a good outfit, one of the better ones. *If he's looking for some sort of compliment, he's come to the wrong place.*

Ryland looked past MacLeod, focusing on his Rattlesnake-class rig. The big ASHUR had a cobra-head look to it. It was painted with an urban camouflage pattern, blacks and grays with jagged blocks of white, with a few small block-patterns of light browns. There was a one-foot-wide checkered band around the mid-section that had nothing to do with camouflage—a mix of black and yellow checkerboard, with some bands being larger than the others. MacLeod knew he was confused by the Clan MacLeod tartan on the rig, most people were. "That's a hell of a rig you have there," Ryland offered.

MacLeod turned and glanced at the ASHUR, then at Swift who grinned. "With all due respect, don't compliment this rig."

"Sergeant?"

Walking up in front of the rig, he patted it just under his Steel Hyena logo, a wild-cartoon-ish hyena decked out with medieval armor. "This armor plate has been replaced three times—and it still doesn't fit right." He reached over to the Mark IA Plasma Carbine. "Corporal Swift here has never been able to fully align the targeting system for my plasma weapon to my satisfaction. My assault ACR jams when I need it the most. Oh, and the left foot is sluggish."

"It's not, Sergeant," Swift said. "I have tested it myself, four times."

"Then how do you explain me falling over in that last firefight?"

She opened her mouth but he cut her off. "That was rhetorical. You can't explain it without impugning my piloting skills, which even the Army acknowledges to be outstanding." MacLeod turned to face Ryland. "You see, sir, when you go and start complimenting my rig in front of its technician, it goes to her head. She's already insufferable and barely able to conduct her duties," he said, turning to her and raising his right lip in a half smile. Corporal Swift only narrowed her eyes down to slits and glared at him with red rage rising under the streaks of grease on her cheeks. *Damned officer coming in here and messing with my motivation session.*

"Is that an external speaker?" Ryland said, nodding at the ASHUR.

"Yes, it is," he said proudly. The speaker was ugly, mounted just over a shoulder. He didn't care how it looked, it worked.

"What is it for?"

"Fucking with the Fish, sir."

"How is that?"

"Think of it as my own personal sonic weapon."

That brought about a puzzled expression in response. "I don't understand. Your Rattlesnake is outfitted with a SW-02X Sonic Disruptor."

"That's the Army's weapon. Mine is psychological."

"You've lost me."

"I blast music in a fight. It scares the Fish, confuses them."

"What kind of music?"

"I've tried it all. There are only two kinds of music that do the trick. First—heavy metal. Not that shiny metallic music-bullshit that kids listen to now and claim is heavy metal, I'm talking the good stuff: Black Sabbath, Twisted Sister, Mötley Crüe, Gwar—you know, the classics. I also do some historic rock, back before it was all synthesized and fake." MacLeod was proud of his collection of tunes he unleashed on the enemy.

"What is the other kind of music?"

"Bagpipes. You put on 'Scotland the Brave' or 'The Black Bear,' the Fish freeze in their tracks in confusion. It's glorious to see." The sound of the pipes was inspiring as it was terrifying.

"Sergeant," Corporal Swift said. "You are the only person that thinks that music works. Maybe the Fish are just pissed off that you play that stuff."

It was his turn to scowl at her. "You are dismissed, Corporal." Swift almost seemed relieved, walking off leaving MacLeod and Ryland alone in the repair bay. *I don't need her negativity here right now.*

"I should have guessed you play bagpipe music—with a name like MacLeod."

"Being Scottish has nothing to do with a last name. It is a state of mind. I'm Scottish alright, but it's because of my way of thinking." He stabbed a finger at his own temple. *It's not about being Scottish as much as it is about being stubborn.*

"Have you told anyone in G2 about the music affecting the aliens?"

"Some damned officer intel spook named Slade. He said they were likely just confused by the noise, that it didn't matter what was being played. The Defense Intelligence Agency—that's a contradiction in terms." There was a part of him that knew that Slade was probably right, but he was not going to concede that.

"The word is you like bucking the system," the lieutenant said.

"Only when the system is retarded."

"You have been promoted over your current rank two times, both times getting busted down."

"That's true."

"You didn't put up any defense when they busted your rank."

"Also true."

"Why?"

MacLeod narrowed his gaze on the slightly taller officer. "Permission to speak freely, sir."

"Granted."

"Why do you care? Am I in some sort of new trouble? Or are you doing a documentary vid on the unsung heroes of this glorious war, sir?"

Lieutenant Ryland cracked a thin smile. "I'd like to know what your issue is with authority?"

Most NCOs knew enough to keep quiet, but MacLeod wasn't a typical staff sergeant—something he was proud of. He didn't know this lieutenant from a hole in the ground, nor did he care what the man thought of him. "The first time I got busted down was because some dumb-as-fuck officer gave me orders that would have gotten me and the rest of the platoon killed. Funny thing, I'm against dying. The second time I defied orders and executed a flanking maneuver on my own authority. I saved the lives of the fire team I was working with in the process."

"I thought ASHUR pilots had a high degree of autonomy in their deployments."

"We do, usually. The officer in question did not appropriately appreciate my assessment of the tactical situation. In other words, my actions made him look stupid."

"And you pointed it out."

He nodded once proudly, reaching up and stroking his four days' growth of stubble that served as a beard. "I most certainly did. The man was a hazard to himself and the people under him. I had hoped he would benefit from my experience and expertise. Instead, he labeled me as insubordinate and busted my balls and ranks."

For a few moments, Ryland said nothing. "Let me ask you something, Sergeant. What is your endgame? What is it you want to get out of this war?"

It was a strange question but not offensive, so MacLeod decided to play along. "Good question. Frankly, I'd be happy to get through this whole thing alive, preferably with all of my body parts intact."

"You have a family of your own?"

"No. I have a sister but she's as pigheaded as I am and we haven't spoken for years." That was the truth. He had come to grips with Agatha and her many issues years ago. After their father died, it had gotten messy between them...mostly because she demanded his share of the inheritance. It wasn't a lot of money to begin with, but for Sutherland, it had become personal. It was easier for him to not talk to her at all than to try to patch things up. He let her have the money and walked away from their relationship.

"So you're a lifer?"

That made him chuckle. "I never thought about it much, but yes, sir, I am, I guess. Taking on the Russians in the last war was a brutal damned experience, but I earned my ASHUR wings and proved to everyone that I was indeed as good as I'd been claiming. They offered me a package after the war, but I decided to stay. Where was I going to go at the age of thirty, when my only appreciable skills were piloting an ASHUR and killing people? Surprisingly, there's not a lot of demand for that in the commercial sector."

"I know the feeling," Ryland said. "When they started reducing the military after the war I could have quit too, but I ended up staying. When you have led people into battle, nothing quite compares to it in the real world."

"Sir, may I ask you a question?"

"Sure."

"Why are you here? Why do you care what I want after the war? You have some sort of suicide mission for me? 'Cause if you do, fuck that."

Ryland chuckled again. "Far from it. I came to you because you have an independence streak that is well known. I have a mission, but it's not about suicide."

"Go on."

"Before I go further, I want your word that what I am about to tell you stays between us."

Who would I tell? MacLeod had to admit that his curiosity was piqued with what he had just said. "Sir, it's clear you've read my records—probably even pulled up my performance evals. I'm not a backstabber or a shirker. I don't have a lot of friends because people I get attached to either try to fuck me over at some point or end up dead. One thing you learn in this man's army is that close personal attachments in a shooting war is a fast path to being put on PTSD meds."

"It can be a lonely life."

"I'm an ASHUR pilot," he said with pride. "I'm used to being the tip of the spear and operating on my own."

"One thing that attracted my attention to you is you often disregard orders. If I remember correctly, you have, on at least four occasions, undertaken missions without authorization."

MacLeod felt his jaw slide forward. "And?"

"Why? I mean the AIZ is a dangerous place. You've gone out on your own, without orders. That's damn peculiar behavior."

It may seem that way to you, but not to me. "What I did, I did for my own personal reasons."

"Which are?"

His jaw set and locked, his crossed arms flexed. "Revenge."

"Revenge?"

"I lost a few friends out there on a handful of missions that went south. Every time that happened, there's a particular Boss out there that is behind their deaths. He's a big-ass bastard. If you must know, I am going out there looking for him."

"How do you know it's the same Boss?"

"It is. I know what he looks like. He's got a scar under that eye-slit thing—courtesy of my plasma carbine. I call him Scarface and that black-skinned monstrosity is my white whale. That rat-bastard has managed to get away every time I have had him in my sights."

"You've fought him more than once?"

"Twice so far. The first time I cut his ugly-ass face. The second time I brought down a building on him—only to see him crawl out of the rubble and get away."

"Why isn't that in your combat summaries?"

"It's none of the Army's damned business why I went out there. Officers like you would piss and moan about not being in the revenge business. Well, that fuckface killed people I cared about, and he needs to be taken down."

"So this Boss is still alive?"

"I think so. The problem is, we have given up so much ground, he hasn't surfaced lately."

Ryland nodded at MacLeod's words and drew a long deep breath before he spoke again. "My reason for coming here was to proposition you, Sergeant."

MacLeod grinned. "Sorry, Lieutenant, you're not my type… no offense."

Ryland chuckled at that. "No, not that kind of proposition. I am putting together a team to mount an unauthorized mission behind enemy lines. I'm looking for the right people, individuals that have a certain moral leniency when it comes to the Army."

He liked the way that the lieutenant was tap-dancing round the subject. *Moral leniency—I will have to remember that one.* "Let's not pussyfoot around this, sir. What is the mission?" The officer shifted on his feet and looked around to make sure there was no one close enough to hear their conversation. "Well, we are looking for your fire support to assist us with a bank robbery in Beverly Hills."

Those were not the words he expected to flow from the officer's lips. *Ryland has a pretty solid reputation.* It seemed as if this entire awkward discussion suddenly made some degree of sense. *If he's talking about robbing a bank, this isn't some pipe dream.*

"What bank?"

Ryland smiled a little more. "Let's find a private place to discuss this in detail."

* * *

The conversation was in hushed tones, low and intense as the pair of them walked around the perimeter of Firebase Dragon. Ryland had spoken as if he were reading a slide show, rattling through bullet points about the bank, the team he was pulling together—everything. It reminded MacLeod of a machine gun firing, the facts and details came so quickly. The lieutenant's entire demeanor became almost like an excited child…as if there was some relief in providing the details of what he was planning.

Sutherland drank in every point even though it was like trying to sip water through a fire hose. Even he had to admit, it sounded exciting. While he would never admit it, he admired Ryland for having the guts to approach him with such a plan. *If it was anyone else, they might turn him in. He did his research in finding me, that is for sure.*

After the steady barrage of words, Ryland finally stopped with a simple question: "So, what do you think?"

MacLeod knew the right thing to say was, "It'll never work. Someone will leak; they always do. And even if they don't, the Army will come after us. We will end up in a military prison, or worse, dead." Those were the right words. Despite that, the staff sergeant found himself caught up in the proposed robbery...though not for the same reasons that Ryland would have anticipated.

"I think it's crazy. You are talking about going miles behind the lines, deeper than almost any other penetration, and hauling out the contents of a vault, back through Army lines. You would have to be a madman for even considering it."

Ryland looked dejected, his jaw opened slightly, as if he wanted to talk but could not find the words. MacLeod decided to continue to speak. "Which is why you need me. Yeah, Lieutenant, I'm in. I'll go with you and be your fire support for this heist."

Ryland exhaled and smiled. "I don't understand...if it's crazy..."

"Look, the money would be nice. I'm not doing this for you and your friends. The last time I saw that Boss, Scarface, it was in Beverly Hills just after the last round of fighting there. I'm hoping he's still there. I'm going with you and I intend to find that asshat and kill him. It's less of me providing support for you as you providing bait for me."

"I—I—"

He's nervous, and rightly so. Sutherland waved his hand in the air. "You're worried I won't be there when you need me, that I'm off on some vengeance quest and that will blur my responsibilities and put you at risk. Don't worry, you'll get the firepower you need. But if I can get a chance at killing that Fish, I'm going to take it."

"I can live with that," Ryland said, extending his hand.

Sutherland took it and gave it a firm shake. "You will. So, I have some ideas to tweak your plan a little. If we are going to rob a bank and face military justice, I think we need to do it with a little style."

CHAPTER 13

Starlight Inn, the Western Front, Le Brea, California, the United States

The conference room table that Spartan Associates used for their planning had the semi-holographic display system covering every bit of it. The system was far more sophisticated than the digital mapping systems that the DoD used...one of the advantages of being a PMC. Where the Army was limited by army specifications, private contractors could purchase whatever they could afford and Spartan Associates had money to spare.

The display showed the latest satellite views of the city, courtesy of Starlink III, enhanced to a 3D light display. With the lights dimmed and the curtains pulled, the map itself was the primary source of light for Dawes and his people. While the Fish came from space, they didn't seem to appreciate the value of satellites. It was just another one of their quirks that Albert Dawes could never wrap his head around. *Maybe they have another way of monitoring us, something we haven't discovered yet. Of course it's just possible that they don't care that we can see them—that they want us to come at them.*

Dawes wore wristbands to control the display. Using his hands to zoom out to the point to show the target as well as the rest of the border with the AIZ. The display's limited holographic capabilities showed the buildings still standing in relief. The cars were still displayed in 2D, but the rest of the map showed the subtle hills and undulations of the terrain that the city had been built on.

His team gathered around the map, staring down at it intently. Dawes stood at the head of the table, arms crossed, surveying the image. "Reaper and I have been looking over this mission with a great deal of scrutiny. We have a few challenges to overcome. First, we have to get to the objective without letting the Fish overpower us. Second, we have to penetrate the vault. Third, we need to have the appropriate transportation to take the contents of the bank with us. Fourth, we must be able to get out of the AIZ without getting killed or raise the suspicions of the Army."

"In doing some digging, we think we can solve the first hurdle by using the Purple Line," he said, using his hand to adjust the map. The metro subway line lit up in relief on the map in a streak of magenta. "The subway was put in twenty years ago and there's a station just outside of Beverly Hills that appears to be clear of obstruction. We can gain access to the tunnels not far from here and work our way right to the edge of Beverly Hills."

"Sir," Guy Hague spoke up to his right. "Seems to me that the fucking subway is either going to be fucking flooded or impassable." Hague's variant and liberal use of the word "fuck" was frustrating at times, but this time it seemed appropriate.

Reaper weighed in with the answer. "The Army and the city pulled the subway cars out of there. It's not a deep tunnel, just under street level, so flooding is not likely to be an issue. The Army's used it a few times themselves. It's big enough for us to drive a dump truck through if we wanted to."

"What are we taking for vehicles?" Treacher asked.

Dawes fielded this inquiry. "Toyotas—short bed Tacomas with four-wheel drive. Four of them. They are small enough to navigate around street level obstructions. More importantly, the city built vehicle access at a number of the transit stations to allow the fire department to get down there in case they had emergencies. If we enter the AIZ at Outpost 35, we only have to navigate about a mile to reach the best entry point, at Pershing Square." With a wave of his fingers to activate the pre-programmed controls, the line of outposts lit up—with 35 highlighted in a circle of crimson light. A dotted line stretched from it, twisting and turning for many blocks, before arriving at the subway station at Pershing Square. All eyes in the room tracked the path, mentally committing it to memory.

"We don't know if the Fish use the subway at all. By the same token, we don't have any indication that they even are aware of it. The fact that the Army has used it tells me that the Fish simply don't give a damn about it. That makes it the perfect hidden highway for us to get to Beverly Hills."

Glancing around the table, he could see the excitement in his people's eyes.

"So we come out in Beverly Hills. Then what?" Diamond Jones asked.

"We make our way up Rodeo Drive and then get to the bank. Once there, Agis Team will form a defensive perimeter around the bank." With a flick of his wrist, he made the image zoom in on the bank and surrounding buildings. "They will assume rooftop surveillance positions as indicated." A twist of his knuckle activated red pulses on the intended building roofs. "The rest of Agis will secure the perimeter at ground level." Dawes let those images sink in.

"Leonidas Team will have to crack the nut," he said, reaching down and pulling up a new image. He'd had the blueprints for the vault and bank interior made into a 3D model that rose a full two feet above the tabletop in full holographic display. "This vault is going to be a bitch. If we went in with explosives, we risk damaging what is inside it. That means we drill our way in. It wasn't easy getting the details of the vault construction. As you can imagine, the companies that make these things don't let their secrets out to the public. We were able to get information from the manufacture of the security system itself, however, which will prove to be useful. We will drill two holes in the vault that will give us access to the electronic system that controls the door mechanism."

"There's no power there, not after all of that time," Fisher pointed out.

"True. When the bank loses power, it automatically goes into lockdown. There's a backup battery, but it only has power for ninety-six hours. The assumption is that no one will have four days' free access to the vault without attracting law enforcement. In our case, we are going to restore power with a battery. From what we have learned, when the system gets power after being down for that amount of time, it resets to the factory defaults settings. Those codes are specific to that vault and we don't have them. All we know is that it is a five-digit alphanumeric code."

"So how do we get in?"

Dawes pulled a flash drive from his fatigues' breast pocket. "I reached out to some guys that I know. They have written a little worm to try the access codes—all of the combinations. There's a port for plugging in the drive inside the vault door, hence one of the holes we are drilling. Worst-case scenario, it'll take an hour to run through the combinations to hit the one that runs the unlock routine and opens the door."

"An hour is a lifetime that deep behind enemy lines," Zack Nunez said, running his right hand over his black hair, slicking it back.

"Fuckin' Fish are bound to find us," grumbled Hague.

"You're right," Dawes said, his words seeming to surprise everyone gathered around the table. He stopped his sweep of the room with Reaper, who cocked a grin. "Normally we would be outgunned if the Fish discovered us. I got us something that levels the playing field a little bit, if not tips it into our favor."

Reaching down, he tapped the control panel and the holoimage of the vault was replaced with an ASHUR rig. Their eyes traced the outline of the rig, from top to bottom, as the holoimage turned in front of them.

"What the fuck…" Hague said. "I know almost all of the rig classes out there. I've never seen this configuration."

"You're right," Dawes replied proudly. "Meet the Phalanx-class rig."

Even Reaper's face washed with surprise, which made Dawes feel a bit proud of himself. *I had to pull every string in the book and write a check that is huge—but worth it.* As everyone eyed the rotating image, it was Treacher that broke the silence. "This isn't like any rig I've seen before."

"That's right. What you are looking at is one of the few commercially available rigs. It was built as a prototype for the Army, but rejected. The official code name for the rig was Irish Wolfhound. The Army rejected it because they claimed it was too slow. The Raytheon guys had three of the prototypes sitting in a warehouse gathering dust. I found that if you waved enough money at them, they were willing to part with one." *They're probably hoping that if it is successful, the Army will reconsider the design.*

"Why Phalanx?" Nunez asked.

"Because we are Spartans." That response got a lot of nods and smiles. *When you pay for something, you get to name it whatever you want.*

"Fuck yeah," muttered Hague with just a hint of awe.

"So who is going to pilot it?" Jones asked.

"I found a pilot that washed out during the final at the ASHUR School of Tactics. She got wounded, lost a leg, and the Army cut her loose. Her name is Trixie Lynch, call sign Brutality."

"A wash up? Chief, you sure that is a good idea?"

He appreciated the fact that his people were willing to question his decisions. *After all, their lives are as much at stake as mine.* "I do. I met her before she got wounded. She has a real chip on her shoulder about failing the final...claims that the system was rigged against her. She wants to prove that the Army fucked up twice—first for failing her to be an ASHUR pilot, second for mustering her out. I learned a long time ago that people who have a lot to prove will do it when you give them a chance. Trust me, she's determined. Trixie's on her way here now, along with the rig."

"That rig had to cost a pretty penny," Reaper said.

"It did. So did the trucks and the ammunition and everything else I'm assembling for this mission. If we find nothing, we still collect from Ratchet, but that won't cover everything. I'm betting the farm here that this is a big payday. Otherwise we may just find ourselves converted into a militia unit and fighting for whatever scraps the Army tosses us." Those words were sobering, as intended. It wasn't an exaggeration. As a PMC, his company had been pretty profitable. When companies needed servers or their precious records recovered, he did it and handed out hefty invoices. It had allowed him to keep his people in top-notch gear and good accommodations. Times were getting tight, though. The job with Ratchet was a fantastic opportunity, despite the risks. *We don't have to score big, but we do have to score or we are going to lose our reputation and our financial asses.*

"Do we have a code name for this op?" Jones asked.

"Indeed we do," Dawes said. "Goldfinger." It had been Wallace's idea for the name, taken from the James Bond film where they had robbed Fort Knox. He saw that at least a few of his people got the obscure reference. *I hope that bank has as much booty as Fort Knox.*

As he surveyed their excited eyes around the display, he was proud of all of them. For Dawes, they were the closest thing to family that he had. He had walked away from any semblance of a normal life years ago, first in the military, then when he left the service and went private. Spartan Associates was something he had built with his own two hands. Before the war, he provided protection to a number of A-List celebrities. Then with the war, he had found a way to make a great profit sneaking behind the enemy lines.

I'm rolling the dice with this operation, and they know it. That's good, though. If we fail, we all will pay a price. It's a powerful motivation for them to do a good job and go the extra mile when the time comes.

CHAPTER 14

Outpost 46, the Western Front, West Los Angeles AIZ, California, the United States

"Before we begin," Don "Coyote" Sims said, "I think we need to work out the percentages of the loot split." A groan rose from the Open Hostility people in the double cargo container building where they had assembled the Sundance raiding force. Someone threw an empty water bottle at the scrounger, whose attempt to duck the projectile failed.

Stevens saw Ryland's eyes roll, and he jumped in before the lieutenant could rebut the scrounger. "Look, Coyote, you get the same percent that everyone else does—an even split of the take."

"I'm not sure that's fair," he said. "I mean, I'm providing a lot of equipment that frankly is hard to get in the middle of a war."

Ryland weighed in quickly, "You are talking about hardware and gear. We are all putting our lives on the line."

"Oh oh," Coyote said, waving his hands in front of him. "I'm going on this little heist with you."

"You're kidding, right?" Stevens asked. He had known Sims for a long time. The man was a profiteer, a modern pirate mixed with a dash of mobster. He wasn't the kind of person to put his life on the line. He was already cringing at having invited Coyote to the meeting, but he had insisted to the point of threatening to pull his support. *I am regretting this already.*

"If you think I am turning over my hardware to you without coming along to look after my assets, you are mistaken."

"Let the little guy come along," Sutherland MacLeod spoke up. "He might be entertaining when the Fish show up. Hey, if he gets killed, he doesn't get any cut. So we have that working for us." There was a lot of sarcasm in the ASHUR pilot's voice that Stevens appreciated. At the same time, he was starting to understand some of the quirkiness that was MacLeod's calling card. *Ryland warned me that this guy was a wild card. Now he's showing it.*

"I'm not going to get killed," Coyote fired back. "I have too much invested in this plan to just up and die."

"Fine," Ryland said flatly. It was clear he wanted to simply end the entire topic. "You can come along and get a cut for both you and the hardware. That is more than fair. But we are not babysitting you. This op is dangerous enough as it is without us having to protect you."

"No problem, I'll bring one of my guys for protection."

"He gets nothing," Stevens said. "He's coming on your dime."

"Agreed," Coyote said proudly.

"Alright then," Ryland said, shifting on his feet. "Back to the plan." The small cadre of the leadership for Operation Sundance had assembled in the common space storage container structure that Open Hostility called home. Gathered around the dull white Costco folding table was Ryland, Stevens, Coyote, MacLeod, Vogal, and Calcutt. It was cramped and uncomfortable, but the best place to make such plans without prying eyes figuring out what was happening.

There had been a bit of finesse with the assembly. Mark had to concoct a reason for his Army liaison, Reese, to not be there when the others arrived. Giving her leave never worked; she simply chose to hang around the firebase on her time off. So he sent her on a mission to obtain replenishment of munitions from the Army depot in Willowbrook. Just getting there and back would take hours, more than enough time for the assembled leaders to work through the nuts and bolts of the plan.

Ryland pointed to the large printout map he had brought with him. "As I had started to say, before being interrupted, I am going to take my Ghost Legion out first, on the premise of running a deep penetration recon op. Lieutenant Colonel Logan wants us to be aggressive, so he will approve it without batting an eye. Open Hostility will follow an hour later with the ATVs and transport out of this base. I will give them a cover op so that their departure doesn't attract any attention."

"What about me?" MacLeod said.

"You will go at the same time that Open Hostility does, but via outpost 30. I will send a signal to the battlespace command saying we need fire support and that will get routed to you, who just happens to be in position to go. From the Army's perspective, nothing is out of the ordinary."

"Cool beans," MacLeod said.

"We are going to rendezvous at the Beverly Wilshire Four Seasons Hotel," he said pointing at the map. "The hotel was blown up in the second battle for the hills. It's not much more than a pile of rubble at this point. It does give us the perfect defensive position, should we need it. It also is right on Rodeo, two blocks from our objective." His finger traced the path from the ruins of the hotel to where the Commerce Bank was located.

"What condition is the building in?" Vogal asked.

Ryland tossed out several glossy printed images. "The most recent satellite views show some minor structural damage, but for the most part that particular block looks like it has been spared a lot of the damage from previous operations." Everyone leaned over the images and studied them carefully. Mark liked what he saw. *If the building is intact, we can hope that the vault is as well.*

"What do we know about that vault?" Stevens asked.

"Almost nothing," Ryland replied. "I was able to determine who the manufacturer was. The thing has so many tripwires and backup systems, it is frightening."

"So we blow our way in?" Vogal asked.

"Hey, hey, hey," Coyote said. "Let's not get crazy. You set off too much in the way of explosives, whatever is inside that vault is destroyed."

"We came to the same conclusion," Stevens said, getting a short nod from Ryland. "As sophisticated as this vault is, in the end it is a big steel box. Rather than use explosives, we are going to cut through the sides of the vault."

"Cut?"

"Well," Ryland said, "technically, we are going to burn our way through. The Navy developed a phosphorous derivative putty for their underwater drone program. The stuff was designed to attach to ship's hulls and set off. It burns hot, *very* hot. It will cut right through up to four inches of steel, melting it like butter."

"And you have been able to get some of that stuff?" the Witch asked.

"I did."

"Is it enough to cut through the vault?" Calcutt asked.

"It should be. If it isn't, we have MacLeod's plasma carbine. We need to burn a hole big enough for us to crawl through without setting fire to what is in the vault. The good news on that front, when the temperature spikes inside, the fire suppression system releases gas to kill a normal fire. That should be enough to prevent our cutting from damaging anything inside."

"Let's hope," Stevens said. Burning through thick steel was not something that anyone on the team had experience with—so it was an educated guess. *It will work; it has to.*

"We will leave some of the team at the rendezvous point to cover our extraction. The rest will be in the vault, helping us load up the contents onto the ATVs and trailers. We will then fall back to the rendezvous team and work our way back to this outpost," Ryland said.

Vogal shifted on her feet, her fists planted firmly on her narrow hips. "If we show up here with trailers of stolen goods, someone is bound to talk. Prying eyes are going to be wondering what we recovered, and sooner or later there's bound to be an investigation.

What good is the prize if we are locked up in a stockade?"

"Fair enough," Ryland replied. He glanced over at Stevens and both of them smiled. The plan that Casper had come up with was brilliant, if they could pull it off. "We understand your concern. Let's just say that we have come up with a way of dodging prosecution."

The Witch looked over at Stevens who gave her a nod back. "You say you have it covered, that's good enough for me." He admired her trust. He had used her as a supervisor back during their construction days and her instincts were always sound. Mark always had her back then, and had done right by her and the rest of Open Hostility since they had become militia.

For a moment they stood in the storage container under the white lights of the LED strips that were attached to the metal roof. Mark could feel the tension mixed with excitement in the room and felt strangely relieved. It was hard for him to put his finger on why he felt so good, given the risks and dangers they were bound to face. As he drank in the faces of the command staff for Sundance, it dawned on him where that feeling was coming from. *We aren't just doing a mission for the Army, or running some op where we don't know why we are doing it or what it contributes to the war. This is for us! For the first time since all of this started, we are doing something for ourselves.*

"So, Casper," MacLeod said. "What's the wrinkle?"

"Excuse me?"

"You know," the stocky man replied. "The wrinkle—the rub—the thing that can screw us over when this goes down. Every mission I've been on has something that can come and bite us. You have done a good plan and all, downright impressive for an officer. No offense. But there has to be something out there that can monkey-fuck all of this planning."

"There's always the Fish," Vogal muttered loud enough for everyone to hear.

MacLeod turned to her. "I like the way you think, but the Fish are a force a nature. They are such a constant threat. Some aspects of them we understand, other times, they behave erratically. We are at a point where their inconsistencies are almost predictable at times. So what's the wrinkle, Casper?"

Ryland adjusted his stance, standing more erect. A hint of pink rose in his cheeks at having been called out. "There might be one. Ratchet, the celebrity that lit this fuse, may have talked to at least one PMC, Spartan Associates."

This wasn't news to Mark; he and Ryland had talked about it. "I did a little surveillance check on these guys, just to see if they were undertaking any actions that might look suspicious."

"What did you find?" Vogal asked for everyone in the room.

"At first, not much. I thought they might be sitting this one out. But two weeks ago, they made an unauthorized run into the city. Their target was the Los Angeles City Hall. I was able to pull up satellite feeds and monitor their activity yesterday." There was a hint of dejection in his voice that was hard to mask.

"Is that a big deal?" Calcutt asked.

Ryland dipped his head slightly as he spoke. "On the surface, maybe not. Then again, the building plans for Beverly Hills are stored at city hall. There's also no reason for them to make a run to that building. Most of their work is for private citizens. The city didn't pay them to go in there."

The words were sobering. Mark spoke up. "They were going in for the plans for the bank."

"It's a distinct possibility."

"So what does that mean for us?" Vogal asked.

Mark took the lead. "There are a few possibilities. One, they were there for some unrelated reason. Two, they are just poking around, wondering if it is actually possible. Three, they are planning their own run in and are committed."

Ryland joined in. "We have to assume they are going to take a shot at the bank."

"Agreed," Stevens replied. "They are a PMC. That means they have money at their disposal, probably enough to fund this kind of mission. God only knows what Ratchet waved under their noses to entice them. Spartan Associates would be a formidable challenger if —*when* they decide to try this."

There was only one option that Mark could think of. "We have to beat them, then."

"I've met Albert Dawes the owner, just in passing. He's ex-Special Forces—if there is such a thing. He has surrounded himself with experienced people. They are mercenaries of a sort, which means they will be motivated by the cash aspects of this."

"Maybe we could partner with them?" MacLeod offered. "I mean, we are all working towards the same goal. Working together would increase our odds of pulling this off."

Coyote threw a bucket of cold water on that concept. "If they are money motivated, they will turn that down. To them, this would dilute what they are investing in this. Worse yet, if you go and talk to them, you'd be tipping our hand and letting them know we know what we are up to. If I was this Dawes, I would make the run immediately just to make sure he didn't have to share a penny with you."

Leave it to a profiteer to bring in a dose of reality. "Coyote is right," Mark replied. "Whatever is there would end up being split three or four dozen ways. Why do that when you can pull it off and keep more of the cash? Besides, they probably have no more of an idea of what they are going to find there than we do. Guys like Dawes, they manage risks. Even if he did partner with us, he'd probably turn us into the Army just to ensure we don't get the prize before he does. We can't risk it."

"So what do we do about it?" Vogal asked.

"We have an advantage right now—we suspect what Spartan Associates is planning," Mark replied coolly. "It's a question of how we use that advantage."

"That's simple," MacLeod said. "We go now—ASAP."

His words hung in the air for a moment with no reaction. "He's right," Ryland said, shattering the silence. "I had hoped that we would have time to do some joint training, so that we all could get to know how we operate and learn to work as a single team. It looks like we aren't going to have that kind of luxury. If Spartan Associates is planning to make their move, it could happen at any moment. If we plan on taking the time to do it right, by the book, we will be left holding the bag. The only sane move is to wing it and go as soon as we are ready."

Mark didn't like the solution, even if it was the right one. He had been one of the chief advocates for the teams getting to train together —but things were different now. *If we don't go right away, we might be screwed over.* "You're right, of course. I hate it, but this is the right call."

"Sounds like fun," MacLeod said, chuckling a little at his own attempt at humor.

"When are we talking about going?" Coyote asked.

"Tomorrow," Ryland replied. "Does that work for everyone?"

Most of those around the table said nothing. Coyote spoke up. "If that's the case, I need to leave now to make sure I have the ATVs ready to roll."

"I think we should go in at midday," Ryland said. "I'd prefer at night, but coordinating our various elements is going to be a bit tricky. Doing that at night would be a little more complicated."

"Agreed," Mark said. No point in adding in more risk.

"I'll have Raffi come here in the morning to pull your people's ID chips. That will take us off the radar of the battlespace commander."

"I'm not chipped," Coyote said. "Glad to say. That the process sounds like something painful."

"You don't need to be so chipper about it," Vogal said. "The rest of us have to deal with it."

"I'm just saying—"

"Let it go, little man," said MacLeod, cutting Coyote off. "From the looks of it, this lady could perform a vasectomy on you without skipping a beat."

Vogal gave a slow nod to Coyote, who recoiled a half step from the table.

"Alright then," Ryland said. "We rock out at 1230 hours tomorrow. I'll see you all at the Four Seasons at 1530. We do this right, and we're all rich. We foul this up, we all hang together." His words were ominous, but underscored the risks each of them faced.

Two hours later...

Warrant Officer Shelly Reese came back to the base and saw the Army unit departing. She recognized their commanding officer, Frank Ryland. *Casper and the Ghost Legion were here? If they were here, why wasn't I present?* She ordered the transport driver over to the storage container lined with sandbags to drop off the munitions then defiantly marched over to Mark Stevens.

The CO of Open Hostility was standing, talking to Vogal as she approached. The Witch gave her a stare as she got closer, one that seemed to say, "Here comes our hired nag." Shelly understood that attitude. She and the Witch had never seen eye-to-eye when it came to her role in the unit. "If the Army wasn't so screwed up, we wouldn't need a liaison."

The truth of the matter was that Reese hadn't asked for this role. If anything, she had asked for a different assignment. Her CO had assured her it was important and necessary, and would be temporary —but months had passed and there was no sign that she would rotate out anytime soon.

Militias were often clumsy groups of misfits, wannabe weekend warriors, or so many reputations claimed. She had been lucky getting Open Hostility. They had been more organized, more professional, more Army-like, than most militia units. Recently however, it felt like the CO of the unit was sending her away often. Now the Ghost Legion had paid a visit. *Something doesn't feel right.*

"Sir," she said, deliberately interrupting their conversation. Stevens turned to her slowly, his face not revealing anything. "Was that the Ghost Legion?"

"Why yes, it was," he replied.

"Why wasn't I informed of their visit? I'm your Army liaison. I should have been in the loop."

Stevens's face seemed to harden. "Calm down, Shelly. This wasn't a big planned event. It was an unscheduled thing. Lieutenant Ryland and his people just stopped by to introduce themselves."

Shelly could feel her face getting hot and red. "Sir, that is highly irregular."

The Witch weighed in. "We're militia...we're the definition of irregular."

Reese kept her gaze fixed on Stevens's face. "I would have liked to have been informed of such a visit. All you had to do was signal me and I would have returned." She had felt that the assignment he had given her was busy work, something that anyone could have done. This, however, was what she was supposed to manage as a liaison.

"Shelly, it really wasn't a big deal," Stevens replied. "We shook hands, made some introductions, nothing special."

Stevens was a master of words—he had given her nowhere to go. That in itself was frustrating to her. "Sir, in the future, I would like to be a part of such a meeting. It's my job. I realize that you and your people don't see the value in it, but that's a decision made above our heads."

"Duly noted," Stevens said, turning back to Vogal.

"What are those ATVs for?" she said, gesturing the four-wheelers parked near one of the storage containers.

"Oh those," he said, returning his eyes to hers. "Coyote is loaning those to us. I'm going to see if they are of any use before I buy them."

That doesn't sound like Coyote. He doesn't do anything for free. "That doesn't make sense sir. I mean, those things had to have cost Coyote a pretty penny."

"What can I say? I'm pretty good at bartering, I guess." He then returned to engaging with Vogal.

Something is going on here. I'm not sure what, but for some reason, he's keeping me in the dark.

Reese took a few steps away, then glanced over her shoulder. The Witch made eye contact with her, grinned slightly, and gave her a bye-bye wave. *They should call her the Bitch...not the Witch.* She accelerated her pace to make sure the munitions she had brought back were being properly stored.

A nagging thought kept chewing at the corners of her brain. *It's like they are hiding something from me. They keep coming up with reasons for me to not be at the base. Everyone in the unit has been more standoffish than usual. Add in these ATVs, and it points to something strange. He's being short with me, not given me any details.*

Something is happening, and I need to find out what.

CYCLE II

Close Captioning Feed— Dale Wharton, Trusted News
Network— November 19, 2040

"Good evening. This is Dale Wharton and I'm reporting from Los Angeles at the headquarters of the 7th Infantry Division's 1st Striker Brigade Combat Team. With me is Lieutenant Colonel Derek Logan, newly appointed commander. Thank you for joining me for a few minutes today, sir."

"Thank you for inviting me."

"The war in Los Angeles has been a series of disappointments for the American people. Since you took command a few weeks ago, we have taken back several city blocks. Do you feel like the tide of the war is turning in our favor now?"

"Well, first off, I wouldn't call it a 'series of disappointments.' Yes, we've had setbacks. Our enemy is utterly ruthless. They don't seem to have fear. An Army squad that suffers thirty percent losses would fall back in a fight. Not the Fish. They will fight right up to the last creature. Where we use conventional weapons, the enemy uses poison gas and other inhumane weapons."

//Footage 282—Visuals of Crab-warriors with La skyline in background//

"Yes, we have taken back several key strategic blocks. We won't know for some time if we have rounded a corner and are in a new phase of this fight. Every time we think we get an upper hand, they come up with a new twist or genetically altered creature to throw at us. The best way I can describe it as a boxing match. We are in round three at this point—and both fighters are throwing some pretty devastating punches."

"When will the American public expect to see tangible results?"

"We have results every day. We can't broadcast everything we accomplish because we don't know what the aliens may be monitoring. Trust me, we are making progress."

"You are asking us to trust you, but the military's track record thus far has been iffy at best. Much of Los Angeles has been laid waste as a result of the fight."

//Footage 881—images of city destruction//

"Look, Mr. Wharton—"

"Call me Dale."

"Fine, Dale—whatever. I think you are characterizing this incorrectly. Yes, some damage has been done to the city. Wars do that. There are still a large number of neighborhoods that remain untouched. And whatever has been damaged can be rebuilt. Look at Berlin, Bagdad, Fairbanks…all rebuilt and vibrant once more. The American people need to stop worrying about property damage and keep their focus on winning this conflict."

"At what point can we expect to see Los Angeles free from the aliens?"

"If you want a specific day, you're not going to get one from me. Only a fool would rattle off a date. If you set expectations that way, you are pushing yourself down the road to disaster. We are fighting street by street, block by block, to take back the city. We have a plan and are executing it. If you don't think I want a free Los Angeles, you are sadly mistaken."

"Many Americans think they have been patient so far."

"We have never faced invasion along our entire coast. We have never faced an enemy with a distinct technological advantage. We have never found ourselves thrown into a mass human migration away from the coasts as a result of war. So while people are impatient, let's all try to remember, this is a war unlike any other we have confronted."

Seven months earlier...

Commerce Bank, Beverly Hills, the Western Front, California, the United States of America

The knock came to his office door. "Mr. Billings, the Army is here," said Pat Lowe, his director of security, as he cracked open the door.

Antoine Billings rose from his red leather chair in his office, dusting the arms of his suit. "You let them in?" he asked as he walked to the door of his office and started to follow Lowe.

"Yes, sir, I thought it best," Lowe replied.

He knows he made a mistake. "We have protocols here at the

Commerce Bank, Mr. Lowe. You know those. No one enters without first entering their PIN code outside."

"I know, sir," he said as the lights flickered again. "It was the Army, though. I left Blevins with them."

As they rounded the corner towards the lobby, Antoine finished his chiding. "In the future, you need to adhere to the procedures we have. Those procedures are what separates us from the other banks."

"Yes, sir," he said, opening the door for Antoine.

Standing in the lobby was a soldier, wearing gray, black, and white camouflage. At his side was security officer Blevins, a hulking figure who was larger than the soldier. Antoine had hired him because he had been a stunt double in films and his sheer size and muscular frame conveyed safety.

The soldier's big assault weapon was being held across his front torso. "Sir, as I told your people here, you need to evacuate immediately."

"I'm afraid that is impractical," Antoine replied, crossing his tailored sleeves as an explosion when off not too far distant.

"I'm not asking," the soldier said. "Those are orders."

"You have no authority here," he quipped. "We are a private institution."

The soldier shook his head. "You clearly don't understand the situation. In a matter of minutes, this entire area is going to be behind enemy lines. The Fish are here and we are falling back. If you don't leave now, you'll be dead."

Antoine forced a smile of confidence on his face. "We are perfectly safe here. You have done your job, you've warned us—

now you may move on." He gestured to the door as he spoke.

"Damned fools," the soldier muttered. "I hope whatever you are protecting is worth dying for," he said as he left.

For a moment, there was quiet in the small lobby as he heard popping and cracking. Antoine had witnessed a shooting once in downtown La. If you lived in Los Angeles long enough, you heard the bang of gunfire and could distinguish it from the other sounds of the city. This was gunfire, rapid and a lot of it, and it was close enough to penetrate the insulation of the lobby. Hearing and identifying the sounds of gunfire added to the tension of the situation, something he sought to suppress.

"Sir," Lowe said. "If he's right, perhaps we should lock everything down and leave."

"I don't pay you to be afraid, Mr. Lowe. You are in charge of security. This minor *incursion* doesn't change your responsibilities."

"With all due respect, sir, this doesn't sound like it's minor. A tank just rolled up Rodeo Drive a few minutes ago. This is war."

"Our customers expect us to look out after their possessions. It is our obligation." Conviction dripped from each word that he spoke.

"I didn't take this job to protect a bank during an alien invasion," countered Lowe. "I have a family that I need to attend to." He took off his hat and placed it next to the espresso machine in the lobby.

"If you walk out of that door, you are fired," Antoine warned him as a massive boom went off nearby, rattling the chandeliers of the small posh lobby. One of the bulbs above them popped. "I will ensure you never work in this town again—mark my words."

Lowe shook his head. "This is just a bank. It's not worth my life.

You can't prevent me from getting a job when you are dead…and that's what you'll be if you stay here." Lowe didn't wait for a response. He moved to the door and departed, slamming it behind him.

Antoine turned to the hulking Blevins and for a moment, neither man spoke. *He owes me; I hired him when no one else would.* To his dismay, Blevins walked to the door. "Where do you think you are going?"

"I'm not going to die here," he said.

"Wait," Antoine called, stepping towards him. "I will triple your pay."

"Your money isn't worth shit if I'm dead," he said. Opening the door to the outside, the sounds of the approaching battle grew loud. He too slammed the door behind him, leaving Antoine alone.

What if they are right? No, that isn't possible. Even if they are, this bank is my responsibility. I will protect it to the end if I must. Making sure the front door was secured, he rapidly walked to his office. Once inside, he moved behind his Scully & Scully desk and opened the lower desk drawer.

The polished walnut gun case lay there, along with two boxes of ammunition and two clips…*no, the man at the gun store said they were magazines.* Unlocking it with a small key he kept in the same drawer, he pulled the cold weapon out, holding it nervously.

Like many of his clients, he had advocated that guns be confiscated by the government—that they were the cause of urban violence in La. It was far easier to blame the weapon than the person. Also like his clientele, he was a hypocrite. Where the actors and actresses appeared in movies that used guns extensively as part of their plots, Antoine's hypocrisy came in the form of a gun purchase for personal security.

The weapon was as blinged out as he could get it. Pearl handle grips and ornate etching and scrollwork covered the Sig Sauer .38. On one side, he'd had his initials etched. He'd had it studded with eight tiny diamonds. The weapon had a special dull golden plating too. The extras cost far more than the gun itself, but he didn't care. If he was going to own a pistol, it had to look more like an expensive piece of jewelry than a weapon. *It's a weapon befitting someone running the most exclusive bank in North America.*

Memories of going out the one time and firing it came back to him. The bang of the weapon, even with the ear protection on, was ridiculous. His wrists had hurt for three days from firing it. It was cold in his hand as he tried to re-familiarize himself with it. No matter how much he held and stared it at, he was still afraid of the pistol.

Another explosion went off, vibrating the entire building harder than ever before. A momentary flash of anger came over him at his security personnel. *No loyalty. At the first sign of trouble, they fled like cowards.* When the bank reopened, he would hire better personnel to protect it.

Antoine heard the erratic banging and popping of gunfire, seemingly much closer. As he sat in the bank, he realized this was a rare moment for him, when he was alone with his family's pride and joy. *If no one else will defend this place, I will.* He took one of the magazines and fumbled for a moment before he slid it into place on the pistol.

CHAPTER 15

Operation Goldfinger, Outside Outpost 35, Los Angeles, the Western Front, California, the United States

The Phalanx-class ASHUR rig had been freshly painted an urban camouflage scheme of random blocks and streaks of white, gray, black, and maroon. Lynch's name was painted under the canopy and her call sign, "Brutality," was painted on a Viking shield crowned with a pair of battle-axes. She had sent Dawes a rough sketch of what she wanted and his people had done an admirable job of bringing the logo to life. On the other torso was the symbol for Spartan Associates, a Greek warrior with a spear over his head, ready to throw. *I think we are the only PMC to have our own ASHUR rig—that alone almost makes the purchase worthwhile.*

Of course you didn't just get to purchase an ASHUR alone. You had to buy the special tools, spare parts, expendables, lubricants, special hydraulic fluid, and dozens of other odds and ends—all of which the manufacturer was more than willing to sell. You needed at least a tech or two to keep it running as well. The Raytheon guys were more than willing to train two of his people to service the Phalanx, but that came at a cost. *It's like buying an attack helicopter or a tank in terms of the costs to keep it running.* Still, there was some prestige that came with owning a one of a kind piece of military hardware.

No one knew for sure if camouflage paint had any effect on the Fish, but no one was willing to ignore it. Dawes watched Trixie Lynch put it through its paces on the cleared street. She trotted it for a block, pivoted almost in place, and then sprinted back up the block in a full run. Running around the corner, she flexed the waist, the arms, seeming to try to get a sense of the range of motion of the ASHUR. The thudding footfalls crunched the pavement and Dawes could feel each step, right up to the leaning skid she made to come to a stop.

Standing before him, he was impressed with the war machine. Lynch used her control sleeves to flex the arms and weapons. She tested the fingers of each hand. Shifting slightly, she raised one leg to check balance, then set it down and tested the other. Dawes watched and learned how a pilot got a feel for a rig and was impressed. *Hopefully it measures up to her expectations.*

The Phalanx was a medium-sized rig. Mounted on top of one arm was a heavy laser. The other arm was ringed with triangular rocket tubes, seven in total. In the torso was the stubby barrel of a grenade launcher on the left and a flamethrower on the right. The rig had big thick legs and a cockpit that was seated deep in the chest of the rig, with very little protrusion jutting forward. *If you turned that thing sideways, it could actually get through a doorway, with a little effort.*

Lynch popped the almost vertical cockpit canopy and stood up.

Her skin was dark, but contrasted with a pair of bionic replacement legs, the right being a full leg, the left starting at the kneecap down. She had passed on the synthetic skin models—her replacements were a flat black in color. He had read about her loss, when a Crab had gotten her in its claw and had crushed her limbs in a brutal clamping motion. From what he had read, she never passed out from what had to be incredible agony—which said something about her character. Lynch's hazel eyes glared down at Dawes as she stood there, facing him. "She's got a good center of balance, but her speed is a little slower than what I am used to."

"The Raytheon guys up-armored it to meet the Pentagon's ever-changing specs. Doing that made it too slow. That was one of the reasons they passed on it. Classical five-sided foolhardiness."

She ran her hand back through her curly black hair and shook her head. "It's good ride. They were stupid to pass on it."

"About as stupid as the Army pushing you into retirement."

Her lean cheeks seemed to tighten with those words. "Just because they tagged me as unfit for combat, doesn't mean that I didn't have a lot to offer. My CO had it out for me. Getting wounded was a perfect excuse for getting rid of me."

"Well, you heard my offer," he said. "From what I saw today, you know how to handle this rig. Would you like the chance to flip the bird off to the Army one last time?"

Reaching over, she ran her hand along the edge of the armored cockpit, stroking it as if it were alive. "When I got selected to try out as an ASHUR pilot, it was the proudest day of my life. Until today, I never thought I'd actually get to take one out again. When you drive one of these things…it's a feeling like no other. It is like having an armored skin, like the rig is part of your own body. I swear, you can feel it just like bare skin." Her mind drifted for a moment, and Dawes let it. *She's hooked, now I just need to reel her in.*

"So, I take it you're on board."

"Mr. Dawes, I'll take your contract. It's not about the money. I just want my dignity back. That, and I want to rub the Army's nose in my shit for cutting me loose."

I wish I had known that, I would have offered her less. "Excellent. You will certainly get a chance to do just that."

"I need a few days to test-fire the weapons, make sure they are properly aligned with the targeting system, that kind of thing."

"That should be possible," he said. "I want to launch this op in the next three days." He and Wallace had just a few loose ends to wrap op. Ted was visiting the Army to get the latest intelligence images. The Fish were constantly on the move, but he wanted to validate the route they had chosen and make sure they could get the trucks through with little effort.

"Have your techs come over and we will get started right away," Lynch said. "I'll make sure she's ready for battle." She powered down the Phalanx, its low hum died off—allowing in the sporadic sounds of battle from deep inside the AIZ.

Dawes heard footsteps near him and turned to see Reaper Wallace walking up to him. "Chief, we need to talk." From the tone of his voice, it wasn't good news.

"What is it?"

"When I was there, I pulled up the latest surveillance footage," he said in a low tone, casting a glance at the nearby ASHUR where Lynch was clearly still in earshot.

"Has someone made a move on our target?" That was Dawes's worst concern and there was no point in hiding it.

"No indication of that," Wallace replied. "But when I pulled up the images, I noticed that someone has been looking at the same images. I dug a little deeper. The same person had recently pulled up our run on city hall. They are watching us, they are tracking what we did when we went to get the blueprints. Hell, they may be watching us right now." He cast a wary eye skyward.

"Who? Who is looking at us?"

"I didn't get a name—that part was secured. What I did see was that it came from someone in one of the Army units."

"Which one?"

"The Ghost Legion—Casper Ryland's unit."

The Ghost Legion was well known. Ryland was a seasoned lieutenant who drew some pretty difficult assignments and pulled them off with amazingly low collateral damage. *They got their name by being able to move through the AIZ like ghosts, that's how good they are. That's probably why they get the hard missions. Why would he be looking into what we were doing? The only reason he would have any reason is if he knew what we were going for.* "Damn it!" Dawes spat.

"It could be coincidental. Heck, I suppose there's a chance that he was looking for some other reason," Wallace offered.

"I doubt it. When Ratchet came to us, she said that she had been given our name by someone in the Army. I'm willing to bet that it was Ryland."

Wallace stood rigid. "What do you think we should do?"

In his mind, Dawes was already mentally processing his options and the list he was coming up with was short. "How long ago was the inquiry made?"

"A few days ago. Why?"

"They are sizing us up…seeing if we are competitors…or if we have made our move. They know we haven't." His words were not intended for Wallace or anyone else other than himself. "They wouldn't have checked if they had already made a run."

"True," Wallace said.

Sighing deeply, he focused his brain on solving the problem. "The choices are not great. Ignoring it is an option—though not one I would ever really consider. We can reach out to Ryland and his people, see if we can partner in this. We can go as planned and run the risk that they make a move before we do. Or, we go now—with what we have, ready or not." As he spoke, he heard Lynch walk in closer. His eyes darted to hers and he could tell that she had been tracking the conversation as well.

"If you reach out to them in any capacity, you'll be alerting this Ghost Legion that we know that they know," she said. "Intel is everything out here, it's the same as ammo in your magazine. If you reach out to them, it becomes a race."

Dawes understood that sentiment. "Partnering isn't great for us. When all is said and done, this is about simple economics. Yes, going in with them increases the odds of us getting in and out, but including another ten to fifteen people in the cut eats up our margins."

"No one can afford that," Lynch added.

She's right. "If we go as planned, they may get the jump on us," Wallace's flat tone replied. "We run the risk of showing up and finding an empty vault."

Damn it! He hated the way his choices were being forced on him. Part of running a successful PMC meant not doing things on the fly. *If we go in now, we are not at 100% in terms of planning and prep. That means we run the risk of this whole thing blowing up in our faces. At the same time, waiting could be worse.*

"Seems to me the choice has been made for us," Dawes finally said. "We go in two hours. Reaper, tell the others. Have everyone go through their checklists, armor up, and get the trucks ready to roll. Lynch, you don't have days to get the Phalanx ready—get it prepped right now."

Both of his people nodded and took off. *Let's hope that this is the only glitch we run into on this mission.*

Five hours later...

Operation Goldfinger, Pershing Square, Los Angeles, the Western Front, California, the United States

Fire Team Agis had the point as they approached Pershing Square. It was a large city block, with a small patch of greenspace that was now little more than tall, dead brown grass. The rest of the square was concrete, flat and long abandoned by mankind. A several-stories-tall, twisted, concrete bell tower was blackened near the base from a fire at some point, and the structure was pockmarked with bullet and shrapnel impacts. Several of the big concrete slabs that made up the square where blown apart, with jagged bits of stone and rebar twisting upward. As Dawes led Fire Team Leonidas in, they hunkered down, using battered stone benches for cover. The nine-and-a-half-foot-tall Phalanx hugged every corner and every piece of modern art for what little concealment it could offer.

The flat gray Tacomas brought up the rear of their formation, carefully weaving around craters and anything that might pop a tire. Dawes was fully alert, his eyes darting in every direction to see any possible threats. *We are already behind the enemy lines. This was our city, now it's theirs.* The tall buildings that flanked Pershing Square never felt as threatening as they did to him then. *They could be up there, in any window, observing our every move.* Some troops didn't think that the Fish were intelligent, that they acted purely on instinct. Dawes and the other seasoned veterans of Spartan Associates knew differently. *They have the technology to travel here from another planet. I doubt they are mindless creatures—we just don't understand how they think.*

Up ahead, he heard three sharp cracks—not gunfire, but something else. They came from where Agis was taking point. "Talk to me, Reaper," he said into his helmet's mic.

"We set off some webbies," came back Wallace's breathy voice. "Jones triggered three of them."

"Roger that, we are coming up on your six." Dawes used his wristcomp to switch to the channel for all of his people. "Be advised, there are webbies deployed in the park. Move slow and watch them."

The webbies, aka spidermines, were a nasty little landmine of sorts that the Fish employed. The softball-sized organic balls exploded when any human got near them. They sprayed out a thick, sticky, stringy goo when detonated. The material immediately set and was as tough as steel wire. If it hit bare flesh, you had to painfully cut it off. If the material hit your body, you were essentially held in place like a spider's web, hence the nickname.

The other trait of webbies is they seemed to have some communications component. When they were triggered, it almost always summoned someone. As he moved forward, he thought about the implications. *This is a wide-open park, huge fields of fire. Good ground for us, but we are not here to fight a battle. If they come at multiple angles, we are essentially in a big-ass kill box.* "Are you able to get her free?"

"Working on that right now, boss," Reaper replied. "We are going to need a couple of minutes."

We may not have that kind of time—shit! Switching to the Leonidas Team channel, he said, "I want us to spread out, get good positions for flanking fire. Get the trucks up here—we need to protect them. While Agis gets Jones free, we are going to form a corridor to the metro underground entrance to the west."

His people fanned out, keeping low and moving briskly. The distant popping of gunfire only added to the tension washing through him, igniting his adrenaline in his veins. One of his team, Dressler, spoke next. "I am at the metro entrance."

Before he could speak a syllable of response, another call came from Wallace. "Contact—movement to the east and north."

"You mobile yet, Reaper?"

"Almost."

"Almost isn't going to cut it."

"Roger that."

Dawes toggled back to Leonidas Team. "Let's get those trucks underground now! Brutality—I want you to move up between us and Agis."

"Visual on those contacts," Wallace interrupted. "We have Crabs and Frogs—a *lot* of Frogs—moving in."

"Alright, people, engage and start to fall back to the metro line."

The Phalanx hummed to life, firing off a power shell with a loud bang, then the hum of the laser capacitor discharging. Near the end of the barrel he saw a flicker of light, no doubt dust in the air being fried. Lynch leaned back and fired a pair of grenades downrange. The flash of their thermobaric explosions mixed with the gunfire from Agis as they made their way to link up with the Leonidas fire team. A pair of oily black pillars of smoke rose downrange from the grenades going off. *Come on, people—move it.*

The gunfire was steady and controlled. Dawes squinted slightly and could see the outline of a Crab starting to move in from the north. Lynch must have seen it as well. She executed a series of sidesteps to get a clear shot with her laser. Another bang of a power shell echoed off the surrounding buildings, and he heard the deep hum as the laser fired again.

Reaper appeared, followed by Fisher helping along a limping Jones. Blood soaked her STG and right leg, and her face was painted with an image of agony, but she was still in the fight. The quick succession of bursts from Nunez's M245 light machine gun dominated the noise. Dawes could hear the low grunting sound off to the east of the Frogs. Most were synchronized, but some were simply grunting and growling on their own.

When he saw the Crab move into the open, he aimed his Wolverine, dancing the laser reticle right on target inside his helmet's visor. He was sure that at least two of his shots hit, but with the Crabs, there was no way to guarantee that they penetrated. The creature's thick hide, combined with its carapace, made penetration difficult.

"Reaper," Dawes said, firing another pair of shots. "Get to the metro entrance. Plant some explosives there. We will fall back and blow the entrance."

"On it," Wallace replied. "Treacher, let's fire off a few grenades and get your ass down here."

Treacher aimed his grenade launcher high and sent three grenades downrange in the direction of the Frogs. The explosions echoed all around Dawes. He knew it wouldn't stop the Frogs; most of their breed were mindless killers. All it had to do was slow them down, even for a few seconds.

Off to his left, motion caught his attention. Twisting, he saw a Crab come into full view. The creature was a pale yellowish on the bottom, blending to a deep crimson on top. It aimed one of its huge claws and Dawes started to squat, to minimize his body aspect. The air between him and the alien rippled towards them in fast successive waves. The sonic weapon's deep reverberation hit at the same time as the deafening tones. For a moment, his vision tunneled and he curled up on the pavement.

Rising seconds later, Dawes couldn't hear anything—his ears had popped. Reaching under his visor and pinching his nose, he blew hard and at least the right ear brought in the sound of another power shell going off as Lynch fired the Phalanx's laser at the Crab. He knew she'd hit. Though he couldn't see the beam, he did witness the result of the deadly weapon. The claw that had been pointed at them flew off, seared away at the joint. Liquid, dark and ugly, squirted out as the Crab twisted in place, darting off to the left for cover behind one of the works of art in the plaza. Dawes didn't care where it went, just that it left.

"Let's go, people," he transmitted in the clear, barely able to hear his own muffled voice. "Everyone, in the metro station—now!" He started to move towards the direction the trucks had gone as well, his right ear hissing for a moment, then popping back. In the back of his mouth, he could taste the coppery flavor of blood. It had happened before when he had been hit by a sonic blaster. Some blood vessel in his nose had burst and the blood was trickling down the back of his throat. Hopefully it would stop. A gurgle came in his right ear and it slowly hissed back to normal hearing.

Lynch thudded on past him in the ASHUR. As she passed, he saw some damage on her right shoulder—nothing serious, but she had been hit by something in the fighting. Fortunately it hadn't managed to penetrate the armored skin of the Phalanx. For that he was momentarily thankful. *If we had lost the rig this early on, we would be screwed.*

When he reached the maintenance tunnel entrance, it was dark and looked more like a cave opening than an access point. The big double doors had been pried open long before his people had gotten there. It was a sloping tiled ramp, designed so that rescue vehicles could reach the metro subway if they had to. In the distance, he saw the red taillights of the trucks, and Wallace was just finishing placing the charges as Dawes got there. Tapping his wristpad, he pulled up the local battlespace view and could see that all of his people were inside.

Turning to cover the opening, he glanced over at Reaper. "Talk to me, Wallace."

"Charges set. Transmit B for Boom on channel five to detonate," the older man said as he rushed past him.

At the far end of the tunnel where they had just come from, the silhouetted figures of several Frogs appeared. They were man-height, standing on long legs with twisting muscles. They moved in hops, some twenty feet at a time, jagged and erratic, difficult to hit. They swarmed down the tunnel right at him as Dawes drifted back. Gunfire roared from behind him as the rest of his people laid down fire.

Pulling up his wristcomp, he switched to channel five and hit B.

It was less of a bang and more of a deep *whomping* sound as the explosives went off. The opening they had come through collapsed, dropping right on the first wave of the Frogs, plunging the entrance into darkness. Dust swirled everywhere and even switching to night vis didn't help. He could taste the dust from the cave-in in the back of his throat, making him cough hard as he staggered back towards the rest of his people. A small clot of blood from his earlier bleeding came up with the dust he had inhaled, and he lifted his visor to wipe it from his lips onto his sleeve. The air was dense with dust as he almost walked into the Phalanx. He could hear the echoes of others in the unit coughing as well.

Slowly the dust settled. When it did, he saw one Frog had somehow managed to make it through. It lay at the base of the debris, flat on its stomach, arms outstretched towards them. It was covered with a dusty film already. It hadn't moved for a few seconds, and he presumed it dead. Suddenly it swelled up, as if it were inhaling air. Its legs recoiled towards the body and it lifted its head.

Instinct kicked in. He swung his Wolverine assault rifle round to fire but the Frog leaped straight at him, its clawed hands jutting in front of it. It was faster than he had been, slamming into Dawes's chest hard, knocking him backwards and down, with the full weight of the alien on top of him. The big jowls of the creature started to swell as he felt the tile flooring grind into his back. *If that thing sprays me at this range, I'm toast.* The toxin that the Frogs could spit was deadly if inhaled or touched, even in a minute amount. Dawes twisted hard but could not get free. Instead, his move allowed one of the sharp talon-like claws of the creature to find a gap in his STG, digging into his chest.

Just as it was about to spray, the massive hand of the ASHUR slammed into the creature, backhanding it. The weight flew off his chest and he saw the Frog hit the nearby wall, right near an *A safe worker is a happy worker!* poster in a case that was mounted there, shattering its glass. The Frog didn't move, but slid down the wall slowly, leaving a greasy smear of whatever it had for blood following it to the floor.

"You okay, boss?" Lynch asked over the tactical channel.

Checking his chest and body for wounds, he slowly got up as Lynch turned on her external lights, filling the tunnel entrance with bright white-blue illumination. *I guess I am fine.* He wanted to check the claw wound, but it didn't feel serious. *There will be time for mending that scratch later.* Dawes rose to his feet. "Thanks for that," he said, nodding at the dead Frog.

Turning to the tunnel in front of him, Albert Dawes knew they needed to get going. *The Fish know we are down here. They may know the other access points too. We need to get moving, fast.* The thought of being trapped in the metro tunnel fighting waves of alien warriors was too frightening for even the stoic Dawes to contemplate.

"We need to keep moving," he said sucking in a deep breath. *The more commotion we stir up out here, the more Fish will come at us.*

CHAPTER 16

Operation Sundance, AIZ, Los Angeles, the Western Front, California, the United States

Ryland's arm still ached where he'd had his ID chip pulled a few hours earlier. Everyone going on Operation Sundance had them pulled. They brought the chips along with them, shielded in a small lead-lined artillery ammo container—which should provide blocking from the battlespace commander. He knew he was going to need them later, otherwise he would have left them behind.

He had gotten permission from Lieutenant Colonel Logan to take his people out on a recon mission, designated by the Army as Operation Bates Motel—227. Corporal King had explained the origins of the op name, otherwise it would have been lost on him. To Ryland, it didn't matter; just as long as they could get out into the AIZ.

Logan had been enthusiastic about it. He had been clamoring for more aggressive patrols and the fact the Ryland had volunteered the Ghost Legion for such a mission only seemed to feed the desires of his commanding officer. "Fantastic—get your people out there and kick some alien ass!" had been his response. Ryland hoped that it wouldn't come to that, but if they had to, they would indeed slaughter the enemy if engaged.

The members of the Ghost Legion moved cautiously through the streets, darting between points of cover while still trying to keep a wide-open field of fire as they went. "Whisper" King was running point with his GRD, using a GHD-9 Greyhound drone out in front of them as they moved. Greyhounds were fast and nimble, though they couldn't carry too much in the way of extra gear. They possessed great sensor packages and cameras that could give them excellent eyes and ears without risking human life to gain their images.

King worked the GRD like a kid playing a video game. He had a reinforced digipad he used to control the semi-autonomous drone, mapping out its general recon pattern. He would pause it every so often to zoom in on something. So far, Whisper and his GRD, which he had nicknamed Astro 201, had not found any indication of living aliens. That alone made Ryland cautiously happy.

As they rounded one corner near a house, the smell of rotting garbage managed to creep its way into Ryland's mask. The house they were moving in front of had a small white picket fence and, in its prime, was probably a great little starter home—a ranch-style bungalow. Now the front yard was filled with garbage bags put in neat rows. The stench of the rotting material filled the air. A horde of flies swarmed over it. Someone still lived there. *They are putting out the garbage as if they expect the sanitation trucks to show up anytime.*

As if on cue, the front door opened and a woman emerged. She wore a light blue house robe, flip-flop slippers, and her salt-and-pepper hair had not experienced a comb in days, if not weeks.

"Hey!" she called out. Ryland held his finger in front of his mouth and shushed her, then moved to the fence where she met him at the gate. As he got closer, the smell of the garbage was worse but not enough to mask the smell of the woman herself.

"Have you guys taken back this block?" she asked.

"We are just on patrol," he said in a curt whisper. "You really should leave and head south…get out of here."

"This was our home for years," she said as the rest of his team continued to deploy towards the next block north. "I promised him when he died that I would stay here."

"It isn't safe."

"The Fish don't seem to care about me. I see them from time to time. They are mostly interested in you Army-types."

Ryland looked at his team, then back to her. "You're in enemy territory. The best thing for you to do is get out of here. Get someplace safe."

"I still have plenty of food," she said proudly. "And what I don't have I take from the neighbors. They're gone—it's not like they care."

"Take care of yourself," Ryland said as he moved on. All he heard from her as he did was, "Yeah, yeah. Don't you worry about me." *Why is it that people choose to remain behind? So she made a promise to a dead husband. He would want her to be safe, not living like some scavenger.* There were some aspects of the human condition that he knew he would never fully comprehend.

Two blocks up, in the middle of an intersection, there were signs of battle—both human and Fish. The rusting burned-out hulks of cars littered the scene. One of the electrical ones oozed a pool of battery fluids still, trickling to one of the open drainage grates. The aliens were not into fire, and most of the block had been gutted by flames at one point—no doubt the result of the Army's efforts. The craters that pockmarked the streets and front yards were human in origin too. From what he saw, it had been a brutal little battle.

Looking over where he saw his alpha fire team, he spied the body of a Crab, flipped upside down. The usually bright colors of the shell had faded to a dull gray. Parts of it had rotted away entirely, but the carapace shell components remained. As Ryland got closer to it, he was still in awe over its size. Its ugly head was shattered and caved in—which he assumed had led to its demise. *When we lose people, teams are sent in to get their remains. They don't seem to care at all about their dead.*

Raffi kicked a long-dead Goblin husk in front of her. It rolled and rattled in the roadway, bouncing off of spent brass shell casings —remnants of the firefight. "Whatever went down here, it happened a while ago."

Glancing around at the burned out structures, Ryland responded to her comment. "Was it worth it?"

"Ya gotta kill 'em, Lieutenant," Raffi said.

"Yes, but we're destroying the city in the process," he said, looking around carefully to make sure they were really alone. "Let's keep this show moving—we have a long ways to go to reach our rendezvous waypoint."

A voice came in his helmet earbuds, "Casper—this is battlespace command. I show you in Grid Gamma-one-eight. Please confirm."

"Roger that, battlespace command."

"Your unit's ID chips are showing you right on top of each other, but I did a drone pass and you are spread out. We are no longer picking up your individual readings either."

He knew why; Calcutt was carrying their ID chips in his ruck. "I don't know what to tell you, we are all present and accounted for." It was a lie, but a necessary one.

"I will do a reset. That will take two minutes. Recommend you remain in place."

"Roger that," he replied, surveying the surrounding structures. Switching to the tactical channel. "Everyone, hold up."

"Problem, sir?" Calcutt called back.

"Battlespace command is rebooting. They can't read our ID chips."

Hollings spoke up with a sarcastic tone. "Wow, that's weird." It was followed by several chuckles.

"Look sharp, Ghosts," Ryland said. "Like they said in the old films, we are in injun territory." As if to make his point, there was a distant banging of small arms fire, punctuated with an occasional grenade blast.

He waited a few long moments, and finally the battlespace commander came back on. "Casper, this is battlespace command. We are still showing you standing on top of each other, no bio signals."

"Sounds like *you* have a problem."

"Operational protocol says you should return to base until we can sort this out. I can't direct artillery fire or any other mission support if there's a glitch with the transponders."

Ryland wanted to point out that artillery support was a rarity. Air support even more so. The United States has blown through their stockpile of munitions in the first few weeks of the war. Even mortar rounds were carefully rationed. "Look, Colonel Logan wants us to be aggressive in pushing at the Fish. Coming back for a computer glitch is going to piss him off and make my life a nightmare. We are proceeding on our mission."

"Understood," came back the now-tense voice of the battlespace commander. "I am noting it in the log that you did this against my recommendation."

"Roger that." *Your ass is appropriately covered.* Tapping his wristcomp, he cut off the channel to headquarters, and back to his unit. "Alright, I've satisfied the curiosity of battlespace command for the time being. Continue to advance."

As he reached the next block, Ryland huddled down next to a Honda hybrid that still had its Lyft sticker in the window, barely visible under the film of dust. A check of the time told him that he should be able to reach MacLeod at this point. He went to the predesignated channel the two of them had set. "Casper to Steel Hyena. Come in, Hyena."

All that came back was silence. He tried again, and again, there was no response. *Come on, MacLeod—say something…*

Operation Sundance, Outpost 46, Los Angeles, the Western Front, California, the United States

"Sir," Warrant Officer Reese said, standing in the open flap of his tent. "Something is going on and I want to know what it is." There was an accusatory tone to her voice, one that Mark Stevens both liked and dreaded.

"What makes you say that, Shelly?"

"I've seen everyone prepping their gear. We don't have a mission on the board for today, but everyone seems to be getting ready for something."

Stevens was a little angry, but kept it in check. *I told people to be discreet, that we didn't want Reese to know what we were up to. Somebody screwed up.* "I think you're mistaken. I'm sure you just saw my people getting their gear cleaned and prepped."

"I saw Ripper put one of the Carl Gustavs into the trailer of one of those ATVs," she said. "It sure looks like folks are preparing for an op."

I'll have to have a chat with Ripper—just not the conversation you think I should have. "I will have to take a look at that. I didn't give any orders to take a Gustaf out of inventory." That was true. The recoilless launchers were old, they had been a mainstay in the Army for decades. They had become highly prized for their ability to inflict damage against Crabs and Bosses and stockpiles of the weapons were rumored to be running low.

"With all due respect, I feel like there's a lot of things going on here behind my back."

"I'm sorry you feel that way, Shelly. No one is trying to make you feel that way," he replied with a stone-faced expression. It was true, no one was trying to make her feel left out…they were simply attempting to keep her in the dark.

"So, there's nothing to the members of Hostility getting their weapons ready as if they are going out on a run?"

"I think you're letting your imagination get the best of you. I know my people are pretty edgy. We haven't had a mission in some time other than manning the outpost here. Even you have to admit, there's not a lot to do here recreation-wise. Open Hostility is a finely honed weapon, but we haven't been getting any meaty assignments." Stevens knew she had to agree with that stance.

"I have noticed some changes with some of the team members."

"We need a mission of substance, if only to break some of this monotony. I'd like you to go to HQ and find a mission worthy of these people."

"I can get on the radio and put in the request right away," she replied with a sense of purpose in her voice.

"No. Go there, in person. Besides, you know their prioritization over there. Our stuff will get shuffled to the bottom of an endless pile. You are the best person to make the case for us to get a good mission. Moreover, it makes a statement to show up live, in their faces."

Shelly nodded. "I'd be happy to."

"Good. Thank you, Shelly," he said as she turned to leave. A slight sense of guilt hit Stevens in that moment. *It's a shame that the last time I will see her, it was based on a lie. But I didn't have a choice. Reese is so rigid and by the book, she would never go along with what we have planned.*

Two hours later...

Operation Sundance, West Los Angeles, the Western Front, California, the United States

As soon as Reese departed, Stevens scrambled Open Hostility for their departure for Beverly Hills. His people didn't just pack for their mission, they brought whatever personal belongings they could carry with them as well. For most, it wasn't much, just some space in their rucks. It wasn't a matter of traveling light. Like him, they had lost a lot in the war. Material things had ceased to have value, especially when you lost almost everything. Almost all of them had been driven from their homes when the invasion began.

As they cautiously made their way out into the city, Stevens found himself to be nervous. There were the distant sounds of fighting—the thunderous booms of manmade explosions that seemed to make the entire city throb. *There's a few firefights going on, hopefully not the Ghost Legion or MacLeod.* The signs of fighting were all around West Los Angeles. Entire neighborhoods were in ruin, either from runaway house fires or from battle. They crossed one intersection that was almost treacherous from the amount of spent brass shell casings littering the pavement. Strangely, there were no alien carcasses, or any other signs of battle—just a slippery carpet of expended rounds. As much as he tried, he couldn't imagine what kind of fight had taken place there. *You would think that the surrounding structures would be scarred up from missed rounds—but there's nothing.* As he carefully skirted the site, he couldn't shake the strange mental image.

Coyote and his shadow, a hulking bodyguard who simply went by Bowers, came up beside him. "I wonder what went down here?" Coyote asked nervously. His finger was on the trigger of his civilian-purchased Wolverine assault rifle, which made Stevens a little angry. He reached out and pulled his finger off the trigger, placing it on the guard. "I wasn't in favor of bringing you along in the first place. The last thing I need is for you to shoot one of us. Exercise safety or you will be put on point." It wasn't an idle threat.

"Sorry," the scrounger said. "It's my first time this far in."

"What is all of that shit on your weapon?" he asked, nodding at it.

"Enhanced laser sights, the tactical stabilizing brace, I even sprang for the muzzle brace and suppressor, LED tactical light—everything they had in the catalog," he said with a hint of pride.

"Waste of money," Stevens said. "You're hauling a lot of worthless weight that you'll never need. You'll wear yourself out with all that shit."

"That's what I told him," the hulking man at his side said. "Amateurs…"

Mark looked over at Coyote's bodyguard. The huge black man was built like a tank and had all of the attitude of a bouncer at an exclusive night club. He also held his weapon in a way that told Stevens he had been in the service at some point. The two exchanged short nods of understanding and respect.

"Watch him, will you?"

Bowers nodded once. "Like I have a choice."

Turning away, Stevens focused on his people. The sound of the ATVs sputtering and the occasional jostling of their trailers added to the apprehension he was feeling. They needed the four-wheelers for transport, but they were noisy. He was used to Open Hostility moving in near perfect silence. The ATVs advanced slowly, which helped keep the noise down, but even the crunching of their wheels on the bits of blasted gravel and spent casings in the street made him cringe.

His helmet's earbuds buzzed for a moment. "This is Casper to Punch List," came Ryland's voice.

"This is Punch List."

"Just verifying that you are on the move."

"Roger that."

"Any problems?"

"None so far."

"Have you heard from Steel Hyena?"

"Negative." MacLeod was supposed to be coordinating with Ryland. *I wonder if something is wrong.*

"I haven't, either. Let's hope he is just running silent."

It was unnerving. The ASHUR was needed if the Fish showed up. If MacLeod wasn't on the move and the aliens showed up in any large number, it would be a deadly encounter for both sides.

"Very well," Ryland said. "I will contact you again in an hour." The channel hissed for a moment, then went silent. Mark climbed up on the remains of a Cadillac Prestige. His boots dented in the hood of the expensive luxury car he was using for a higher vantage point. *This was a very expensive car, and now it is just abandoned junk.*

Making his way to the roof, he surveyed the surrounding area as his team continued to creep north.

From what he could see, the signs of damage were diminishing for the next few blocks. It was strange how the war seemed to skip some blocks or buildings, and devastate others. The slight breeze carried a chemical aroma with it, one that overpowered the stink of rot that usually dominated the city. Mark gave it some attention, simply because it was different. *Is this some alien weapon, a gas or some byproduct? Or is this simply something leaking from a factory somewhere nearby?* Mentally he noted the smell and then climbed down.

Open Hostility moved slowly and quietly north, hugging every bit of cover they could find. Up ahead, his people had stopped—and that was always a possible source of concern. "Corvin—talk to me. Why have you stopped?"

Corvin's voice came back "It's Nardo, sir."

"She see something?"

"No, sir. She's just having a moment."

Mark crouched low and hurried up to the point, not sure what was happening. He found Nardo, on her knees, crying. She was surrounded by her comrades like a protective shell of armed flesh. *Nardo never cries—she rarely showed any emotion other than raw anger. What the hell is getting to her?* She had also retracted her ECH's visor, which was another thing that seemed out of order. Stevens moved up slowly to where she was, and bent down beside her, putting his hand on her shoulder.

"What is it?" he asked.

"That was my Pop-Pop's home," she stuttered between sobs. Stevens lifted his head and looked up at the small 1950s bungalow in front of her. It was still standing, but ugly black burn marks rose up out of the shattered windows. Most of the roof was gone, either burned or caved in.

There were no words that were going to make Nardo feel better. "Was he able to get out?" he asked, risking the answer he might get.

Nardo sobbed more, and shrugged. "We don't know. My mom has been checking the camps, but there are so many…I just don't know." She sniffled hard and used her gloved hand to wipe the tears off her face. "I'm sorry."

All of the times we were in the AIZ, she never asked to come this way—to see her grandfather's house. That was a testimony as to how unselfish and tough Nardo was. He squeezed his arm and hugged her a little closer. "You don't have a damn thing to be sorry about."

She drew a deep breath, then turned to him. "I'm fine. We should move on."

"Do you want to go and check the building?" he carefully asked.

Her tear-streaked face was caught flatfooted with his question. He could see that part of her wanted to look, another part of her was afraid of what she might find. Nardo's eyes darted to the burned out home, then back to Stevens. "No," she managed, slowly rising to her feet. He mirrored her rise, taking his arm off her shoulder. "I don't want to look."

Stevens nodded, fully understanding. "You need another minute?"

Nardo shook her head. "No, sir," she replied, gripping her

Hawkeye sniper rifle tightly to her body. "I'm fine." It was a lie, one that they both knew, but neither acknowledged. Stevens glanced once more at the burned house. *Every one of these buildings has people attached to them, people who have lost loved ones, homes, or their jobs. The Fish have a lot to answer for when this is over.*

"Alright, people, let's move on. We have miles to go before we reach the rendezvous," he said as Nardo took her position near the front of the formation.

* * *

Shelly Reese huddled low behind a minivan which was resting on one inflated tire, and three hopelessly flat ones. She rose only enough to get a glimpse of Open Hostility, stopped for some reason in front of a burned-out house. Nardo was on her knees, which made her wonder if the sniper had been injured, which added to Shelly's tension. After a few moments, she saw her rise. Shelly zoomed in her view and could see that Nardo was visibly upset, and apparently crying. It was confusing and Shelly wished she could hear the conversation. *I wonder what happened? I've never seen Nardo show anything other than attitude.*

Reese had left Outpost 46, just as Stevens had said, but she had not gone to HQ. Instead she had circled back to the base to see what was going on. Open Hostility had departed just a half hour after they thought she had departed, taking the ATVs and trailers. It had taken a few minutes for her to get her gear on. Tracking their movements proved easy; the ATVs left tire imprints in the dusty streets. Being out alone in the AIZ was unsettling at best—it was the stuff of paranoid nightmares. Shelly moved fast to catch up with her unit, not just out of curiosity but for protection in case she encountered the Fish.

He lied to me...I knew it! Something *was* going on. When she spied Coyote in the mix, her stomach knotted with more rage. *If that black marketer is involved, chances are it's not something legal. I'll bet that weasel is behind all of this—it smacks of his kind of thing to pull.*

With the ATVs, she wondered if they were planning on looting something.

The feeling of betrayal ran deep. She had implicitly trusted the CO of Open Hostility and that had been paid back with treachery. What bothered her with the same intensity was the fact that they thought she was stupid, that somehow they had pulled the wool over her eyes. *Was he really that arrogant to think that I didn't know something was up?*

Shelly had held Open Hostility up among the militia groups. She had even bragged to other liaisons about what professionals Mark Stevens and his people were. Now she was seeing them making an unauthorized mission into the AIZ. *They are just like so many of the other militia units—out for themselves. I wonder how long they have been planning this behind my back?*

It was tempting to rush out and confront Stevens before things went too far, or contact the battlespace commander and call in Army support to have them arrested, but she held herself in check. *If I show myself now, I'd be doing it without evidence. It would be his word against mine. The Army isn't going to be worried that they sprang a mission without authorization. But if they are out here looting, well, that's a chargeable offense.* She resolved to follow them farther, to catch them in the act.

I will make him pay for playing me the fool.

CHAPTER 17

Operation Sundance, Outpost 30, Los Angeles, the Western Front, California, the United States

Standing in his leg control sleeves of his Rattlesnake-class rig, Sutherland MacLeod glared down at the second lieutenant who was standing in his path. "Sir, I'm going through your checkpoint. I'm on a bit of a time schedule and already running late."

"Not without authorization, you're not," she fired back. "I checked with battlespace command. They have no op that you are assigned to. That makes this mission unauthorized and illegal." If they were standing eye to eye, he had no doubt that the muscular blonde officer would be intimidating. *She seems to have forgotten that I am in a rig and can blast my way out if I opt to.*

"I do this all of the time," he offered. *Though never on a mission quite as entertaining and fun as this one.*

"Not through my checkpoint," she barked up at him.

This day had not been going well at all for him. When MacLeod had gotten to his rig in the morning, he found that his tech, Swift, was realigning the plasma carbine and had the charging assembly in parts. It had taken a half an hour for her to get it back into one piece, though she complained about it every step. She told him that his communications system was also not fully operational—that its range would be limited, which added to his inner rage just a bit. Damned techs, always taking stuff apart when you need it the most. It was hard to blame Swift, she had no idea that he was going to need the rig for a covert run, but he focused his anger on her, more out of convenience. "Before you start taking shit apart on my rig, check with me first!" Having started early, the unexpected maintenance had eaten into his buffer of spare time…not the best way to start the day.

MacLeod had set out from his firebase for Outpost 30, and immediately got bogged down by a long convoy of dull green Army transports that clogged the main roads, and the secondary roads. It was good to see supplies coming in, but it made movement nearly impossible. He had navigated the Steel Hyena through neighborhoods that were still semi-populated with civilians— civilians who'd parked so awkwardly that his ASHUR had to be turned around several times to get even a block of progress. He scraped and damaged a few vehicles intentionally on one street; in his mind the equivalent to giving the locals a warning. *It's technically their fault. They shouldn't live this close to a war zone. Evacuations were called for months ago.*

After the loss of precious time, he arrived at Outpost 30 and this very loud second lieutenant decided to stop him from making the passage into the AIZ. He considered the option of moving farther down along the front line and finding another place to cross, but chances were good that this lieutenant would send out warnings about him in advance. Not only that, but searching for another crossing point would take time—time he already didn't have. "Look, Lieutenant, I need to go into the AIZ. It's cute that you believe you can stop me, but I assure you, I'm going through."

"Staff Sergeant," she called up, emphasizing his rank. "Need I remind you that I outrank you. You do see these bars, don't you?" She tugged at her sewn on uniform lapel. "You do understand what these stand for, don't you?"

"That you were once a member of the Royal Order of Trained Cowards?" His slur reference to the ROTC struck home like a rocket. Her face went past red and jumped into fiery crimson. MacLeod knew he should hide the smirk that was forcing its way onto his face, but he decided to let it out to play instead.

"I will call the MPs over here."

He chuckled. "Do you really think they can stop a fully armed ASHUR? Come on, surely you aren't that ignorant. Call 'em up, it should be entertaining."

"That's it!" she roared. "I've had enough of your disrespecting a superior officer."

"For what it's worth, Lieutenant, I haven't begun to insult you yet."

"Get your ass down here right now, Sergeant!"

"I would love to, but as I said when we started this wonderful little chat, I am behind on a time schedule. So I will decline your kind offer, and you will step aside."

"Are you insane? This is a court-martial offense."

"You are aware of the war, aren't you? While you coddle your precious regulations, I am going to go and kill the enemy. That's how wars are won. Our new sector commander wants progress, results. I'm going to deliver on that. You…you are a speed bump. So if you want to call the new commanding officer and tell him that you were preventing a trained killer from doing his job and trying the bring this war to an end, I encourage it. Otherwise, get the hell out of my way." He dropped back against the padded seat and hit the retract button on the cockpit canopy. The pistons hissed slightly and lowered it into place.

She stood there, in front of him—dazed and confused by the concept that anyone would defy her direct orders—let alone do so with such style. He toggled on the power-up and the ASHUR around him hummed to life, the monitors flickered on.

Still, the lieutenant stood in front of him, defiant.

He took one solid step forward, the pavement crunching under the big footpad of the rig. The lieutenant held her arms out wide, as if they might somehow block him. *I don't have time for this bullshit.*

Reaching down, he turned a small knob to the right, then used a keypad to make a selection. With a gentle push, he hit a play button.

The external speakers roared with the blare of electric guitars. Then came the words from the Black Sabbath classic… "I am Iron Man…"

The sound was so loud he could hear it clearly inside of his rig cockpit. It shook the lieutenant enough for her to back up. He started to walk, as if she was not there, heading straight for the gate. He grinned broadly as the music roared and she finally darted off to his left, moving out of the way.

When he reached the checkpoint, the corporal on duty lifted the gate—no doubt he had been listening to the debate and wanted nothing to do with MacLeod. His rig walked through the checkpoint and as it did, he dialed down the volume of the song blaring through his speakers. After the song ended, he shut it down entirely. Playing the music now might draw the enemy to him, but it would put him behind schedule even more. There will be plenty of time to irritate the Fish later on. For now, he needed to make up time.

* * *

A lot of people thought you couldn't maneuver an ASHUR with any degree of stealth. Sutherland prided himself on his ability to choose his footing well and to minimize his noise. His Rattlesnake was already running its ACS system, making it difficult to see, but sound could be an enemy that defeated visual cloaking. There were times when loud music was called for, but much of the time in the AIZ required silence. The problem with silent movement was that it was slow. MacLeod had to thread the needle carefully between being slow and remaining invisible, moving just fast enough to link up with the other raiders.

As he moved through the mostly abandoned neighborhoods, his mind did drift for random moments. Coming on this mission meant that he could possibly encounter the big alien Boss that he had fought before, Scarface. The last place he had seen him was in Beverly Hills. Memories of that fight were short and brutal, with the hulking alien managing to get away. *I owe him for the deaths of my alpha team.*

Other thoughts he toyed with that were far more pleasant was what he would do with the money. He liked his job in the Army—after all, he was in one of the most prestigious roles as an ASHUR pilot. Walking away from that was something he was not prepared to contemplate. Having money would mean that he had options. *I always wanted a RV...to drive around the country to see all of the sights.* Purchasing a big RV was simply a pipe dream on a soldier's pay. In the recesses of his thoughts, he liked the fantasy of taking a large recreational vehicle to see the parts of the US where the Fish had not gotten to yet. *Best to see it now, before it is all behind enemy lines.*

When he arrived at a huge apartment building that was mostly in rubble, he opted to go through the debris rather than around it. Moving through the rubble was tricky, but he liked the challenge. As he started down the far side of the debris field he spied a shadow, not much, but the outline of something that looked like an alien Fox.

Freezing in place, he used his controls to zoom in his cockpit's view of the image. It didn't move, but he could see that it certainly looked like one of the creatures. *If I move, I'll make noise. If it's a Fox, the last thing I need is for him to bring his heavily armed buddies here. I am still a good two miles from the rendezvous site.* His eyes stayed locked on the shadow, looking for some verification that it was, indeed, an alien.

The shadow moved. Not much, but the dark silhouette turned and he could see that it was definitely a Fox.

"Bingo," he said in a low breathy voice.

His tactical training and skills took over. Surveying the rubble, he mentally mapped out how to move, swinging wide around the creature. *If it's a Fox, it's going to break for the street to go and get away or to get an angle of attack on me.* He would angle the Steel Hyena around to get a good firing position on the street.

The Rattlesnake wasn't the fastest ASHUR, but he knew how to get the most out of it. Mentally he counted down from five, and when he hit zero, he launched into motion. The strides the ASHUR made were huge as he darted across the rubble of the apartment building. Swinging around, he saw the creature do what he thought it would, jump down from its position onto the street.

For a few milliseconds, the Fox glared at him as he raised his Mark IA Plasma Carbine, firing off a power shell. The capacitor light on his weapons display went green with a surge of power flowing into it, and the low hum gave him audible confirmation. The bang of the shell didn't startle the Fox. It lowered its head towards him and extended its huge arms. *He's going to come right at me…fantastic!*

The alien planted its claws onto the pavement and used its arms to swing forward, angling slightly to the right. MacLeod zoomed back out and brought his targeting reticle onto the alien as it landed. The Fox was faster than he was—it launched off again, angling right at him this time. Leaning forward to brace for the impact, his sight came right at the approaching creature and flickered green.

He fired. The weapon discharged a magnetic pulse that held the superheated plasma in a stream, searing white hot, stabbing right at the Fox just before it collided with him. He held the trigger and angled the stream of searing energy downward. The Fox slammed into the Steel Hyena hard; there was a crunch of outer armor and his sheer thickening plates stiffened to diffuse the energy of the hit. Its cumbersome hands tried to grapple with his rig's hydraulic hoses, intent on ripping them out. *Clever little beastie, aren't you? Well, two can play that game.*

MacLeod instinctively twisted hard and fast to toss the creature away. Its face, with its ugly jutting lower jaw, collided with his transparent aluminum cockpit canopy, its big fangs scoring deep marks right in front of him as he threw it aside. It stopped trying to grab at his hoses and held on strictly to avoid flying off.

The creature released some sort of gas as it scraped his canopy, a sickly gray cloud. MacLeod reeled around hard, tossing the Fox clear in the process as he stepped back. The Fish had a lot of different organic gases. Some were aerosol organic acids, others were bacterial agents that devoured organic tissue on contact. He wasn't sure what the Fox had fired, but simple preservation instinct had him back away from the gas.

The Fox rolled onto its side as MacLeod brought his heavy ACR into play—firing off three fast rounds right into the thick hide of the beast—in one side and out the other. It was then that he saw that the Fox was missing one of its big forearms. A blackened mark showed where his plasma weapon had cut it off. The momentary sight of it made him feel good.

The Fox rolled over and started to rise, though it wobbled in place. *How is that thing still alive?* MacLeod used that momentary wavering to fire another three rounds into its squat throat and torso. The large rounds punched hard and deep into the Fox's thick leathery hide. Squirts of a grayish green fluid came out like little geysers as the alien reeled back. The huge maw opened and it uttered an unholy sound, a roaring cry that was a mix of lizard hissing and bear growling. It was frightening, especially since he had never heard one of the Foxes make any noise, let alone a wail like that.

MacLeod wasn't impressed or intimidated. Squeezing the trigger of the ACR in his arm's control sleeve, he sent two more bullets into the Fox. The alien flopped over backwards on the street, its remaining limbs going limp.

Swinging round in place, he made sure the Fox was alone—that reinforcements were not closing in on him. The street seemed silent and abandoned, as empty as any in the AIZ. Moving forward to his fallen foe, he raised his right leg and then drove it down on the Fox's face, grinding it hard into the pavement…just to make sure that the Fish was indeed dead. He could hear the crunching of its bones and carapace under the footpad and it was strangely satisfying.

For a few seconds, he stood and forced himself to relax. His breathing had been controlled through the entire encounter, but he could not control the flux of adrenaline in his system. Bit by bit, the edge began to fade.

Lowering his ACR to his rig's side, he docked it and the auto-reloader clicked, replenishing his magazine. Pulling his arms from the control sleeves, he reached out and refreshed his mapping system. While the battle was satisfying, he was behind schedule. Checking his route, he oriented himself and prepared to move out.

Before he started out again, he glanced down the long avenue where he had just killed the Fox. There was nothing out of the ordinary—no signs of alien activity. All he saw was the severed arm of the Fox, its shoulder stump still releasing fine white wisps where it had been cut off from its host body. A part of him secretly hoped that his nemesis, Scarface, might be approaching. Seeing nothing was disappointing, but MacLeod reminded himself that the day was still young and he wasn't in Beverly Hills just yet.

As he started out, walking past the dead alien, he muttered to himself, "This is a hell of a way to afford buying an RV…"

CHAPTER 18

Operation Goldfinger, Beverly Hills, the Western Front, California, the United States

When Spartan Associates had reached the metro station for Beverly Hills, they found the exit blocked with debris. Fortunately ASHUR rigs were well equipped for heavy work, and thanks to Lynch's efforts, they were able to roll the trucks out after about fifteen minutes' heavy lifting. Then they began the slow five-block trek to the Commerce Bank.

The signs of previous battles for the area were everywhere. Buildings had gaping holes blown in them. The dead husks of alien body parts were evident, along with craters and the debris of fighting. They passed a massive Buford tank, its hatches left open and its turret looking as if it was melted in several places. Its tracks had not been hit by enemy fire; they looked as if they had been ripped off and thrown in the street around the crippled vehicle. The massive gun barrel was bent, and as he passed, he could see the claw marks of a Boss that had done the deed. As Dawes maneuvered his people closer to their objective, he could not help but get an eerie feeling of dread and doom. *A lot of people before us fought and died here—and lost.* While he didn't believe in ghosts, if he did, this was a place that had to be haunted by the events that had taken place there.

When they reached Rodeo Drive, another battle scene unfolded. Several crushed Jolts and a trio of Schwarzkopf-class fighting vehicles were tossed about as if they had been thrown by a giant child playing hard with his toys. Chunks of pavement were furrowed by their skidding, and heavy armor plating looked as if it had been peeled off. There were no signs of human bones, but helmets and blast plates and spent ammo casings were scattered everywhere. As they moved into the area, Dawes could hear the wail of a cat, no doubt feral at this point.

One of the big Bosses lay dead, its dried husk of a body draped over a Jolt where it had fallen. One leg was missing. *I hope the bastard suffered.* The large dead alien was easily fourteen feet in height when alive. While it had been onyx black at one point, it was now an ashen grayish color. Where it had once been a massive knot of muscles, it looked dehydrated and strangely shriveled. The deflated and dried armored-hide-skin pulled taut over the head of the Boss seemed to indicate some sort of bumpy bone-like structure underneath, making the face look even more creepy. Dawes had always been told that the aliens were essentially organically grown inside a suit of armored flesh. Seeing a dead one, he realized they had a complex bone structure, dissimilar from a human's. There were bulges that made no sense, no doubt organs of some sort. The head of the creature seemed to have a series of jagged bumps under its hide. *I wonder if they can operate outside of their skin—or what kind of organs they have.*

Looking around the carnage, Dawes was glad that he was no longer in the Army. *I get to pick and choose my own missions. Good men and women died here. If I had stayed in the service, this is the kind of place that they would have sent me.* Kicking a few of the spent cartridges, he felt strangely lucky to have plotted the course of his life the way he had.

"Sir," called out Rice over their tactical channel. "I think we found it." With a rapid beat of his eyes, he pulled up the tactical topographical view of where Rice was. It took him another five minutes to reach it.

Rice stood at a nondescript metal doorway, heavily decorated with ornate inlay. She nodded at it as Dawes and Fisher approached it. There was no sign over the door, but one of the framing stones bore the words, "Commerce Bank." Rice spoke up with a nod towards the door. "This is the right spot, but it doesn't look like much."

Dawes glanced up at the three-story building. The upper floor windows were cracked with a spiderweb of damage, but were still in place. Armored glass. There was some damage, mostly small arms fire—though some cracks ran up the stucco from foundation stress. "It's the right place, alright," he said, tugging at the door which refused to budge.

"Get the torch up here and start cutting," he said firmly. If it had been a normal structure, he would have used a breaching kit. Having reviewed the blueprints for the bank, he knew that such an attempt would be a loud waste of time. "Everyone, per the plan, I want you to assume a defensive perimeter. Get the trucks up close here and under as much cover as we can provide them. Eyes on the rooftops." Looking down the small curved roadway back to Rodeo, he saw the Beverly Wilshire Four Seasons Hotel. In its prime, the structure had consisted of two seven-story block towers interconnected by a thin structure in the middle. One wing, a block-like tower, still stood, though it stretched the definition of standing. It showed considerable damage, with several large holes blasted into interior rooms and perilous cracks running skyward like jagged dark lightning bolts.

The remaining tower and the center connection structures had succumbed to the wreckage of one or more of the battles for Beverly Hills. The lower two floors were still intact but impassible, clogged with debris from above. The interior of the structure had collapsed inward—no doubt as a result of either artillery or one of the Fish's sonic blasters. The upper three floors were gone, and jagged pieces of the exterior wall jutted skyward one or two floors. *That will provide a good defensible position as well.*

He saw his people begin to move into position on the display inside his helmet's visor, moving smartly. *We made it this far with minimal damage. I wonder how long our luck can hold?*

* * *

Whoever had built the door to the Commerce Bank had been a devious genius. Even with heavy duty grinders, it took almost an hour to finally shear off the bolts on the hinges and to pry open the doorway. Given their exclusive clients, Dawes understood the need for such security. Climbing over the toppled door, he entered the lobby and waited a moment for his eyes to adjust to the near darkness.

A chandelier lay in the middle of the lobby area—a jumble of shattered crystal and metal. Otherwise the interior looked remarkably pristine. The narrow profile of the building meant that only the upper floors had windows. Dawes pulled a Maglite out and swept it around the room. The marble tile floor had a few cracks but other than a thin film of dust, the room looked remarkably intact. When he spotted the expensive espresso and coffee bar, he shook his head. *Espresso…there's something I haven't had in a long time.* Up until that moment, he hadn't realized how much he missed the little luxuries in his life.

Walking across the lobby, he passed the two small walnut and brass teller booths. A large paneled door dominated the back wall, one he knew from the blueprints. Tugging it open, Dawes looked down the darkened hallway, illuminated only by his Maglite, and saw the large circular vault door. *Jackpot!*

"Jones, Treacher—get here to the vault and bring the drill and cutting torches," he ordered. Walking forward, he stood before the massive door, reaching out and caressing it. It was tantalizing for Dawes, knowing that only a few feet away were treasures and money. Getting this far had cost him a fortune, and he was literally betting the future of Spartan Associates on what might be on the other side of the door.

Jones got there first, her wrapped wound from the spidermine seeping a little through her field bandage. She went to work setting up a portable light that was almost blinding in the space. Treacher arrived a few minutes later with some of the tools. "You remember where to drill in?" he asked.

"Yes, sir," Treacher replied. "It's a small spot, but we will triple measure it before we start to try to cut in."

Even with the diamond bits, cutting through the steel and concrete door, just to get to the internal mechanisms, was going to take precious time. Doing it right was important. "Alright, get at it." Jones was already breaking out the tape measure and a laser level from her ruck.

From outside the bank, he heard a rumble. It sounded like thunder, but instinct told him it was not a storm...there hadn't been a cloud in the sky all day. *No, that's the sound of fighting, and it's close.*

Moving through the lobby, he toggled his communications set in his helmet. "Someone want to talk to me?"

Reaper's voice came back. "Sorry, sir, things just got complicated out here." Three loud cracks of gunfire followed his words.

"What do you have?"

"Crabs, about four of them, along with two Foxes. Coming from the northwest. I think it's safe to say they know where we are."

Damn! Clutching his Wolverine, he made his way to the door leading to the street. Now the pop-cracks of gunfire were clear and distinct. Looking across the street, he saw Lynch in the Phalanx, starting to take strides towards the signs of battle. He moved in beside the hulking war machine, flanking her down the street to

Rodeo Drive.

As she rounded the corner, the stance of the Phalanx shifted slightly, even before Dawes saw the enemy. Lynch was bracing herself as she raised her arm and released one of her rockets. The heat from the rushing projectile washed around him as he rounded the corner and saw it streak downrange. It missed one Crab, hitting the pavement just a few feet behind it. No doubt it caught some of the shrapnel, but luck had favored it that the shot was off by a matter of inches.

Bringing his own Wolverine to bear, he fired at the next Crab in line. It appeared that his shots were hitting their target, but whether they were doing any real damage was hard to see, even as he zoomed in his display view of his helmet's visor.

The Crabs were different colors. The one he fired on was a pinkish hue on top blurring to a cream color. Two were green on top fading to a yellow. The last one was a dark gray fading to a pearl-white sheen. *It's like they have no sense of camouflage...that or those colors mean something to them...something we don't understand.*

Nunez was poised in the next building down on the rooftop. His grenade launcher *thunked* three times fast, raining explosives down on the advancing Crabs and Foxes. The explosions were savage, throwing hot metal shrapnel and bits of Rodeo Drive in every direction as they went off. One was a direct hit, landing on the lead Crab's back. The detonation tore into its armored tail section, peeling back two of the shell-like plates. The rest of the tail whipped around savagely, hitting a utility pole and wrenching it half out of its foundation.

That Crab aimed one of its claws up at an angle towards Nunez. A stream of hyper-compressed water stabbed up at the building. The beam devastated the low parapet that Nunez was using for cover, showering the ground with bricks and stucco that had been blasted. A check of his tactical display showed that Nunez was still alive, moving back from the edge.

Another Crab unleashed a sonic blast that rippled in the air from them up Rodeo Drive. The few windows that still had glass lost them in the deep, chest-throbbing rush of sound energy. Dawes turned his back to the wave, but it was to no avail. The rippling air hit him and despite the sound protection of his helmet, he felt like his brain was attempting to punch its way through his temple.

Dust swirled in the air as he pivoted back to continue pressing the attack. At his side, he heard the loud bang of a power shell going off. Lynch aimed the large laser and the weapon hummed. The dust in the air between her weapon barrel and the target flickered for just a moment, a shimmer of green-white light. The beam seared a hole in the side of the raised body of one of the green Crabs, flashing through and burning a blackened streak along its body. The Crab swung around, clearly in pain as an explosion tore into it, no doubt fired by a repositioned Nunez. It looked as if it were curling into a ball for a moment, then pointed one of its large claws forward.

It fired something—a blur—at the building across the street where Hague and Reaper were firing from. The projectile was a liquid that splattered like a basketball-sized glob of snot, spraying the front of the building. Some of the splatter hit the Phalanx which thankfully had protected him. The smell of the goo was horrible. It reeked of rotting flesh, rotten eggs, and left a metallic taste in the back of his mouth—even through his filters. Glancing up at the Phalanx, he saw wisps of smoke rising from where the rig had been hit.

"Nice try, fuck-stick!" Hague called, pushing out through what had been a window and firing several controlled bursts.

Three quick metallic *thunks* came from the ASHUR's heavy grenade launcher, spraying the street. One Fox dove for cover, just in time, but the crimson Crab caught the full fury of the hits. One of its maneuvering legs was blown off, hitting the building next to it. It dropped hard on the roadway, then sprayed a cloud-like mist into the street. The cloud rolled up the street, pale gray and ominous.

"Fall back," Dawes called out. The cloud could be any number of nasty biotech weapons in the Fish's arsenal. It could be a flesh-eating bacteria, an aerosol of their corrosive acid, a paralytic, or something else. Lynch backstepped the Phalanx and Dawes darted back behind the building corner. Even from his cover, he saw the mist dissipate right in front of him, washing past Lynch's ASHUR.

Explosions rang out along with gunfire, still attempting to halt the enemy advance. Once he was relatively sure it was safe to move out of cover, he did. The Crab that had fired the gas was dead. In fact, only the dark gray one was still visible. Gunfire hit it steadily—he could see some of the shots ricocheting, others seemed to hit and stick—though there was no sign of real damage. The Foxes were gone, no doubt moving around the flanks.

The remaining Crab held up a claw and an organic vein-like

growth spat three objects in Dawes's direction. One came at him and narrowly missed. Two slammed hard into the Phalanx, with a hard crunching sound. It was one of their needler weapons that fired slender bone-like needles that were embedded with metal. The only weapon that was close to it was the rail guns, though the Fish-versions were organic. Dawes saw the shattered pieces fall to the feet of Lynch's rig as she fired off another pair of grenades from her torso launcher. Even though they were composed of bone, the alien projectiles could punch through armor if they caught it at the right angle. It showed her grit that Lynch did not flinch or dive for cover, but instead returned fire. *I picked the right person for our pilot.*

The explosions were louder because they were closer, close enough for him to feel the blasts with his teeth grinding together. Wheeling around the corner, ready to fire, through the haze of the explosions, there was no target. More disturbing, one of the Crabs he thought was dead, was no longer in the street. "Are they bugging out, or moving to flank us?"

Nunez's voice came over the comm channel. "I have zero eyes on target. With these buildings blocking my line of sight, they could be doing anything."

The Fish were known to engage in a circular pattern in battle. It was rare that they retreated. Where humans had common sense and survival instincts, the Fish were not built with those. They would push on despite losses or injuries. When they did fall back, it was temporary—not to build up courage, but to summon reinforcements or draw in their prey. It was not an endearing feature in Dawes's mind.

Glancing behind him, he spied the trucks parked in front of the bank. *We've already kicked the hornet's nest. More are bound to come now.* If this had been a typical mission, he would have called it then and there—fall back. This was not a typical mission, though. This was for all the marbles.

"Any wounded?" he asked.

Reaper replied from across Rodeo Drive. "Conroy is down. That gas got him."

"Is he alive?"

"You better come over, sir," came back Wallace's solemn voice.

Crouching low, he ran behind the Phalanx and into the building where Reaper had set up. The counter of the small boutique had been turned into a bed, and Conroy was laid out on it. His chest was rising and falling, so fast it looked as if he were running a marathon. His left eye was closed, but the right one was wide open and dilated. His left cheek sagged downward, like a balloon with the air let out of it. His skin on the left side of his face was pale and waxen. Two spent EpiPens lay on the counter near him.

"He looks like he had a stroke," Dawes said in a hushed tone.

"Paralytic gas of some kind," Reaper said. "I didn't think it got him, but it must have. Just touching his gear and I've got three fingers that are asleep right into the palm of my hand. We shot him up, but he's not reacting to it. I put one of the portable AED meshes on his chest and it has fired off twice." The bulky patch with its battery operated EKG and defibrillator automatically diagnosed cardiac arrhythmias and tried to correct them. The fact that it had gone off twice was not good news for Conroy.

Before he could offer any medical advice, Conroy started to convulse. The AED mesh fired off another shock to him, and while it twitched, he didn't stop his violent tremors. Wallace reached down to try to hold him steady on the table, but suddenly the convulsions stopped. Conroy's open right eye twitched, then stared blankly at the ceiling. Wallace tried CPR on his chest, despite the risk of getting more of the residue gas on his hands.

There was no response. Conroy was gone. From what Dawes had seen, he was gone before he had even crossed the street to see his body. Once he got hit with the gas, there was little chance that he would ever recover. Dawes had been prepared for some losses. The only thing that helped him cope was the thought that if he lost people, it meant that the survivors' shares of the loot would be larger. It wasn't the kind of thing a commander said out loud, but it was all he had to mentally cling to.

"Reaper, you did all you could," he said as Wallace frowned. "We will mourn him later. Right now, we need to prepare for another attack. We have got to protect the trucks and buy the people in the bank time."

"Right," his second-in-command said, shaking his frustration over Conroy's demise. "I will get another team rooftop and a sniper over to Four Seasons."

"Good," Dawes said. *Hopefully Conroy is the only person we lose on this job.*

CHAPTER 19

Operation Sundance, Beverly Hills, the Western Front, California, the United States

The sounds of battle hit Ryland as they carefully approached Rodeo Drive. The steady crack of gunfire, the occasional explosion of grenades—it was a siren's song, luring him and the rest of the Ghost Legion up the street. The thunder-like roar of the alien boomers— their sonic blasters—shook the air of Beverly Hills once again. The sounds were disturbing on multiple levels. Either it was Stevens and his people slugging it out with the Fish, or it was Spartan Associates. In either instance, there was no good news in the echoes of the battle that reached him.

"What do you make of it?" Staff Sergeant Calcutt asked as he came up beside him as they moved along the sidewalk. Small wisps of smoke rose in the distance, right in the direction they were headed.

"Trouble."

"It might be a good time to break communications silence," the sergeant suggested.

That's what he liked about Calcutt, he wasn't afraid to offer his suggestions. "Hold up here," he said, holding his fist upright for anyone that may have missed his message. Using his wristcomp, he switched to the channel that he, Stevens, and MacLeod had agreed on to coordinate their activities.

"This is Casper to Punch List. We are on Rodeo and closing on target. We're hearing gunfire; is that you? Over."

For a few seconds, there was no reply which only ratcheted his tension. Then came a hiss and Stevens's voice. "Casper, this is Punch List. We are coming up on the target from the south, hearing the same thing. It's not us stirring that pot. Over."

Ryland soaked in those words. He hated complications, especially ones that were setting off explosions and attracting far too much attention behind enemy lines. One option was to sit back and wait. The emotion was there and tangible. *If Spartan Associates have engaged with the Fish, let them sort it out.*

The problem was, they were humans fighting the same enemy that he and his people had been waging war against for months. *Even if they are the competition, it would be wrong to let them hang out and die when we could save them.* It would be tricky—the last thing he wanted was to have his people fired on by Spartan team members. At the same time, he didn't want to tip them off that they were nearby too soon. *They might take whatever they have gotten from the vault and bolt.* The best plan was to contact them when his forces were about to engage.

I hate goddamn complications! "It's tempting to let whoever it is to bleed off the enemy for us, but we can't risk them doing something rash. Let's continue to advance on their position. Once we are ready to engage, I will reach out to them and let them know."

"They're starting a fight we may have to finish."

"Roger that. See you at the rendezvous."

Ryland turned to his people. "Alright, people, there's a fight going on up ahead. Assuming they are fighting our Fishy-friends, they are our allies. We are going to advance on our waypoint at the Four Seasons. Keep sharp and hold your fire until I give you the word."

His anxiety reared its ugly head. In the back of Frank's mind was the persistent feeling that he should have known better, that he should have created plans to deal with this contingency. With the brain-wracking mental equivalent of angina was a feeling that he had somehow failed.

He checked his ECH feed from the battlespace command but saw no sign of MacLeod's ASHUR. That wasn't entirely a surprise. Per the plan, he was going to disconnect the IFF transponder. What was disturbing is that he had tried twice to raise him on their tactical channel, but those efforts had garnered only static.

Time to try again. He switched to MacLeod's channel. "Steel Hyena, this is Casper. Come in. Over."

Unlike his call to Stevens, this one did not bring any response. MacLeod was known to be a loose cannon. *Maybe he didn't push off at all, or got ambushed. Maybe he just got drunk and forgot.* He tried again as they walked up the street. Again, no response. Another deep thudding *boom* and *whoosh* of alientech roared, this time closer— more ominous.

I should have known it wouldn't be this easy...

* * *

Mark Stevens and the rest of Open Hostility were on South Beverly Drive, two blocks from the Beverly Wilshire Hotel, when they spied their first glimpse of the enemy. A recon Fox was huddled behind a crushed microvan that was half-on and half-off the sidewalk a block ahead. It rose quickly, then scurried off down a side street before anyone could even squeeze off a round.

Corvin's dejected voice confirmed what Stevens thought he had seen. "Sorry, boss. That Fox bolted before I could get a bead on it." Gunfire banged and popped ahead, and from the rising dust and smoke—he knew he was almost in range of the troops who were already slugging it out with the enemy.

Foxes did that. They seemed to be the scouts for the Fish. It was better when they stood and fought. When they ran, it almost always meant that the humans would be hit with a larger force. "Alright, people," he broadcast to the entire unit. "We've been spotted. Watch the rear and flanks—they are likely to come at us from any angle." His grip on his own ACR tightened, if only a little.

His team moved forward cautiously, and for Stevens, it felt as if there were dozens of alien eyes on him, simply waiting for him to walk into whatever ambush they had planned. The waiting was the hardest part, followed by what happened when the trap was eventually sprung. *We are in their territory. Yeah, we built this city— but they own the streets and have for months.* Reminding himself of that was something that helped keep his brain focused.

At the corner of Charleville Boulevard, his people on-point stopped, fists in the air. "Contact. West, a Crab," Corvin said in a whisper.

"Contact east, two blocks," said Guideon said. "Holy shitballs…"

"What do you see?"

"A whole lot of Frogs, heading right this way," came back the nervous voice of Guideon.

"Numbers?"

"Fifty-ish…heavy on the ish."

Stevens's tactical experience kicked in. Across the street was what was left of a California Pizza Kitchen on the ground floor, part of a sturdy concrete structure that showed little damage. Two blocks down was a jumble of cars and trucks, burned-out husks. In one area, he spied a dump truck that had been long abandoned.

The restaurant's double front door had been ripped off, meaning that the ATVs could be driven in for their protection. It wasn't the best defensive position he had ever seen, but it would have to do. "Everyone, cross the street, secure the pizza place. Ripper, get your machine gun positioned on the second or third floor at the corner—concentrate on those Frogs. Get the ATVs inside where they can be in-cover. Vogal, get high, on the roof if you can. Use that grenade launcher on anything that gets close. Remember—keep them distant, take them down before they get in close." Memories of the Frogs spitting on Clarkston on the roof of the mall were still fresh.

Everyone moved with purpose and in a matter of seconds, the pizza restaurant had been converted into a fire position. Tables were upended and moved to protect the ATVs. Nardo went upstairs and the shattering of a window indicated she was in position with her sniper rifle. Stevens knelt behind one of the large windows, the brick providing him some cover and the ledge giving him a perfect place to rest his weapon. He adjusted his targeting reticle on the inside of his visor and braced for the inevitable assault.

The Fish seemed to sense that there was a battle coming and rushed forward. The Frogs closed the gap the quickest. Most hopped in an erratic pattern, crisscrossing the street, some using the abandoned cars or debris for cover, others landing on hoods and vehicle roofs with each bound. They grunted loudly, a deep gut-vibrating noise, almost all of them in unison as they came forward like a wave flowing right at Open Hostility's position.

The gunfire came from the restaurant both on the ground floor and above. The purring of the Ripper's M245 machine gun in short but deadly bursts was joined with a series of explosions as Vogal rained down grenades fired from on high. Other members of the militia joined in with controlled shots at the incoming Frogs.

One Frog was cut in half by a short burst of machine-gun fire. Many others were hit. It wasn't that they were impervious to the shots but like so many of the other aliens, they appeared to be immune to the pain. Stevens hit one in the shoulder, tearing out a chunk of flesh in the process, leaving the arm limp. If it had been a human, there would have been wails of agony. In the case of the Frog, it simply hopped on forward, its limp arm covered in whatever grayish-black ooze it used for blood, grunting with the others.

The explosions devoured a number of Frogs at once, but as soon as the smoke cleared, those that were wounded simply clawed and crawled forward, still intent on attacking. Ripper's machine gun severed the long muscular legs off one Frog. It flopped to the pavement, and dragged itself forward with its clawed arms until someone else concentrated several rounds into its head, exploding it.

His head was throbbing with each rolling pound of his heart as Stevens continued to fire. Three Frogs defied the odds and got in close. The sacs behind two of them swelled and they unleashed globs of their sticky venom inside the California Pizza Kitchen. Stevens saw them go down under concentrated fire. The third leapt in through the large long-shattered window, swinging one of its big claws at Bigalow and tearing into his STG, knocking him back into a wall and cratering the drywall with an impression of his body. As Bigalow dropped, Roth fired three fast rounds into the neck of the Frog, decapitating it.

The sounds of the battle, even with his suppression earpieces of his helmet, were deafening, amplified by being in a structure. Dust from the explosions formed a khaki cloud and bits of concrete bounced off his STG as the tempo of the firing intensified. Frogs kept coming—and the grenade barrage devoured them a handful at a time—as did aimed shots by Stevens's people. That wasn't the only threat, though. *Please tell me someone took out that Crab.* Turning to the gunfire at his left, he saw the massive reddish creature unleash its slicer weapon. The intense cutting beam of highly pressurized water went over the heads of his people into the kitchen area of the restaurant, destroying anything it touched. Stevens rose long enough from cover to empty his magazine into the creature's raised torso as it closed the distance with their position. Unlike the Frogs, the Crab's carapace and hide took most of the shots with little evidence of damage.

Bigalow rose from where he had been recovering on the floor and pulled his shotgun out, firing off several rounds at the Crab as it reached the front of the building. The large scorpion-like tail coiled, then lashed out at the front of the restaurant. It slammed into the thick concrete support between two of the now-open window bays like a battering ram, knocking it out and throwing chunks of the support, complete with rebar, inside. For a fleeting moment, Stevens wondered if the entire structure might come down with damage to the support, but defying gravity, it seemed to hold.

Coyote was near the back of the restaurant, his weapon trembling as he fired. With the visor down on Coyote's helmet, Stevens couldn't see his face, but he didn't have to. No doubt it was a mask of total terror. Bowers, the hulking bodyguard, stood next to his employer, firing a steady but controlled stream of shots out of the front window at the Crab.

Above him, he heard fresh bursts of machine-gun fire but with no reaction from the Crab, he presumed it was dealing with the Frogs or some other threat. His body moved as if it had a mind of its own, sidestepping around an ATV as he put in a new magazine in his ACR. Raising the weapon he fired five more rounds, his ears roaring from the bangs. One hit oozed a streak of black liquid, hopefully a penetrating wound.

The Crab's tail recoiled, preparing for another swipe. His brain screamed, *get cover!* and he did just that—springing behind where the soda machine still stood. The crash of the tail whipping and stabbing all around him sent bits of the restaurant raining down on his prone position. *This is not how I planned on going out, in the middle of a California Pizza Kitchen.*

* * *

Shelly Reese took up a position in a lingerie shop some 200 feet from what was left of the California Pizza Kitchen. Despite her efforts to move silently, she had attracted the attention of two Frogs that had attempted to rush her. Even in her near-panic, her training held true and she hit one in the head—blowing its large lower jaw and part of the base of its skull off. It flopped down hard on a display of once-colorful G-strings covered with dust.

Its partner spat at her as it reached forward with its deadly clawed hands. The dangerous glob of venom was a near miss—some hit her STG-U's left shoulder plate as she tried to move to the right in hope of dodging it completely. The ACR she held tight rocked back over and over with each squeeze of the trigger.

Two shots missed completely, zipping across the street. Four slammed into the Frog with a distinct *thwack*. One bullet had shattered the left arm of the alien at the elbow, blowing out the back with bone and gore. The other shots hit the body of the alien, twisting it as it sprang at her. With a sharp twist of her own body, the Frog flew right past her, sprawling on the white tiled floor of the shop.

She could see the exit wounds, big and nasty, squirting out the alien's black-gray blood. For a moment, she thought it was dead, but it proved her wrong by pushing up with its one working arm, attempting to roll over. *Jesus! What do you have to do to kill these things?*

The question was rhetorical—the answer was to keep killing it. She fired five more rounds into the alien as it contorted near her feet. Out of sheer force of will and malice, it rolled over and reached out to grab her with its one remaining arm. She shifted before it could, sending the last two rounds from her magazine into the Frog's head. It dropped with a flop on the floor, a puddle of ooze creeping out from the many holes she had put into it.

Reese was furious—not at being attacked, but by being where she was—in Beverly Hills. Mark Stevens had lied to her and had pushed off on some unauthorized op deep into enemy territory. He had kept her in the dark about it. Now Open Hostility was engaged in a major firefight, alone and behind enemy lines. *Damn that Frog-fucker! He owes me an explanation. I could have been killed.*

She stepped over the dead Frogs and moved to the window. The street outside was littered with dead Frogs and parts of dead Frogs, shot and blasted apart. The shrapnel from the grenades fired at them had actually hit her right chest during the peak of the fighting. Fortunately her STG and blast plates had stopped it. *It had to be Vogal using that grenade launcher.*

Looking over at the California Pizza Kitchen, she saw a crimson Crab slashing its spiked tail into the interior of the restaurant with a crashing and crunching sound. Reese put in a new magazine and took careful aim at the Crab from behind firing several controlled shots at the creature. *Come on and die, you asshat. Once you're down, I can confront Stevens about all of this.*

* * *

The Crab refused to give ground. It was clear to Stevens that if it had to bring down the building around them, it would do so without hesitation. One claw jabbed at the interior, throwing tables and chairs at him. One chair slammed into his leg hard enough to make him shift his position. He fired another two shots at the alien, both seeming to deflect off its crimson carapace.

Vogal must have seen the threat directly below her, sending two grenades down, aiming so that the creature would block most of the shrapnel from hitting her own people. The explosions made Mark's left ear pop; they were that close. The air was clogged with dust and debris as they all turned from the Frogs and emptied their magazines into the Crab.

The creature reeled, mostly from the grenade explosions, once more lashing at the ground floor of the structure with its deadly tail. The deadly curved barb at the end stabbed deep into the structure, catching Bigalow as he tried to dive for cover. The brute of a man cried out in pain as the spike drove into his shoulder and out his back.

The Crab blasted at Vogal's position above him with its slicer, raining more debris down in front of the now devastated pizza restaurant. Stevens steadied himself for a moment, aiming at the head of the Crab, and fired off five fast rounds. One hit the small eye of the Crab. Black liquid spray erupted like a tiny geyser where the dark orb had been. The alien recoiled, jerking its tail back, and in doing so, slid the barb out of Bigalow's shoulder…his body dropping with a thud on top of an ATV.

By now the Frogs had been eliminated and every bit of the firepower of Open Hostility focused on the Crab. The impacts of well-aimed spots washed over it in waves. It was hurt, he could sense that, but not dead yet. It pulled back one massive claw, no doubt planning to jab it into where he and his people were positioned. Another grenade went off right on the rear of the head of creature, proof that Vogal was still alive above him. This explosion tore into the hide behind the head of the alien, squirting the oily black ooze all over, with droplets hitting anyone near the devastated front of the structure. Bits of torn flesh flew, additional indication of damage. The Crab slumped forward, its head slamming onto the pavement hard. Three of its remaining shorter legs quaked, a hopeful sign that it was dead. With the aliens, you could never be sure.

Stevens wiped the dust and splatter from his helmet's visor and glanced down the street toward where the Frog assault had been. There was still movement, but none of the enemies were standing. The aliens that were alive were doing everything they could to drag their bodies up the street.

"How are we, people?" he transmitted as Wrench and Roth began to check on Bigalow.

"I got some bumps and scratches—but I'm good," Vogal's tense voice responded.

"I think I set a record for kill shots," Nardo signaled. "That freaking slicer almost got me, though."

"Keep your eyes peeled. We made a lot of noise. Chances are

that was just the start of the circus."

"Bigalow is in a bad way, boss," Wrench called over. Stevens hurried over and saw that they had pulled off Bigalow's helmet. He was breathing in rapid, short breaths. His skin was pale and the wound he had was oozing blood. Someone had gotten a freezer pack and an auto-suture on it, but he was still bleeding. There was something else mixed in the blood, something orange-ish. *That stinger must have secreted something.* He had learned a long time ago, anything that the Fish oozed or spat or sprayed was bad. "Hang on, Charlie."

"Sorry, bossman," he apologized. "Despite the warnings—I think I got a case of the Crabs." It was a feeble attempt at humor—something Stevens expected from Bigalow.

Kneeling, the commander of Open Hostility kept close eye contact with his wounded man. "We'll get you patched up—just focus—stay conscious."

Bigalow's body trembled as if he was awash with a sudden chill. "Hurts like a bbb-bitch," he stammered. His arm that had been hit in the shoulder was a ghastly white color.

Roth cut off his STL and shirt on Bigalow's good arm with his tactical knife, then attached an emergency IV pad onto his skin. The plastic pad pumped saline solution into the victim based on sensors. It took a few seconds, but it seemed to slow Bigalow's trembling and his breathing became more regular.

Glancing over at Roth, the younger man shrugged. "That's almost everything I know about combat first aid."

"You did good, Barry. Stick with him."

Bigalow spoke up. "I'll be fine, boss. I might have to spend my cut on a bionic replacement—but I'll be fine." His voice was still weak, but sounded a little stronger.

Glancing off to his side, he saw Coyote and Bowers emerging from the kitchen area. Coyote was trembling almost as much as Bigalow had been, and Bowers raised his visor and used a handkerchief to wipe the sweat from the wrinkles of his face. Both men looked exhausted, and in the case of Coyote, possibly mentally scarred for life.

Vogal came down from the stairs at the rear of the restaurant. "Hell of a redecoration job," she remarked, glancing around at the carnage. Stevens wanted to counter with a quip of his own, but his brain was focused on their objective and their current position. "We need to load up and get to the Beverly Wilshire."

"Is the Ghost Legion there yet?" A distant explosion indicated that the fighting two blocks away was still raging.

Tapping his wristcomp to get the frequency, Mark Stevens intended to get that answer. His mouth opened to transmit, when he saw a figure cross the street in front of him, storming right at his position. It wasn't alien, it was a human. Even by the way the person wore their STG, he knew who it was. His stomach clenched.

The visor of the new arrival raised and the beet-red face of Shelly Reese appeared. "Goddam it, Stevens! What are you doing here?"

* * *

The Ghost Legion had come in behind the three Crabs that were advancing up Wilshire towards Rodeo Drive. It had taken remarkable restraint to not open up on them, especially since they were advancing towards the sounds of battle that had been bouncing around the AIZ in the vicinity of where they were heading. Engaging in a firefight without coordinating with the other friendly combatants was a dangerous proposition. Still, these were Fish, and the sight of them perfectly exposed and unaware was a temptation that he could not pass up on for long.

In his mind, he had been trying to find a way to not reach out to the other humans that he presumed were Spartan Associates. *The minute we start talking to them, the entire game is flipped. They are going to know what we are here for and that could become deadly all on its own. There's no rules out here, behind the front lines. What if they turn on us?*

One of the Crabs reached the standing structure of the Beverly Wilshire, their objective. It did something that he had not expected— it began to climb. Extending its tail down and pushing off with it, the Crab scaled the side of the hotel that was still standing, stabbing its legs into the stone, through smashed windows, or even jabbing them into cracks. *There must be a gun position up there. I have got to do something.*

He switched to a clear open channel. "This is Lieutenant Ryland of the Ghost Legion to any and all troops in Beverly Hills. We are approaching the Beverly Wilshire from the southwest and will provide you fire support. We've got three Crabs scaling the wall towards the rooftop. Inform your people that we are approaching and to not fire on us. Over."

He switched back to his Legion's channel. "Alright, Ghosts, this is Casper. We take these guys out one at a time. Let's go for that climber first. Weapons hot—fire at will."

CHAPTER 20

Operation Sundance, Beverly Hills, the Western Front, California, the United States

The Steel Hyena rounded the corner at Dayton Way and North Beverly Drive when MacLeod saw a sea of dead Frogs and Frog parts covering almost every bit of the paved surface. Down the street, he saw two Crabs heading towards an ASHUR. As a pilot, MacLeod knew every model of ASHUR rig there was—hell, he even knew the models of the underwater Trident suits. The unknown rig's ACS flickered from visible to transparent, a sign that it was just about overloaded. The rig that he saw standing knee deep in dead Frogs was a model he had never seen before…and in that instant, he was intrigued.

The Hyena's communications system had been a hot mess thanks to his tech Swift prior to the mission. MacLeod was receiving messages just fine, which added to his frustration. The battlespace commander had been calling for him to respond—demanding to know what he was doing in the AIZ. He couldn't respond if he'd wanted to. There had been a few calls for him to respond from Ryland, and not being able to respond to those frustrated him to a point of near-rage. Having run the diagnostics, he saw that he was limited to laser comms, short range, line of sight only. It had made his journey more nerve-wracking. It had been extra frustrating when he got the signal in the clear from Ryland that they were engaging to the west. *The situation is getting leaky—that's for sure.*

Watching the ASHUR rig raise its weapons, he knew he had to help. One-on-one with a Crab, a rig was a fair match. Two-to-one, not so much. *Time to be a hero!* He broke his Rattlesnake into a sprint and fired off a power shell for the sonic disruptor.

Running over the dead Frogs deadened the thuds of his footpads as he sprinted. Several times he slid, as the pulverized aliens' fleshy goo turned into a lubricant under his rig's footpads. The hum of the weapon told him it was ready. When he reached a hundred feet from the target, the other rig fired a rocket at one Crab, the explosion engulfing the alien momentarily in an orange and crimson ball of fire.

MacLeod stopped and fired. The sonic disruptor throbbed a repeating *whom-whom-whom* and the air between his raised arm and the back of the other Crab rippled with each wave. His entire rig throbbed with the weapon's pulsating noise bursts. The sonic waves were strong enough to toss some of the tiny blasted bits of Frogs downrange in their pulse waves. He knew that the friendly ASHUR was going to be aware of him now, some of the sonic spillover was destined to hit it as well, but the brunt of the attack hit the alien.

The Crab seemed to tense up, its legs curling under the attack, its claws contracting as the raised upper torso swung around to face him. The alien pivoted in place toward him, and MacLeod grinned inside his helmet. *That's right, big boy, there's two of us on the field now.* The disruptor didn't show physical damage, but from his training and experience, he knew it had inflicted serious pain on the Fish—and that was good enough for him.

With a twitch of his forefinger, he fired off another power shell, this time shunting the excess energy into his Mark IA Plasma Carbine. The Crab aimed one of its big claws at him and fired a blast of acid at him. MacLeod juked right, dodging most of the spray, though some hit the shin of his left leg. He ignored the damage indicator screen telling him that his armor had been hit—he knew that from the mist that drifted up in front of his cockpit canopy. Nothing was going to shake his concentration from aiming as he drifted his arm gently at his approaching target.

Squeezing the trigger, the plasma carbine unleashed its deadly spray. A long molten stream of superheated plasma stabbed at the Crab. It used one of its big claws to block the incoming yellow and orange bolt of superheated particles. The plasma splatter seared deep into the claw, hissing, and some of it splashed onto the alien's torso and even its head carapace.

The Crab reeled and screeched; its reaction was dramatic. While the unknown ASHUR engaged its partner, MacLeod stayed focused on his target. Bringing his ACR-30 into play, he fired off devastating .50 caliber rounds into the creature. One shot missed entirely—but the next three hit the head of the armored body of the Crab. Small rounds might get stuck on the thick hide or glance off the carapace— but the ACR-30's rounds punched in. Squirts of blackish blood shot out and the Crab sprayed another blast from its acid sprayer in a wild diagonal sweep. It was a shot of desperation, only a little of the spray hit his right thigh armor plates, and he chose to ignore it as he had the first attack. All that mattered now was the kill.

MacLeod switched to full auto and emptied the large magazine of the ACR into the Crab. The bloody black holes stitched into the torso and lower head. The twitching of the alien gave him immense and immediate satisfaction. The Crab fell onto the dead Frogs, smoke still rising from where the plasma cutter had burned into its now-mangled claw.

His attention shifted to the remaining Crab and ASHUR. That alien had sprung at the rig, and was clamped onto one of its arms by a massive claw—seemingly oblivious to the fate of its comrades. *All the better.* MacLeod didn't take time to slap another magazine into the ACR, instead he fired another power shell and held the trigger for the plasma carbine.

The molten stream of plasma squirted into the back of the creature like a long glowing scar right up to its raised torso. Where plasma sank into the hide of the Crab, jets of superheated blood and goo burst out as it went in. *I'll bet that hurts like a bitch.*

The Crab released the ASHUR in front of it and turned to face him. MacLeod sidestepped, matching the turn, slamming the ACR against the side of its leg where it synced and reloaded. As it turned, the other ASHUR fired a power shell and aimed. A momentary flash happened and a large smoking hole seared through the raised torso. *A laser…a damned big one too.*

The Crab seemed to freeze in place then dropped down, limp, right next to its fallen partner. Moving around, MacLeod checked his tactical screen to make sure that the enemies had indeed been taken out and that no one was approaching from behind him.

This cockpit sound system came on. "Who the hell are you?" a female's voice demanded.

"You're welcome," he replied, using his laser system.

"Thank you," the voice replied. "I hadn't expected anyone to show up. Certainly not another rig."

"I'm Sutherland MacLeod." Pride oozed in his words. "Call sign Steel Hyena. I'm here with the Ghost Legion. My apologies for taking so long, I had a little firefight of my own and my wideband comms are on the fritz."

"Trixie Lynch. Call sign Brutality. I just got the squirt that you guys were in the battlespace."

"You okay, Brutality?" he asked, surveying the crunched armored plating on her rig's left arm where the Crab claw had tried to pinch it off.

"Still operational. My STL pads in the arm are compromised." She extended the arm out so she could see it from the cockpit of her rig. "It looks a lot worse than it is. I had a minor hydraulic leak from the Frogs hitting me, but I've been able to compensate for it. You?"

His eyes had just lifted from the damage display. "Some acid damage—nothing serious."

"It looks like we have cleared this street…for now anyway."

"They'll be back," MacLeod assured her. "They always come back." It was a grim reality of life in the AIZ.

"I appreciate the assist."

"Assist? I think it was a little more than that."

"I had the situation under control."

"It didn't look like a lot of control with two Crabs almost on top of you."

"I could handle them. You *do* see all of the dead Frogs, don't you?"

That made MacLeod grin. "Frogs? You're an ASHUR pilot. Frogs are an annoyance…slimy cannon fodder. Organic target practice. You don't need a rig to take them out."

"There were a lot of Frogs," she snapped back. Her rig's arm gestured to the street filled with dead aliens.

Body counts didn't impress MacLeod. He had been in combat far too many times, killed more aliens than he could even begin to count. The fact that this pilot was impressed with the numbers told him that she was green…that and she had allowed the Crabs to close with her to danger-close range. His patience ran out relatively fast with the conversation. "You had two Crabs almost on top of you. We both know that was not a desirable situation. A simple thank you will do."

Lynch said nothing for a moment, then replied in a low tone. "Thank you."

"See, that wasn't so hard." The moment he spoke the words he knew he had rubbed it in a little too much. It didn't bother him, MacLeod simply acknowledged it.

"Have you always been this arrogant?" she snapped.

"According to my mom and my CO, yes. Enough of the formalities between us. I have a bigger question for you, Brutality."

"What's that?"

"What the hell are you piloting?"

Operation Goldfinger, Beverly Hills, the Western Front, California, the United States

The Ghost Legion…damn it all! It wasn't that Shredder Dawes didn't appreciate the additional firepower, but he also knew that the Ghost Legion had been tracking their movements. *They are here for the same thing we are.* It was a complication that he had hoped to avoid.

The situation had been brutal for almost an hour. The Fish had showed up in force. First had been three successive waves of their suicidal Frog troops. The bodies were stacked high and deep along Wilshire to the west of the Commerce Bank, where he had posted Lynch in the Phalanx. On two occasions, that had overwhelmed her position, but she had managed to kill them all, having to physically peel their dead off the outside of her ASHUR.

Crabs had been coming in threes and fours, hitting from the north and east. One of his best snipers, Merndon, the Iron Infidel, had lost most of a leg, thanks to one of their slicers. Quick medical attention had saved his life. To prove how tough he was, he was still in the Beverly Wilshire, using his Hawkeye rifle to hammer the Crabs.

We've been gassed, sprayed, and splattered—and we're still here. There was a feeling of pride in that, especially given where they were fighting—deep in the AIZ. The thought of some assistance from other humans was a relief and curse. *They will want a piece of the pie when we get that vault opened.* His people in the Commerce Bank said progress was slow but there was progress. Dawes didn't have the time to go and check on them—his job was to protect that team and their transports.

I have to respond to this call. If we start shooting at each other accidentally, the situation will get even messier. He switched to the same open channel. "Ghost Legion, this is Shredder with Spartan Associates. We appreciate the assist. My people are listening in and will watch their fields of fire to avoid targeting your team. Recommend you approach from the south."

"Roger that, Shredder," came back Ryland's voice. "We are converging now on the Beverly Wilshire."

"I have snipers up top."

"We know. We're trying to save them right now."

Save them? What is going on down at the Wilshire? His focus shifted from the east and to the remains of the hotel. To his dismay, he saw a Crab climbing the side of the building, heading right to where Merndon and Kerrigan were positioned.

Gunfire streaked up from below, hitting the Crab and peppering the exterior of the building. It was steady, persistent, and deadly. At first the alien seemed to ignore the attacks as an annoyance; it continued to climb up past the third floor, closing on the Spartan Associates' perch. It stopped, turning toward the Ghost Legion who were shooting it, and it sprang away from the building with a powerful leap.

Dawes had never seen that before. Yes, Crabs jumped but not from a height. The creature dove for the ground with its claws open before it. He couldn't see where it landed but the increase in gunfire told him that it came down quite alive.

Operation Sundance, Beverly Hills, the Western Front, California, the United States

The Crab landed on a UPS delivery truck, crushing it under its weight with a sickening metallic moan. One of the claws unleashed a stream from a spiker tube that was grown on the exterior of the beast. The shots came with *thwift* sounds as the deadly spikes zipped through the air at his people. Ryland watched as Hollings got hit and flew backwards from the kinetic impact. Grant and Raffi dove for cover. Avery twisted hard, an indication that he had been hit as well.

Ryland's fired one shot after another as the Crab crawled down from the crushed UPS vehicle. Its tail whipped, aiming apparently for Winston who was hunkered down by a fire hydrant. Winston sprang back into a window for a small bakery, shattering the glass that remained there as the tail hit the hydrant and tore it from its fittings, sending it flying down the street. There was a gurgle and a momentary surge of rusty brown water into the air, then nothing. The water system in the city had been off-line since the start of the war.

Calcutt was mostly visible as he overloaded his ACS by running. He dashed out, connecting two stackable grenades as he ran, then threw them at the Crab. The grenade bounced and rolled under the creature and went off with a blast that made Ryland's ears ache. Bits of the street and parts of the UPS vehicle comingled with the shrapnel, some hitting his chest plates hard enough to make his STG packs stiffen.

The dust and smoke obscured the damage done, and he held his fire until he had a good target. Calcutt's ACS was off-line, no big surprise. As it cleared, he could see that the explosion had nearly torn the Crab in half. The lower legs and tail were twisted to the right, where the upper body was contorted to the left. The rear of the creature lay limp, but the forward portion, with the head and deadly claws, was attempting to pull itself along. It was still attached to the rest of its body by ugly gray organs and bits of body carapace, and it dragged them along—apparently unfazed by the damage it had taken.

Raising its weapon mounted claw, it fired another burst of spikes at Calcutt who huddled behind a car. The spikes punched neatly through the vehicle and out the back—and Ryland was unsure if the sergeant had been hit or not in the process. The rest of the legion fired away, riddling the part of the Crab that still showed signs of life. It collapsed a moment later.

The other two Crabs were under attack farther up the street—not by his people but someone else, either Stevens's or Dawes's people. A pair of explosions went off, the sound bouncing off the buildings and stirring the dust that seemed to cover everything in La. Slowly, the gunfire died down. Ryland started up the street, finally standing in front of what was left of the Beverly Wilshire. Glancing to his left, he saw the curve of Rodeo Drive, and the front of the Commerce Bank. The door had been removed and in front of the building were several pickup trucks. He found himself gritting his teeth at the sight. *I was right about them...they are here to hit the bank just like we are. I wonder if they've breached the vault yet.* That feeling made him tense. It wasn't just about the money—it was being able to put to rest the compulsive anxiety that consumed him. *If they already robbed the place, am I going to be able to get to sleep?*

As he got closer, the fear that he felt wasn't of the aliens—it was that they had gotten there too late.

* * *

Stevens ordered his people to start moving again, trying hard to ignore Shelly Reese's demands for information. His liaison wouldn't let go; she practically screamed at one point. *She's a pit bull, locking her jaws onto me and shaking until I give up.* The roar of distant gunfire seemed to get louder with each step. The noise bouncing off of buildings was deceptive, making it sound like the fighting was all around them—and significantly louder. Alien sonic boomers went off—and the rattle of machine-gun fire. *Whoever it is, we are closing on them. It sounds like it's on the far side of the hotel.*

"Damn it, Stevens," she said, moving right in front of him and blocking his stride. "You need to tell me what you are doing out here."

"Reconnaissance," he muttered, trying to sidestep her. Reese shifted and blocked that path as well. *She's consistent—I'll give her that.*

"Bullshit," she spat. "Do you want to tell me what this is about, or do I have to squeeze it out of one of the others?"

"That wouldn't be my first choice," he quipped in response to her question.

"What?"

"You asked if I wanted to tell you—" he paused, realizing that she would not appreciate his attempt at humor. In all the time he had spent with Reese, she had not demonstrated a hint at levity. In his mind, he wondered if it was worth trying to keep her in the dark. *She's not going to fall in line and stop demanding answers. It's against her nature.*

He opened his visor for a moment and stared into her face. "I didn't expect you to follow us."

"Surprise."

"Alright," he said with a deep sigh. "We are here because there's some exclusive bank here, the kind of place that celebrities store their stuff. We are going to liberate it." As he finished his sentence, he started to walk past her. This time she did not sidestep in front of him and block his path.

"You're robbing a bank?"

"More or less. If it makes you feel any better about it, the bank is a bunch of rich people's—a private little business catering to the famous beautiful people. We're not so much as robbing it as relieving it of some of its contents."

"That's looting, no matter how you try to paint it. You'll get sent to prison for this."

As they reached the corner of Wilshire, there was a huge explosion from down the block in front of the hotel. Dropping his visor, he motioned for his people to spread out. They were coming up on the scene of the fighting. With a simple gesture, he motioned for Vogal to take her fire team across the street. Stevens raised his ACR and right at his side, Reese did the same. Vogal and her people hunched low and moved quickly across Wilshire, jumping into a small clothing boutique and using it to cover them.

Two Crabs were heading right at his people. They were a block and a half down, moving away from dust stirred from another part of the battle. *We have space between us and time.* "Alright, people, controlled shots. Ripper, it's time to bring Carl out to play."

"Roger that, Punch List," he said. Ripper's ACS system was operating, but the shimmering movement of his figure was visible as he darted out behind a sedan in the street. Ripper readied the Carl Gustaf as the rest of Open Hostility opened fire. They only had a few rounds for it, but the recoilless launcher was highly effective. Stevens fired five rounds at the Crab on the right. While he was certain he was hitting, there was no way to see if his shots were doing damage at this range.

A loud *ba-bang,* like an artillery piece going off, filled the air as the Carl Gustaf sent an 84mm round streaking downrange. It slammed into the Crab on the left, engulfing the creature in a ball of orange flames. Oily black smoke rolled skyward from the blast. Stevens watched it, half wondering if he'd see the Crab emerge from the flames still alive. It was a scene he had witnessed before. There was no such emergence.

"Everyone, concentrate on the remaining Crab," he ordered. "Hold up on another shot, Ripper, we are limited on ammo."

"Gotcha, boss," Ripper replied, lowering the tube and switching back to his M245—firing short bursts at the remaining combatant.

The remaining Crab started to pick up speed as it headed for them. Raising one of its huge front claws, it unleashed a spray of spikes that filled the air between it and its human targets. The spikes shattered against buildings, forcing Stevens to recoil for cover around the edge of a wall. Where Ripper was, the car he used for cover was punctured with a dozen holes, in one side and out the other. Ripper dove for the street and lay flat. The boutique was hit so hard with the burst, the dust it kicked up obscured all view Stevens had of it.

Without hesitation, he swung back around the corner and resumed firing. Reese knelt at his side, doing the same. He could see the muzzle flashes from the boutique, signs that at least most of his people were still in the fight.

The Crab was a half a block away when Ripper rose and sprayed it with a longer burst. The shots tore into the upright torso of the alien, flailing away huge pieces of its carapace-armored hide, chewing deep into the creature's flesh. Shots were raining down from behind the alien as well now, coming from whoever had been engaged in the fighting at the hotel.

Wheeling around, the Crab seemed confused, with gunfire hitting it from all sides. It fired back at the upper floors of the hotel with its spiker weapon, spraying the façade of the structure, shattering windows and sending chunks of the exterior plummeting downward. For a moment, the gunfire farther down the block ceased as they dove for cover.

Open Hostility did not hesitate; their gunfire intensified. It was impossible to tell whose shot was the one that downed the creature, but suddenly, the body of the Crab stiffened, then it went limp—falling over.

Stevens moved out onto the street and waved his people to

follow. A strange quiet seemed to fall over their part of the city. In the pit of his stomach, he knew the lull was temporary. He started down the street towards the hotel. Reese came up beside him. "We are not done talking about this," she said.

"There's not a lot more for me to say, so I appreciate the quiet," he replied.

"You can't just waltz into the AIZ."

"Look around you," he said as he picked up the pace. "I would say that your statement is false. We are here in Beverly Hills."

"The Army will fry you for this."

Stevens chuckled.

Operation Sundance, Beverly Hills, the Western Front, California, the United States

Through the light haze, a figure walked towards Ryland. The man was tall, muscular but not to the point where he looked like a juiced-up pumper. His blond hair and beard were visible with the visor of his mask raised. He had light gray eyes and as he approached, his face offered no hint of his emotions or intentions.

"You Lieutenant Ryland?" he asked.

Ryland walked up to him. "That's right. And you are?"

"Albert Dawes, Spartan Associates. Call sign Shredder."

Eyeing Dawes carefully, Ryland wasn't entirely sure how he felt about finding them there. They had engaged the enemy, forces that would have gone up against him and his people. Before he could reply, he heard the crunch of ASHUR footpads in the distance. Behind him, he heard voices, not his people. Craning his head around slowly, he saw Mark Stevens of Open Hostility approaching along with the rest of Open Hostility. "I'd say it's good to meet you, but I think we are both here for the same reason."

"Ratchet?"

"Ratchet."

The stomping of ASHUR footpads in the distance gave Ryland some hope. Glancing over, he saw the outline of MacLeod's Steel Hyena come from a cross street into his view. It was followed by another ASHUR, one he had not seen before.

Dawes brought his own ASHUR. This is about to get very complicated.

CHAPTER 21

Beverly Hills, the Western Front, California, the United States

Ryland looked at the circle of troops that had assembled. Stevens and Vogal were present, along with Reese, Open Hostility's liaison. MacLeod was there as well, having climbed down out of his ASHUR. Dawes was there along with someone he introduced as Ted "Reaper" Wallace. Once the introductions were done, an awkward silence fell on them.

He hated long silences, they made him edgy, and being in Beverly Hills at all was nerve-wracking enough. "Look, we all know why we are here."

Dawes crossed his beefy arms. "Unfortunately you are late. We already got to the bank and my people are working on the vault. So it looks like you wasted your effort."

Stevens shook his head and grinned. "This isn't like calling 'shotgun' for the front seat in a car. You don't get to lay claim to the bank simply because you got here first. It wasn't a race."

"It was in my mind," Dawes countered. "And we won it."

The Witch, Kris Vogal, spoke up. "If that's your position, we could just take it from you." From the tone of her voice and the icy resolve on her face, Ryland knew she was not joking.

"You could try," Ripper Wallace said. "And you could die."

This is getting us nowhere fast. "The Fish are going to come back and we need to sort this out. I propose that we set up a defensive position around the bank right now, before they strike again. That will give us some time to sort through the…other details."

Dawes gave a reluctant nod. "My people will take the north, Dayton Way and Beverly."

"I'll take a posting to the east farther along Beverly, if you'll post your ASHUR at your far end of the line. That way we can support each other, if need be," MacLeod said.

"I think that can be arranged."

"I'll take the south," Stevens volunteered.

"Ghost Legion will take the west," Ryland said, looking over at Calcutt who gave a nod of agreement. Stevens motioned for Vogal to come over and whispered something in her ears, which got a nod from his second-in-command. Calcutt, Vogal, MacLeod, and Wallace departed to begin to deploy the troops. Ryland was pleased. Reducing the number of voices in this conversation will be helpful. All that remained standing in front of the remains of the hotel were Dawes, Stevens, Reese, and himself. Stevens ordered Reese to assist Vogal, which only seemed to add to her anger. She bitterly narrowed her gaze at him and stomped off.

"She's full of piss and vinegar," Dawes remarked, watching her storm off.

"She eats, sleeps, and shits by the book," Stevens replied. "I just wish she hadn't followed us in."

"We appreciate your help in defending this position, but I want to assure you, it isn't necessary," Dawes stated his stance.

"We've shed good blood to get here," Stevens countered. "I'm not going to tell my people that this was all a big-ass waste of time. Yes, you got here first, but if you think we're going to let you trot out of here and leave us with nothing, you are sadly mistaken." The resolve in the militia commander's voice was inescapable.

Dawes turned to Ryland who decided to reinforce the point. "I've risked my career in the military for this. My people will not take it kindly if you take from them what they have fought for."

Now for the kill shot. "We will get word to the outposts that Spartan Associates have been engaged in a looting incident in Beverly Hills and are to be arrested and secured the moment they attempt to come out of the AIZ."

Dawes tried to deflect his words. "Your people are here too. You'd be slitting your own throats."

Ryland didn't flinch, but did crack a thin smile. "You'll find that we are on an authorized mission here I cut those orders myself. You are not. My version of events will be that we learned of your illegal looting and deployed to intercept you. We are the good guys in this scenario. Who do you think the Army is going to believe? Mercenaries with trucks loaded with stolen loot, or a distinguished officer with a spotless record? You don't have to answer because we all know how this will play out."

Dawes's cheeks went red and his jaw set. "If you play it that way, you don't get anything either."

"I would prefer that to you ripping us off."

From what Ryland could see, Dawes was grinding his teeth in frustration and anger. The silence was cut by Stevens's voice. "We're not ripping you off. All we want is an equitable split."

After a few more seconds of thought, Dawes finally nodded. "Damn it—alright, fine. We split this three ways. But know this, the contents of box 435 is part of our split. I won't negotiate that point."

"Ratchet's box?" Ryland asked.

"Yes."

Glancing over at Stevens, he got a single nod of agreement. "We can live with that."

"Alright then. Let's go see what progress my people are making." He started off towards the bank, followed by Ryland and Stevens.

* * *

Shelly Reese took up her position as assigned by the Witch. It wasn't much, a mound of rubble in the collapsed tower of the hotel. She preferred it to being in the standing structure, though. That part of the hotel had taken so much damage, it looked as if it could collapse if hit a few more times by the Fish. It was tempting to turn on her ACS system, but it might be out of juice by the time the battle started. At least in her pile of rubble, there was a chance of mobility. *The last thing I need is a building coming down on me.*

The betrayal she felt was deep and personal. Stevens had always seemed so upright, so just. He had brought his people into the war to help them, to put some money in their pockets. He had acted out of loyalty—and his people paid that back. Reese had respected that about him, even if she had never said it out loud.

Now he's selling out—now he's just some amoral looter. It galled her that he was willing to flip. He was risking everything, including military prison, for this. Why? Then the answer came to her. *He's taking care of his people still. This isn't about profiting, it's about giving them a life outside of all this.*

That realization bothered her, but in a different way. *It's a violation of the rules...it's breaking the damn law.* For Reese, the rules of the game were everything. *If we don't follow the regs, we are no better than the Fish or men like Dawes. People worked for what is stored in that bank. It belongs to them—not to whoever takes it out.*

Complaining to the nearest officer wasn't going to do a bit of good. Clearly Lieutenant Ryland was an architect of this entire plan. If she waited to report this until after they got back, it would be too late. *They will scatter with what they take—and there's not a lot of resources to go and look for them.*

For long tedious minutes, Reese pondered the state of affairs, looking at it from different angles, as if it were a Rubik's Cube in her mind, thinking through all of her options. None of her choices looked promising. *There's no guarantee that we will get out of here alive. We are deep in enemy territory and they know we are here. Stevens was smart to set up a perimeter because they are bound to come for us.* As she shifted in the rubble and checked her field of fire, she wondered if she had made a massive mistake in following Open Hostility into the AIZ to begin with. *What good is it to be right if you end up dead?*

There was some additional guilt she struggled with—thoughts of what she could do with some of the contents of that bank. *If it really is where the rich and famous stored their prized possessions, the contents must be worth a fortune.* What could she do with wealth, *real* wealth? The Army had been her home for almost a decade. Being a warrant officer was some sort of purgatory for her—trapped between the enlisted and officer ranks. Shelly had always viewed the Army as her career, but with the war on, it could very well be a death sentence one day. Sooner or later, the Fish might kill her. That was inescapable.

With a share of the contents of the bank, she could afford to leave. *Would the Army even allow that, though?* Rumors abounded that the military was not letting personnel retire, citing the war. *Am I trapped here?* Having money might make escape possible. In her brain, she took several minutes to consider what she would do with a share. *I could get a ranch—buy some horses...I always wanted to learn to ride horses.* Then there were her parents. She could afford to get them some place safer, deep in the heart of the country.

Drawing a deep breath, she refocused her thinking. *No, it would be wrong to take a share of a robbery.* As tempting as it was to play a child's game of daydreaming about wealth, she had to keep focused on the realities of what she was facing.

She picked up several bricks and piled them up so she had a better firing platform to rest her ACR's rail on. There was only one solution that she centered on that seemed viable—contacting the Army now. They would be compelled to send in a relief force. Then she would be able to expose Stevens, Ryland, and Dawes for what they really are.

* * *

As Ryland climbed over the heavy metal door that had been cut off and followed Dawes into the bank, he was immediately impressed. The interior had been beautiful, truly unlike any bank that he had ever been in. Marble floors with expensive carpet, crystal chandeliers, every detail in the dimly lit room screaming opulence.

Dawes gestured him to the back, past the teller stations. The air carried a hint of ozone in it as he got closer. Two of his people stood with an industrial drill and Maglites, staring through a fist-sized hole that had been bored into the massive circular vault door.

"What's the word, Diamond?" Dawes asked.

One of the people turned to him, a dusky woman with the name patch, Jones, and eyed both Ryland and Stevens in the process. "We think we got it, boss. We had a couple of failed attempts, but Treacher says he's got it. Who are these dudes?"

"New friends," Dawes replied. "Partners."

"I thought we were a solo act."

"Things have changed."

She eyed her holstered sidearm, then Dawes. Holding his hand out, he gestured for her to calm down. "Trust me, Diamond, while you've been in here, things got interesting outside."

"So it seems. Regardless, we think the third time's going to be the charm."

"Dazzle me."

She leaned back with a small box in her fingers that had a yellow and red wire leading into the hole they had bored. Another set of wires led to a heavy truck battery on the floor. Jones hit one of the toggle switches on the box and there was a loud snapping sound, and the whir of a motor somewhere in the vault door.

The door seemed to come alive. Something was clearly moving and the two troops working on it moved back a few feet. A thud in the door was followed with the door popping open, swinging just a bit.

Dawes walked over and grabbed the handhold. Ryland and Stevens joined him. It was heavy, and took a moment to get enough momentum to open it. As soon as they did, they were greeted with a smell, a rotting flesh aroma that stung at his nostrils. The room beyond was dark until one of the Spartans brought in a lantern. The stark white light lit up the chamber beyond and for a moment, he was both awed and somewhat disappointed.

Given the décor of the lobby, he expected that the vault itself would be spectacular. Instead it was a bank vault. Row upon row of safe-deposit boxes of three different sizes comprised the side walls and most of the back. There was an inner barred cage with a table with something stacked on it—he assumed it was money, but it was covered with some sort of green cloth. The steel floor had several boxes mounted in it as well.

Leaning up against one wall was the source of the rotting aroma that still lingered heavily in the air. It was a man, in what had been a nice suit, sitting against one wall. Being locked in the vault for months had left him in a semi-mummified state. His body fluids had oozed out onto the floor and it was stained a strange mix of colors, yellow, pink, and maroon. The man sat seeming to stare at them as they came through the door. Next to one hand was a pistol, a bronzed Sig Sauer .38. Ryland walked up to the body, closing his mask so that the air filters in his visor could do their job and block the smell. Bending down, he picked up the weapon. It was magnificent, with pearl handles, ornate scrollwork, and what looked like diamonds studding it. *There's a story here, how this man ended up in the vault —why he chose to die here rather than leave. We'll never know it.* He tucked the .38 into one of his pouches.

Dawes walked over and checked the dead man's pockets. After several seconds, he pulled out a ring of keys—not normal keys, strangely shaped ones. "Bingo—the master keys. This poor sap must have been the manager." It was a callous comment, but one that Ryland understood. *Being in this war has made us all a little numb to death.*

"There's a lot here," Stevens said. "Enough for all of us."

"Sure," Dawes replied. "I've got trucks outside."

"We have ATVs with trailers," Stevens replied. He then sent a message to his people to have them brought up to the bank.

"Each one of these boxes has to be pried open," Jones said, looking around the room. "It's going to take some time."

There was a rumble in the distance—not thunder, but the sound of battle, creeping in through the opened vault door. Ryland looked that way, then back to Dawes. "It doesn't sound like we are going to have a lot of time to divvy this stuff up."

"It's best to leave the stuff in the boxes. My people will be prying them out and putting them in our trucks. You're responsible for your own."

Ryland used his wristcomp to switch channels to his team. "Avery, get over to the bank. You work with whoever is here from Open Hostility to get stuff put on the ATVs." Corporal Avery acknowledged the order, though the signal strength was low and Ryland turned to his forced partners in crime. The sounds of small arms fire started outside as well—proof that the aliens were making another assault on their position. Signals started coming in from Calcutt, though it was hard to make out. In the vault, his helmet's display could not get an accurate picture of the battlespace, and communications were spotty. *I belong out there, not in here salivating over treasure.* "I need to get back to my people."

"Same here," Stevens said. Dawes nodded in agreement and moved with them through the vault door and into the dim lighting of the lobby.

Ryland didn't trust Dawes—he had no reason to. He stopped when they reached the exterior door, reaching out and gently grabbing Dawes at the elbow. "No tricks," Ryland said.

"What do you mean?"

"Exactly what I said. If you think for a moment about stabbing us in the back or double crossing us, you had better squash that thought. My Ghost Legion will hunt you down like wild animals. You and yours will never get a chance to enjoy a bit of what is back in that vault." Ryland didn't make idle threats, and the deeper tone of his voice seemed to emphasize the gravity of what he was saying.

"If they don't get you, my people will," Stevens added. "The lieutenant here, he has a set of rules. We're militia. We make our own rules. I'll turn the Witch loose on you. You betray us and they will never find your bodies if we get to you first."

Dawes chuckled a little. "You gentlemen need to relax—I have no intention of going back on my word."

Ryland nodded as he heard the sentence, but he was still not convinced. *I need to warn Avery to keep sharp.*

* * *

It had taken Reese a long time to muster the courage for what she had to do. *I swore an oath to defend the Constitution of the United States against all enemies, foreign and domestic.* She hated the fact that Stevens was breaking the law, but in her mind—he set her choice in motion. From the looks of it, Lieutenant Ryland was doing the same. *I need to get in contact with someone higher up in the chain of command...let them know what is happening here.*

There was regret. Outside of this incident, Mark Stevens had been a very good commander. He had chaffed at having her assigned to him, she knew that. It wasn't personal. He simply didn't feel the need to have additional Army support. Stevens treated her with respect...the same as he did for the others in Open Hostility. In reporting him, she was going behind his back, turning him in for prosecution. *There's no other choice. If I turn a blind eye to this, it's the same as me being part of it.* The remorse weighed heavily on her as she lay on the rubble, watching for signs of the enemy.

There was an explosion to the west—the sound of a grenade going off. Gunfire started. *If I don't do it now, I never will.* She used her wristcomp to get a signal directly to battlespace command. "Foxtrot battlespace command, this is Warrant Officer Shelly Reese. I need you to patch me through to Lieutenant Colonel Logan— priority one."

The voice came back. "Understood. I am showing you…wait… what the hell? WO Reese, confirm your position please."

"Grid 10 A—Beverly Hills. I need to talk to Colonel Logan, now."

"What is going on? I show your unit and the Ghost Legion both there. You are a solid three miles behind the lines. Who authorized this op?"

"I don't have time for this," she fired back. "Put me through to Colonel Logan now, priority one."

There was a hissing response. She could hear bits and pieces of what he was saying. "…authorized…enemy for…too far forward…" then it faded to nothing but static. Reese repeated her order—but got nothing back. *It has to be something with the comms system.* Reaching up, she banged the left side of her ECH where the comms system was housed, then repeated her message. Once more, the only response was static. *Figures, the damned equipment would fail the one time I need it!* A new level of frustration hit her. She started to remove her helmet and noticed someone standing behind her.

It was the Witch—Kris Vogal. In her hand was a signal jamming unit.

"Hand it to me," she said, nodding to the helmet in her hand.

Reese narrowed her gaze and did so slowly. Vogal reached into the helmet and pulled out her comm transmitter. "You'll get messages now, but not be able to send." She tossed the helmet back to her.

"How'd you know?" Reese asked.

"I didn't. The boss-man did. He told me that you might try to bring in the brass. We can't have that kind of interference…not now."

"I hate you," she managed.

"I know. I don't care—but I know. If it had been my choice, I would have hogtied and gagged you. The boss clearly thinks a lot of you. You chose to pay him back with betrayal. I suggest that you focus on the Fish. This will all sort itself out after we are out of here." The gunfire sounded like it was getting closer, enough for Vogal to look off to the west. "When this is all over, you can track me down and we can settle up. I'm fine with that. We didn't invite you along on this trip, but we expect you to kill the Fish all the same. Understood?"

Reese jammed her helmet back on and refused to give the Witch the satisfaction of an answer.

CYCLE III

Headquarters, Foxtrot Sector, the Western Front, West Los Angeles AIZ, California, the United States

The Army Corps of Engineers had turned the warehouse where battlespace command was centered into a bunker, and with good reason. The coordination of the battlefield was done from that location. Resources from artillery to air support were directed from there, as well as assessment of enemy strength and movement. It was the eyes, ears, and command voice for any field commander that were fighting the Fish.

Lieutenant Colonel Derek Logan stormed in and went right to Captain Weiser who had contacted him a few minutes earlier. "Captain, explain to me how we could have mounted a major operation in Beverly Hills without my knowing about it?"

Weiser was clearly nervous, his face tensed up. "Sir, both Open Hostility and the Ghost Legion were on recon missions—fairly standard. We have a glitch with tracking them. Their chips were not relaying biosignatures and were very tightly clustered. I reset the presumed it was a glitch in the system, especially when they stopped responding to my signals. Procedures call for them to fall back. I was focused on the current op, zoomed in on that one, and assumed they were heading home." He was admitting he screwed up, which took a lot for an officer. *Most would try to cover their asses—this guy owns his shit.*

"It's okay, Captain, we all make mistakes. How did you find out they were there?"

"I got a garbled voice message from Open Hostility's liaison. It was just bits and pieces. I did a check on her position and that's when I started to piece it together. By the time I was able to access a Predator to validate their positions, they had converged on Beverly Hills. Now I have detected another force, Spartan Associates—a PMC. All of them are in Beverly Hills."

Logan looked at the holographic display and was dismayed. *Three miles in behind enemy lines! We've been slugging it out for a block or two at a time. These people have punched a hole deep behind the front. God bless them for that!* "What's their situation?"

The image zoomed out and he could see the identifying dots of lights of the alien forces, all starting to shift towards his people's position. "I'm not getting bio readings from the units, I only know they are there. Spartan Associates aren't chipped; I had to figure out who they were by reviewing satellite feeds of their movements.

"The Fish are sending in the heavies—Bosses and Tanks. It's like throwing chud to the sharks. They are going to get hit and hit hard."

Logan stood erect and crossed his arms. He wanted to know why they were that deep behind the lines—but that could be sorted out later. And Ryland—he had underestimated the lieutenant. *This is exactly the kind of aggressive commander we need at the front.* Memories of what happened to his predecessor rose to the forefront of Logan's mind. *He didn't make any progress and they transferred him away. I'm not going to face the same fate as him.*

Captain Weiser broke his thoughts. "Sir, I have tried to order them out of there, but neither Lieutenants Stevens nor Ryland are acknowledging my messages."

"You want them out of there? Why would you want that?"

"Sir, look at the display. They might get wiped out if they don't fall back."

"To hell with that. What support can you provide them?"

"Sir?"

Logan stared at the holographic display that was projected vertically in front of Weiser's workstation. *He sees this as a mistake. This is an opportunity. They have punched a hole in the lines and have established themselves deep inside the enemy lines.* "Son, we are not going to pull them out, we are going to drive right to them and redefine the front."

"Yes, sir," the captain replied.

"So, what can you do from here?"

Weiser scrolled through several virtual windows in the air in front of him. "I can direct bombing and strafing runs on the alien force. It won't stop them—but it will slow them. We have enough for a short rocket bombardment as well from Charlie Battery. As you know, sir, we are limited by the munitions shortage."

"Not enough. We need a *thrust* to Beverly Hills. I want all of my platoons to thrust out and link up with them."

"Yes, sir," Weiser replied. "Sir, that will leave the front line with no defense. Not to mention there's a lot of enemy forces sitting between our lines and where our people are dug in."

"Damn it, we are redefining the front lines. Let me deal with that. This is too perfect for us to not take advantage of."

"Two of your platoons are still recovering from their ops yesterday. That leaves you with three we can throw in right now. I have one additional militia unit in this sector, the Savage Penguins, which I can mobilize as well."

In his mind, Logan was looking at the map and performing the mental calculations of war. The force was enough to reach Beverly Hills, but not to hold it. *I don't want to get there and give it up to the Fish. We need to change the front—and this is the opportunity to do that.* He had been waiting for the right opportunity to change the game in Foxtrot Sector, and now he had it. The problem was, he didn't have enough resources to fully exploit it.

He arrived at a decision, one fraught with risks, but worth taking. "Contact Golf and Echo commands. Patch me through to their COs."

"Yes, sir," he said, his fingers flying on the keyboard.

It took a few minutes, but he soon heard the voices of his counterparts on the flanking fronts. "I'll cut to the chase. I have a force that has made it in as far as Beverly Hills. This is an opportunity to retake a big chunk of the city—but I'm going to need more resources than I have. Can you spare any troops that can help me exploit this and breakthrough to our people?"

Colonel Gomez spoke up. "I have a platoon of armor that I can get to your sector within the hour."

Armor...perfect. He knew Gomez was a no-nonsense commander. "Thank you, Dan."

Colonel Hollifield of Golf Sector was on the call, voice only. "Most of my people are tied up in an operation here. I have one unit that I can send your way—militia."

"Are they good?"

An image flickered on the conference call screen of the logo for the unit. It spoke louder than any words that Hollifield could say out loud.

"Damn—thank you, Klaus," Logan replied with a hint of relief in his voice. "Have your people coordinate with Captain Weiser, Foxtrot's battlespace commander." The call came to a quick end and Logan patted Weiser on the shoulder. "That should be more than enough," he said to the junior officer.

"Yes, sir." The unit that Hollifield had offered up was a shot in the arm in terms of confidence.

"I'm going to get my gear on. You will need to relay to me directly in the field."

"Sir?"

"I'm going in with the troops."

"Sir, that is most...irregular."

Logan flashed a smile. "I know my job is here, but I want to be on the scene in case this situation turns south." Like it or not, the sixth battle for Beverly Hills was already underway.

Seven months earlier…

Commerce Bank, Beverly Hills, the Western Front, California, the United States of America

Antoine Billings stood in the lobby as the rumbles of the battle grew in both volume and intensity. He had never felt more alone. The security guards had left and the Army had come by again to tell him to evacuate. His refusal had sounded impressive enough when he had spoken it, but as soon as the soldier left, he had rushed to the restroom and thrown up. Now, judging by the sounds of the fighting he heard, there was little hope of getting out. *If I open that door, I'd be stepping into a battle.* Glancing down at his own body, he had to admit he'd be the best dressed person in the fighting, but that would likely make him an easy target. Setting the locks on the exterior door, the lights once more flickered.

The power was going to fail soon, he knew that. Reaching into his jacket pocket, he felt his Sig Sauer pistol and touched it enough to give him a sense of confidence. Even if power failed, there was a backup for the vault. The door could be opened from the inside. The vault now represented more than the holdings of his clients, it represented perhaps the only safe place in all of Beverly Hills.

As he walked into the vault, he heard a nearby explosion outside of the bank, one that made the entire building quake. Once inside, he opened the small panel and entered his code to close the door. The big circular steel door slowly swung closed. On the inside, he watched the locking bolts slide out, sealing him in.

Billings looked around and realized the only furniture were some chairs used when counting was done or when someone was accessing their deposit boxes. In the stark white light, he pulled over a chair and sat down. It was in that moment, he realized that he had not brought any food or water with him.

He remembered the specifications of the vault. It was airtight, but there was a fifteen-hour air supply. The fighting had to be over by then. He settled into the chair, and the lights went off. A cold wave of fear washed over him. Then the emergency backup lights, much smaller, much dimmer, came on.

Even sealed in the vault, he could hear distorted rumbles of the fighting. Billings forced a smile to his face, an act of false bravado for his own satisfaction. He had never been in a war before, let alone one with aliens. *The Army will drive them away; it will only take a few hours. Once they are gone, I will open the door and step out.*

He absentmindedly checked his phone but saw he had no signal...*of course, I'm in the vault.* He wanted to chuckle, but couldn't. For a short time, he flipped through the pictures on his phone and tried to take his mind off the deeply muffled noises he heard outside. Then it hit him—he might need his phone once he got out. He powered it down and put it in his jacket pocket.

There was nothing to do but sit and think. His clients would be coming as soon as he reopened. *They will want their holdings that we have for them; it's perfectly natural.* In his pocket were the master keys for the safe-deposit boxes or to make withdrawals. It required two keys to open them, but there was a set of master keys that could be used—for emergency situations. Different master keys went to different boxes, an additional level of security. They were necessary; sometimes clients forgot their keys, or outright lost them. *They will come, and I will be here to greet them. They will be thankful for what I have done for them. I will be able to raise prices and they will pay them without even flinching. That is the true measure of the service that I provide.*

Time passed strangely for Billings. He had no idea what hour it was. For a while, he paced the vault. There were periods of long minutes where he heard nothing, perhaps a sign the fighting was over. Then it would start up again.

At one point he settled down on the floor, lying up against the wall. Pulling his coat tight, he eventually was able to close his eyes and get some sleep. It was not easy at first, but slowly he drifted off. His last thoughts were of the work he would have to do to repair the damage that the fighting likely had done to his business…his legacy. He never noticed when the backup power failed, or that the stagnant air in the vault had been exhausted.

CHAPTER 22

Operation Goldfinger, Beverly Hills, the Western Front, California, the United States

Dawes heard the rumble of something approaching from the northeast, coming down Dayton Way. The thuds of the feet didn't sound like the approach of any alien he had faced before. It was a rumble, like that of a stampede, the ground rattling under him. His first thought was that it could be one of those Megas—a Cthuga, as they had been dubbed. Like most people, he had seen images of them on the net. They were gigantic creatures, usually used against targets deep in the interior. No, this was something else.

"Anyone have eyes on whatever that is?" he asked.

Calcutt's voice came online. "It's one of their Tanks," he said. "Confirm one coming down Dayton, with three Bosses on it."

"I've got four Crabs coming down Brighton," came Rice's voice.

The words were ominous. A single Boss alien was a major threat —three of them was terrifying. In the back of his mind, he wondered if it was worth cutting and running. They could escape with whatever was loaded in the trucks and leave Ryland and Stevens holding the bag. The only thing that held him in check was that it had only been a few minutes since he had left the bank. *My people haven't had enough time to get enough of the boxes out. We need to buy them time.*

"Concentrate our firepower on that Tank and the Bosses," he said. "I'm on my way."

Trying to move fast through the clutter of abandoned vehicles and debris in the street was difficult, but he pressed on. As he rounded the corner, he saw the charging Tank. The alien was a massive cross between a turtle and an elephant. The legs were huge, at least a yard in diameter, and moved with blazing speed as the creature rushed straight down the street. Where Dawes had been forced to move around cars littering the road, the alien simply plowed into them, hurling them aside. It had a massive low-slung head with a huge thick armored plate protecting its skull and acting like a plow blade. Its lower jaw jutted forward with a row of jagged teeth. A spiky fin started at the back of its head up the curve of its huge body, and down its back to the tail. The alien's tail jutted out a good six feet and flattened out to a paddle that was covered with white bone-like spikes. The fin seemed to flex, almost as if it were tied to the alien's breathing. As it charged, the tail flicked side to side, slamming into cars and flipping several, so strong was its run.

Hanging on to the turtle-shell-like bulky body were three of the obsidian-black Bosses. They were roughly humanoid shaped, but all muscle. Each had a strange tattoo-like pattern on their massive bodies, and two that he saw had tattoos shimmering bright red. The head of the deadly aliens narrowed to a slit where its eye, a shimmering crimson glow, was set. They all released at once, jumping off. Standing at a dozen feet in height, with highly pressurized suit/skins, they landed with thuds of their own, grinding into the pavement.

Aiming his Wolverine assault rifle, he targeted the charging Tank, aiming at the head. The shots were hitting. He saw flickers of some shots being deflected, others may have penetrated—he couldn't tell. Grenades were thrown in the creature's path and the explosions were violent. At first, they seemed to have no effect. One grenade, a stacked one, went off under the jaw of the creature as it charged. That one made it skid to a stop, shaking its head violently.

The Bosses fanned out, firing their weapons at his people. One unleashed a spray of a gas cloud, no doubt one of their deadly toxins, at the building where Merndon was huddled. The gunfire stopped there, and Dawes hoped it was because the Iron Infidel was falling back and repositioning.

Another Boss aimed downrange towards him and fired a spiker. The small bony white spikes sprayed the area where Dawes tried to dive for cover. He felt an impact on his right leg in the thigh as he ducked, the shot's kinetic hit spread out by the shear thickening fluid. His leg ached and he glanced down and saw his STG had been ripped where the projectile had hit. It was clear that his blast plate was shattered, but it had done its job. For Dawes, it only cemented how dangerous the situation was.

He rose and fired at the Tank-alien as it pivoted in place, using its tail to whip the abandoned cars like projectiles into the buildings around it. He kept his shots low, aiming at the legs. He could see the flesh quake under the impacts but otherwise he saw no indication that his shots were digging deep. As he emptied his magazine, he dropped down behind a car and reloaded, then pulled out two stackable grenades.

Attaching them was as simple as a twist to join them. Flipping off the cover of the firing stud, he hit it and then rose. He threw the conjoined grenade and it spun in the air, landing near where the creature's tail connected with the body. He was ducking down as it went off, devouring the alien in a huge fireball and riddling it with thousands of bits of deadly shrapnel.

As the smoke cleared and the churning ball of flames and smoke rose skyward, Dawes could see that the alien was still alive—still furious. Huge chunks of flesh were missing from its tail, and a muscle-like tissue, grayish white, was oozing out through the gaps. The Crab seemed to turn and look right at him with its narrow-slit yellow eyes as gunfire rained down on it from several members of his team.

A deep, rolling, continuous, almost throbbing, sonic roar tore through the haze of the street. Dawes ducked again as bits of dust and debris hit him. What remained of windows on the street shattered, raining glass shards everywhere. The Boss fired a sonic blast, its undulating ripples tearing through the air. His eyes ached and his ears felt as if someone were sticking a hot poker in them. "Brutality—we need you here, now!" he called out, not sure what the volume of his voice really was.

As the blast finished, the huge Tank alien started to charge straight at him. Dawes squeezed off two rounds then broke into a run, heading for a building. Leaping into the store, he ran towards the back. A dozen strides in, there was an enormous crash as the massive creature smashed into the storefront. He reached a back door only to find it locked. He fired two bullets into the lock plate and slammed it hard with his shoulder. As he half-fell through the opening, spilling into the back alley, the tank-sized creature hit the front of the structure again. It tore through the brick and stucco as if it were barely an obstacle. The sounds of crunching, grinding, and moaning all around him only propelled Dawes to run farther and faster. Getting distance between him and the Tank was all that he could focus on.

The building started to collapse on the alien, which stopped its charge and seemed to turn in place, shaking off the tons of debris that came down on top of it. Dawes wanted to run, but his leg ached as if he had been kicked by a horse, compounded by the fact that the STL armor was still stiff from the impact. He rapidly limped down the alley as the structure slowly crumbled, aided by the violent swish of the big alien's tail. As he spilled out onto the street, he was passed by the Phalanx ASHUR heading towards the battle.

The ASHUR slowed its run, leveling its arms at the alien in the middle of the collapsed building. Dust rolled out at almost head-height in every direction from the collapse, but Lynch held her ground, aiming carefully as the Tank turned and twisted, throwing off debris in every direction. *Bang*—she fired a power shell, re-popping Dawe's ear that he hadn't known was popped in the first place. The large laser flickered, like a camera flash. The shot seared a black mark on the armored body of the beast, searing deep into its hide. Smoke rolled out of the hole, making the alien stop its contortions and turn to face this new threat.

Lynch juked aside, unleashing two rockets into the creature. The armor-piercing high-explosive rounds hit with a pair of loud *ka-whomps*, flashing bright orange and yellow as they punched deep. Bits of the creature's armored shell flew off, spinning and flailing in the air from the penetrating blasts.

The massive dinosaur-like creature twisted again, hard. Its massive mouth opened wide and roared. The sound was not like anything Dawes had ever heard before—it was a strange mix of a whale call, mixed with a bear or lion, which did something rare—it made him feel afraid. It was good that the creature was hurt, but a wounded animal was a dangerous one.

Despite being half covered in debris, the creature hunched down then sprang into the air. Dawes was unable to process what was happening. *It shouldn't be able to jump—not with all of that mass.* It sprang right at the Phalanx. Lynch turned, raising one arm to deflect the impact, and the alien hit her like a runaway cement truck, knocking her rig back so hard, it flew into the side of building, leaving an almost perfect imprint where it crunched through the wall's stucco. Dawes fired again, at the side of the beast, from much closer range this time. Wet areas gleamed on the creature's legs and side, near the burn marks from his grenade. He hoped it was blood, that the alien was dying.

As he ducked to reload, he saw Lynch stagger to her feet. The front of the rig was crumpled, some of her armored plates were twisted outward from the impact. The Phalanx's cockpit canopy was bent from the blow, but she was still in the battle. Her grenade launcher banged out five rounds fast and furious, sending them straight at the beast's head, only a dozen yards away. The rolling explosions continued as Lynch staggered a few steps, still attempting to get her footing.

The Tank-alien darted its mouth at her, its huge jaw open, as if it meant to get to her and bite her. Dawes saw that one of its legs was badly damaged by the grenade blasts…bits of flesh were missing as if something had taken a big bite out of the knee joint. What may have been bone, an ebony hard thing in the center, was visible and apparently shattered. The thrust with the jaw fell short, by only two yards, positioning the head right in front of Lynch.

She crouched, leveling her laser and banging off a power shell. The laser was a flash of green, thanks to the dust in the air making it visible. It seared into the huge beast's head as Dawes squeezed off two round from his ACR into the blackened laser wound. The entire creature trembled for a moment, almost as if it was quivering either from cold or fear, then slumped flat to the pavement with a dull *whomp*. For a millisecond, he got a jolt of pleasure from the blast.

Dawes's focus shifted to the closest of the Bosses—emptying his magazine in a series of precision aimed shots. They hit their mark, but did not seem to even attract its attention. It fired another burst of spiker shots into one of the buildings, where some of his people had been sniping from. The entire storefront was chewed up with the organic ammunition. The shots that hit solid brick and didn't penetrate exploded, showering bits of brittle white shrapnel in every direction. Dawes reloaded and as he slapped in another magazine, Lynch moved past him—holding her ASHUR's left arm out. The forearm was covered in triangular rocket tubes and she fired one shot, then another at the Boss.

The first round slammed into its upper torso a few milliseconds after it cleared the tube, the explosion seeming to force the creature to stagger sideways a few steps. The second shot went low, hitting the Boss in the knee. The concussion from the two blasts made Dawes's chest throb and his head pounded angrily as the onyx alien toppled over.

One down. Rising, he targeted another Boss, about a half block down. He missed with one shot, but three more hit the lower body of that creature. Without warning, the one that Lynch had downed started to shift, using its forearms to pull itself up. The leg that had taken the rocket was a mangled and twisted mess just below the knee. It was spraying an oily liquid out like a garden hose on a jet spray setting. *No, that's not possible. He should be dead.* The alien reached down with its large claw-like hands and looked as if it was trying to suppress the injury.

It grappled with the lower limb and twisted it aggressively clockwise. With a pop and hiss, the lower leg came off. The flow of liquid ceased. The Boss reached up to a car next to where it fell and hoisted itself up, its big hands crunching through the hood and fender as it rose upright. Lifting one arm, it sprayed a cloud at Lynch's ASHUR, quickly engulfing the rig in a gray fog-like mist.

Dawes was in shock—he had never been this close to one of the living Bosses, let alone seen one that simply remove a damaged limb and continue to fight. The gas attack didn't deter Lynch; she moved forward, through the spray, opening up with her grenade launcher as

Dawes ducked for cover. Four fast rounds *thunked* out of the stubby barrel at the Boss. It reeled under the new explosions, toppling over onto the car it had used to climb up. The staggering weight of the creature blew the front tire out with a bang and it smashed through what was left of the hood. This time the alien did not rise.

The odds were more favorable, but still were not great. *What good is it if we take these guys out and we're too crippled to get back?* "Sit rep," he called on the tactical channel.

"Merndon has an arm injury," Reaper called back.

"I'm hit, but can move," Kerrigan called.

Hague's voice chimed in next. "I twisted my fucking ankle in a bad fucking way."

One of the Bosses unleashed another sonic blast that rippled down the street in his direction. A flying chuck of brick slapped into his visor, damaging his display. Dawes struggled with the pain; it was as if his forehead was about to explode. He felt something wet on his lip and licked it. Copper. His own blood, drizzling out of his right nostril. Sucking back, he could taste more of it now flowing down the back of his throat.

Lynch sent another rocket downrange at one of the Bosses as he focused. The explosion was muffled as he realized that his ears were popped. Fighting the aliens up close and personal was not the desired way. Suddenly there was a massive explosion—not artillery, something larger. The blast devoured the farthest Boss, along with four surrounding buildings. Bricks and bits of lumber from the structures clattered and rained down everywhere around his people. The concussive force of the blast was enough to nearly knock Dawes off his feet.

His agonized brain grappled with what the source was—a bomb. *Air support. We got air support!* As his people struggled with the rolling debris rising out of the crater that marked the demise of one Boss, he saw that the remaining one had been toppled over, face first, onto the road. Flames roared from several cars and the center of the blast crater.

Elation over the support faded quickly for Dawes. Air cover meant that the military knew they were there. *What else do they know?* Was their robbery of the bank now in the open? While he appreciated the bombing run, a rarity indeed in the AIZ, it might mean that more military forces were heading his way. *If the Army gets here, driving out with our trucks loaded up with the bank vault boxes is going to be problematic.*

The remaining Boss rose to his knees slowly, no doubt staggered by the force of the explosion that still was billowing white-gray smoke into the sky over Beverly Hills. The large alien struggled to his feet as gunfire from Spartan Associates pelted it from every angle. It took an almost drunken step forward, raising its arm to fire.

Lynch beat it to the draw. A power shell banged, though for Dawes the noise was muffled. He didn't see the laser fire; few people ever did get a glimpse of that happening. What he saw was a smoking hole, several inches deep, in the Boss's gut. Steam shot out of the hole, superheated and pressurized from the hide of the creature. The alien reached down to the hole with a claw, feeling where the laser had burned, almost as if it were caressing the wound. Then it fell forward, crunching onto the road, unmoving. While that creature was down, it didn't mean that the Fish were calling it quits. *They will come again, they always do.*

The sounds of battle thundered all around the Hills as Dawes contemplated their next step. He had never planned on letting his new "partners" get a fair cut. It had been his intention to load his trucks up and then they could have whatever was left. The problem was that the fighting might not have bought them enough time to clean out most of the vault. Using his wristcomp, he signaled Diamond Jones on a private channel. "Where are we at, Diamond?"

"Honestly, sir, we could use another couple of hours. We've pulled the target box and are dragging out the others, but there's only two of us here—it's a slow go."

"How much have you pulled?"

"Only about a third of the boxes. Two trucks are fully loaded already. These things take up a lot of room."

A third…not great, but definitely worth the risk. "Step it up—we are going to start to fall back towards your position."

"Yes, sir."

Lynch signaled him as he finished with Diamond. "Sir, there's a lot of activity down North Beverly. That Rattlesnake is engaged down there. I request permission to provide assistance."

He wanted to say "no," but didn't. She was a recent addition to Spartan Associates and that meant he wasn't sure how she might react to him betraying his word to Stevens and Ryland. *I don't want to raise any suspicions with Lynch that we are abandoning these people until we actually do it.* "Permission granted. Keep yourself positioned to come back and reinforce us if needed."

"Roger that," she said, and the ASHUR took off towards where MacLeod was fighting.

They'll call me crook, a douchebag, and a traitor when this is over. The key is not caring. I'd rather be a rich traitor than a poor hero any day of the week. Dawes opened a channel to his people, blocking the signal to Lynch. "Listen up, Spartans, we need to start falling back towards the bank. We do this gradual, steady—with suppression fire as each fire team makes a move."

"We're falling back?" came the surprised voice of Reaper.

"That's right, Ted. We're going to load up what we can and get out of here."

"Boss, you promised to help these people."

"And we did. This is about the bottom line. Now, gather up our wounded and start to fall back before any more of the enemy show up."

CHAPTER 23

Operation Sundance, Beverly Hills, the Western Front, California, the United States

Mark Stevens watched with a hint of joy as the pair of Crabs swiftly rushed into the kill box that he and his people had formed on Charleville Boulevard. It was just west of where they had fought so hard at the California Pizza Kitchen and his people had held their fire from their positions in the buildings and rooftops flanking the street. As much as a part of him was happy about the enemy he intended to kill, he also understood that when it came to the Fish, few things went as planned.

His own position was behind a burned-out dump truck that was resting on its charred wheel rims. Stevens had climbed into the back of it, relying on the thick metal sides to provide him better cover than a late model Prius on the street. There was some stagnant water pooled in part of the truck bed, complete with the stench that came with it—but he tuned all of that out.

Also in the back of the dump truck was Coyote and Bowers. Bowers was wet with sweat, his camouflaged shirt dripping perspiration from under his STG. Every aspect of how he fought was just like any other member of Open Hostility. Coyote was nervous; it showed in the way he jerked and twitched at every sound. Despite his fear, the professional scrounger somehow summoned the courage to stand up in the truck bed and aim out.

"Sir," came Vogal's slow, tense voice. "Please tell me it is time to unalive these things." In his mind, he could see her looking down the sights of her ACR, lining up the shot.

"Alright, Hostility, you heard the Witch. Kill 'em."

Gunfire rang out simultaneously from three different directions. The Crabs jerked in response for a few moments, then proceeded down the street, right at his position. His shots were single, well-aimed, right at the head of the lead Crab. A trio of grenades went off at the rear Crab, kicking up debris and smoke that cast a haze everywhere in the kill box.

The lead Crab fired a squirter, sending a large glob of greenish acid right at the dump truck. Stevens ducked instinctively, as did Bowers. Coyote almost didn't, but Bowers reached up and pulled his employer down hard onto the bed.

The acid hit the side of the dump truck and some splattered over the top, hitting the far side. It hissed, and the white smoke rising off it reminded Stevens of paint remover. Even with the filters on his mask, it stung his nostrils and at the back of his throat. Looking up between where he and Bowers had dropped, he saw a sizzling hole form where the corrosive was eating through the metal. It started out small, like a ping-pong ball, then the eroding corrosive patch grew to the size of a beach ball, filling the truck bed with the stink of its handiwork.

Coyote looked at it and even with his visor down, Stevens could see the man's jaw dropping.

"Don't touch any of the edges," Stevens told him. "It'll burn you even an hour from now."

He rose and fired three more shots at the lead Crab as it turned to the left and unleashed another spray of globular acid at a storefront. The turning gave Stevens a fresh angle on the raised torso, and his shots all hit the shoulder joint for the large left claw. He knew he must have penetrated the flesh, because the Crab turned violently, stabbing its tail right at the dump truck. For a moment, it felt as if he were inside a bell, the entire truck bed rang loudly as he was diving for cover. The deep thud was followed with a scraping noise, no doubt from the tip. Looking up, he saw that the impact was visible in the side of the vehicle.

Bowers pulled out a grenade, pulled the tab and hit the activation stud. Rising a little, he tossed it out onto the street. He ducked down and a few seconds later the grenade went off, once more making the bed of the dump truck ring like a bell. Another blast went off before he could rise and shoot again, no doubt from another grenade.

Rising up, Stevens aimed his ACR, but saw that the Crab was no longer moving. Three of its shorter legs used for propulsion were twisted and gnarled by one or more of the blasts. The oily ooze for blood was already starting to spread from under it.

"Good work, people," he transmitted. Glancing down the street and felt his stomach tighten. There were two of the massive Boss aliens rushing down the street toward where the Crabs had been blown up. Each thud of their feet was audible, even from the two-block distance. *Things just got worse.*

Instead of rushing into the kill box as the Crabs did, the pair split up, each taking one side of the street. On the left, the alien paused, using a slicer, opening up on the storefronts where Open Hostility had taken their positions during the initial ambush. The high pressure water beam chewed through the buildings as if it were a surgical laser beam—searing deep into the interior. The occupants of the dump truck fired away at the creature, but nothing seemed to distract it from its task. Concentrating its efforts on one storefront in particular, the Boss took out enough of the internal structure on the ground floor that the entire front half of the building collapsed with the sickening sound of pulverizing concrete.

The other ebony Boss sprang at the parking garage where Wrench had been set up on the roof. Using its massive arms and webbed clawed hands, the alien hoisted itself up the side of the garage. On one metal guard rail where it planted its foot, it bent the pipe down visibly, a testimony to its incredible weight. Despite its size and bulk, it scurried up the structure. When it didn't find a handhold, it simply drove a claw into the structure, punching it deep enough to secure a grip.

"Wrench—run! Get out of there," Stevens ordered in the closest thing to a panic that he had felt in a long time.

In two beats of his heart, the alien reached the roof. Shots came at it, some from within the structure as it climbed, others from across the street, but nothing seemed to deter its onslaught. Once on the roof, it bounded in two controlled jumps. For a moment, it was out of sight. Gunfire from at least two people roared from the rooftop—a cacophony of fully automatic carnage. *God, I hope Jon gets away…*

* * *

After Vogal had torn off her transmitting module, Reese had considered simply leaving. The problem was that she was far safer staying with Open Hostility than risking the long trek back to the friendly lines alone. She hoped that her message had gotten through to someone in the Army's command structure, but there was no way to know for sure. Of all her options, staying and fighting with her unit was the safest choice…one that offered the best chance for survival.

Stevens had ordered her to the parking structure and she had angrily stomped her way there. The killing of the Crabs had proved hard enough, but now the Bosses were coming. They were not moving into the kill box, but down the flanks. *They are smart—they used the Crabs to flush out our positions. Now they are coming to kill us all.* That realization, that the Bosses were intelligent, was terrifying. So much of what the Fish did seemed animalistic. Throwing in thoughtful tactics was a frightening proposition.

Reese was poised on the third floor of the parking structure and saw the huge Boss scaling the side of the building. The scrape of its claws digging into the structure itself was chilling as she moved away from her position on the edge. It appeared right in front of her as it climbed. Moving perpendicular to its ascent, she emptied a magazine into it at point-blank range as it rose to the floor above her, the roof of the parking structure. The shots hit the beast's hide, but she could not see any indication that any rounds had penetrated. The alien didn't slow to see her, which she was thankful for. Several bullets fired from the rest of the team missed the obsidian creature and ricocheted around the parking deck enough to make her duck for cover. Then she realized that she wasn't the target it was going for. *Aw shit—Wrench!*

Wrench was on the roof, alone, one floor above her. She liked Offerman—but against a Boss, he was horribly outmatched. Reese sprinted to the stairs. She feared that she would be too late. The crack of gunfire from outside the structure told her the alien was still very much alive.

Racing up the stairs, she nearly stumbled on the last few, managing to catch herself from falling on her face. Reese slammed into the door that led to the roof of the structure. Offerman was twenty feet from the edge of the building where the Boss stood, firing away with his ACR as he drifted back.

Standing her ground, Reese fired a series of aimed shots at the creature, hitting it in the neck and upper body. The bullets made impact—she could see the faint ripples on impact—but none seemed to do any real damage. Several hits oozed a trickle of grayish ooze, but it was impossible to know if that was significant. Wrench drifted towards her, swapping in a fresh magazine as he moved.

The Boss jumped at Wrench, its webbed feet landing so hard that the concrete cracked under it. The leap was so big that Reese was only a few yards from the creature—and she realized that this was closer than she had ever been to a Boss before. Panic tried to overtake her, but she backstepped as she fired, making her way back toward the staircase.

The Boss lunged and swung one clawed hand through the air, leaning in at her. The claws on the large hand ripped at her STG, tearing at the Kevlar outer layer and sending her flying into one of the cars on the same level. The vehicle's alarm blared from her impact on it. The shear thickening fluid stiffened in her lower back where she collided with the door of the Fiat, crumbling it inward. Her neck and back throbbed, and the air was knocked from her lungs, forcing her to gasp for breath. While the panic tried to surge and take control of her, Reese managed to keep it in check.

Getting air in her lungs was a struggle, but she finally managed to get a gasp of air. The Boss lunged at Wrench with one clawed hand, sinking the four-inch, sharp, bone-like spikes right into his chest. His helmet flew off and his gun went limp. *No!* Her own hands fumbled for her ACR as Offerman seemed to go limp. He wasn't dead—he moaned in agony as the Boss pulled the claws free, then grabbed him with both hands by his shoulders. The alien lifted him up to eye level and Wrench looked as if he were trying to twist free, but to no avail.

* * *

For a moment, there was no sound at all from the parking structure, to the point where Stevens was hopeful that the alien had been taken down. There was gunfire on the roof of the building, the sounds of at least two weapons firing quickly. Then the gunfire ceased. The Boss returned, both arms held aloft. In its grip was the bloodied body of

Jon "Wrench" Offerman. With his free arm Wrench was futilely striking the alien's forearm. In that moment, Stevens knew that he was going to throw him down the four stories to the street below and there was nothing anyone could do about it. Helplessness hit him harder than any alien weapon in that moment.

The Boss didn't throw him down, instead his arms pulled away from each other. It was a struggle, but then he ripped Wrench in half. Intestines and blood flowed down on the black hide of the alien, and it seemed to revel in it for just a moment. Then it unceremoniously tossed both halves of his man down onto the abandoned cars on the street. The thud filled Stevens's ears despite the gunfire filling the street.

He had known Jon for five years—hired him when he had been down on his luck, living on the streets. Offerman had some basic carpentry skills, but working for his construction company, he had found his place in life. His trim work was exceptional, everyone on the team acknowledged that. When the war had come, his family had fled to relatives in Kansas for safety. Jon had needed work, that was why he had stayed with Stevens when he had proposed forming Open Hostility. It was not a profession for him, it had been a way to put food on his family's plates.

And now Mark was going to have to tell them he was dead.

"Sprang—break out Carl and kill that bastard," he ordered.

"On it, skipper," Sprang replied. The Boss stood at the edge of the roof of the parking structure as shots riddled it, almost as if it were bravado—as if it were taunting the militia. Then came the bang of the Carl Gustaf that Sprang fired. The shot hit the Boss in the chest, punching into its outer shell and exploding. The blast was massive, throwing the alien backwards in a ball of red and orange flames and an explosive spray of gray organic material from within the creature.

* * *

The heat from the explosion made Reese cringe. The STL layer of her armor stiffened from the blast and her face, even through her visor, felt sunburned. She had seen the alien blown up in front of her and the bio-matter released had showered her in a luke-warm gray-wet film. Her ears rang from the explosion, adding to the pain in her back. Glancing down at her legs, she saw some sort of organ or gland was splayed across one of them as the alien's twisted lower torso collapsed forward, tumbling to the street below where he had thrown the pieces of Wrench.

Her gloved fingers trembled as she flicked the tissue off her leg. Moving slowly through the shock, her back throbbing from the pain of being hit, she checked her STG. The razor-sharp claws had cut through her webbing, leaving one of her ballistic plates exposed with a scratch across it.

Straining and fighting back a wave of nausea, Reese got to her feet, thankful for the STF that was still rigid on her back. *If that stuff hadn't worked, my spine might have been broken.* The image of Jon being ripped in half by the creature was something that was now imprinted in her mind—a memory that was destined to haunt her forever. Her first two steps were awkward, imbalanced, a mix of the pain she felt and the almost crippling fear that grabbed her. She made her way to the stairway door and started down. To her, the stairwell felt safe, though the gunfire she heard from the street told her differently.

Wrench's death is on Stevens's head. He's responsible for it as much as that Boss. If he hadn't brought the unit into the AIZ, Offerman would still be alive. The image of her teammate being ripped in half still made her stomach knot. Those thoughts, mixed with the pain she felt, made her resolve even stronger, and her hate for where she was and why she was there surge. She had seen deaths before, but this one hit her harder, punching her already battered soul.

This whole war is as fucked up as a football bat. We have no idea what these aliens want or why they are here. They just want to kill us and we want to kill them. No matter how many we slaughter, more show up. Is there any end to this?

As she reached her former floor of the parking structure, she paused. *There's got to be a way out of this living hell. I can't take this—first being betrayed by the CO, and now seeing Wrench killed right in front of me. Goddamn it—I am covered in the guts of that alien!* She stopped and pulled a plastic bottle of water from her side pouch. It had miraculously not burst in the melee. Taking a sip, she noticed that her fingers were still trembling from the adrenal rush. The sound of the gunfire prodded her to move on, to rejoin the fight —but she hated the fact that she was doing it. *I don't want to end up like Wrench.* She checked her magazine and saw she had three rounds left according to the side indicator. *Come on, Shelly—get your head back in the game. This battle isn't over—not by a long shot. When the dust settles, you need to find a way to make this right —if not for Wrench, then for yourself.* She took another sip of the water, stowing the rest of it back in her waist pouch.

In that moment, Shelly Reese realized she understood Mark Stevens and why he was undertaking the mission. *He probably feels the same way I do. This war is just going to result in more dead people...his people. This is his way to get out of the war, not for himself, but for the entire unit.* It angered her that she understood his motivation, simply because she now shared it. Wrench's death had changed her—it had opened her eyes. *His reason is wrong, but he's doing it for the all the right reasons.*

Does that make it right?

* * *

An icy resolve filled Mark Stevens's body as he watched the mangled torso of the Boss hit the street, slightly cratering the sidewalk where it fell. It landed on the gore of Offerman who it had torn in half. For a moment, he had hoped that the death of the alien might ease the rage and pain he felt at the loss of one of his people. It didn't at all.

Movement farther down the street caught his attention. Crabs... at least three...and another Boss. *I can't catch a damn break.* "Boss," came Vogal's voice. "You seeing what's coming?" His experienced gaze saw that the Bosses were starting to climb the buildings. One of the Crabs broke off at an intersection, no doubt starting to move to flank his team.

The decision was simple—stay and fight with an enemy that likely knew his positions and would avoid his kill box, or redeploy to better ground. He switched to his unit channel so everyone could hear. "Alright, people, we are moving. Head north to the Beverly Wilshire. Vogal, you and your team get in that wing of the building that is still standing. You have the high ground. The rest of us are going to take positions in the rubble. We need to move, people, hoof it!"

CHAPTER 24

Operation Sundance, Beverly Hills, the Western Front, California, the United States

Frank Ryland saw the greenish-brown lumbering Turtle-Tank creature coming at him down Wilshire Avenue. He had faced one of these garbage truck–sized creatures before and had hated every moment of the encounter. The one rushing towards the Ghost Legion's position was moving like a charging rhino. Whenever a car or a dumpster was in its way, it would collide with it head-on, flicking it aside with its powerful neck.

On its own, the creature was intimidating. What made it more imposing was the fact that holding on to its side was a Boss alien, skin as black as the night sky. They were at least coming down the street, giving his Ghosts good crossfire opportunities. Sergeant Calcutt had his fire team poised in the sushi restaurant and small French bakery across from his fire team. Winston was on top of a building a little farther down, his sniper rifle no doubt tracking the incoming threat. Ryland's remaining fire team were spread out in three different buildings. In the center of the street he had poised Corporal King, his GRDs, Mullins, and Finn were hiding behind a bank's armored car that had been blown onto its side during one of the other battles for Beverly Hills.

"Listen up, people," Ryland said. "We need to take down that Tank first, then the Boss. Take your time, get good aim—watch your distance as they close. Mullins, Finn—break out the heavy gear and prepare to engage."

King's three GRDs consisted of two Husky haulers that had brought their heavy weapons—a battered Carl Gustaf and three precious rounds of ammo, and a light rail gun. His last drone was a Tarantula, good for short range fire with a back mounted chain gun, and held in reserve. *Hopefully we won't get that close to where we need that one.*

As the charging aliens reached a block and a half out, Ryland knew he had them entering his kill zone. "Alright—Mullins and Finn, take your shots. The rest of you engage when they cross El Camino."

He glanced down the street to his left where the pair stepped out. Mullins had the recoilless launcher and Finn brought out the bulky rail gun. Both took a moment to settle into position, kneeling, and aiming carefully. Ryland turned his gaze to the approaching enemy.

Mullins fired first. The round hit above the head of the Turtle-Tank with a large explosion that tore off one of the armored shell plates on the alien, sending it flying behind. The blast was enough to dislodge the Boss that was holding on. It fell and rolled along the pavement—slamming into a long abandoned car, demolishing it with a sickening metallic grinding noise.

The Tank alien's charge was not stopped but definitely slowed. As it emerged from the blast smoke, he could see that it had taken a hit. The hole the round had left was smoking white and the alien shook its head, no doubt stunned by the explosion. There was a bang of a power shell going off from Finn, and a second later, a blur raced down the street, slapping into the body of the creature not far from the first hit. The hole it made was not large, but there was a gush of black-green fluid that shot out of it. *That's going to leave a mark...*

The rail gun round was enough to make the beast halt, if only momentarily. It opened its huge jaw and roared as the gunfire broke out from both sides of the street. The sound was grotesque, deeply disturbing—unlike any one Earth creature. There was a mix of different noises, twisted and contorted into a sound that sent shivers up Ryland's spine.

Another bang went off as Mullins charged for another shot. The conical metallic projectile slammed into the front knee of one of the big legs, blowing a hole clean through the limb and spraying the street with bits of flesh and gore, some of which splattered the Boss, who was in the process of rising to its feet.

Despite the damage, the Turtle-Tank rushed forward with an erratic limp, then lunged off to the side, whipping its massive spiked tail into the building next to Ryland's where Private Canton was poised on the roof. The tail swept into the structure, ripping out the supports of the lower floors as the team poured more shots at the abomination. The lower floor of the three-story structure moaned for a moment, then collapsed, bringing the large portions of the upper floors down with it. Dust and debris rolled into the street, blocking all vision as it rode up on a California breeze. *Canton!* He could only hope at this point that his sniper had somehow managed to survive the collapse of the building.

The dust-filled air clogged his visor's filters and all he could hear was the tail of the creature swiping back and forth across the street where Calcutt's people had taken position. The clatter of bricks spilling in the street and the crunch of glass grinding on the pavement filled his ears. *I can't get a good shot at this damned thing with all of this dust.*

The moment he glimpsed the alien through the haze, he fired— aiming at the neck. A grenade went off near the creature, adding to the chaos and carnage below. The wounded animal thundered past Ryland, down the street, heading for Mullins and Finn's positions, whipping its deadly tail, tearing into buildings as it ran. Suddenly it stopped, skidding to a halt on the pavement. The tail thudded to the ground. *Apparently someone's shot hit something important.*

As he turned back to face the Boss, a blast of hyper-compressed water hit the building where he was in, sounding like the crackle of thunder before the boom. The beam was like a grayish laser, destroying whatever it touched as it slashed horizontally through the building. His right shoulder was hit as he dove for cover, and he felt the armor stiffen as he fell. Looking over, he saw that his tactical gear had been cut off, along with his shoulder blast plate. There was blood on the severed uniform sleeve, but not much. *An inch in either direction and I would have lost the arm.*

Ryland ignored the pain and rose, aiming at the Boss and emptying his magazine in a series of short precise shots. The Boss turned away from him as if he posed no threat at all, spraying the other side of the street where his people were poised. It walked forward almost casually, as if its human opposition was a mere annoyance.

Ryland advanced to the broken window, swapping in a fresh magazine as he walked. The bangs of his gunshots mixed with those from the Ghost Legion who were still in the game. One of his rounds penetrated enough to elicit a large squirt of the alien's grayish black blood out from the hole, a bit of satisfaction. It was enough to make the Boss stop mid-stride, and slowly turn towards him.

Then came the explosion. The shockwave was enough to knock Ryland back on his ass, hard. The hair on his face—especially his eyebrows—got seared from the heat as he fell. His gloved fingers patted his skin on his forehead to make sure he still had some there. Mullins was still in the fight. While the Carl Gustaf was an excellent weapon against armor, what it did to the Fish was always impressive. Ryland's head throbbed as he scampered to his feet to see if the Boss was still there.

One large leg stood upright still, but had nothing else attached to it from the hip up. The other leg lay behind it, also severed. The head, shoulders, and arms of the Boss were splayed out on the street, unidentifiable organs lying between them and the legs. A large piece of the creature was simply gone, blasted into tiny bits everywhere. The smell was a mix of Fish and raw hamburger mixed with a hint of a burning wood aroma…sickening and inhuman.

"Nice shooting, Mullins," Ryland managed, his eyes transfixed for a moment on the upright detached leg looking so weird and out of place to him. "Sergeant Calcutt, we need to see if we can find Canton in that debris."

"Yes, sir. Grant, Raffi, get on it."

Ryland stepped through the window frame of the building he had been using for cover and surveyed the street. There was no other sign of the enemy, giving him a much needed minute to address his wound. From his med-pouch, he pulled out a wound binder patch and peeled the adhesive strip, placing it as best he could on the cut on his shoulder. It ached but he ignored it. *It hasn't killed me…yet.*

He moved over to where the building had been destroyed and saw Grant and Raffi pawing through the rubble, calling out Canton's name. Ryland ran over and joined them, pulling up large pieces of the debris and tossing them behind where the building had been. His wounded shoulder protested each time, but he ignored the throb of pain.

Then he heard it, a loud whistling noise overhead, followed by a thud. Then came another. Out of the corner of one eye, he caught a momentary glimpse of something—an object lobbed from the south towards the street. The Fish had their own artillery, though their shells usually were gas or a deadly organic fluid. There were no booms, only the thuds of something hitting the street.

"Casper," came Calcutt's voice. "You seeing that?"

"Yes, I am," he said firmly. Zooming in his helmet's visor, he glared down the street where the projectiles continued to land, just a half-block up from his position. There was a swirling of dust and debris in the street—then he caught a glimpse of them. Shiny, golf ball–sized orbs with legs and teeth. Intermixed with the tiny creatures were larger ones, roughly the size of baseballs. That was something new that the Army intel briefings had prepped him for.

The aliens had used them as weapons of terror when they had first made themselves known, unleashing them on unsuspecting communities. They were like amped-up sand fleas crossed with piranhas. Attracted to motion and sound, they moved in swarms. Within minutes, they could devour an unprotected human, ripping their victims apart with venomous-coated jagged sharp teeth. Since they had invaded, the Fish had taken to tossing them at troops. The official designation for them was Class IV Alien Species, but they had a half-dozen different names. Most troops in the field simply called them Goblins.

A human in full standard tactical gear was fairly well protected from them, but they could get at your neck, bite your hands, and find any gaps in your armor. It was like they could track soft flesh, exposed skin, eyes. Worse, as a swarm, they were hard to kill, given their speed and erratic jumping. Ryland and his people had dealt with them once before, and several of his team still bore the scars from the encounter.

"Grenades," he called out the Ghosts on the unit tactical channel. "Drop them in front and behind them." He took his own advice and pulled out a grenade and hit the firing stud. Lobbing it hard and long, he got it on the ground between two clusters of the Goblins. One swarm moved to it, clearly unaware of the threat. The explosion sent them flying in every direction. Two more grenades went off, throwing more into the sides of buildings or farther up or down the street.

The survivors were undeterred. They sprang in the air, hopping on the sidewalks, pavement, cars, anything they landed on.

One swarm jumped into the rubble where Grant and Raffi were working. Grant opened up on full auto, the bullets ricocheting every direction. That kind of attack was futile but there was no point in telling his people that—they had to try something to take them out. Emptying a mag on full auto might only hit a few, but a few was better than none.

King's Tarantula GRD was abuzz, its mini–chain gun firing controlled bursts as the drone hopped from one pile of rubble to the next, seeming to take on one swarm all on its own. When hit, Goblins exploded with each tiny burst it unleashed, and its movement only seemed to draw in more of them onto the drone. King himself joined in, letting the drone engage in autonomous mode, firing off several blasts from his personal shotgun. The sawed-off barrel made it worthless against larger Fish, but against the Goblins, it devoured several with each booming blast.

Another few of the shells carrying the Goblins came down, this time behind his unit as more grenades were cast. A trio of the Goblins emerged from the explosion, springing right at Ryland. One latched on to this protective right knee guard, while one tried to chew through his STG chest plates. The last crawled up his chest and was attempting to get in under his visor.

He grabbed the one trying to gnaw at his face and pulled it off, throwing it on the ground with a crack. If it was injured, the Goblin didn't show it, because it sprang right for his legs. Ryland twisted off the one on his chest as it attempted to bite his fingers. This time he dropped it then stomped it hard with his boot. It crunched and squished. Bending down and snatching at the others, he crushed them all.

Rising, he noticed his breath was out of control, almost hyperventilating, it was so fast. Training kicked in and he started to take air in through his nose and slowly out through his mouth. As he twisted back toward Raffi, he saw her with one of the larger baseball-sized Goblins clamped on to her hand. Flicking her hand hard, she couldn't shake it free. Blood squirted out from where its jagged teeth did their worst work. Ryland darted over to her and grabbed the alien with both hands, jerking it free from her now bloodied fingers. Larger than the trio that had hit him, this one was softball sized. It squirmed and twisted in its hands as it tried to take bites out of his flesh. "Get something heavy," he barked to Raffi who pulled out a shattered cement block.

"On three," he spat. "Three, two, one—" he tossed it on a piece of broken lumber in front of her. Raffi brought the brick down synchronized with his toss, crushing the legs of the Goblin with the block. The alien was still alive. It attempted to roll, gnashing its jagged white teeth at them, but was unable to move.

More grenades went off to the rear of the Ghost Legion as they attempted to fight off the new Goblin wave. *They will whittle us down if we stay here and try to kill all of them.* "Ghosts, this is Casper. We are redeploying north, toward the bank."

Glancing over at Raffi and Grant, he saw the latter rise up—"I've got him! I've found Canton." Raffi moved over to him and helped remove the last bits of debris, carefully pulling their teammate out of the rubble. His helmet was gone, as was his weapon. Everything was coated with gray dust. The only sign of life was that Canton coughed. "No time to check his injuries. You two move—I'll cover you," Ryland said. Both Raffi and Grant slid under Canton's limp arms on either side of him and took off, the wounded man's boots leaving drag marks in their wake.

Ryland followed them. The four of them cut down a narrow alley between two buildings. It was shaded and cooler, and he checked his six every few seconds. The Goblins seemed to re-form in the street, returning to whatever constituted a cluster to them—and started to follow. Ryland was halfway down the alleyway when they came, filling the space, bouncing off the walls and the ground, coming right at them. *I can't catch a break today.*

Pulling one of his grenades, he tossed it in their path—doing the mental calculation as to where to place it based on their speed. "Fire in the hole," he called out just before the grenade went off. The blast turned the alley into a dangerous echo chamber. Both of his ears popped, despite his helmet's protection. A ripple of debris rolled towards and over him and he pressed on, catching up with Raffi first, feeling her shoulder with his hands as the debris blocked his vision.

Ryland, Raffi, Grant, and Canton in tow burst out on the street, and he saw the rest of the unit a few yards away. His left ear popped first, and he could hear gunfire and explosions to the north, from the approximate area where Spartan Associates was posted. Likewise there were blasts going off to the east towards Open Hostility. *The Fish are pressing us on all fronts. We need to link up, form a single cohesive defensive position.*

His own people were firing at something near the ground just a few yards up from his position. At first, he assumed it was more

Goblins—but as he moved forward to see their targets, they were larger, scurrying on the ground like rabid rats, coming right towards the gunfire tearing into them. Their bodies were segmented and round, like an armadillo's. They had large slender slicing teeth, their ugly jaws menacing. Their speed was remarkable, no doubt thanks to their legs with the wide webbed claws that allowed them to push off. *Dillos—just want we didn't need.* Like the Goblins, they were swarming creatures whose bites were toxic to humans. Ryland brought his ACR to bear, firing at several of the creatures. He missed more than he hit, but the ones he hit were knocked back hard by the impact of his rounds. One died, but it took two bullets to kill another. It exploded, more than it should have, spraying a light greenish color of what he assumed was blood. One creature managed to dodge enough to reach Winston, locking its teeth on to his shin. The tall Texan let out a deep moan as Calcutt swung the stock of his ACR like a club, hitting the creature and sending it flying.

Winston's leg was bleeding—not a good sign. "Damn, it feels like it's on fire," he said, as the last of the Dillos was blasted. Winston was shaking, not from adrenaline, but from the effects of the venom.

"Hit him with a shot of Narcan," Calcutt ordered. The medication used to treat overdose had proven to be effective against the venom that the Dillos secreted. Raffi, a former nurse, came over and injected him. The shaking seemed to slow. "Can you walk?" Ryland asked.

Winston nodded, then gingerly tested the leg as Raffi helped him to his feet. "I'm still with you, Casper," he said, weak.

Tapping his wristcomp, he broadcast in the clear. "This is Casper, we are falling back toward the bank. What is your situation?"

"We are on our way there now," came back Dawes's voice.

"We just began our movement to the hotel and were going to set up our position there," Stevens replied.

A pair of Goblins burst out of the alley, one going for Calcutt, another at Raffi. Both soldiers paused, Raffi dropping Canton in the process, and pulled the aliens off, crushing the bony bodies under their boots. *It's a hell of a way to fight a war. I'm not sure if the Fish are trying to kill us, or if they are using the Goblins and the Dillos to herd us.*

"Very well, we will form up between the two of you. MacLeod, are you there? What is your status?" Nothing came back. He had complained of having comms issues…and that was what Ryland hoped it was. Then again, MacLeod was a bit of a loose cannon. *God only knows what he's up to.* "MacLeod, if you can hear us, we are falling back to the bank and hotel. Link up with us there."

CHAPTER 25

Operation Sundance, Beverly Hills, the Western Front, California, the United States

Sutherland MacLeod stood in the middle of North Beverly Drive in his ASHUR, eyeing the approaching threat with a deep inner resolve. A trio of Bosses were coming up the street one and a half blocks down, zigzagging, moving briskly to close the distance with him. Reaching out to his display controls, he zoomed in the image on the inside of his canopy for just a moment. *Come on—be one of these bastards.* He looked at each one of them in the face, searching for a distinctive mark.

Bingo!

One of the Bosses had a scar, a diagonal slash down from its forehead, across its vision slot, on its cheek.

"Is it I, God, or who, that lifts this arm?" he muttered, quoting one of his favorite books. All three of the aliens had bright green pulsating tattoo-like patterns on their body. The last time he had seen Scarface, he had an orange light coming from the pattern. There were a lot of rumors as to what the colors meant, everything from a means of communicating to some sort of rank markings. MacLeod didn't know nor did he care. All that mattered was lining the enemy in his sights and firing.

He raised his rig's SW-02X Sonic Disruptor and fired. The alientech version of the weapon was far more devastating and had a longer range…he was catching the enemy at the maximum reach of his version of the tech. At the long range, the ripples of sonic blast would hit all three of the Bosses. The air went out like a pebble thrown in a pond, only focused down the street. The air swirled with particles, hoisted and boosted by the blaster. MacLeod held the trigger down for a full five seconds, carefully watching his power levels as he did.

At first the Bosses seemed to ignore the ripples of deep, low decibel throbbing that hit them. After several moments, they started to react. One held up its arms to block its head. Another used his hands to bat at his head, no doubt because the attack was hurting it. The third, Scarface, leaned into the blasts in sheer defiance. *That's right, you fuckfaced bastard, it's me again.*

One of the Bosses held out its arm and unleashed a spray of spikes from a tube that ran to the back of the creature. MacLeod started to move as the arm came up, but several of the projectiles plowed into his ASHUR. One hit near the cockpit, shattering on the armor plating there. Two more dug into the legs of his rig. He felt them hit, hard enough to make him wince. According to the amber indicator on his damage display, one had penetrated his right shin but hadn't damaged any systems.

He hoisted his huge ACR, holding it with both hands of his rig, and brought the weapon to bear at his hip, aiming with the targeting reticle inside of his cockpit. He fired at the lead Boss as its pace in running increased. The large bullets tore into its lower body. One hit a thigh mid-step, and the impact was enough to topple the alien face-first on the street—grinding into the asphalt hard.

It was enough to make MacLeod crack a smile.

Another Boss unleashed a slasher beam at him. It fired over his right shoulder, then slashed down as MacLeod turned to target him. The beam tore into his ASHUR, cutting a furrow into his armor and searing a nasty mark across his cockpit canopy. It held, but MacLeod knew what it was, a warning. He could die quickly out here, behind enemy lines.

He brought his ACR to bear on the alien firing the squirter. His shots banged loud, slamming into the broad shoulders of the ebony-skinned alien. The hits were enough to make the rock-like skin of the creature ripple under the impacts—one punching through and spraying out a plume of black-gray ooze. The wounded Boss sprang to the side of the street, breaking his target lock. It began to scale the side of a building. *He's going for the high ground...smart move.* "Oh no, you don't." He moved the targeting reticle onto the creature and fired the last three rounds of the magazine as it reached the second floor. The shots hit the side of the Boss hard enough to make it lose its grip and fall to the street.

Scarface was undeterred. It jumped over the first Boss, who was rising to its knees, and sprinted straight at him. "That's right, you slick bastard...it's me!" *We have unfinished business.* He brought the ACR to his side and synced it to its ammo feed. The metallic snap of shells reloading into the magazine was assuring.

In a heartbeat, all three of the Bosses were once more on their feet. One resumed its climb up the side of a building, while the other two bore in on him. "Time to thin the herd," he said, raising his ACR again—this time aiming at his old adversary. Each shot was precisely aimed, and he savored each shot that he sent into his foe. The jolts of impact showed his aim was true. He knew he'd scored a hit on one arm, because it twisted backwards and sprayed a plume of alien blood in the process.

Scarface dropped to one knee, skidding on the pavement. An upraised arm fired a glob of caustic horror right at MacLeod, hitting his left arm and shoulder. The acid hissed loud enough for him to hear it in his cockpit—not a good sign. His damage indicator flickered with several spots of amber and there was a hydraulic warning light, flashing crimson, demanding attention that he could not provide. White wisps of smoke from the chemical reaction obscured his visual check of the damage. It didn't matter—MacLeod had no choice but to battle on.

He fired his remaining shots into the other rushing alien as the Boss who had been climbing started to jump from rooftop to rooftop, bypassed MacLeod's position, closing the distance on the troops at the bank. MacLeod began to backstep down the street, if only to trade space for time. Diverting energy to his sonic disruptor, he lifted his undamaged arm up and squeezed the trigger in his control sleeve.

Scarface kept low, using the other Bosses to obscure his movements as he rose and slowly started forward. The ripples of sonic waves had less distance to travel and raked the two Bosses advancing on the street level. It tore into them with more damage. One was forced to duck down behind a microvan for cover. Scarface stopped advancing, holding its arms up as if to block the assault. He leveled his ACR and unleashed another trio of shots into his foe. One dug deep, sending a momentary geyser of grayish ooze squirting from the wound under high pressure. "Hurts, doesn't it? Ye bawbag suckin' pile o'jabby!" Eventually Scarface dove into one of the buildings to get out of the waves of agony that the rig was unleashing.

The rooftop alien stopped, raining down a spray of deadly projectiles from above and behind him with its spiker weapon. One hit his rig's right foot, two more slammed into the damaged arm, this time digging deep because the armor was eaten away by the acid spray. Using the control sleeve, he swung the big ACR into action again, but this time his human arm strained under the flex. The damaged hydraulic system was starting to make itself known. It took a lot of work to bring the weapon in line with the reticle in his cockpit. With a stepping turn, he brought the weapon up to his new target, and the moment he lined up the Boss on the roof, he fired off four rounds quickly. At least three collided with the alien, making it twist, then fall down, out of his line of sight. "I'm not going to assume you are dead—not yet."

Shifting his targeting back down at street level, MacLeod fired another burst at the Boss that emerged from behind the microvan. It blasted away at him with its slasher beam. Most of the grayish spray went wide, but the last bit of the swipe tore into his rig's lower torso, right under the cockpit. Bits of his armor gave way, and he could feel the rig stiffen as the STL tried to resist the cutting force. From his cockpit's lower window, he could see the damage, mangled armor plates and warning indicators of power relays needing to be reset.

In his mind, he knew he had only a few minutes of use of his damaged arm before it would be impossible to move. Lowering the weapon, he re-synced and reloaded the ACR. Sweat rolled down his face as he strained to lift the weapon. Even with the aid of his functional arm, it took every bit of his strength, fighting his arm's control sleeve every second.

He drifted the shot at the alien that had fired the slasher, and fired four controlled bursts. The first shots hit low on the torso, rocking the creature under the bullet impacts. For a moment it looked as if it was going to dive for cover—but the next burst hit its chest, spraying alien blood.

The creature seemed to turn its gaze to face him—and two rounds hit its head. The Boss staggered back, lifting its hands up to its head. Then it fell over with a thud.

"Sucks to be you," he said through gritted teeth, struggling to keep the ACR ready for action.

Another burst from the rooftop sent spikes slamming into his rig as MacLeod continued to backstep down the street. There was no sign of Scarface, but he knew that his old foe was not going to break off—not yet. A spike hit his cockpit canopy, sending a few shards of transparent aluminum flying at him. One hit his right thigh, stopped by the Kevlar III weave there, but barely.

As he brought his good arm into play, he heard something move beside him. His tactical display showed it as another ASHUR rig—undetermined class—its call sign flickering under it, "Brutality."

"Mind if I help, Hyena?" came the voice of Trixie Lynch.

"I've got this," he said.

"Not from the look of that arm," she replied.

The Boss on the roof sprayed the two of them with a stream of deadly projectiles. MacLeod twisted, letting his rear armor deal with some of the damage as Lynch fired off one of her rockets. It angled high and hit the building façade in front of the alien, turning the blasted structure into shrapnel, spraying the Boss, forcing it back for a moment.

"Thanks," he managed to say. The damage indicator for the Steel Hyena showed that the damaged arm was off-line for mobility, making the ACR it held impotent. The hand of the rig still clutched the weapon, which told him it was the hydraulics in the elbow and shoulder that had been compromised. There were tricks of the trade for dealing with such damage, but most required being outside of the cockpit and jury-rigging the hoses manually.

Suddenly he saw a blur. An obsidian figure emerged from a side street, leveling its weapon at Lynch and firing. *Scarface!*

Pushing off with a leap, he hit Brutality, knocking her down on the street with his rig on top of her. The spray caught his already damaged arm and the ACR, turning the weapon into a melty looking piece of worthless metal. "What are you doing?" she said, twisting as he rolled off and came to his knees. As he rose to face her, he was sure she could see the damage. "You took that shot for me…"

He was going to respond, but the alien from the rooftop had jumped to the next closest rooftop, firing a shot down and narrowly missing MacLeod's battered rig. Lynch wheeled on it, unleashing her last two rockets in quick succession. From his cockpit, he saw the explosions and the body of the big Boss plummeting to the ground, landing on a lamppost on the way down. The metal moaned and bent as the Boss lay across part of the bent metal post, unmoving.

"Nice shot," he said, angling to where he had seen Scarface, but his foe was missing. *He's close…damn it.*

The thud of rushing footsteps to his right caught his attention. As he turned to the threat, he was hit hard, like a truck driving right into the Steel Hyena, knocking him to the ground. Every joint on his body protested, then ached from the hit. The five-point harness dug into his chest and at his crotch. Scarface loomed in front of his cockpit, closer than it had ever been before.

His foe rose, planting its massive foot on the cockpit, making it groan and crunch under the weight. MacLeod twisted and tried to move, but couldn't. He angled his free arm and the plasma carbine mounted there, bringing it up, but Scarface saw the threat and planted the foot on it before he could aim and fire. He discharged a power shell regardless and stored the energy. He could barely see Lynch and heard her rig fire its own power shell. Scarface whipped one of its arms around, hitting her with what appeared like a whip. The weapon shimmered blue-white, charged with electrical energy. It slashed onto the front of her rig and sparks arced all along the body of her ASHUR, as if it were struck by lightning.

The weapon was known to MacLeod—they were called power whips. If they hit a human, it was pretty much a guaranteed death by electrocution. For an ASHUR, it could do a lot of electrical damage. Panting, he waited for her laser to fire, but it didn't. Her rig didn't move, didn't react. It was as if it had become a statue, right next to him.

"Lynch," he called out.

"My systems are all black!" she called out. Panic tinged every word she spoke. *She must be broadcasting on her helmet's comm system.*

"He's tripped your power systems; you need to reset the masters," he said as the footpad of Scarface crunched and ground deeper into his cockpit, inching closer. MacLeod kicked his feet, attempting to toss the Boss off him, but to no avail.

"I don't know how—what do I need to do?"

Instant confusion hit him as he twisted again, trying to get his rig free. "Open your master power panel."

"I—what does it look like?"

"Small panel—it's probably down by your hips."

Sparks flickered hot and white on the whip that was still attached to her rig. Scarface twisted his heel into the cockpit canopy again, bending it inward even more. *Another few seconds and I am toast.*

"Got it! There's six toggles here. Oh shit-fuck, he's raising his squirter." Above him, between the claws, he could see the Boss lifting its arm. At this range, he couldn't miss.

"Focus, Lynch! Throw them one at a time—if you throw them too fast, you'll cascade the system again. Start with power then to motivation and then weapons. The moment you hit the last one, move and fire. You've got this!" *I have to buy her time if I can.*

Reaching down to his sound system, he loaded the first song that he had queued. The external speaker of the Steel Hyena crackled then unleashed "Kickstart My Heart" by Mötley Crüe. He cranked the volume all the way up. The guitar riffs wailed into the streets and skies of Beverly Hills.

Scarface paused, whip in one hand, half raised squirter in the other. Its battle-worn face seemed to look down at MacLeod under its feet. He wasn't sure, but the tip in its head made the Boss look confused. "That's right, ye dirty dobber."

Lynch said nothing for what seemed like an eternity. Scarface's arm moved slowly, as if it were going to savor destroying Lynch's ASHUR. Only a few inches in front of him, Scarface's clawed foot twisted again, bending the canopy of his Rattlesnake inward even more. At any moment, it was going to give way, and when it did, there was nothing MacLeod could do but die.

There was a flash that he saw above him, near Lynch's Phalanx. It was only for an instant, white, like an intense strobe light. The feet lifted off his cockpit and arm as Scarface staggered back from the two ASHURs.

"Got him!" Lynch called as she moved out of his field of vision.

His targeting reticle couldn't project on the bent and mangled cockpit canopy. "Gotta do this old-school." He rolled his rig to the side, managing to come up on one knee. He pointed his crumbled but functioning arm and its plasma carbine at Scarface, who had released its whip from Lynch. A perfect half hole had been cut into its left shoulder as if a paper-punch had taken out a three-quarter moon slice of its flesh…the handiwork of Lynch's laser.

He aimed by iron sights as best he could, holding the carbine in front of him. He squeezed the trigger in his control sleeve and held it. His weapon hummed as the energy sprayed the superheated blast of plasma on a magnetic beam, right at Scarface.

The plasma splashed as he sprayed it at the Boss, searing deep into its chest. The alien twisted then dropped to its knees. MacLeod rose to his feet and looked over at the alien as he fired another power shell for the kill shot.

The Boss reached up to its head and the fine claws seemed to touch on several points at its face where the plasma had seared through. Jets of searing hot steam erupted as they burned deep, hissing loud enough for him to hear it from inside the cockpit.

With his operable hand, MacLeod clawed at the Boss's face, sinking his rig's mechanical fingers into the holes he had burned, furrowing them deep. Using the control sleeve, he clenched the fingers into a fist. The resistance was fierce, but he gave it every ounce of his energy. The fingers tore into the thick sharkskin-like hide and he jerked the arm back. An explosive blast of high-pressure oily black ooze sprayed on his canopy, blurring his view for a moment.

As the spray ceased, he saw a skull-like feature. It was knobby, almost jagged, yellowish in color. It had a massive jawbone-like bone that formed a thick chin. There was an almost metallic shimmer to the bone-like material, unlike any internal bone he had ever seen. Scarface wrenched itself hard, breaking his grip on the thick flap of skin that he had torn at.

This was the true face of his enemy. MacLeod looked at the visage and could see the raw anger and rage that it represented. His usually mouthless enemy stared at him through lifeless eye sockets, its mouth open in a rictus roar. Sprayed viscera and spittle dusted his canopy.

The sound of its final death scream was like that of an elephant mixed with a tiger's growl and the scream of a banshee—all weirdly twisted into one. It was a noise that MacLeod knew he would never forget. The kind of sound that would haunt his sleep for the rest of his life.

Leveling his weapon, he fired again into the face of the evil he had been pursuing for months. The hot plasma ended the wailing. It burned through the thick bone. Scarface toppled over with a dull crunch onto the street, unmoving, smoke rolling out of the side of his face that had been torn open.

MacLeod felt exhausted, both physically and mentally. For a few moments, he looked at the charred face of the dead alien—the red light eyes were now sunken pools of dark black gore. Once he was satisfied that his foe was indeed dead, he realized that tears were pooling around his eyes, making them sting. His focus on vengeance and on the Boss had been all-consuming. Now that it was dead, it was as if a huge weight had been lifted. Pulling his arms out of the ASHUR's control sleeves, he wiped the tears from his cheeks. Then he slowly turned his rig to face Lynch.

"You saved my life," she said.

"We saved each other," he replied with a ragged breath. "How's your power?"

"I'm at fifty-two percent. You?"

MacLeod checked. "Forty-six." Power was the constant struggle for ASHUR pilots. "We need to move steady—no sprinting—give the fuel cell time to build up more of a charge."

Before Lynch could respond, a new message came in on another channel. "MacLeod, if you can hear us, we are falling back to the bank and hotel. Link up with us there." The voice was that of Lieutenant Ryland. *Things must be going to shit for them to fall back.*

"My people are falling back near the bank," he transmitted to Lynch.

"Spartan Associated is heading for the bank too." Lynch paused for a moment. "If you don't mind—I will go back with you."

"Fantastic," he sighed. "Keep your eyes sharp. Something tells me this isn't over just yet."

CHAPTER 26

Operation Goldfinger, Beverly Hills, the Western Front, California, the United States

Spartan Associates fell in around the trucks outside the bank, taking positions in some of the nearby buildings. After their initial wave of attacks, the Fish seemed to be focusing on his forced comrades of the Ghost Legion and Open Hostility—something he was thankful for. Lynch was still several blocks away, fighting. Hopefully she could link up with them once they left.

When he arrived, he looked in the beds of the trucks and saw they were filled with stainless steel metal safe-deposit boxes—some big, some small—all packed like a Tetris game in the beds of the trucks. Three trucks were filled, and the last one had just a few boxes in it.

Glancing over to his right, he saw the ATVs and trailers that Open Hostility had brought with them. Two of their trailers were loaded, though mostly with the smaller metal boxes, allowing them to be packed with more. Larger boxes were strapped to the backs of the ATVs. *They should have planned better...brought better transport. Not my problem. It's their loss.*

He ran through the door, passing one of the Hostility crew

carrying out two boxes. Dawes ignored them, he needed to get to his people. When he arrived at the vault, it was a scene of controlled chaos. The hundreds of box doors were in various stages of being opened. Several deposit boxes were piled up, others looked as if they had been tossed aside. The vault was warmer than the last time he had been in it, and the air reeked of perspiration.

"Jones, where are we at?" Dawes asked as he raised his visor back into his helmet and slung his Wolverine ACR over his shoulder.

Diamond spun to respond. "We still have a hundred or more to go."

"What about box 435?"

"Front seat of the lead truck," she replied. "First one we pulled."

"Good," he said, leaning against the open vault door for a moment. Dawes bit his lower lip, doing some mental math. *We could stay, take more—but run the risk of being holed up here when the Fish come.* He knew that the other two groups were engaged with the aliens and were already starting to fall back. *Our path to the north looks open, at least for now.*

It wasn't an easy choice for the PMC's owner to make. Dawes wanted to leave. *We've got the sharks circling around us already, and there is blood in the water. Staying here and fighting a battle of attrition behind enemy lines is a losing proposition.* Taking what they had and running was the smart move. *If Open Hostility and the Ghosts want what is left, they are welcome to it. We have nothing to gain by helping them fend off the next wave of attacks.*

Dawes knew it looked cowardly, but he didn't care. *If we don't leave soon, we may never get out of this place.* "Grab one more armload," he said. "We are bugging out." He went over and grabbed one of the medium-sized boxes. Whatever was inside was rattling around against the metal.

"Wait a damned minute," spoke up a corporal who wore the patch of the Ghost Legion. "Our people are heading this way. They will need help to hold off the Fish. You can't just pack up and leave."

"'Fraid I can," Dawes replied. "This is your circus and your monkeys. If your CO has an issue with that, he can try to track me down after he gets out of here…*if* he gets out of here."

"You're a coward," the corporal fired back, his face flush with hot anger. For a moment, Dawes wondered if he was going to pull his sidearm—but he seemed to hold himself in check.

"I never claimed to be brave. I came to rob a bank. If your bosses want to win medals or bonuses, good luck to them. We are leaving." From outside, he heard the rumble of explosives going off not far away. *The clock is ticking.*

Dawes moved smartly outside, putting the box he carried with him in the bed of the truck while several of his team put a cheap Harbor Freight blue plastic tarp over it, securing the load down with tie-down straps, ratcheted tight.

"Alright, people," he broadcast to his entire team. "We are heading out the way we came in, to the north. Get our wounded on the trucks first. Everyone else, lie low and keep your weapons ready. We'll get out of this battle zone and head for the Metro."

Reaper approached him, his visor up, his visible brow wrinkled and a look of concern on his face. Wallace leaned in so that his voice wouldn't carry. "We are leaving the other teams holding the bag?" he asked in a low whisper.

"We didn't come to kill Fish."

"I know that. Look, both of us are ex-mil. We both bled up in Alaska for the cause. You know you don't hang good men and women out to dry like this." Wallace was close to pleading in his tone, clearly struggling to keep his voice low when he really wanted to shout.

"You just said it, we are *ex*-military, Ted. This is about business. Staying here and fighting some last stand against the enemy isn't why we came. We came to recover some goods and get out. That's what my people signed up for, and that's what we are going to do."

"This is wrong and you know it." Reaper had never showed an inkling of insubordination before, but now it was plain and out in the open. "We are talking about abandoning humans to fight the Fish without our support."

"It isn't our problem."

"Damn it, Albert," he said louder than before. "Stabbing these people in the back is morally wrong."

He's never called me by my first name before. "Morals? This isn't about morals. If the tables were turned, Stevens or Ryland would make the same decision."

"You don't know that."

"Neither do you. Right now, we can get out of here and that is what is best for the company. If you want to quit and stay with these people and lose your life, you are welcome to. My obligation is to my company, and I am going to do what is best to save what lives I can."

For a moment, Dawes wondered if Wallace might take him up on his offer. From the expression on his face, he clearly wanted to stay. In Dawes's mind, it was a stupid reaction for Ted to consider, but that was not his responsibility. Eventually, Wallace nodded. "Damn it…I came in with you, I'll go out with you. But this is the end of it, boss. I'm leaving once we get back."

"You have to do you. Right now, I need your head in the game. Get these vehicles ready. I want to be out of here in five."

He set his comms channel to that of the Phalanx. "Brutality, this is Shredder. What is your ETA?"

Lynch's voice came back. "I'm with Steel Hyena and we just finished a fight. We have enemy movement. It's going to take a few to work our way towards you."

"We are bugging out in five, swinging back to the north then cutting east to the Metro. I need you to link up with us."

"Are the other units leaving?"

"Not your concern, Brutality. Link up with us or find your own way home." *She needs a kick in the pants. I want her to get out— that ASHUR cost me a pretty penny.*

"Understood," she replied in a solemn, slow tone. "I'll do what I can."

Dawes turned his eyes back to the Commerce Bank with a sense of satisfaction. *I wish I could take it all, but hopefully we got enough to allow everyone an early retirement.*

Beverly Hills, the Western Front, California, the United States

Two Crabs maneuvered along the north side of Beverly Drive as MacLeod held up his arm, angling the sonic disruptor and aiming by eyeballing it. "Alright, Brutality—when I fire this, it will stun them for a moment. When they stop, take your shot."

"Roger that."

"Game on." He squeezed and held the trigger in his arm's control sleeve. The weapon pulsated, sending ripples of deep throbbing sonic waves down the street. Both Crabs were caught in the sonic pulsations and stopped their advance, coiling up slightly.

He heard the bang of a power shell off to his right as Lynch blasted away with her laser. While he didn't see the beam, he did see the searing hole in the large claw of the lead Crab. As MacLeod released his trigger for the disruptor, Lynch fired four grenades from her launcher downrange, blasting the same Crab.

MacLeod aimed his rig's plasma carbine, this time using the secondary targeting screen inside of the cockpit to bring the reticle on the other Crab. It was harder to use but the primary reticle for the inside of his canopy was worthless, thanks to the near collapse of the cockpit on him. It was at the long range for the carbine, but with the sonic pulses ceased, the Crab was once more trying to close the distance. Locking onto the center mass, he unleashed the searing white plasma stream. It wasn't like spraying water from a hose; the plasma rode a magnetic beam and stabbed out like a knight's lance at the Crab.

The searing hot blast struck the creature in the head, molten plasma splash-raining over the front of alien. The creature shrieked like an amplified lobster tossed into boiling water. Contorting violently as the shot ended, the Crab crashed into a nearby building, no doubt to avoid being shot again.

As the smoke and haze cleared, the first Crab that Lynch had fired on was also falling back and moving onto a side street, leaving a wet oily scar of gore to mark its path.

"Got 'em," came Lynch's voice.

"Not for long. We need to link up with our people."

"About that," her voice came back. "Spartan Associates is leaving."

"Leaving? What kind if fucknugget move is that?"

"They want me to link up with them."

MacLeod had no fear of being alone—he had come into the AIZ by himself. He had a hunch that Lynch wasn't a fully trained ASHUR pilot. Her not knowing how to reset the power systems had been his first clue. Her piloting a rig he had never seen before only added to his suspicion. "Are you going to go?"

There were a few moments of hesitation. "I should. Dawes gave me this chance. It's his rig."

"That's herpa derp if I ever heard of it. You're a frigging ASHUR pilot. That means you make your own call on something that messed up."

Another pause came back. "I'm sticking with you."

MacLeod grinned. "Alright—let's make our way down the block before the Crabs decide to make another attempt."

Operation Sundance, Beverly Hills, the Western Front, California, the United States

Ryland and his team crossed Wilshire Boulevard just as Open Hostility was taking up their defensive posture in the ruins of the hotel. Stevens came over when he had spotted them closing in on the bank. As soon as he caught up with Ryland, the two of them headed for the bank. It was then that he noticed the Spartan Associates trucks were missing.

"Are you okay?" Stevens asked, glancing down at his wounded shoulder.

"Yeah—I'm fine. Where in the fuck are the trucks?"

Stevens spun in place looking for some sign of them, his jaw slightly agape. "You don't think…"

"You know exactly what I think."

Corporal Avery emerged from the bank holding two safe-deposit boxes. He hurriedly put them on the back of one of the ATVs as Ryland and Stevens hustled over to him. "Where are Spartan Associates?"

Avery stopped, clearly flummoxed by the question. "They got out of here about five minutes ago. I thought you knew."

"Son of a bitch!" Ryland cursed. Tapping his wristcomp, he linked in Stevens to the last channel he had used to speak with Dawes. "This is Casper to Shredder—what is your position, over?"

Nothing came back. He repeated it on an open channel, broadcasting in the clear. Again, no response. Turning to Stevens, Ryland did what he could to pull in his rage. "They either can't respond or are refusing to respond."

"We both know the answer."

"Right. Okay then. How loaded are our transports?" he asked of Avery as he glanced at the ATVs.

"We have gotten just about all we can on them, sir."

"You thinking of bugging out too?" Stevens asked.

"I'm not sure we can. We were engaged and forced to fall back here."

"Same with us. I've got wounded too."

Gunfire chattered from the hotel just across the street from the small roadway where the Commerce Bank was located as Open Hostility began to engage the approaching enemy.

"Some of my people are injured too. Right now we have good firing positions and can support each other. If we start moving out, we might not be able to mount a good defense—depending on the ground."

"We could call in the Army."

Stevens's suggestion was ominous, laden with risks and an infinite number of complications. Ryland had given it some thought, but had dismissed it. "I'm not sure they would risk sending units this far into the AIZ. If they got here, there's a chance they would see why we were here, and that has some, shall I say, legal complications. I think the only way we get out of this mess is to get kinetic on their Fish-asses."

"Agreed. The Fish are likely to ignore the ATVs—they tend to go after humans. We cover them up, then we hunker down and stack their bodies."

"Pile them high and deep, brother." The use of the word "brother" was genuine, now that they were fighting for the same ground, against a common foe.

As the Ghost Legion shifted into the buildings, everyone calling "clear" as they entered new rooms, he got a signal from Winston, who, despite his wound, had already taken position in the upper floors of a building across from the bank. "Casper, the Fish are coming in-force. I count, eight, no, make that ten Crabs—at least two Bosses coming in from the southwest."

Vogal came in on the same channel. "Punch-List, we have problems from the southeast. We have a wave of Frogs coming in fast. I make it well over a hundred, possibly more—a lot more."

Stevens whistled. "That's a hell of a lot of Frogs."

Ryland drew a deep breath through his nose, held it, then slowly let it out of his mouth…just so he could focus his thinking. "We're going to need some more firepower." He keyed in the channel for MacLeod. "Steel Hyena, please fall back to the bank and hotel area. We are about to get hammered here."

A voice came back, female, a few seconds later. "This is Brutality—I'm with Hyena. His comms system is not great but he got your message. Our ETA is five minutes."

Our? That's the other ASHUR. Why didn't she go with Dawes? There was a story there, but he knew it would have to wait for later. "Glad to have you join us, Brutality."

Ryland looked over at Stevens. "You think you can hold?"

The militia commander nodded. "It's a good position—but that is a hell of a lot of Frogs. If we get pressed too hard, we will cross the street and join you there."

Ryland then turned to Avery. "Cover the ATVs with tarps and put some debris on top of them. It's not much protection but if we are forced back here, I don't want them damaged if we can avoid it. Choose debris that can work as armor and soak up damage."

He turned his attention to the growing growl of battle that filled the air. Flexing his arms, his wound still throbbed in the shoulder and his joints all wanted to protest even the most basic of motions. Ryland's nostrils picked up hints of his own body odor and the ever-present stink of garbage that somehow lingered in the air of La. *Is this the ground I am going to die for?* He wondered how many other treasure hunters looking for riches died in foreign lands over mankind's history. *Will they remember us? Or will we be forgotten like so many others?*

The odds were not in their favor; it was a fact that he grudgingly accepted. Dawes and his people had fled, either making them cowards and geniuses. Only the coming fight would tell for sure. Glancing over at Avery as he covered the ATVs, Ryland wondered if robbing the bank was the easy part...if the getaway was the real obstacle.

CHAPTER 27

Operation Sundance, Beverly Hills, the Western Front, California, the United States

Looking down Wilshire Boulevard, Mark Stevens was stunned. Blocks away to the west, it looked as if a gray-green wave was surging forward. The knowledge that it was not water, but a mass of alien Frog fighters, made his stomach clench. They worked in masses, but this was the largest he had ever seen. Hundreds of them. The only good news about the Frogs was their bunching was so tight, it was keeping the Bosses farther away. "Enemy coming down Wilshire," was all he could muster from his position on the third floor of the hotel. He had pulled the ragged curtains down and used his ACR stock to remove the last bits of glass that still clung in the window frames.

"Contacts, sir. We've got more coming up Beverly from the south," Vogal replied. "I see some Bosses bringing up the rear too."

Ripper's voice cut in. "On Wilshire, I see some Crabs behind the Frogs—multiple contacts." It wasn't what he wanted to hear, but it was the reality they were facing.

"Alright, people," he said firmly on the channel. "Don't engage until they are in optimal range. They are only dangerous if they get close. Vogal, you and Ripper get to the corner so you can use that grenade launcher and the M245 to cover both approaches. The rest of you, don't waste your boom-booms, only throw them when they are close and clustered. We need to take out as many as we can with each blast."

"Sir," came Sprang. "I can plant a few remote charges on cars that have fuel in them. They will give us some extra fire down there."

"Good idea, Coastie, get on it and move fast—they are closing with us," he replied. "We need to hold this line. The Ghosts are going to be holding our rear. We need to whittle them down. Make your shots count. Engage at your discretion." Glancing again, he saw that the mass was closing. He adjusted the range on the targeting reticle that projected on the inside of his visor to automatically calibrate for the distance. Leaning out, he took aim and waited until he was sure of a clean hit. The problem was the Frogs' movement was not straight at their position. They moved erratically, at odd angles, making anticipating them difficult. It was best to catch them on the landing…it was the longest they were in one spot.

The sound was as disturbing as the wave of deadly flesh encroaching on their position. The Frogs bleated out a deep toad-ish growl. Individually, it was loud. For some reason, they synced up as they advanced. Each sound was amplified, low and grunting, intense. Each time the noise reached him, it served to remind him that these were inhuman creatures—not living organisms of this world.

Shots rang out from the floor below him. Frogs were hit; whatever they bled sprayed as a mist as they were hit. Some fell and stayed down, others twisted under the impact of the shots, and a few dropped only to rise back up. Frogs were relentless killing machines.

Stevens fired, hitting one Frog in the head, downing it permanently. Its comrades simply hopped over the downed creature without a hint of respect to its fallen comrade. His second shot hit in the body of one Frog. It curled up, then rose to hop again, landing awkwardly. His next round tore one Frog's lower leg off at the knee. It fell to the pavement, then pulled itself along with its long arms and claws. Another Frog sprang over it, only to catch two rounds in the head from Stevens and fall dead.

Sprang detonated the first car when the mass surged past it. The fireball rolled in a ball skyward and that least five Frogs were doused in flames. Black smoke twisted and coiled in on itself as it billowed high. The second explosion was less effective, but the flames did serve to force the Frogs into a narrower corridor on the street. Several of his shots hit one alien then passed through them into another. One shot seemed to hit four in a row, only instantly killing one.

Vogal unleashed the grenade launcher. The explosions rained down on the front and middle ranks of the Frogs, throwing shrapnel and body parts into the air. The short bursts from Ripper's machine gun rang out, but he didn't see the impacts—a hint that he was firing at the group approaching from the south. More explosions followed from grenades, but nothing seemed to shatter the will of the Frogs. They continued to come forward.

The Tarantula GRD scurried out from cover, its mini–chain gun cutting a swath through the mass of Frogs. It darted back and forth across the street, switching to shorter bursts, falling back as it moved.

Maybe they don't have wills—maybe they are programmed to do what they do, or they are simply devoid of souls. Stevens didn't care. He emptied three magazines with controlled shots. As he reloaded, he noted that he was almost out of ammo, meaning he had to make his shots count. The tempo of the shots fired was a symphony of death and destruction, punctuated by explosive blasts—like bass drums. The echoes through the war-torn streets of Beverly Hills only amplified the sounds, making the fighting seem even worse.

The lead Frogs reached the rubble of the hotel, where they were dropped by a hail of outgoing fire. More surged, and they were shot, filling the air with a bloody mist. A few crawled forward—oblivious to the damage they had taken. After a few minutes there was a low wall of dead and dying Frogs forming around the east side of the Beverly Wilshire Hotel. The Frogs had to climb or spring over their dead, only to be shot and join the pile.

There were blasts from across the street at the bank where the Ghost Legion were dug in, fighting their own battle.

"Witch," he signaled on a private channel. "How we looking?"

"I'm down to my last drum of grenades," her breathy voice came back. "We are holding them to the east, but to the south, those Bosses are almost on top of us."

In Stevens's mind, he contemplated falling back to the bank. The window for that move was closing fast. *Either we stay here and fight or we move over and join the Ghosts.* He keyed in to broadcast to his entire unit. "Listen up, people, we are going to fall back to the bank.

We do this fast, maintaining a good masking fire as we go." He fired two more shots, then headed for the hallway.

"Ryland," he said as he reached the staircase and started down. "We are redeploying to your position."

"Suggest you take the buildings across from the bank—we have formed up on the bank-side of the street."

He almost slipped on the last landing, the plaster dust on the polished concrete making it treacherous. Stevens caught himself on the guard rail. He found himself frustrated that he had gotten so sloppy in his rush to get down. Memories of his time serving in the Army during the last war came rushing to him. His grizzled old staff sergeant had that line… "It always gets worse before it gets worse." *Let's hope that old fart was wrong…*

* * *

The open street between the hotel and the block where the Ghost Legion was fighting was terrifying for Reese. She had used up half of her ammo on the wave of attacking Frogs and it was hard to see the results of her efforts. For every alien that she had hit, there seemed to be another dozen that surged forward and took its place. As she rose out of the rubble, she saw Guideon sprint across, firing up Wilshire.

She had been focused on the force to the south. Glancing off to her right, she saw a long pile of dead Frogs, erratically piled almost three feet high. Behind the blockade cutting off the road, she saw more of them coming, visible as they hopped. Claws reached up to the top of the mound as the aliens pulled themselves up and over. Shelly had killed Frogs before; she knew their mass-attack tactics, but not on this scale. For a few milliseconds, she was transfixed by the chaos and horror below.

Three Frogs bounded over the wall. Guideon fired into one of them, almost severing its neck. It dropped some twenty feet from her and jarred her back into motion. She lowered herself and started across the street, raising her ACR at one of the other Frogs that had leapt over their dead. More surged over the pile of the dead.

Reese picked her target, aimed, and fired. One shot hit the Frog's arm, tossing the remainder of its body back under the impact. Another shot tore flesh out of its muscular leg. The Frog was unfazed by the hits. It limp-jumped haphazardly to the left, and she fired, missing. It sprang at her with two short hops. Adjusting her aim, she pulled the trigger.

Nothing happened.

Empty magazine! Her hand dove for her leg ammo pouch as the Frog rushed right at her. Her fingers fumbled to get a grip on the magazine as the Frog lunged for it, its claws coming at her like eight little daggers. Reese twisted to deflect the impact but couldn't deflect it enough. The Frog hit her hard and she could feel the points of two of the claws dig into her right breast as she fell backwards on the pavement. The impact was amplified by the weight of the Frog right on top of her. Using her ACR as a lever, she tried to pry it off, but the creature had a grip on her chest armor and would not budge. The sacs behind its jaws inflated. It sprayed her head with a sticky goo, covering her visor. The stink of the material hit her nostrils and stung. Fear gripped her as she lunged even harder with the stock of her ACR, knocking the Frog off her chest.

She scrambled, arms and legs, one hand unhooking her helmet and tossing it. The Frog squatted on all fours as she put a few feet between them. For a moment, it actually looked like a Terran frog, the way it sat. It tracked her, turning as she moved and got to her knees. It was going to spring again. She ejected the empty magazine and grabbed a full one, but in her mind, she knew it was too late.

The Frog's rear legs flexed, then shots rang out from behind her. Bullets riddled the creature's head at the moment it began to leap, toppling it over backwards onto the street in a mist of its dark blood. Reese turned and saw the Witch standing behind her with her ACR still trained on the Frog. A second later, Vogal fired an additional round into its head for good measure.

Vogal lowered her weapon and extended her hand as Reese coughed, then grabbed it, rising to her feet. She had breathed some of the Frog's toxic spit, which was bad, and some of the goo had hit the skin of her neck and was still on her STG. She saw her helmet and decided to leave it, it was coated with the spray.

"Thanks," she said, finishing reloading. She coughed again. "I got some of that shit in my lungs." She saw Coyote and a large black man dart between her and the Frog-wall. The scrounger ran firing full auto, hitting more dead Frogs than live ones.

"TDDB. Haul your ass across," Vogal said, firing a steady spray of shots at the Frogs attempting to crawl over the wall of dead to get to them.

The Dead Don't Bitch…equivalent to the more archaic, "But did you die?" She got the clue and closed her mouth. As Reese ran, each thud of her boot on the pavement made her right breast ache, reminding her of the Frog's claws hitting her. She would have to check the wounds there when she got the chance. She slowed only once as she crossed the street, pausing to fire three rounds at a Frog that had risen to stand on the wall of its dead comrades, raising its arms in what looked like a motion of defiance. It crumpled forward, adding to the pile.

Crossing the street, she saw Stevens and he pointed to a small store next door to the bank. Reese wanted to chew his ass. *We wouldn't be here if he wasn't so damn greedy.* There was a part of her that wanted to tell him that this was all his fault…but she knew that she had come on her own accord. *Hopefully we'll survive this long enough for me to tell him what I think of this clusterfuck.*

* * *

Ryland's position was three stories up in a building two doors down from the Commerce Bank. The street itself was on a small knoll, rising above the rest of Beverly Hills, giving him a good vantage point. He could see the Crabs that came in from the west and took time to make each shot count. The beasts' armored hide made his shots seem ineffectual, but experience told him that looks could be deceiving when it came to fighting the Crabs. He concentrated his shots at the head of the greenish creature at the lead of the cluster of Crabs as they approached. Each squeeze of the trigger was hope that the alien might drop.

Finn was on the adjoining rooftop hoisting the hulking rail gun. There was a bang of a power shell, and a plume of superheated air roared out of the barrel as the slender round sped downrange. It collided with a Crab, tearing a long jagged scar down the creature's side, peeling back some of the armored hide plates in the process. The gash squirted the oily blood out but only for a few seconds. *Damn things don't have the decency to just up and die.*

A big boom roared from another building down the line—the distinctive sound of Mullins unleashing the Carl Gustaf was followed with the instantaneous explosion of the lead Crab. The blast blew the Crab into two big pieces, right at its raised upper torso. The Crab's body stood as it did before the explosion, but the head and large upper claws were obliterated, reduced to unidentifiable chunks and wet goo. Entrails, like exposed intestines, draped over the back of the alien.

"Good shooting, Mullins," Ryland said on a discreet transmission.

"Thank you. I'm down to two rounds though, sir."

That wasn't good. The bang and rumble of grenades going off and the flashes as they burst near the Crabs were encouraging but Ryland knew they had a finite supply of explosives. "Make your tosses count, people—it's not like we can resupply."

In the corner of his visor display, he saw that he still had four more rounds in his magazine, and he was determined to unleash them. As he leaned out, he watched as a Crab jutted out both of its big claws, unleashing a huge gaseous cloud of gray smoke-like substance. The sight of it made him recoil. The gas cloud was likely the airborne bacterial spray that the Fish used. It was a rapid flesh-eating bug that consumed its target's flesh and, in the process, secreted acid. Breathing it in meant your lungs and internal organs were at risk. It was so fast-acting and there were no good treatments short of amputation of affected limbs to stop it.

The male scream he heard from outside the window made his heart sink…one of his people had been hit with the spray. The battlespace image inside of his visor was not complete and without the biochips, he couldn't check status. "Who was that?"

It took a few long moments for an answer to come back. "It's Mullins," came the voice of Finn in a near panic. "Oh God…" In the background, Mullins's wailing screams flooded the comms channel.

The protocols for such injuries were heartless. "Don't touch him —that bacteria can go through your gear."

"There's got to be something we can do," Finn called back amid the agonizing cries.

Ryland rose and aimed his ACR, hitting the Crab that had shot the blast…it seemed the only appropriate response. The creature started to climb up the side of the building, pushing off with its tail and sinking its legs into the stucco façade. Someone must have grabbed the recoilless launcher that Mullins had. There was a massive booming sound and the Crab's head exploded in a mist of gray and a ball of fire that twisted in on itself as it rode skyward. The alien toppled back, landing hard on one of its comrades.

There was another bang-crack from above as Winston's larger caliber Hawkeye sniper rifle hit the Crab that was crawling from under the body of its dead war-mate. Winston's shots were akin to a surgeon operating—precise and perfectly aimed. The round hit one of its large claw shoulder joints and punched deep, riding the weak spot in its hide and into the alien. A gush of grayish gore shot out of the hole, then the claw went limp.

The Crab that had been hit by the railgun unleashed a spray of spikes from its claws-projectors, raking Ryland's and several other positions. They made a *ffifft* followed by a cracking noise as they came, hypersonic and deadly, at him and his people. Three projectiles missed him, coming up into his room, hitting the ceiling, and passing on up into the floor above him. Plaster dust sifted down from the holes like fine snowflakes.

One fragment from a bony projectile that had shattered, stabbed into his forearm on his already injured left arm. The kinetic force broke his grip on the ACR for a moment, twisting him as he tried to step back for cover. His hands shook as he turned and looked at the arm. His armor had mostly stopped the penetration…his STL made even bending his arm difficult for a few seconds. While his STG had protected him, the sign of blood told him that it hadn't been fully protective.

The glistening white projectile was slender, like a pencil, but hard and was stuck in his forearm. Slinging his weapon slowly, he reached over with his free hand, grabbed it, and girded himself for the ripple of pain he knew was coming. With a single jerk, he extracted the alien projectile that was wet with his blood. As the gunfire continued outside, he pulled the release tabs on his STG and pulled off his arm protection to check the wound. It wasn't bad—a two-inch cut, no arterial injuries. There was no time or need to wrap it. Instead he pulled on his armor again, cinching it tighter so that the blast plates and pads would act as a pressure bandage. It hurt, but hurting was merely proof that he was still alive.

Returning to the window, he saw that a Crab, the one with the damaged claw, was now unmoving—presumedly dead. The other Crab fired more sprays of the deadly bony needle projectiles into his people's position. Ryland lined up his reticle and fired a string of shots into the body and legs of the creature. Another shot from the portable rail gun flashed a plume of air and sent a metallic needle into the creature's back. When the needle hit the armor, it had enough resistance for the metal to collapse in on itself, instantly superheating, melting, and punching through the hide-plates. It formed a small volcano of flames roaring as it ate into the alien's back. The Crab's tail stiffened straight out, something that he had never seen with a Crab before. Its fore-claws jutted out as well, and from his perch, the creature looked more like a scorpion than he had ever imagined possible.

As a twisting smoke rose from the still-glowing hole, the Crab's support legs collapsed and it fell dead on the ground. Ryland let the air out of his lungs that he didn't even realize he was holding in… relief washed over him. The thunder-like rumble of gunfire stopped on the backside of the bank, but the noises from the front still raged.

"Corvin—what's the view up-front?" He had positioned Corvin's fire team to the front of the bank.

"Hostility is across the street so we have good crossfire, but I'm not sure that's enough. I've never seen this many Frogs. It's a meat grinder out here."

"Winston—you, Finn, and I will shift the front to provide additional fire. The rest of you have the back door here, keep your eyes out for another assault and keep me posted." Twinges of pain radiated from his wound, despite his attempts to ignore it. Ryland checked his ammo status as he started to briskly move to a room that faced the front of the bank.

CHAPTER 28

Beverly Hills, the Western Front, California, the United States

As the Steel Hyena edged around the corner of the block, MacLeod was stunned by the image of what he saw, enough to make him backstep into cover—almost colliding with Lynch who was right behind him.

"What is it?" she asked.

"We are coming in behind more Frogs that I ever knew existed. They are pushing on the bank."

"Let's get them!"

"There's two Bosses in the middle of that mess. We need to take them out first." The Frogs would realize they were behind them soon enough and turn to face them. The Bosses, those were the real threats from an ASHUR pilot's perspective.

"Right," Lynch replied slowly. "Okay, you call the play."

They had fought their way through a small cluster of Frogs and Dillos on their way to this position. The risks to them in ASHURs had not been great, but it had taken time to kill the aliens…precious time. It had also cost ammo and power—the lifeblood of an ASHUR. It was the kind of opportunity every soldier dreamed of, being behind the enemy, undetected. *Yeah—our rigs are beat up—my ACR has no use and the arm is dead weight—but we still have ample firepower. More importantly, we have the element of surprise.*

Mentally he processed what he had seen in that brief glimpse around the corner. "They are a block ahead of us—a thick mass but are facing the other way. We will step out in unison. Target the Boss on the right first—both of us. We need to hit him and take him down. We aim and shoot together—accuracy counts. Once we open up, they are going to turn on us and there are a lot of them, over a hundred that are bound to react to us carving a new anus in one of their big guys."

"Roger that—say fire and I will fire with you."

All his Rattlesnake had left was his plasma carbine and the sonic disruptor. The carbine was his weapon of choice, but he knew it would be less accurate at long range. MacLeod exhaled slowly, then drew a deep breath. "Alright—it's fuck-shit-up-o'clock." Scrolling through his playlist he opted for a rock song, toggling up Molly Hatchet's "Flirtin' with Disaster." He stepped out onto the street, bringing his carbine up and using the small secondary targeting screen to aim his shot—then broadcast the song at full volume.

The aliens didn't even know they were there. Lynch's Phalanx stepped out beside him, raising her large laser for firing. "On three," he said, locking the reticle on the middle of what he assumed was where a spine would be on the ebony Boss's back. "Three, two, one —boom!"

Their power shells went off in perfect unison. Her laser fired first —a flickering white-blue flash then a dull glowing orange hole the size of a melon just between the Boss's shoulder blades.

MacLeod fired, holding the trigger in his control sleeve. The superheated white-hot plasma sprayed out in a perfect beam, almost like the old sci-fi movies where blasters blazed away. The stream shot out in a tight stream, barely affected by gravity. It hit the alien's back, splattering as it did. He released after a few moments, giving the barrel the time to cool as the hot spittle of plasma seared deep into the alien's hide. Some of the spray hit the nearby Frogs that were packed in around the Boss, and one dropped entirely from view.

The hulking Boss fell forward, crushing several Frogs.

There was no time to rejoice—the untouched Boss realized the new threat, and turned, knocking two Frogs down in the process. *That's right—you're not alone, you dickfuck.* "Go for number two."

He fired off another power round and checked his power level, artfully shunting the power to the carbine slowly so as to not overheat the capacitor coils. Lynch fired off another round as well, blasting with her laser at the Boss. The shot hit the hulking alien in chest and shoulder as it completed turning, shimmering yellow from the intense heat, and sending a white mist rising from the hole.

The Frogs realized the threat to their rear as well, and the whole rear mass of creatures began to reel about to face the pair of ASHURs. It took a heartbeat for the carbine readiness indicator to flicker to green. Aiming his reticle at the alien's chest, he fired once more as the Boss rushed straight at them.

His plasma shot hit the shoulder that was already damaged and sprayed and slashed diagonally down the body, hitting several Frogs.

The Boss reached one clawed hand up to the wound, jerking it away from the hot plasma that scored deep into its hide. *Hurts, doesn't it?*

MacLeod moved to the side of the street beyond Lynch, moving behind her. Now the Boss and at least a dozen Frogs were starting to break off from the group and converge on them. He brought up the targeting reticle for his sonic disruptor, aimed and fired while Lynch cycled to her grenade launcher, firing the rounds downrange at the charging threat.

The deep throbbing ripples of sonic energy pulsated down the street. The Boss craned its head to the side, no doubt feeling the pain. Burst of high pressured water and biological ooze sprayed out in a mist from the holes that the shrapnel had torn on the Boss. The Frogs that bounded towards them began to bleed, mostly from their eyes. Several dropped, others were blinded and bounded into cars, other Frogs, or in one case, a building.

Lynch's explosions blew holes in their ranks and sent hot shrapnel into the Boss. The hulking alien stumbled through the smoke and flames from the explosions, clearly suffering. Its pain made MacLeod feel good. *That's right, keep coming. You can join your buddy in whatever hell your people believe in.*

The alien lifted its damaged arm, clearly struggling with it, and fired a deadly squirter. The beam initially missed Lynch, then slashed it across the front of her ASHUR. MacLeod saw bits and pieces of her armor flying off as the high pressured cutter did its nasty work. Lynch turned to deflect some of the damage, which helped.

"He's pissed," she said.

"Madder than a bull eating a cheeseburger," he muttered, firing off another power round. "Chew on this."

The plasma carbine hummed as the spray stabbed out, hitting the Boss below its face and across its torso. It raised one claw up right into the path of the plasma, losing most of the big hand in the process—burned clean away. The stump of the hand sprayed a huge burst of liquid out like a garden hose, if only for a few moments. Smoke rolled from the heat as the big Boss toppled over. MacLeod felt the thud through his ASHUR's footpads as it dropped.

The Frogs were still rushing forward. Glancing at his power levels, MacLeod winced. Twenty-seven percent. *If this keeps up, I might be dead in the water before this fight is over.*

Lynch stepped forward at the advancing Frogs and unleashed her flamethrower. Unlike his plasma carbine, there was an arc as she sprayed the street side-to-side, hitting almost all of the Frogs that had been charging them. When she stopped, greasy black smoke rolled off the flames, forming a wall of fire.

Through the flames, several Frogs jumped at them. Three in total —and two were on fire from the attack. Lynch dunked a single grenade downrange at them, the blast and shrapnel tearing through their burning bodies, leaving two dead and one twitching creepily in the middle of the street.

"Nicely done," MacLeod said. Through the rippling heat from the flamethrower, he could see that more Frogs were turning, breaking off from the rest, turning to face them.

"Your orders?"

"We advance on to the bank, killing as many of these hackit

arseholes on the way as possible."

Operation Sundance, Beverly Hills, the Western Front, California, the United States

The small narrow lane that led to the Commerce Bank was filled with Frogs—surging forward. The ATVs were covered with the aliens, dead, alive—and some caught in between. The aliens were pressed, packed in, and climbing over each other in a mad scramble to get to them, reminding Ryland of a zombie film he'd seen as a kid. They broke down doors and surged in through shattered window frames, pushing to get to the troops who held the street.

Across the street, Open Hostility rained down fire too, but there were far more targets than bullets. Ryland had ordered his people to aim for the creatures' heads, if only to not have to waste multiple rounds per Frog. He threw his last grenades into the mass, killing many, but as soon as the explosions opened big gaps in the crowd, the surviving Frogs flowed in, standing on their dead.

The air reeked—stinking of the aliens, their caustic spit, and the aroma of fired rounds of ammo and smoke. The stench of the battle hung like a haze over the aliens. He could hear their grunts from the lower floors of both buildings and immediately stopped firing, closing the door to the hallway and dragging a sofa from the small flat that he was occupying to block the door. "Everyone, be aware they are getting into the buildings. Make sure you barricade your access points." None of his people replied—they couldn't—this was a full-on battle—with all of the hallmarks of a last stand.

Sweat stung at his eyes as he returned to the window, only to see that the carnage was continuing—and that the Frogs, standing on their dead and wounded, were getting closer. He emptied his magazine in a series of single shots, then fell back into the room to reload.

Pausing, Ryland pulled a water bottle out and took a hot swig of water, crumbling the plastic as he finished.

The grunting in unison that the Frogs did was like a drum, beating into his ears and head. It was ominous and frightening, one they did not stop despite their losses. The noise surrounded him as much as the aliens did.

My damned fixation is what caused this! My obsession with the bank and robbing it may get all of these people killed. Regret washed over him in that moment, and as he stood there, he realized he was rocking side to side, just as he had as a child.

Closing his eyes, he reached deep in his brain and soul—searching for the strength to get on top of the emotions seeking to consume him. *My people are counting on me. I can't fold, not now. This is when they need me the most.*

His people—that thought centered him, allowed him to push the mental pressure back, holding it at bay. Ryland moved forward, forcing himself to take each step, reaching the blasted out window. He numbly lifted the ACR and aimed, firing shot after shot, then reloading his last magazine of ammo. *So this is what the endgame looks like…*

An explosion went off down the street at Rodeo Drive, then another. Through the vapor of the battle, he saw two hulking

ASHURs enter the narrow twisting lane where they were huddled, blazing away at the Frogs with wild abandon. *MacLeod!* One unleashed a sonic weapon—the deep pounding bass rippled into the mass of the Frogs and forced him to move away from the window as it made his own brow throb with each pulsation. Explosions followed as the weapon ceased, and as Ryland leaned in, he saw a flamethrower spray deep and long into the Frogs, lighting up so many that the black smoke blocked his line of sight.

Hollings from the next building down sprayed into the flaming mass with several bursts of machine-gun fire from the M245. More explosions went off into the Frogs—grenades fired from the Spartan Associates ASHUR—followed with another long stream of fiery death from the flamethrower. On one rooftop, King's Tarantula emptied its last bit of mini–chain gun ammunition, the whirring of the empty barrels mixed with the carnage.

Then he heard something else—a fifty-caliber machine gun's distinctive noise. *What the hell? We didn't bring a mah deuce with us. Where is that coming from?* Leaning farther out of the window, he saw something that stunned him. An old M1 Abrams tank, no doubt dug out of mothballs by some National Guard unit, moved in behind the AHSURs. Its machine-gun tracers showed that it was firing between the ASHURs a hot spray of full metal jacketed death that mowed down the Frogs like a scythe through autumn wheat.

Troops spilled out around the tank, forming up around the pair of ASHURs. Explosions ripped into the Frogs and Ryland fell back from the window as bits of debris from the street along with bits of Frogs, splattered into the flat that he was using for his firing position.

Then there was nothing—no sounds other than the rumble of the tank's engine. The grunting of the Frogs was gone. There were strange noises, faint, muffled—not quite moans, more like injured animal whimpers—drifting up from the street below.

Leaning out into the miasma, he saw no standing Frogs. There was movement in the deep pile that filled the street, but it was feeble and weak. Leaning his ACR against the wall, Ryland moved to his door and pulled the sofa away from the opening. The moment he did, the door flew open and a Frog stood before him. *Shit!* He knew his ACR was too far for him to reach. The Frog stood there, filling the door, its neck sacs inflating as it prepared to blast him with its toxic spit.

His hand found the Sig Sauer he had pulled off the body in the vault. In a fluid motion, he chambered a round and fired. The first shot punctured the right sac, squirting its spit-toxin all over the sofa. His next three shots tore into the Frog's head. It staggered back a step, then collapsed, hitting the hallway wall as it fell dead. His mind strangely stirred a memory from his training on urban combat… *"Hallways and stairs are death traps."* His instructor had been right.

Ryland grabbed his ACR and started downstairs, his senses even more heightened after the attack he'd just survived. When he reached the bottom, he saw that there was three feet or more of dead Frog flesh filling the street. The reek of their spit and blood leaked through his facemask's filters and made him momentarily nauseous as he slowly made his way to the doorway and stepped out on the dead bodies of the aliens. It was an awkward footing, and his eyes watered, but he made each step to get out into the street.

Glancing over to his left, he was pleased to see the ATVs were still there—hidden under tarps and debris. Looking down the street, he saw several troops coming out, walking on the same dead mass that he was. Across the street, he saw Mark Stevens and several of his people emerge from their buildings. The ones with raised visors looked dazed, almost drunkenly numb. It was in that moment he knew he wore the same expression on his own face.

The fresh trooper leading his people up the street approached him. He was a large black man with a chiseled face. His uniform was militia, leftover uniforms from the last conflict. The patch worn on this right sleeve provided instant recognition. It was a bloody knife against a Fish with its head cut off in a small pool of blood, with the words *We gut 'em* below it.

Above the patch were two distinct phrases. *Fifth California—Colton's Cutthroats.*

The cutthroats were legends from the very start of the war. They were better than many Army units in terms of their ability to slaughter the Fish. Militias aspired to be them. Seeing the patch and the face, the recognition surged in him. *This is the legend—this is Antonio Colton.* "Who's in charge of this?" the man asked in a deep tone of voice.

"I am. Lieutenant Ryland."

A short, muscular, young Asian woman moved up alongside of Colton, holding an ACR fully tricked out with a suppressor, light amplification kit, and a custom stock. The weapon had so many notches on the stock, it looked chewed up. Her STG was scarred and battered yet strangely efficient. She had the grim, stern expression of someone who had been in battle far too often, given her age. "We need to get on these rooftops," she said, nodding at them.

"Make it happen, Little Doll," he said to her, then turned to Ryland who was joined by Stevens. "We are going to need to form a perimeter around this position while the armored troops secure the flanks. In the meantime, Colonel Logan's on his way here—he's going to want to debrief with you while we firm up a defensive perimeter."

"We've got wounded," Ryland said.

"Transport's still a few blocks back. There's some Army medics that came in with us, they can help you get them mobile." Colton paused and surveyed the carnage that he stood on. "This was one hell of fight. You folks pulled off a damned miracle."

"We were highly motivated," quipped Ryland with a chuckle... the first he had experienced in a long time.

"Well, your folks can stand down. Battlespace command says that most of the local opposition is some distance from here. That should give us some time to expand our defensive perimeter. We can handle it from here," Colton said, nodding to another Abrams tank that drove past on Rodeo.

Ryland loosened his grip on his ACR and his shoulders ached as he purposefully relaxed his muscles. More infantry appeared, riding in on old Humvees, unloading and deploying on the streets. Then a weathered Bradley Fighting Vehicle rolled up down the block, its gray urban camouflage scored in several areas revealing the arctic camouflage paint underneath...a survivor of the war in Alaska. *Having old hardware is still better than having no hardware. In that respect, those National Guardsmen are better off than we are.*

Stevens walked over to him, extending his hand. "I thought we were goners for a few minutes there."

He shook the militia leader's hand. "Me too." Behind Stevens, he saw the battle-worn Shelly Reese sidle up just out of earshot. "Our original plan to get out of here is hosed." They had planned on scattering their ID chips in the rubble of some building—something that the Army would never recover because they were so far behind enemy lines. Now the front lines jutted up to Beverly Hills—*because of what we did.*

"Don't worry," Stevens said. "We'll get a chance to get out."

Suddenly a voice boomed, "Ryland! Ryland—get over here!" Lieutenant Colonel Logan stomped his way into the dead mass of Frogs. "You and I need to have a conversation—right now!"

CHAPTER 29

Operation Goldfinger, Beverly Hills, the Western Front, California, the United States

Dawes's team huddled around the trucks as they started the trek down into the Purple Line metro tunnel at the Wilshire and La Cienega station. It had taken a while to clear the rubble out of the way of the emergency access ramps they had to use to get the trucks in…made harder by the fact that, for some reason, Lynch had not shown up with her ASHUR. *That rig cost me a great deal, and it sure would have helped with this removal.* The rubble had been light but deep—the debris of an apartment building that had collapsed during some of the earlier fighting in the city. Moving it so that the trucks could pass took precious time.

Their departure from the battle had gone better than he had hoped. The Fish had been drawn more towards the bank, allowing Spartan Associates to stealthily creep to the north then swing in a long arc to the east. They had come across a dozen or so Frogs but had managed to avoid engaging them. Dawes didn't want to get into another battle if he could avoid it. From the nasty, intense sounds of the fighting behind their exfil, he was glad that he had ordered his people out.

Not everyone agreed, he could see it in their eyes—though none of them were willing to say anything out loud. Wallace only glared at him when they made eye contact, same with Kerrigan. Several of his people had been wounded in the fighting and were glad to be on the move out of the AIZ. Blood did that to a person. It either propelled them into being a vicious killer or made them want to get to safety and recover. *The ones that are pissed will feel differently when we pry open all of these boxes. Money has a way of healing wounds.*

Diamond Jones drove the truck he was in. On his lap as he sat on the passenger seat was safe-deposit box 435. The metal box felt heavy and it was hard for him to not imagine what was in it. *There will be plenty of time for me to see that once we get out of this hellscape.*

The metro tunnel was not deep underground but was pitch black. The trucks crept forward slowly and steadily, avoiding detection by the Fish. "Sir," came Wallace's voice. "If you remember, we sealed the end at Pershing Square."

"I know, Reaper. We are going to exit at the Wilshire and Western station. It may mean some tricky street navigation, but it'll save us having to dig through the debris we brought down at Pershing Square." Wallace didn't reply. *I know Ted—he's still fuming. He has a misplaced sense of duty and obligation. This isn't about humanity against the Fish, this is about making a score—and we did just that.*

It was difficult to judge distance underground. They had come in via the same tunnels, but that didn't help. The trucks were using their headlights, which made the use of nightvis less than optimal. The abandoned train tracks were dull and what few markings they did have were not helpful. Only when they came to an abandoned station did they have any sense for where they were under the streets of Los Angeles. The air was stuffy, even with the windows down on the trucks. Without the ventilation systems running, the tunnels got hot and the trucks they drove weren't electric, so the stink of their exhaust hung in the air. *It's a small price to pay. We're not far from our exit point.*

Diamond suddenly pressed the brakes.

"What is it?" he asked, squinting ahead.

"I'm not sure. I thought I saw movement."

"What kind of movement?"

She shook her head, leaning forward in the driver's seat. "I don't see it now."

Ted signaled over his comm channel. "Problem, boss?"

"Diamond thinks she spotted something." As he spoke, Jones crept the Toyota down the tunnel. The fact that she was cautious caused Dawes to start to check for the emergency ladders to the surface. It always paid to know how to get out, should things turn south.

"Contact. I've got motion in the rear," came Hague's voice from the bed of the rear truck in the column. "Something is fucking coming in behind us."

"You have visual?" Dawes asked.

"Negative. Something low. I've got my fucking light on and can't see it, but I hear something."

They're just nervous. After fighting with the Fish, they are strung out and now we are down here in a long dark tunnel and they are getting jumpy. "Alright, people, we have just another station to go and we are out of here."

A few moments later, gunfire erupted at the rear of the column. Hague's voice was almost screaming. "Dillos—hundreds of them!" The cracks of the gunfire in the confines of the metro tunnel made them seem even louder. Some of his people were going full auto—the purr of their ACRs echoed around him.

"Shit!" Diamond called, hitting the brakes. Looking out, he saw four Crabs coming at them in the tunnel. One was on the curved roof of the tunnel. They were close, far too close. She hit reverse and slammed into the truck behind her, jerking Dawes hard in his seat. "We have Crabs to the front," he called out, pulling his sidearm and holding it out the window, blasting away at one of the Crabs that was approaching along his side of the vehicle. Emptying the magazine, he quickly put in a fresh one.

"Sir," Wallace came over an open channel. "They knew we were coming…they had to have. We've gotta get out of here…now!"

He hated what he was hearing, but agreed. The Fish had never demonstrated much thinking to him, but this smelled like an ambush. *We can abandon the trucks—they have no use for the contents. We'll come back and recover the stuff—it's the best way.* "Everyone, grab a deposit box and head for the nearest ladder out of here." Clutching box 435, he opened his door, banging it into the sidewall. It was tight, but Dawes squeezed out.

Diamond started to slide across the console to his side of the vehicle when the windshield exploded inward, turning into thousands of tiny bits of glass. Glancing back, he saw the spike at the end of a Crab's tail had punched through the glass and into Jones's chest. Her eyes locked on his as he got free of the truck. There was no life in her gaze, only confusion. The curved spike recoiled fast, pulling Jones out of the vehicle, slamming her limp lifeless body into what remained of the windshield, showering glass on the hood. With a single flick of the tail, her body thudded onto the Metro train tracks.

Panic gripped Dawes as he ran past his truck and across the tracks to the ladder up to the surface, holstering his M19. He saw feet going up ahead of him as he reached it and looking up, he saw Reaper, already steps ahead of him. Gunfire roared in the tunnel and screams echoed all around him. Clutching the deposit box, he started up the ladder.

Wallace pushed open the emergency hatch and sunlight flooded downward as he scampered up the ladder and out to the surface. He slid the box in front of him. "Take this," he ordered, and Ted obeyed. Dawes, now able to use two hands, managed to get up one more rung when suddenly he felt a searing pain in both of his shins.

A massive claw crunched his STG, cutting deep into his flesh. He held on to the rung with his hands as the claw pulled hard, attempting to bring him back into the darkness of the tunnel. Reaper looked down at him. Setting the box down, he reached for Dawes's hands to help pull him up.

Dawes flexed his arms hard as the Crab pulled, and reached up with one hand to Wallace. At that moment, the claw jerked. His grip evaporated and his chin slammed hard into a rung on the way down. The cracking sound in his ears was from his jaw shattering under the impact.

He didn't know he had fallen, only that the world was suddenly vertical and his side and ribs ached. Being dragged along the tracks added to his agony. It felt as if his legs were on fire. Dawes managed to get his pistol out of its holster and fired at the Crab that held him. There was a snapping sound, followed by another, as the claw clamped down and severed his legs off. The pain was excruciating, worse than any he had ever felt. *This can't be happening—I was so close...*

The M19 felt heavy in his hand and his vision tunneled. The last thing he heard was a scream...only to realize that it was his own.

Operation Sundance, Beverly Hills, the Western Front, California, the United States

"Damn it, Ryland, this is a hell of a lot more than a reconnaissance in force," Lieutenant Colonel Logan said as Ryland saluted him. Logan gave him a fast salute back before he could even muster an excuse as to why they were in Beverly Hills.

He still couldn't tell if Logan was pissed off or happy, so he quickly decided to assume a positive stance as to why they were there. "You told us to be aggressive and bold. I knew if I told you what I was thinking of doing, you might hesitate, sir. The gamble was big. If it worked, you got to claim all of the credit. If it bombed, well, that was all on me."

"Son, you've blown this sector's front line all to hell, but in a good way. This salient you've formed and the number of Fish you've killed will allow us to keep a firm grip on the Hills this time."

Ryland wanted to say more, but he knew that every word he spoke could potentially hang him. That was the kind of experience that the Army gave an officer—the understanding of when to shut up. "Sir, this is Mark Stevens, commander of the militia unit Open Hostility." He gestured towards Stevens. "They deserve as much praise as my Ghost Legion for this little venture."

Logan firmly shook Stevens's hand with both of his own. "It is a distinct pleasure to meet a militia leader with the guts to do what you have done."

"Um—thank you, sir," was all that Stevens could muster at that moment...still coming down from the excitement of the battle.

Logan glanced around. "We got some National Guard folks here with some older hardware, but it should be enough to keep the Fish at bay. My God," he said surveying the dead Frogs that filled almost every inch of the street. "I've never seen a body count like this."

"We were fortunate enough to have two ASHURs with us," Ryland added. "A lot of credit needs to go to those pilots—especially Sutherland MacLeod."

Logan turned and made eye contact with each of them gathered around the commanders. "You've all earned some R&R out of this, not to mention some medals for bravery. We have been looking for a victory here in La, and you just handed us a beauty of one. I'm damned proud of all of you."

Ryland tried to squash the guilt he felt over the praise,

smothering it with a sense of irony and a bit of humor. He saw Warrant Officer Reese step forward. "Sir, there's more going on here than these folks have let on." She shot an icy glance at Stevens, then over at Ryland. *Here it comes—she's going to rat us out.* His mind raced with possible ways to deflect what Reese was going to say, but none of them came fluidly.

"I'm sure there is," Logan replied. "And there will be plenty of time to review all of that later. For now, we should get your people out of here and get your wounded tended to." The lieutenant colonel cut off Reese completely—and he saw the crimson rise to her cheeks as she realized it. Reese's jaw set, then she turned and stormed off, almost falling over the dead Frogs as she did. It was hard to hold back a sigh of relief.

His commanding officer took off to look over the battle scene himself, leaving Ryland with Stevens and a smattering of their people. "Your liaison is pissed."

"Reese will eventually let this go, but it's going to take a while. She lives her life by the code of conduct. I've never seen a warrant like her."

The rumble of the old M1 Abrams echoed all around them, forcing Ryland to lean in and raise his voice. "I thought we could fake our deaths and count the booty. It looks like that plan is shot."

"We've got four ATVs," he said. "We split them up. After we get our heads clear, we can meet up and divide what we have."

"Sounds good," he replied wearily. "My people have been through a lot, and we need to tend to our dead."

"Same here." As he spoke, he surveyed the scene, watching the strange ASHUR from Spartan Associates wade into the sea of dead Frogs. "I never thought it would end like this."

"No plan survives contact with the enemy. We got screwed over by those Spartan rump-humpers. When this is over, I'd like to give that guy a piece of my mind."

"I'd like to beat him bloody—but that won't change anything."

"You're probably right. Still, it would feel good."

That it would. "Let's round up our people and get moving."

They walked in a long wide arc around Logan, who was busy handing out orders to the newly arrived troops. Colton's Cutthroats were moving out of the area—and tired COs had to avoid a lot of contact with them as well. In death, the Frogs took on a distinctive smell, a swampy, wet, algae-like aroma with a hint of rotting fish. Ryland hated the stink, but knew it was going to get a lot worse. *They will have to soak the dead and burn them before the rot sets in.*

It took long minutes to finally and discreetly reach the ATVs. When they arrived, they saw that the debris and bodies had been removed, and the tarps had been pulled off. More startling, one ATV and trailer were missing.

"What the fuck?" Vogal asked. "Someone stole what we stole." There were tire imprints on the dead Frogs, leading south, out of Beverly Hills. *With those tanks and other vehicles passing by, we didn't even hear the ATV. I should have put someone on the ATVs to guard them.*

"They did it right under our noses," Stevens said. "Where's Coyote?"

"Right here," a man said, stepping forward, covered in the blood of the Frogs. Behind him was a hulking black man wearing a face of exhaustion. With his visor up, Coyote's face was smeared with dirt, sweat, and even a little splatter of blood. He no longer looked like a person out of place…he looked like a veteran.

"Do we go after them?" Stevens asked.

"We need to do a headcount," Ryland said. "It wasn't someone in the relief force, they had no idea what was in those ATVs. This was one of our own. Somebody stabbed us in the back."

Vogal spoke up once more. "I say we figure out who it is, track them down, and kill them." *Now I know why her call sign is the Witch.*

Ryland looked at the remaining vehicles with their contents. "There's been enough bloodletting today. When we get back to safety, we can figure out if it was worth going after them or not." Only Vogal looked like she was willing to offer a rebuttal, but even she held her tongue...for which, Ryland was thankful.

"Let's get out of this place, and get our people to safety."

CHAPTER 30

Ryland and his people arrived the next day at Open Hostility's base. It was amazing how much a hot shower, food, and sleep could change people. His ranks were thinned, and that served as a reminder of what he had done. Mullins had died before he could be put in an ambulance. The flesh-consuming bacteria had eaten most of one of his arms and he had sucked in enough that his lungs were gone, reduced to an acid slush. Fisher had been exposed but had lived, though it had cost him his hand in the process. Canton had died before the relief column had reached them. Almost all of the survivors had been wounded, either physically or emotionally.

Ryland felt good because he had slept. The burden that his compulsive obsession with the heist was gone, as he had hoped. It hadn't been a long sleep, six hours, but it had happened. Now he was plagued with the thought that it was his obsession that had led to the loss of lives. He caressed those thoughts with the knowledge that Operation Sundance had been more than that. *This was a chance for everyone to get something out of this war that was more than medals and surviving.*

Calcutt had suggested sending one of the Ghosts over to stand guard on the loot the night before. Ryland had dismissed that thought. "We trusted Open Hostility with our lives. I'm not about to betray that trust now." Calcutt pointed out that none of the Ghost Legion were missing. "Whoever stole that ATV had to have come from Hostility." That was a point he had to concede, but it was not enough for him to change his mind. It struck him as strange how the possibility for wealth twisted a person's thinking.

When they arrived, Vogal escorted them into one of the container units where the survivors of the militia unit remained. Their numbers had been thinned even more by the previous day's events. On the table before them was a neatly stacked pile of safety deposit boxes—none showing signs of having been opened. Ryland made quick eye contact with Calcutt, who only offered a shrug. *I told you so, Sergeant.*

Mark Stevens looked ragged still. The bags under his eyes almost mirrored those that Ryland had. "It took a lot for us to not open these before you got here."

"I bet."

"So how do we divide this up?" asked Coyote from across the table filled with the boxes.

Stevens looked to Ryland for his lead. "Well, the liquid assets get divided up equally. Whatever else is in there we can parse out as equitably as possible." There were no murmurs of dissent to the plan.

The opening of the boxes reminded Ryland of Christmas

morning when he had been a kid. Without any guidance from their leaders, the gathered group opened them one at a time, each person getting a turn. Calcutt took responsibility for keeping track of what they found. The first box had some jewelry, personal papers—nothing too exciting. One box was packed full of antique currency—most of it sealed in plastic cases and rated. Another box was filled with usable cash—to the tune of over a million dollars. One box was filled with designer drugs, hopelessly illegal. Another had three Grammy awards in it. *Those are bound to be worth something on the open market.* One hefty box was filled with small silver ingots—hundreds of them. One had a single gold bar that was passed around to each person who savored hefting it. One small leather pouch was full of diamonds that fascinated everyone that carefully inspected them. Other boxes proved worthless—filled with paperwork, photos, or other ephemera that had no value to anyone other than their owners.

Each box that was pried open elicited something that Ryland hadn't seen in a while—joy. There were oohs, ahhs, and outright boos. Sutherland MacLeod had showed up with a stranger in tow, bringing the alcohol for the gathering—ten cases of ice-cold brew… making him the unofficial hero of the evening. The beer was broken out and the two units became as one, celebrating each box with an almost childlike glee. Looking over at Winston, he noticed that the sniper's twitching fingers were steady and true. *Maybe this was all worth it, not for the treasure, but for the happiness. For the first time in this war, my people are enjoying themselves.*

The funniest moment was when one box produced a purse.

According to the documentation, it was a diamond Himalayan croc Birkin bag. It was bright colored and clearly had never been used; no surprise, given that it had so many little diamonds on it. Raffi claimed it, immediately stating that she was going to use the tricked-out bag to carry her spare magazines.

It took over two hours, with some of the boxes putting up more of a fight than others. The members of the Sundance Operation joked and laughed and drank. There was plenty of booty for everyone by the time the last box was opened with a crowbar. It was no longer about the money—it was about the victory.

"Look at 'em," Stevens whispered in Ryland's ear.

"Yeah—they earned this. Why not be happy? They're all walking away quasi-rich."

I love that word...I'm going to have to remember that. "Money doesn't go as far as it used to with the war going on. Still, they are happy, and maybe that's what really matters. What are you going to do with your share?"

Ryland had been nursing that thought carefully. "I had planned to go MIA and find a nice place to spend the rest of my life. My CO is insisting we are some sort of heroes for regaining Beverly Hills. He's got the media lined up to interview me and is planning some sort of ceremony for both of our units to pin medals on them."

"So, disappearing isn't going to work for you."

"No. I am going to leverage this to get leave for the unit. Even the Army wouldn't deny that of its latest heroes. My people will get a chance to spend some of this, get a chance to recharge their batteries at least. What about you?"

"I did this to take care of my people. Most of us are getting out of here once and for all. A few of them are likely wanting to stay in the fight—their patriotism outweighs survival instinct."

"If they want to stick around, I will find a place for them in the Legion," Ryland offered.

"Thank you."

"So you are going back to civilian life?"

Stevens nodded, but not enthusiastically. "I need to be away from all of this shit. I don't know for how long, but it will be for a while. I've got to clear my brain and get the blood off my hands. If it was a year ago, I would have opted to sit on the beach and get drunk—but with all the beaches being war zones, I think I might settle for some time someplace safe, maybe Wyoming or North Dakota."

"Are you coming back?"

The leader of Open Hostility grudgingly gave a nod. "I wasn't going to. No plan survives first contact with the Fish. I'm putting in for three months' leave. Whoever comes back, comes back. A few of my people want to return to some sense of normalcy. I have come to the conclusion that this war isn't going to just go away. Having won the last battle, maybe it's better to be a part of the fight rather than let someone else die for me."

It was a sentiment Ryland completely understood and shared. "I always wanted to buy a classic hot rod. Now that dream is shot. I mean, where would I drive it? Where could I keep it safe?" *No place is really safe now, which means the things we used to want...the things that we thought would make our lives whole, no longer have any meaning.* In that moment, he came to realize that what they had earned through their robbery of the bank was not material—but emotional.

"There is no safety anymore. I thought money might change that, but it doesn't—not really. Besides, your CO is lining up a bunch of media stuff—interviews, vids, that kind of thing. Suddenly Open Hostility is a hot commodity, at least that was what he said when he called this morning. It's better for me to stay in the fight—after some downtime."

"I just wanted some sleep," Ryland replied in complete honesty. "Last night was the first night in weeks that I got some actual shut-eye. I'd become obsessed over this entire operation. With it over, I will at least be able to sleep—until the next thing for me to obsess over comes along."

Sutherland joined them, holding out his beer for a casual clinking toast. The three of them took a long cold swig and Ryland savored it. Stevens popped one of the questions that neither of them had broached. "Whatever happened to those dickbags from Spartan Associates?"

Ryland shook his head. "I did a check around 1300 and no one had seen them. They didn't show back up at the hotel they use as a base."

"You think the Fish got them?"

MacLeod nodded. "Trixie Lynch, that young lady I brought with me, she was their ASHUR pilot. She went to their base and there was nobody there, other than the logistical staff. From what she told me, they were all in full-on panic mode over there. They've been trying to raise them on comms but have only gotten static back."

"Couldn't have happened to a nicer set of asshats," Stevens snorted.

"True enough," Ryland said. "Spartan left us to die."

MacLeod gave a nod of agreement. "She was telling me that she washed out of ASHUR training. She got wounded and the Army booted her. Funny thing is, when we were out there, she saved my life. She's got a lot of fight in her and is finally not having to prove a thing to anyone about what she can do. Her employer has disappeared into the ether and she is orphaned."

"She won't be for long," Ryland replied. "With an ASHUR rig, any militia unit would be happy to pick her up."

Stevens's grin broadened just a moment. "Don't let her leave without me having a few minutes with her."

Ryland returned to the original subject. "Spartan Associates left us to get screwed over—that much is true. None of that reflects on Lynch. She did the right thing, where they took the coward's road out of town. As much as I want them to fail, I have to admit, I'm a little torn about it. Anytime we lose fighting forces to the Fish, it's a bad thing. They were humans, just shitty ones."

There was a moment of silence between the three men. MacLeod leaned his beer in between them. "You're right, Lieutenant. Dying out there in no-man's-land is not the way anyone should go. A toast then. Let's hope that some of them got out. To Spartan Associates."

Ryland and Stevens both knocked at his bottle top with theirs and they all finished their beers. "That only leaves us with one big unanswered question. Who took that last ATV? The only one I can't account for is Slocum, but one of my people swears they saw him get torn up by a Crab."

"I have two people unaccounted for," Stevens said in a low tone as Ryland huddled a little closer to him. "Bishop Grant. We lost track of him in all of the fighting. No one saw him go down. I have a hard time believing it was him. He was the only member of the unit that was a regular churchgoer."

Sutherland sneered. "Sometimes those church types are the biggest hypocrites."

Stevens shook his head. "Not Grant. I've known him for years. He was just some punk kid when he joined my construction crew. He didn't even have a place to stay when he came to the west coast—I let him crash for a few weeks on my couch until he got settled. It wasn't him."

"Who else?"

"Shelly Reese, my Army liaison," he replied, cocking his head as he spoke. "She was always straitlaced, by the book. I hate saying it, but it had to be her. I put in inquiries. No one in the sector has seen her, and her ID chip isn't registering at all."

"She didn't strike me as the type to double-cross anyone."

"She was never in on the plans. In fact, we went out of our way to keep her in the dark. None of us knew her really well, other than Offerman. Maybe his dying pushed her over the edge, or the fact that we all got hailed as heroes. I don't know. Maybe she took it as evidence for our court-martial. If she's smart, she'll never surface. If Vogal finds her, it's going to get ugly—pulpy-beaten-dead-flesh-ugly. Whatever she did with the stuff, she's up and disappeared."

"Good for her," Ryland said with a low chuckle and a toast of his glass.

Laugher spilled from the gathered team, loud, drunken, and boisterous. Ryland looked over and could not help but grin. *Maybe it wasn't just the sleep I've been missing. Maybe it's this—the camaraderie.* He tossed his empty bottle into the recycle bin and headed over to where the cases chilled on a small mound of ice. As he twisted off the top of a new bottle, he decided to let himself enjoy this time…because he never knew when such moments would ever come again.

Epilogue

The DoubleTree Hotel, Orange, California, the United States

Ted "Reaper" Wallace was ushered into the suite by a professional security person wearing a pristine suit. Ted wore his best combat jumpsuit and as his eyes followed the man, he remembered when that had been the business of Spartan Associates…when *he* had been the man in the suit.

It had been a week since the Sixth Battle of Beverly Hills, though it seemed as if a lifetime had passed. Only he and Kerrigan had gotten out of the Fish's ambush alive—and Kerrigan was in the hospital with multiple wounds. A nasty infection had set in, and while Wallace was hopeful Kerrigan would survive, each day the prognosis looked grimmer.

Wallace had a limp himself, a reminder of the ambush. Everyone thought that it was alien projectiles or vomit or whatever that caused injuries. He had twisted his ankle in a pothole. The debris and not being careful caused far more pain than the Fish did. It was a sprained ankle and was well wrapped, but each step served as confirmation that he was, indeed, alive.

Surviving made him the only surviving owner of Spartan Associates—a PMC that only existed on paper now. Memories of their retreat from the Hills shamed him still. *We lost almost all of our people, all of our gear, and for what?*

Entering the suite, he saw Ratchet sitting at the small table. Reaching out, he put safe-deposit box 435 on the table between them and took a seat.

"I thought that Mr. Dawes would be bringing this to me," she said.

"Dawes is dead. Our entire team, other than two of us, are gone." *Left out there to rot in that damn tunnel. All for this…*

"That's too bad," she replied as if they were talking about a restaurant being out of pico de gallo for her chips. The three words hurt Wallace deeply.

"People died for this. I only hope it was worth it."

His words clearly didn't move her. "Have you opened it?"

"No." He pulled out a pry bar and put it on top of the box.

Ratchet nodded to one of her security people, who went to work on the lid. It took two minutes for him to finally get the lid to pop off. Lifting the long lid open, Ratchet pulled out a large book. "Perfect!" she said, caressing the cover.

"A scrapbook?" Wallace said as she opened it. There were photographs, ticket stubs, and little comments in pink and green ink on the page.

"My mom made this for me. She's gone now. That's why I kept it someplace safe."

It wasn't gold, silver, bonds, cash, or jewels. *Everyone died and for what…a photo album?* He felt his face redden. He wanted to scream. Wallace wanted to rattle through the roster of names from

Spartan Associates that had perished to get the box to her. Looking at the joy on her face as she flipped through the pages of the book, he knew that Ratchet would never understand. *Her kind don't appreciate what others have to do to make them happy.*

She pointed to one of her security people, who handed him a plastic wrapped block of currency. Wallace hefted it in his still-sore arms. *So this is what a million dollars feels like…our blood money.* "Thanks," was all Ratchet said, then flicked her hand, gesturing to the door.

Wallace squeezed the block of bills into his large rucksack. He couldn't form words for the inner rage and the horrible sense of loss he felt. *I'm the only surviving officer of the company. Maybe I can rebuild. But do I want to?*

The last question was one that Reaper was ill-prepared to answer.

Al's RV Superstore, Lancaster, California, the United States

Sutherland MacLeod stood in front of the RV and touched the warm metal with his hand, as if to caress the skin of the vehicle. It was his first day of a much deserved leave and he wanted to fulfill a dream. Colonel Logan had hailed him as a hero and there was talk of promotion and medals, but he didn't care about that. *I went into that fight to kill that Boss and I did it. The money, well, that's just icing on the cake.* Looking at the RV longingly, he was able to focus on something other than vengeance for the first time in months. *I'm going to take her east, out to Wyoming or South Dakota, far from the war and all the shit associated with it.*

The salesperson who had introduced him to the selection sidled up next to him. "She's a beaut, isn't she? The Starrunner is the top of the line when it comes to luxury. It has a fireplace, a wet bar, every amenity you could ever want. You name it and this babe has it."

He eyed the long length of the RV and turned slowly to face the salesman. "How much?"

"Well, we should sit and go over the numbers. We have a number of payment plans that I am sure will fit your budget."

"Will cash work?" another voice spoke up. MacLeod turned to see Trixie Lynch walking up, a backpack slung to her back, and a thin smile on her face.

"Cash always works," the salesman answered her. "We should go over to the sales office. We will be able to draw up the paperwork there. You really picked out the best we have on the lot, Mr. MacLeod." He started off for the distant office, while Sutherland turned to Trixie.

"I'm surprised you came."

"Not too surprised, I hope."

"I figured you would be settling in with Open Hostility."

"They all needed a break, and so did I." She eyed the big RV for a moment. "So, where are we heading?"

"Someplace where the only Fish I care about are the ones dangling on the end of my line."

"Sounds great," she replied.

MacLeod started walking toward the sales office with Lynch at his side. For the first time in a long time, he was at peace and looking forward to something that wasn't related to the war.

The St. Regis Resort, Aspen, Colorado, the United States

Shelly Reese looked out of the window of her suite at the mountains in the distance. Winter was coming, and soon she would be able to enjoy the slopes. She was looking forward to skiing. She hadn't done that since college.

Sitting down on the couch, she nursed her bourbon and ginger ale as the news came on. A familiar face was on the screen, Mark Stevens. Next to him was now-Captain Frank Ryland. The banner under Stevens read, *Open Hostility Commanding Officer.* Her curiosity piqued, Shelly turned up the volume. As Stevens spoke, she noticed a paracord bracelet on his wrist—Clarkston's. It struck her as strange, until she realized he wore it out of respect for the dead man.

The interviewer practically gushed over her guests. She peppered her questions with labels like "heroes," and praised them for handing the US "a stunning, much needed victory." To their credit, neither Stevens nor Ryland played into that. They downplayed what they had done. She was one of the few people on the planet who understood why. *They don't have a choice. They wouldn't be hailed as heroes if the rest of the country knew what they'd really been doing in Beverly Hills.*

Shelly's decision to take an ATV and leave had come in a mental tornado of spite and despair. The Army didn't want to hear the truth —that Ryland and Stevens were bank robbers. The Army wouldn't have even known they were there if it hadn't been for her. *I was the one that called the battlespace commander...I led to the Army showing up.*

I created them!

When she realized that no one cared about the truth, she had taken the ATV and left. She had cut out her ID chip, crushing it under her boot. As far as the Army was concerned, Shelly Reese was just a statistic, another MIA soldier in a war that continued to slough on.

The safe-deposit boxes she'd liberated were the keys to her new life. She had checked into a cheap hotel in Anaheim, California, after getting out of the AIZ, and had spent an entire night opening them. Money, jewelry, and even an Oscar were now hers. Shelly had converted the material goods to cash. With the Oscar, she contacted the actress that had earned it, claimed she had found it, and wondered if there was a reward. It all added up to one thing— freedom.

She had not indulged herself in wild spending. She had sent $10,000 to Jon Offerman's family, simply signing her name. His loss still tore at her. He was the one person in Hostility that was a friend. Sending Offerman's family something was more to ease her pain than theirs. *Now I now know the truth; I was never really a part of that unit. They saw me as a necessary evil. They embraced Coyote more than they did me.*

Shelly put her time in the Army into her own mental deposit box and threw away the key. *I did everything by the book, and in the end, the cheaters won.* In her mind, there was only one solution—become the very thing she had stood against. *I have earned this, maybe more than Stevens or Ryland. I did what was right, and all it got me was frustration.*

As the interview finished, Shelly lifted her glass in a toast to them. *You may have pulled off the heist of the century, but someday, everyone is going to learn the truth about what you two did. I'll see to that myself...when the time is right.*

About the Author

Blaine Pardoe is a *New York Times* bestselling and award-winning author. He has been an author and designer in the gaming industry since 1985. He has written countless sourcebooks for games including the Star Trek RPG, Space 1889, the Robotech RPG, BattleTech/MechWarrior, Twilight 2000, Renegade Legion, and Leviathans. He has authored numerous science fiction novels in the BattleTech/MechWarrior universe. His political thriller, *Blue Dawn*, was an Amazon bestseller in its category. Outside of the gaming industry, he is an accomplished historian and bestselling author in the military history, business management, and true crime genres. He has twice won awards from the Military Writers Society of America and was awarded the Harriet Quimby Award from the Michigan Aviation Hall of Fame for his contributions to aviation history. He has been a guest speaker at the US National Archives, the Smithsonian, and at the US Naval Academy.

About the Creator

Brent Evans is a long-time illustrator and award-winning art director. As an artist, he began freelancing in 1987 and worked in many genres including political cartoons, comics, and children's books. In 2005 he was hired by gaming visionary Jordan Weisman to work on several games, and immediately distinguished himself as one of the core illustrators for the *BattleTech* franchise. His creative design and project management style inspired his elevation to Senior Art Director in 2009 for many legendary gaming franchises including *BattleTech*, *Shadowrun*, D&D's *Dragonfire*, *Valiant RPG*, and many more. From 2017-2019, he took on the additional role as line developer leading the overhaul of the *BattleTech* product line, catapulting the brand into the industry-leading global success that it enjoys today. Of Brent, it is said that his "superpower" is the ability to recruit and develop creative talent.

Additionally, Brent is a graduate of and serves as a board member for the Game Design & Development program for the University of Washington.

www.ingramcontent.com/pod-product-compliance
Lightning Source LLC
Chambersburg PA
CBHW050916030726
47503CB00007BB/2325